Opposites Ignite

At the moment they may be like fire and gasoline, but something in his eyes said Reno Wilder was a man worth fighting for. And Charlotte's heart was more than willing to take a chance.

His gaze swept her face, lingered on her mouth, then came back up to her eyes and held. His thick, dark lashes lowered on a slow blink. When she thought her heart would knock through her ribcage, he cupped her face with his strong hands, lowered his head, and brushed her mouth with his warm lips.

"I'm sorry you had to fight for your father's attention," he whispered against her mouth. "But you definitely have mine." Then he kissed her so slow and sweet she thought her hammering heart would shatter.

By Candis Terry

ANYTHING BUT SWEET
SOMEBODY LIKE YOU
ANY GIVEN CHRISTMAS
SECOND CHANCE AT THE SUGAR SHACK

Short Stories
HOME SWEET HOME (FROM FOR LOVE AND HONOR)

Coming Soon

SWEETEST MISTAKE

CANDIS TERRY

Anything
BUT SWEET

AVON
An Imprint of HarperCollinsPublishers

AVON BOOKS
An Imprint of HarperCollins*Publishers*
10 East 53rd Street
New York, New York 10022-5299

Copyright © 2013 by Candis Terry
ISBN 978-0-06-223722-4
www.avonromance.com

First Avon Books mass market printing: July 2013

Avon Trademark Reg. U.S. Pat. Off. and in Other Countries, Marca Registrada, Hecho en U.S.A.
HarperCollins® is a registered trademark of HarperCollins Publishers.

Printed in the U.S.A.

10 9 8 7 6 5 4 3 2

*For the remarkable Amanda Bergeron,
editor extraordinaire, and one of the nicest people
I've ever had the pleasure to know. Without you, my
stories would exist only inside my chaotic imagination.
Thank you so much for helping bring my characters
to life and for being so much fun in the process!*

Acknowledgments

$\mathcal{M}$y sincerest gratitude to Marine Sergeant Kelly Aldrich for answering my numerous questions so clearly that I got a real glimmer of what it was like to be a Marine—without the whole boot-camp thing! I knew from the moment we met you at that Steelhead game so many years ago that you were a special young man. Over the years, you've become even more impressive. From the bottom of our hearts, thank you for your service to our country and for continuing to display such honor. You make us all proud.

Thank you to Pat and Frank from the Eagle Ranch in Boerne, Texas. Your hospitality was delightful, and your guesthouse was the perfect place to stay while we researched the area. We shall return!

Also thank you to Randy of the Bergmann Lumber Company in Boerne, the helpful folks at The Boerne Wine Company, and all the amazing people we met on our visit to the Texas Hill Country. Your lively stories and willingness to give us the true flavor of the area really helped shape this book.

Anything
BUT SWEET

Chapter 1

*T*rouble rolled into downtown Sweet on the spinning wheels of a yellow Hummer. Inside the gas guzzler, the crew for cable TV's makeover show *My New Town* waved their arms out the windows to the legions of enthusiasts extending a big Texas welcome.

On an ordinary day, there wasn't much to attract outsiders to a town that progress had ignored. No interstate to bring in the tourists—just a poorly paved road with too many ruts to be comfortable even in the most luxurious limousine. With the exception of Goody Gum Drops—the candy store painted like a peppermint stick—most of the town's cedar-sided shops were faded with age. Their metal overhangs more rust than steel. Their signs in various stages of chip and peel.

A few years back, Mayor Gary Gleason had promised to put a little zing into the ancient buildings that lined Main Street. Talk was he never got any further than the side-street boutique rumored to have a back room that sold naughty lingerie and large quantities of AA batteries.

Frustrated with the mayor's lack of gumption, the over-seventy crowd who met on a daily basis at Bud's Nothing Finer Diner for coffee, pie, and gossip, put their gray-haired heads together. They conjured up the outrageous idea to contact a reality makeover show to come in and give the town a face-lift.

The harebrained proposition churned up gossip for weeks and kept the town abuzz, like the hive wreaking havoc below the marquee at the Yellow Rose Cinema.

So on this steamy summer day, with wildflowers dotting the meadows and a curtain of brilliant blue draped across the sky, Tinsel Town came calling.

Everyone was excited about the change.

Everyone except Reno Wilder, who stood in the shade of the warped overhang above Wilder and Sons Hardware & Feed watching the parade of trucks and trailers thunder down Main Street.

Dust and gravel kicked up in the wake of the intruders as the community jumped up and down like they were at a Rangers doubleheader.

Arms folded across his chest, Reno leaned a shoulder against a rough-hewn post and crossed one booted ankle over the other. The muscles in his neck tightened as he shook his head.

He wanted no part of this insanity.

There wasn't a damn thing wrong with his hometown.

Sure, it was a little weathered at the wings. Tarnished at the joints. But that's what gave it character and charm. Yeah, maybe the place had been established in the mid 1800s, and all the downtown buildings were original. What was wrong with that? He liked historic. Traditional. If folks wanted new and trendy, they could go to Austin. He liked his little town just the way it was—like his favorite pair of boots. A little worn at the heels but real comfortable.

"They've all lost their minds." The statement came out a grumble.

"Come on." Former Army Ranger Aiden Marshall chuckled as he dumped the bag of dog food he'd just purchased into the bed of his truck. He reached through the open window and gave the golden retriever and border collie waiting in the cab a rub between their ears. "This is the most excitement we've had since I came home from Afghanistan."

Reno raised a brow. Within weeks of Aiden's return, he'd reconnected with Paige Walker, the love of his life. Word had it a wedding was in the works. An invasion from Hollywood hardly seemed a fair comparison.

"Yeah, well, that would be the *Army* part of your brain working in the wrong direction."

Aiden laughed out loud. "Then I guess that means the former *Marine* part of your brain is working overtime."

"Semper Fi, my man."

The good-humored ribbing they tossed back and forth wasn't unusual or meant to be unkind. Didn't matter what branch of the military a man served, they were all brothers in arms. The joking helped bury the memories they'd rather forget. Eased the pain that still lingered.

After one of the darkest days in America, many enlisted. That list included Reno and his brothers. Aiden and his best friends. Some came home. Some didn't. Reno knew that grief too well.

"Think they brought any good-lookin' women with 'em?"

In unison, Reno and Aiden glanced down at the bald pate of the old codger standing between them. At eighty years old, Chester Banks was every bit the skirt chaser he'd been all his life. Reno didn't know if Chester had been a handsome man in his youth; today he was all nose and sunken eyeballs.

"Doubt it," Reno said. "Looks like you'll have to stick with Gertie Finnegan. I hear she's taking fox-trot lessons over at the senior center just for you."

"Pfft." Chester waved an arthritic hand. "That woman ain't got no sense. She should be learnin' that cha-cha like they do on *Dancing with the Stars*. 'Course, Gertie ain't built like those hot little dancers."

"Don't expect she is." Reno squinted against the glare bouncing off another truck bearing the TV show logo. "Hard to maintain a killer bod when you're pushing ninety."

Chester's hopeful smile slid into the abyss. "Ain't that a fact."

"Paige mentioned something about the designer host's name being Charli," Aiden said.

"Probably light in the loafers." Chester gave an all-knowing nod.

"That's an awfully big assumption," Reno said.

The old man looked up at him. "I don't see you pitchin' a hissy over polka-dot chintz or chandeliers with them dangly little crystals."

"I'm not much into fabrics or lighting," Reno agreed. "Unless my sheets need washing or my Maglite needs new batteries."

"Exactly." Chester said this in the same way one would holler, "Eureka!"

"Why are y'all standing over here?" All three men looked up as Paige Walker—honey blond ponytail swinging—jogged toward them. "The party's across the street." She came to a stop in front of Aiden, grabbed hold of his T-shirt with both hands and pulled him in for a kiss. Paige had always been a take-what-she-wanted kind of girl. Not that Aiden seemed to mind.

"We can see fine from here," Reno answered. Not that she was really listening. Reno's heart cramped as he watched his buddy's arms go around the woman he loved.

He'd had that once. That crazy, can't-get-enough-of-her fire in his blood. Like everything else, he'd lost it. Tragically. Horribly. Unforgettably.

Never one to take no for an answer, Paige lifted her head, wrinkled her nose, and zeroed in on the weak link of the bunch. "Chester? Don't you want a better look?"

"Ah." He waved a shoofly hand. "I ain't interested in no girly men."

Paige laughed. *"Girly* men?"

"You know," Chester said, doing a little dance on bowed legs. "The tiptoe-through-the-tulips type. Like that Charli fella."

"You mean Charlotte Brooks? The designer?"

Chester's rheumy hazel eyes widened. "Charli's a *girl?*"

"Was the last time I saw her on TV." Knowing she'd won at least one of them over, Paige gave a victorious grin. "She's kind of a knockout too."

"Now you've done it," Reno said, as Chester found a sudden giddy-up to his get-along.

"Y'all come on." Halfway across the street, Chester waved the three of them over. "In case I have me a heart attack."

"I'm good right here," Reno mumbled. He had no intention of setting foot anywhere near those who planned to seek and destroy his quiet, humble little town.

"No, you're not." Paige grabbed both him and Aiden by the arm. "And if y'all are having any ideas of taking off for the hills, think again," she added, "I've got on my running shoes."

Didn't matter that the front door to his hardware store stood wide open, Reno knew better than to mess with any female who had Texas running deep in her veins. They built them strong in the South. And when a Southern woman used *that* tone, they meant business. A lesson he'd learned years ago and would not soon forget.

Paige hauled them across the street and pushed them toward the front of the crowd, where the big yellow Hummer and parade of trucks had rolled to a stop at the curb of what the folks liked to call Town Square. In reality, it was only a patch of grass with a few trees, picnic tables, and a gazebo with half the roof gone from a random windstorm last spring. Yet more weddings and birthday parties took place there than anywhere else within a ten-mile radius.

With the mayor directing the Hollywood interlopers, the Hummer cleared the curb and drove up onto the lawn, mashing the grass Ernie Mc-Greavy had spent hours the day before meticulously mowing. Like a swarm of killer bees, the crowd of locals surrounded the yellow monstrosity and let out a cheer when the doors popped open. Cameras were already rolling when four passengers stepped out—a tiny blonde with a studious look and a clipboard hugged to her chest and a ragtag trio of men who looked as though they'd pounded a few nails—or heads—in their day.

The last to emerge was the driver—a brunette in a snug skirt that hit her midcalf and a blouse that molded like a second skin over high, firm breasts, and a narrow waist. A tall, *curvy* brunette, whose ankles wobbled when she stepped down from the vehicle. A tall, curvy, *smiling* brunette, whose sky-scraper heels sank deep into Ernie McGreavy's per-fectly clipped grass.

Reno covered a laugh with a cough.

Looked like *Charli* was going to find out fast that her big city ways—and shoes—wouldn't fly in this small Texas town.

"Whoops!" She giggled as the mayor reached out to steady her. Then she looked up with wide eyes, and asked the crowd, "Do you mind if I dispense with propriety?"

The crowd responded with a cheer.

Reno watched in surprise as she reached down, pulled off her shoes, and instantly shrunk several inches. She wiggled her painted pink toes in Ernie's grass with a long "Ahhhhhh." Then she flashed an-other smile through full lips tinted a soft coral.

Paige had been right.

The woman was a knockout.

Appearances could be deceiving. Anyone knew that. While Reno had to admit that *Charli* made a pretty package, it wouldn't take long for the rest of the town to realize what he already knew. They'd made a huge mistake. They'd send her and her co-horts packing faster than roaches out the kitchen door of Mabel's Grits and Grog.

"This is going to be so much fun." Beside him, Paige practically vibrated in her white sneakers. She grabbed hold of Aiden's arm and grinned. "Maybe we can even pick up some design pointers for our B&B."

For what seemed like the millionth time that day, Reno shook his head. If Paige took so much as a hammer to Honey Hill, her Aunt Bertie—the elderly relative from whom she'd bought the place—would pitch a hissy all the way from the Texas Rose Assisted Care facility.

A loud screech of feedback ripped Reno's attention back to the mayor and the TV star. After brief introductions, she took the microphone like she'd been born to hold one in her hand. Reno imagined that manicured hand had probably never seen a day of hard work. Most likely she used it for pointing and ordering others around.

As she addressed the crowd, Reno watched her perfectly bowed lips break into another smile, which flashed her straight white teeth. You could tell a lot about a person from their smile—though these days it was hard to tell with all the collagen, Botox, and veneers going around. He ran his tongue along the slight chip in his front tooth—a gift he'd received during a tussle with his brother about fifteen years back. Not everyone came perfectly put together. Some folks were a little rougher around the edges.

All the better in his mind.

The makeover star made eye contact with several eagerly nodding folks in the pack of humans squished together, vying to be in a camera shot. In Reno's book, direct eye contact spoke volumes about a person. If a man—or a woman—wouldn't look you square in the eye, you'd best figure out how to defend yourself. He'd learned that the hard way. Had the scars to prove it. There were other wounds inside him too. The ones in his heart might be invisible to the eye, but that didn't mean they weren't just as devastating.

After several syrupy comments from Ms. Brooks about how happy she was to be there and how those on the show planned to give Sweet a shot in the arm and help turn it into a wonderful tourist destination, Reno had had enough. He started to back out of the crowd, only to be stopped by the woman who'd raised him.

"Where y'all going, son?" Jana Wilder stood barely tall enough to reach the bottom of his chin, but she wielded a mighty sword that he and his brothers yielded to—if they valued their hides. And they did. On most days.

By the flash in her bright blue eyes and the tilt of her big blond hairdo, he knew he was about to be on the receiving end of a lecture. "Left the door open on the store," he said. "Need to get back."

"This is Sweet, sugarplum." She reached up and

patted the stubble shadowing his jaw. "Who's going to pay attention?"

He angled his head toward the makeover crew. "Strangers in town."

"Oh pooh. Don't be silly. These nice folks came here fixin' to help. Not rob us."

"That's a matter of opinion."

His mother smiled. "Don't be such a fuddy-duddy."

"Yeah." Paige gave him an elbow nudge. "Lighten up a little."

Reno looked for a little masculine support from Aiden and Chester. Knowing they'd be wasting their breath, they both shrugged. Tempted to go the battle alone, Reno put on his best glare. "Y'all might want to reconsider your enthusiasm before this town you love so much disappears. You let something like this in, next thing you know you'll have a McDonald's and Walmart on every corner."

His mother chuckled. "Didn't your daddy ever tell you that life was just one big ol' adventure, and you'd best snatch it up with both hands?"

"Yes." *The day before he died, in fact.* Reno fought back the huge sense of loss that remained as powerful today as the day two years ago, when they'd buried the man who'd saved his life.

"Then turn around and grab it," his mother dared with a big smile.

As Reno turned back to the circus, he found *Fancy Pants* leaning into that big gas guzzler. Her efforts hiked up her skirt and gave him, and anyone else who cared to look, a splendid view of the backs of her firm thighs.

Chester let out a wolf whistle. Paige gave the old skirt chaser a poke in the ribs. Reno had to admit that as much as he did not want change in his little town, he was a man. One who recognized a gorgeous woman even as everything inside him tried to ignore the warning bells and whistles.

The gathered crowd waited with hushed whispers until the TV host backed out of the Hummer with something in her arms. That *something* happened to be a tiny, apricot-colored poodle sporting a sparkling rhinestone collar.

Charlotte Brooks took a step forward, coming close enough for him to catch a whiff of her sweet perfume. Her brown eyes traveled down the length of his body and slowly climbed back up to his face. She flashed him a grin that seemed to say she approved.

"Hold Pumpkin for me, won't you, handsome?" Her voice was the kind of sexy low and husky a man wanted to hear in the bedroom. Whispering his name. As she begged him to take her again and again.

The sensual spell she cast crashed down as she thrust her prissy pooch in his arms, then sauntered away to continue wowing the crowd.

Pumpkin?

Reno glanced down at the pathetic excuse of a dog shivering in his arms. For Christ's sake, it had glitter-painted toenails on its raccoonlike feet. Who the hell would do that?

Chester elbowed him, leering and nodding like a bobblehead figurine. "She likes you."

Reno could barely think beyond the irritation

burning through his veins. That was when something warm and wet spread across the front of his
shirt.

Shocked, he stared down into bugged-out brown
eyes that silently said, "Oops."

Chapter 2

Charli successfully extracted herself from the initial meet and greet in the little town square that needed a lot of her love and attention. It hadn't taken more than a quick glance to realize the place had plenty of potential and that it was probably one of the most important locations for her to renovate. *This* was where the community gathered, and she had to make it extra special. While her producer might not feel the location was important enough to put on the list of places to spruce up, Charli would fight to the last donut to make it happen. All within her squeaky budget.

Earlier, in a quick glance around the crowd, she'd seen faces both young and old, eager and excited about the changes to come.

That was when she'd spotted *him*.

Tall, with stiff broad shoulders. Dark, with

slightly curly hair. Handsome, with eyes a deep chestnut that glared at her as though she bore a triple-six tattoo on the back of her skull.

He was exactly the type of man she was attracted to and equally the type she'd sworn herself to leave alone.

For months, she'd been on a boy bust. A hunk hiatus, so to speak. At least until she figured out why she kept choosing the same kind of man over and over. At least until she learned to be attracted to members of the opposite sex who weren't looking to break her heart or bail like a Recon paratrooper.

Yet, as she looked into that striking face, something wicked inside her busted loose.

Those narrowed eyes had issued a challenge.

And she'd *never* been one to wuss out.

Charli didn't understand his reasons for such a dark frown in a crowd full of smiles, but she sure as hell planned to find out. In a moment of sheer madness, she'd chosen *him* to hold her little traveling companion. Because, really, who wouldn't want to cuddle with an adorable fluff of fur?

Oh sure, she could have held on to Pumpkin herself, but *he'd* thrown down the gauntlet. And, thanks to a hot wave of hormonal lunacy, she'd decided to pick it up.

While the rest of the crew chatted with the community and listened to enthusiastic ideas on how to renovate the town, Charli slipped away to rescue Pumpkin. She'd only meant for the scowling dark-eyed hunk to hold on to her doggie for a few minutes while she gave the residents a quick rundown on what to expect in the coming six weeks. Instead, he'd stomped off in a large pair of cowboy boots toward Wilder and Sons Hardware & Feed.

During her years in design, Charli had learned that first impressions were critical. And Main Street—the heart of Sweet, Texas—was in desperate need of a better first impression. As they'd come through town, the hardware store's sun-bleached cedar siding and rusted metal roof had caught her eye. Though the white paint on the window frame had peeled like a bad sunburn, the place had charm. It just needed a little spiffing up.

As she wobbled across the road in the ridiculous high heels the show's wardrobe consultant had insisted she wear, a strategy sprouted in her mind. Because of a bad economy and budget cuts, shows like theirs were always on the edge of extinction. Charli had a lot to prove. She'd always been known for tackling the impossible—like trying to impress her father—or renovating a former hospital into low-cost apartments for senior citizens. In her mind, the bigger the challenge, the better the satisfaction when the project was complete.

Aside from the numerous large projects on Main Street, there was the hardware store. Which might not be big in size, but something told her a lot of heart had gone into those walls. And she planned to make them prettier.

When she opened the front door, a little bell jingled her arrival. While she waited, she looked around. Everything on the inside appeared as ancient as the outside. Like maybe the items for sale had sat on the shelves since the turn of the nineteenth century.

Finally, from a back room, Mr. Tall, Dark, and . . . yep, still Grumpy, emerged. To her surprise, his big hands were busy buttoning a plaid shirt over a spectacularly tan, naked chest with a light layer of hair that looked soft and inviting to fingertips that were tactile sensitive. Like hers. Below those amazing pecs came a set of rippled abs. Not the overdone variety, like the ones displayed in the gym where some men seemed to have nothing better to do than pump and preen. The abs on Mr. Grouchy looked like they'd been cut from hard, sweaty man work.

In a moment of sheer indulgence, she dropped her gaze lower to the fine dark hair that swirled his belly button, then formed a line that disappeared into a pair of jeans slung over narrow hips. What went on below *that* looked to be equally interesting.

Sadly, with each button he closed, the magnificent view disappeared. She forced her eyes upward with a mental reminder that she was on a man ban. Looky, but no touchy.

"How can I help . . ." He glanced up. "You." While his last word dropped off on an accusation, those dark eyes sliced and diced her like a Ronco Chop-O-Matic. Something in her stomach did a funny side shuffle and a little heel kick.

Down girl.

"You stole my dog," she said, as soon as her senses rolled back up into her brain.

Those incredible eyes narrowed just a fraction. "First of all," he said, "that's *not* a dog. Second, I didn't steal it. *You* dumped it. And third, you owe me a shirt."

"A shirt?"

"Pumpkin had a little accident."

"Oh." Charli covered her mouth to hide her smile. "Sorry. Good thing you sell shirts." She glanced around again at the products available for sale. "And coffeepots. And yarn. And candles. And pet supplies. And . . ." She squinted her eyes. "Are those silk poppies in that apple basket?"

"You got a problem with fake flowers?"

"In a craft store? No. In a hardware and feed store? Don't you think that's a little . . . odd?"

His wide shoulders came up—making him look even larger and infinitely more intimidating. "I think what's *odd* is why you want to come to this town and fix what isn't broken."

"No one said Sweet was broken. But don't you think it could use a little livening up?"

"If you've ever been to Seven Devils on a hot summer night, you wouldn't ask that question."

"And Seven Devils is . . . ?"

"Local bar. Not someplace someone like *you* would frequent."

"You know nothing about me, Mr. . . ."

"Wilder." He gave a nod toward the front window. "Like the sign says."

"So, then, where are your sons?"

"You sure ask a lot of questions."

"And you're pretty good at dodging them." That almost got a smile. Or not. "Where's my dog?"

"That pathetic excuse for a canine is in back. If Bear hasn't eaten her for a snack."

Bear? Images of sharp teeth and claws shot panic up Charli's spine. She headed toward the back room. Mr. Grumpy with the fabulous physique stepped in her way and filled her senses with a delicious scent that was clean, warm, and all male.

"Can't you read?" His voice resonated in a deep rumble that vibrated over her skin like a hot caress.

She looked up over the door. EMPLOYEES ONLY. "Are you holding Pumpkin hostage until I pay for your new shirt?"

"Hadn't thought of that." He glanced at a rack of plaid apparel and the sign that read $19.99. "But it's not a bad idea."

"I left my purse in the Hummer. You'll have to take my word that I'm good for it."

"Now, while it might be easy to figure that a woman who owns an expensive vehicle like—"

"The expensive vehicle belongs to the production company. *I* drive a MINI Cooper."

"Still presents a problem." He folded his arms, and biceps bulged beneath those short sleeves. "Because, as you said, I don't know you."

"I'm not going anywhere for six weeks," she said. "And I promise you twenty bucks is no big deal." She brushed past him. All her fears washed away when she found Pumpkin playfully nipping at the ears of an Australian shepherd several times her size. The other dog lay there with a tilt to his russet eyebrows that said, "Please remove this pest from my personal space."

"Pumpkin! Stop that." Charli swooped up her little dog, then looked up at the big, tall man beside her. "Your dog is very tolerant. Probably a lot more so than his owner."

Turning on her heel, she headed toward the front door, where her earlier idea burst into full bloom.

Behind her, his boot heels came to a halt near the sales counter. She stopped and turned.

"Just so you know," she said in her most confident voice, "at the reveal meeting tonight in the community hall, I plan to present the big plan. I want to do *you* first."

That dark gaze traveled up and down her body like a singles-party cruise.

He was a big strong man. A man's man. With a NO TRESPASSING sign embedded in those dark eyes. Probably burned into his heart as well. She knew the type. Too well. Women loved him, and he knew it. And he'd love them. Then move on.

As his eyes came back up to her face, a smile appeared from within a five o'clock shadow and flashed a deep set of dimples Charli would never have guessed existed. The combination of dark and light on him was magnificent and devastating.

"Well, now, Ms. Brooks, that's a mighty fine offer," he drawled. "But I hardly know you. And I've never considered myself a one-night-stand kind of guy."

Of course he didn't. He was probably more like a *half*-a-night-stand kind of guy.

"I meant I'd like *your store* to be the first makeover we do," she rushed to clarify.

He moved out from behind the counter and came toward her. His boots thudded on the ancient wood floor and stopped mere inches away. Again, she was overwhelmed by his size and pure masculinity. One that foolishly made her want to wrap her arms around his wide shoulders and nuzzle against that strong neck.

He was not a pretty boy by any means. His face

was all man—accented with a few lines at the corners of his eyes. This close, she also noticed a few silver hairs at his temples. Experience and maybe some heartbreak too were etched on that face. It all came together in a curiously gorgeous package that made her want to dig deeper.

"Never," he said.

She blinked away the forbidden fantasy that had begun to romp through her imagination. "I beg your pardon?"

"You will *never* touch this place," he said. "Not on my watch. Not in my lifetime."

The low, deep tone in his voice stopped just short of a growl and sent a shiver up her spine. Unfortunately, the chill wasn't of the Little Red Riding Hood vs. the Big Bad Wolf variety. And reckless girl that she could often be, it intrigued the hell out of her.

She tilted her head and studied him. The intensity in his eyes. The tension in his jaw. The stiffness in his spine. "Why on earth would you be against creating a better shopping environment for your customers?" she asked. "In the three towns our show has renovated, data indicates that afterward, business picked up, and profits increased. Who in their right mind would be opposed to enhanced customer satisfaction and a higher bottom line?"

"Satisfaction has never been an issue," he drawled in a tone that suggested his comment had nothing to do with hardware. Then he reached behind her and opened the door. "Have a nice day."

With a lift of her chin, she took the not-so-subtle hint, tucked Pumpkin in closer, and stepped out onto the boardwalk.

The door closed in her face.

Charli glared through the glass and watched his very fine backside disappear into the stockroom.

"*Never* is a very long time, Pumpkin." She looked down into her dog's big brown eyes and ran her fingers over the fuzzy topknot tied up with a yellow bow. "And, unfortunately for him, I'm on a tight schedule."

Chapter 3

"*I*f y'all are done talkin' amongst yourselves, we can get down to business." Gladys Lewis—current senior center and Sweet Apple Butter Festival president—spoke too close to the mic with her red-smeared lips, and a screech of feedback ensued.

Reno rubbed his fingers over the intense headache hammering him between the eyes. How the hell he got himself talked into things, he'd never know. One minute, he'd been closing up shop and heading home, the next he'd been dragged to an event he'd planned to avoid like a case of the swine flu.

Somewhere between a chunk of his favorite meat loaf and a thick slice of homemade strawberry-rhubarb pie, his mother had sweet-talked him into driving her back into town for the meeting from hell. He wasn't buying that she'd scratched her cornea with a flake of alfalfa and couldn't drive.

So there he sat in the community hall with the

rest of the gang, trapped on a cold metal chair between his mother and his brother Jesse—both of whom believed the town *face-lift* was a grand idea. Realistically knowing there was only one way out of the building, Reno searched the white cinder-block walls in vain for a hidden escape route.

Gladys Lewis's cottony blue hair bobbled as she banged her gavel down on the podium like she was in charge of an unruly courtroom. "Ms. Brooks will now give us the list of lucky businesses chosen to receive the renovations." The audience—a standing-room-only crowd—applauded politely.

His mother nudged him with her elbow. "This is so exciting, don't you think?"

"Electrifying." He turned to Jesse, who sat with his long legs stretched in from of him and his arms folded across his white veterinarian jacket. "You up for a beer after this?"

Jesse shrugged. "Sure."

"Boys," their mother said in the same tone she'd used when she'd caught them hanging from tree limbs, or chasing cows, or heading off into the woods with their BB guns slung over their shoulders. "Pay attention, please."

At that moment, surrounded by her crew and a couple of guys in suits, Charlotte Brooks stepped up to the podium. She'd toned down her earlier skintight blouse and skirt with a pair of khakis, a snug white tee, and a fitted navy jacket. But she still had on those big-ass high heels. Her brown hair had been pulled up into a sleek ponytail that dangled between her shoulders. And the frown Reno had left her with as he'd closed the door in her face had been replaced with an enthusiastic smile. She radiated energy.

Reno sucked in a lungful of air.

God, the woman was as effervescent as a glass of newly poured champagne—all bubbly and ready to go.

"Now, *that* is a knockout," Jesse murmured.

"Out of your league, little brother."

A slow smile spread across Jesse's face. "I don't mind talking her into mine."

Reno opened his mouth to respond and was cut short by the TV host's thanking everyone for coming.

"First of all," she said, "we want to thank everyone for your hospitality in opening your homes to us for the duration of our stay. We've never been in a town without motels before."

Everyone gave an obligatory chuckle.

Reno leaned toward his mother. "What the hell does that mean?"

"There aren't any motel rooms to rent, so the community is opening up their homes," his mother whispered. "Gertie West is hosting the little blond assistant."

"What about the B&Bs?"

"Guess there weren't enough rooms to go around."

"The proximity of the places we're staying are quite a ways apart," Charlotte continued, "but we promise that won't interfere with our ongoing discussions as we complete these projects. And . . . we promise not to steal ashtrays or towels."

Another obligatory chuckle rumbled from the crowd.

A snap of impatience hit Reno. He glanced at his watch and looked around again for that hidden exit.

"As you know in the past, *My New Town* has chosen three businesses with the greatest need of renovation." Charlotte looked out over the crowd and made eye contact with several in the front row. "While our budget is tight, we always aim to give the town the most bang for the buck. After touring Sweet earlier this afternoon, I had a talk with the producers, and this time we've decided to up our game."

A low rumble of murmurs spread through the audience.

"I *knew* it."

Reno looked at his mother. "You knew what?"

"I knew she'd really listened to what the town told her. She knows the needs. And I knew she'd do what was necessary to fulfill those needs. She's a good girl."

Reno doubted that. "Have you even spoken to her?"

"Not yet."

"Then how would you know she's a *good girl*?"

"Instinct, son." His mother turned her head, her eyes cut directly to his. "When you're the mother of five boys, you learn it real fast."

"Amen to that," Jesse murmured.

"This time," Charlotte Brooks said, "the producers have agreed to double the number of makeovers." The announcement received a standing ovation.

Reno stood solely out of obligation, but he refused to go so far as to clap his hands.

"So without further ado," Charlotte continued once the crowd quieted down, "I'm proud to reveal the winners. Though please note these are not specifically in the order in which they will be addressed."

Agitation and dread twisted in Reno's gut while he resettled in his chair, and the provocative TV host unfolded a piece of paper.

"First on the list is the Sweet Senior Center."

A collective gasp filtered out among the gray-haired troublemakers who'd brought the makeover show into the town that had been his safe haven when he'd been an abandoned child and when he'd returned from the war.

"We promise," Charlotte Brooks said, "we'll turn that run-down building into a fun place you will all be able to enjoy for years to come."

Reno hated to admit it, but the senior center could definitely use a little help. The roof had needed replacing years ago, and no one was quite sure how to describe the ugly shade of green paint.

"Second on the list is Goody Gum Drops. We know you gave it a good effort, Mrs. West, and we promise to help you fulfill your dream of making your shop stand out . . . with a more subtle approach."

What was wrong with the red-and-white-striped candy store? Reno frowned. One look at the place, and you knew exactly what you'd find inside.

"Third on the list," the way-too-eager designer continued, "is Sweet Pickens Bar-B-Q. You had the right idea, Mr. Carlson. We'll just help you refine it a bit. Next is the Harvest Moon Mercantile. Mr. Bodine, we know this store is over a hundred years old and has been handed down through the generations. We want to make sure it stands for another hundred."

Then *Fancy Pants* got an even bigger smile on her face, if that was even possible. "For a special surprise we've chosen . . . Town Square." A raucous cheer from the crowd lifted the roof. "We plan to give you a new gazebo, benches, picnic tables, *and* we're going to add a playground in the northeast corner."

That announcement brought the folks to their feet. Reno relaxed. Guess she'd gotten his not-so-subtle hint that he wanted no part of her makeover shenanigans.

While the crowd rejoiced, Charlotte Brooks stood at the podium, looking quite pleased with herself. She didn't understand what she was doing, and it wasn't Reno's job to educate her. But he sure wished someone would before it was too late. Drastic structural changes couldn't be as easily undone as switching your lunch order from a burger to a BLT. And God knew that a small number of tourists passing through could be beneficial, but an entire slew of them would disrupt life as they knew it.

Finally, the crowd quieted, and Ms. Brooks began to fold the plan of attack in her hands. Abruptly she looked down and reopened the pink sheet of paper. "Oh!"

Uh-oh.

"I almost forgot." Her coffee-colored gaze skimmed

over the crowd until it landed on him like a heat-seeking missile. "Last but not least, we are super excited to include in our makeovers, Wilder and Sons Hardware & Feed."

Shit.

A smirk lifted the corners of those full pink lips, and a spark flashed behind those brown eyes. "Congratulations, Mr. Wilder."

Anger spread through his chest in a hot flush.

"Well, big brother . . ." Jesse clamped a hand over his shoulder. "How about we make that a whiskey instead of a beer?"

Reno narrowed his eyes at the brunette standing at the podium with a grin a mile wide that proclaimed she'd just declared war.

While everyone in the hall stood and began to mingle and chat excitedly about the changes to come, he and Jesse gave their mother a good-bye hug, then headed toward the exit. The closer he came to the metal doors, the more he felt her eyes on him. Reno glanced over his shoulder to find the troublemaker still at the podium. Smiling.

Damn city girl.

He shook his head and shoved open the steel door.

She'd learn quick enough not to mess with Texas. Or *him.*

Hours later, Charli passed through large rock columns and an ornate, electric, metal gate. She drove up the gravel drive through a canopy of live oaks that shaded the road and cast shadows on the tall meadow grass. Within moments, she'd parked near a big barn and stepped down from the Hummer.

The day had been long, and she looked forward to a hot shower and a good sleep. She grabbed her purse and Pumpkin off the passenger seat, then turned to look across the wide driveway at the ranch-style home. It wasn't a huge house, but she could imagine a family of four or five living there comfortably.

A rock face gave the home an immediate sense of character. Dormer windows dotted the second story, and a covered veranda held gorgeous glazed pots brimming with red geraniums, bluebonnets, and yellow lantana. Two crimson rocking chairs on either side of a small rustic table tempted her to sit and unwind. Though exhaustion drained every muscle in her body, she could think of no better time to thank her hostess for the temporary housing.

The woman she'd spoken with on the phone had been warm and friendly and more than happy to loan out the little apartment over her barn. Charli knocked on the front door. When no one answered, she figured her hosts must still be at the post-announcement punch-and-cookie reception. Though she'd missed an introduction there, she'd make sure to meet them and offer her gratitude as soon as possible.

Initially, she'd been given the choice of several places to stay—a couple of bed-and-breakfasts, even the six-bedroom home a few of her crew had chosen. But the idea of a little space and privacy after working side by side with her crew and the community every day, six days a week for six weeks, sounded more appealing. When the small apartment had popped up in the mix, she'd reached out and grabbed it.

Shading her eyes against the setting sun, she scanned the area surrounding the house where dozens of cows in assorted shades of black and brown grazed in the tall grass. Live oak and elderberry dotted the landscape at the back of the property in a picturesque pattern. The entire landscape was pretty enough to photograph and display. No makeover necessary here. The place was nicely done and well loved.

With Pumpkin snuggled in her arms, she walked around back and found another covered veranda equally inviting as the front. A nice-sized backyard spread out to where an arbor and a weathered grape-stake picket fence as well as an eight-foot wire fence enclosed a sizeable garden. Charli kicked off her shoes and walked across the neatly mown lawn to the wooden gate that hung between the arbor posts.

She inhaled the freshly turned soil and the crisp scent of foliage topping zucchini, peppers, onions, and an assortment of other delicious vegetables. She'd always wanted a garden, but it had never been in the cards. First, as a kid, she'd moved around too much. Now her job required a good amount of travel for long spurts at a time. She was rarely home at her ultramodern Studio City apartment anymore. To even attempt keeping a single tomato plant alive would be futile.

"It's pretty here, isn't it, Pumpkin?"

Her dog gave a girly bark.

"Good thing there's a fence, though. Otherwise, you'd be up to no good." She gave the dog a little rub on the head. "Let's go check out our temporary digs, shall we?" Charli went back to the Hummer, grabbed her suitcase, then climbed the stairs on the inside of the barn. She set aside dog and suitcase and, as instructed, retrieved the key from under the HOWDY doormat.

From the moment she opened the front door and set down her suitcase, she felt right at home. Pumpkin trotted into the living area—a space decorated with soft leather furniture. Big enough to be roomy but not overly large so as to feel cavernous. Granite countertops highlighted the open kitchen and island bar. Above the room were exposed beams that gave the whole place a country vibe. Although there were no deer heads or stuffed jackalopes—which apparently were a bit of inside Texas humor.

She wandered down the hall to find a large master bedroom with a king-sized bed and heavy but tasteful furniture. Past the master, she discovered a smaller bedroom surprisingly decorated in happy shades of pink and purple. A toddler-sized bed adorned one side of the room, while a toy chest overflowing with stuffed animals and Barbie dolls occupied the other. The large back wall had been embellished with a mural of a stone castle with golden turrets set in a field of bluebonnets. A white pony with a flowing mane stood on a grassy hilltop, while a smiling goldfish jumped from a bubbling brook. Also on that grassy hilltop stood a fairy princess in a sparkly pink gown and her Prince Charming, who was properly outfitted in a suit of shining armor.

Charli walked up to the mural and trailed her fingers lightly across the surface. "Ahhhh. Hand painted." Not like the mass-produced products they purchased for the show. Whoever had created this original art had amazing talent and obviously loved the little girl who lived in this room very much. While Charli hoped she wasn't putting a child out of her home, she couldn't help but let a small sigh whisper from her chest.

The princess-themed room struck a chord. It was exactly the type she'd dreamed of as a kid. But her father's military career meant they were rarely in one place for very long, and making a military house into a permanent home had been a senseless effort. Or so her father had said. Until she turned eighteen and set out on her own, Charli had become like the walls she lived within—beige and bland.

For most of her life, she'd been invisible to her United States Marine Lieutenant General father. From the moment her brother Nicholas had been born a mere eighteen months after she'd come into the world, the situation deteriorated. When her mother died, it had become even more apparent.

Charli had been only eight at the time, and the loss had devastated her. Her mother had been her safe haven in a world of heavy boots and sharp-spoken words from a father who barked orders instead of engaging in conversation.

For years, she'd played to her father's whims, pretending to be a good little soldier, doing whatever she could to get his attention. She might as well have saved her energy. Her father was either never home or never *there*. One removed him from her physically for months at a time. The other removed him from her emotionally.

She didn't know which was worse.

At the end of the day, she didn't know much about the man who wore a hard expression on his handsome face. She only knew that the military had not made him that way. He'd brought that cold, hard heart with him when he'd enlisted. Which always made her wonder what her whimsical mother had ever seen in the man. Her mother had been the only one who could cajole away his bad moods. When her mother was gone, there'd been no one for the job. Still, Charli had tried.

Inarguably, men were complicated creatures. A detail she'd determined at the age of ten, when her father had come home from a yearlong deployment and merely patted her on the head. Yet later, at the welcome-home party their nanny had thrown, he'd proceeded to tell his fellow officers what a wonderful little girl his Charli was.

How did he know?

Did he really care?

And maybe it didn't matter as long as he paid her any amount of attention.

Sadly, she realized that even now, at the age of thirty-one, she was still vying for her father's attention and approval. And, much like her mother, she'd often sought the company of men whose hearts were voluntarily unavailable.

Miraculously, her brother—now a lieutenant deployed to Afghanistan—had grown up to be much like their mother. He had a beautiful heart and soul and a smile that lit her up on the inside.

Charli turned away from the adorable little bedroom and went back into the master, where she hung her clothes in a walk-in closet beside stacks of jeans and freshly laundered shirts. Men's XL shirts. Other than some tutus tossed on the little toddler bed in the next room, there was no women's apparel to be found.

Though curiosity nibbled at her imagination, the accommodations weren't hers to question. She was only grateful for the king-sized bed and fluffy comforter that awaited her. The one on which her dog had managed to curl up and currently snored like an old man.

Desperate to join her pooch in a nice sleep, Charli went into the roomy bathroom to take a hot shower. Tomorrow's activities included a 5:00 A.M. wake-up call and some demolition on the senior center. Since the seniors had been the ones to initiate contact with the show, she felt they deserved the first swing of the hammer. And as she'd learned several years ago when she'd turned an old hospital into retirement apartments, a happy bunch of senior citizens meant a happy working crew. Bless their hearts for all the homemade cookies and steaming pots of coffee.

After several minutes of standing beneath the hot stream of water, Charli reluctantly got out and dried off. She tossed the towel on the nearby hamper and pulled on the fuzzy pink robe that always gave her a sense of home even if she was thousands of miles away from her apartment near the Hollywood Hills.

While the summer night outside might be hot and humid, the air in the apartment was cool and crisp. The perfect sleeping temperature. She couldn't wait to snuggle down beneath that comforter and catch some badly needed Z's.

She'd just pushed Pumpkin over to make room for herself and turned down the covers when someone knocked on the door. Anxious to meet the lovely woman with the deep Texas drawl she'd spoken to on the phone, Charli padded barefoot to the door. She quickly unbolted the dead bolt and swung the door open wide.

At the click of the dead bolt, Reno turned toward the door. Everything inside him froze, then heated back up like he'd been tossed into an electrical storm.

Great. Looked like Jackson had already put the moves on the new girl in town. His younger brother rarely hesitated to use his charm and movie-star looks to turn a pretty head. *Fancy Pants* had obviously succumbed quicker than most.

Her smile slipped, then just as quick pushed back up into place. "Come to collect your money?"

Her warm brown hair was pulled up into a messy tumble of damp curls on top of her head. A coconut scent that made him think of hot tropical beaches danced across the air between them. And she was wrapped up inside a big fluffy pink robe that made her look as delicious as a marshmallow peep.

Was she naked under that robe?

"Well?"

He lifted his gaze from her painted pink toes to those smoky eyes. "What?"

"The money. For the shirt Pumpkin piddled on?"

Piddled?

Okay, there was a word he'd *never* used in his entire life. "What the hell are you doing here?"

She braced her hand on the doorframe, which inadvertently thrust out one slender hip. "I could ask you the same, Mr. Wilder."

He leaned in and glanced around the empty living room. "Where's Jack?"

"Jack?" Her head tilted. A long dark curl escaped the tangle on her head and draped along her cheek. "Who's Jack?"

"My brother." He folded his arms and rocked back on his heels. "Since you're standing in his apartment half-dressed . . . I'm guessing he's somewhere inside . . . half-dressed."

"Excuse me?" Tinkling laughter escaped those perfect, plump lips. "Are you actually standing there accusing me of jumping into bed with your brother—whom I have never even met?"

"Why else would you be standing in *his* place . . . half-naked?"

Without warning, she whipped open the robe, revealing a snug white tank top and short shorts. The cooling night air hit her fast, and the hard pebbles peaked beneath the soft cotton left no question that she did not wear a bra.

That jolt of lightning hit him again.

"*Not* half-naked, Wilder. And for your information—not that I owe you any explanation—I'm here because a very nice lady loaned me this place for the duration of my stay."

He narrowed his eyes. *"Which* nice lady?"

"I only caught her first name. Jana."

"Shit."

"Excuse me?"

"That's my mother."

"Then why is she loaning out your brother's apartment?"

Reno shook his head and dropped his gaze to the scuffed-up toes of his boots. "Good question." When his head came back up, a smile played about the corners of her mouth.

"And from your total lack of enthusiasm, my guess is this presents a problem for you."

"You have no idea."

"Which would explain why you're looking at me like that."

"Like what?" he asked. "Like I want you to leave?"

"Yes."

"Because I want you to leave."

"Well . . . you didn't invite me here. Besides, it's late. I'm exhausted. And I have a six o'clock start in the morning."

He rocked back on his heels. "Not my problem."

"And it's really not your problem that I've been given permission to stay here while we're shooting."

"You might not want to mention shooting. This is Texas, after all."

"Filming then. And it's really none of your business where I stay, is it?"

He leaned in, just slightly, and caught another whiff of tropical beaches. "Now *that* is where you're wrong, Fancy Pants."

One manicured hand slid to her hip. *"Fancy Pants?"*

Heart pounding like an oil rig, Reno turned and headed down the stairs.

"Hey. You don't need to be so rude." She stepped out onto the landing. "Where are you going?"

"Home."

"Which is where exactly?"

He kept walking and pointed toward the open barn doors.

"The ranch house is *yours*?"

He could almost feel the rush of air push from her lungs and sweep across his back. "Yep."

"Crap."

"Exactly." When his boots hit the gravel he kicked a rock across the drive.

"Have a nice night, Mr. Wilder." The hint of laughter in her tone coiled around his spine.

He turned and glared up at her standing in the doorway of the apartment he rented out to his brother. "You still owe me twenty bucks," he said. "And rent's due on Friday. *If* you're here that long."

"I'll be here. *And* I'll gladly pay."

He gritted his teeth and turned. *You bet your fuzzy pink robe you will, sweetheart.*

Chapter 4

"What the hell were you thinking?" Frustration tightened the pit of Reno's stomach early the following morning while his brother leaned back in their mother's kitchen chair casual as you please.

"Any of us ever win an argument with Mom?" Jackson asked, popping open a can of Dr Pepper and taking a good long slug.

"Not that I can recall," Reno answered.

"Then why would I start trying now?" Jackson tipped his chair back on two legs and forked a hand through his brownish blond hair. "Mom had *Southern hospitality* written all over her face. I might like the occasional adrenaline rush—"

Reno lifted a brow. "Occasional?"

Known for his act-first-think-later nature, Jackson laughed. "Like I said, I might like the occasional adrenaline rush, but I do *not* have a death wish. Me standin' in the way of Mom's opportunity to show her sweet side? Uh-uh." He shook his head. "Ain't going to happen. You like tangling with a tiger so much, you tell Mom the lady isn't welcome."

"Tell who, what?" Their mother chose that moment to pop into their conversation. Not that she hadn't heard them squabbling all the way from the back of the house. It wasn't unusual for them to gather in her kitchen for a meal. Though they all had their own places spread out across the large ranch, none of them were foolish enough to pass up their mother's cooking.

"Reno here doesn't want the lovely Miz Brooks staying at my place for the next couple weeks."

"I can speak for myself, jackass." The beginnings of a headache began to hammer Reno between the eyes.

"Watch your language, son."

Their mother slapped Jackson's booted feet off a table scarred from years of abuse from the five boys who'd eaten their meals there. "And *you* . . ." She thrust a finger at his six-foot-two little brother. "Watch your manners. Both the Marines and I taught you better than that."

"Sorry."

Reno chuckled. There was nothing funnier than when one of the other boys got reprimanded. Just proved you were never too old to be mothered. At thirty-four, Reno didn't mind that at all—circumstances with his past being what they were. In fact, he considered himself damned lucky.

Jana Wilder pulled down a mug from the cupboard and filled it with steaming coffee. She stirred in three spoonfuls of sugar, then sat down at the table between him and Jack. She took a careful sip, set the drink down, then glared, while he and his brother waited patiently for her words of wisdom.

And let there be no doubt the woman would spew them like Shakespeare—Texas style.

"Now, Reno, what's got your tail all in a knot about us being hospitable with the TV folks?"

"Where do I start?"

Arched brows pulled together over her sharp blue eyes. "I expect at the beginning is a good place."

"Changes." Reno shoved away from the table and stood. He thrust his hands on his hips and huffed out a frustrated breath. "Damn woman wants to change everything that's good about this town. And you want to let her stay in Jack's place for six weeks? Where's *he* going to stay? What about Izzy?"

"I have four empty bedrooms in this house. There's plenty of room for your brother. And any chance I get to spend time with my granddaughter, well, that's even better."

Reno refused to sound any more like a petulant child than he already did. So instead of pushing out the rest of his frustrated rants and raves, he bit his lip.

"If he turns any redder, we're going to have to call 9–1–1." Jackson chuckled. "I think he wants to know why you didn't invite the lovely Miz Brooks to stay *here* instead of at the apartment."

Since he'd been nine, Reno'd had a leg up on the dark, threatening glares. Hell, he'd practiced them for hours, weeks, months, just to get one up on his brothers. Lucky for him, Jack picked up on the hidden message behind his narrowed eyes.

"Huh. Look at the time. Got cattle to check. Gotta

go saddle up." Jack stood and gave their mother a kiss on the cheek, then clasped Reno on the shoulder. "See you out at the barn. *If* you survive."

When the kitchen door slammed shut, Reno glanced back down at his mother, who looked much as she had the time she'd sat him down at this very table and told him that under no uncertain terms would he ever be taken away from her and his father. They'd held true to their word. But that didn't lessen the anxiety doing the two-step in his stomach.

"Well, now," she said with a little pat on his arm. "I figured Ms. Brooks would want some privacy. A little peace and quiet. No place better for that than the apartment. Some days, I wish I could move in there myself. It's so nice and serene."

"*You* are welcome," Reno said. "*She* is not."

"This is all about the hardware store, isn't it?" His mother gave his arm a tug, and he sat back down. "She put you on the list, and you don't like that."

"The shop is exactly the way Dad left it." His heart took a wobbly sidestep. "There's nothing wrong with it."

"Except that your daddy had plans to make some changes. He just up and died before he got them done, sugarplum. I promise you, he wouldn't mind your spiffing the place up a little."

Reno shook his head. "I worked beside him in that store every day. I saw the look on his face when he'd walk around and dust or add new items to the shelves. It was pure pleasure. The way things are with that shop, it made him happy." He paused. Took a breath. Let the pain subside. "I feel him there. Like he's watching me, approving of the way I'm taking care of the place for him. I'm afraid if I . . ."

"Oh, son." His mother stroked his cheek and gave him a smile. "Nothing stays the same. I know it's been hard on you since we lost Jared, then your daddy. Not to mention Diana."

No matter which way Reno turned, he faced a reminder of all he'd lost. Including the woman he'd loved to a horrific accident just two years ago—a mere two months after his dad died. Not that he suffered those losses alone or selfishly slighted anyone else's grief, but sometimes he wondered if there would ever be a day he didn't feel the pain so deep inside that he often couldn't breathe.

The coolness of his mother's fingers on his cheek kept him grounded to the conversation. The moment. But it did not ease the ache.

"But, sugarplum, we all have to learn to move on," she said. "They'd want us to. Everything and everybody changes. You just need to get on board is all."

Reno looked up, and as much as he wanted to please this woman who'd taken him in and raised him as her own, he could not. He laid his hand over hers. "I'm sorry, Mom. That train is going to have to leave the station without me."

Roofing. Siding. A new door. Paint. And that was only the beginning of what needed to be done for the exterior of the senior center. Those projects didn't even begin to count the list of improvements necessary for the inside. Charli stood back, arms folded, and watched her lead contractor climb the ladder to the roof. A crew of at least twenty volunteers had shown up to help in any way they could. Just one of the many things Charli loved about small towns. Whenever anyone needed help, someone would be there to answer the call without question or expectation of compensation.

"Ms. Brooks?" Sarah Randall, Charli's assistant, came up beside her with her ever-present clipboard plastered to her chest and her pretty blue eyes hidden behind a thick pair of black-rimmed glasses. "We have a volunteer who is offering us a forklift at no charge if you're interested."

"No charge?" Charli laughed. "Get his name and number before he changes his mind. We have to squeak in five buildings plus Town Square on a three-building budget."

"Yes, ma'am."

"Sarah? How long have we been working together?"

"Nine months, ma'am."

Charli sighed and grabbed the girl in a quick bear hug. "Then when are you going to quit calling me ma'am and stop acting like I'm going to bite?" She leaned back and looked into the girl's wide eyes. "Have I ever yelled at you? Cussed you out? Lost my temper?"

"No ma— . . . Ms. Br—"

"Charli. You call me what everybody else does. Okay?"

"Hey, Charli," the contractor called down. "You sure about that roof color?"

"See how easy that is?" Charli grinned. "Tell you

what. I'll give you permission to call me *mud* if I can't pull off this makeover on time and on budget."

"Or you can call her unemployed."

Charli turned toward the new addition to the conversation—Max Downs, the field producer, and just one more in a line of many she needed to please.

Sometimes the growing list overwhelmed her. Those were the times she had to remind herself that she'd auditioned for the job. On a whim. Well, a dare actually from one of her Beverly Hills clients, who'd thought Charli would be perfect. Charli had thought it would be fun.

The day of the audition, she'd been clueless. Other than the occasional hamming it up for her brother for his photography class, she'd had no experience whatsoever in front of a camera. She'd had no idea of blocking, cues, or which lens to look into when she'd either read from cue cards or improvise a take. She'd not known the difference between a cinnamon roll and B-Roll.

The producers had been patient, and they'd given her more than a few extra chances when others might have thrown in the towel. What had once been a long, grueling learning experience had now become second nature.

She loved her job, but her dream had never been to be on television. She'd never imagined she'd have to turn away the clients she'd worked hard to please because she'd be on the road for six weeks at a time for over half the year. Six weeks seemed like forever when all you really wanted to do was wander into your own kitchen for a midnight snack.

She'd lived her entire life on the move. When she'd

become a designer, her goal had been to create environments where families could spend time together. Where singles could have cozy rooms in which to welcome friends. Where people could gather and stay a while. Her dream had always been to settle down in a quaint little town close to a bigger city where she could set up shop. She didn't want the big-city life. She wanted to wake up every day and walk out into her own yard. To be surrounded by the things she enjoyed and the people she loved.

Finding Pumpkin had been the start of finding that comfort. Charli had needed someone to come home to, someone familiar to chase away the solitude on those long, lonely nights. Pumpkin had happily filled the bill.

Hosting the makeover show had merely been a way to achieve her goal—to get her name and style out there. To save enough to buy her own home. Her own design studio.

At the end of the day, she'd fallen in love with the little towns she visited and renovated. They'd become her passion. And sometimes the towns and the people who lived there offered that missing element she'd searched for all her life. If the show ended tomorrow, she'd be sad and would miss all the amazingly talented people she worked with. In the end, she'd take what she'd learned right back to one of those little towns she'd come to love, and she'd fill her life with beautiful things and even more wonderful people.

"Morning, Max," she said, taking no offense at his underlying threat. "You come to put in a full day of sweat equity?"

"No." In his crisp button-down shirt, he handed her a Styrofoam cup. "But I brought you this. It's the closest I could get to a double-shot skinny latte."

While Sarah and her clipboard wandered off to corral the off-camera painters, construction workers, and various geniuses that made the show work and look good, Charli lifted the lid from the coffee and took a whiff. "What is this?"

"Black coffee, sugar substitute, and low-fat milk."

"No Starbuck's in Sweet?"

"Couldn't even find an espresso machine. A cute little waitress at Bud's Nothing Finer Diner made that for you."

"Ah, then it looks like I'll be ordering a machine off the Internet. Which reminds me, where will our deliveries be made? I found some really nice fabric online for the curtains inside the senior center, and I need to get it here pronto."

Max glanced up and scanned the buildings down Main Street. "Best place looks to be the hardware store. They've got a decent-sized lot in back, where lumber and supplies can be stacked."

Charli glanced down the street to the biggest target on her to-do list. "You mean Wilder and Sons?"

"Sure." Max shrugged. "Seems logical. Guess we'd better clear it with the owner first, though."

"I'll do it." Wow. That hardly came out sounding too eager.

"Great." Max readjusted the ball cap that covered a bald patch the size of a dessert plate. "I'm going to talk to Abraham about camera angles and setting up some B-Roll."

"Meet you back here in . . ." She glanced down at her watch. "An hour."

With some quick instructions to the crew, Charli put her sneakers in motion and crossed the street, with Pumpkin trotting happily alongside. She didn't know why facing the grumpy Mr. Wilder gave her such a thrill. Maybe it was because he was only on her "to-do" list and not her "to please" list.

The challenge of reviving the hardware store was too good to pass up. Still, in no way did she think it would be an easy task.

She felt sorry for his wife. Not that she'd seen a woman around when she'd left the apartment that morning. But the house, yard, and surrounding acreage were immaculate and well tended with a caring hand. One glance around the dusty falling-down hardware store would convince anyone with half an eye that the man didn't much care for aesthetics. And that led to only one conclusion—a *Mrs. Grumpy* was hiding somewhere in this town.

Charli was both eager *and* leery of meeting the woman who'd tolerate that darkly disagreeable man. Even if he did happen to be devastatingly handsome.

The bell over the door tinkled, and, in a blink, Charli was joined in the store by the man himself. His perma-scowl remained intact. Foolishly, she wondered what would turn him into Mr. Happy.

"Come to pay me?" Humor danced within those dark eyes.

"Rent isn't due till Friday. That's what you said last night. Have you changed your mind?"

"About your leaving?" He tilted his head, and

those delicious dimples popped into view. "I believe it's a woman's prerogative to change her mind. Mine? Steady as a rock."

"I'll take that as a no."

He leaned in just enough to where she found herself leaning too. Like he had some kind of magnet attached to his gorgeous chest. Those dark eyes glittered. "But you do still owe me for the shirt Pumpkin *piddled* on."

"Oh." The spell cracked and shattered. She patted the pockets of her jeans shorts, even knowing she never carried money there. "Well, once again you've caught me without cash. So I guess I'll just have to give it to your wife later when I get back to the apartment."

"You fishing, Fancy Pants?" He smiled.

Good Lord, stop with the dimples. Her heart—and her self-initiated ban on men—just really couldn't take it.

"Because if you are, you're going to need a bigger hook."

"Fishing?"

"Do I look like the marrying kind?"

The directness of his question should have made her squirm. It didn't. Because something deep and really twisted inside her couldn't help but be relieved that he was unattached. Well, *unmarried* at least.

Did he look like the marrying kind?

She studied his face—looked into eyes so dark she could almost see her reflection—and read what she found there.

"Yes. You do."

Obviously surprised at her response, his brows pulled together. "What can I do for you today, Fancy Pants?"

"You can call me Charli. *Not* Fancy Pants." She scanned the store to keep from getting caught up in everything that made him the man he was. Especially off-limits. "And you can allow us to use this address for our deliveries."

"Now why would I want to do that?"

"Laughing at me won't change my mind," she said. "Your store is perfect." She walked toward a shelf packed with rows of fasteners, picked up a box of machine screws, and gave it a shake. "In return for the courtesy, we'll be happy to purchase whatever supplies are possible from your store. We'll have deliveries of lumber and other bulky items. You have a large yard in the back where they can be stored until we need them." She had the urge to give her chin a "So there" jerk.

"That doesn't answer my question."

"It's simple, Mr. Wilder." She set the box back on the shelf but in a different spot. Then she took a few other boxes and rearranged them too. "You'd be helping your community."

"There's nothing wrong with my community."

"As far as the people go, you're right. They're wonderful. And hospitable. They genuinely care about each other *and* this town. And I can't believe a man such as yourself would deny his neighbors the right to comfort or for their businesses to succeed."

His beard-stubbled chin came up. "You don't—"

"Don't you believe that those who've worked hard all their lives and use the senior center as a place to gather deserve a decent roof over their heads?" she continued. "Or a place to enjoy a simple meal together? Most of them are alone, and lonely, and they use the center for companionship and camaraderie. Would you deny them that? If so, how could you face them afterward?"

His sensuous mouth flattened.

Gotcha.

Charli felt a victorious smile push at her lips. "You strike me as an intelligent man, Mr. Wilder. One who most likely has a heart. Somewhere. You don't look the type to kick puppies or steal walking canes from the elderly. Call me crazy, but I choose to believe that not even *you* could be such a stubborn ass.".

For a moment, he remained silent. His penetrating glare dared her to back down.

He'd wait a long time for that to happen.

Being the daughter of an emotionless military man had taught her patience. Too bad for Mr. Wilder, she'd perfected it. Backing down did not exist in her vocabulary.

Beneath his intense scrutiny, she casually took another handful of boxes, blew the dust from the tops, and replaced them on the shelf. In a completely different order.

"What the hell are you doing?" He snatched the remaining boxes from her hands.

"You have them stocked wrong."

"How long have *you* been in the hardware business?" he grumbled. "These boxes are exactly where they're supposed to be."

"Really?" She looked up. "You don't think you should have them stocked according to type and size? They're pretty much just a hodgepodge collection the way they are now."

"I like the way they are." He shoved the boxes back onto the shelf. "Stop touching my stuff."

Charli laughed. "Well, there's something you don't hear a man say every day."

"Did you come in here just to annoy me?"

"Maybe." In her mind, she did a little celebration dance. "Mostly I came to tell you we're going to have our deliveries made to your store."

"So now you're *telling* me? Not asking?"

"You had your opportunity to say yes."

"You're a pushy woman, you know that?"

"You're not the first to relay that bit of information. But it's not going to stop me either." She reached out and tapped him on the chest. "It's a man's world out there, Mr. Wilder. And it's my job to make sure they know they're doing it all wrong."

She turned on the heels of her Nike Flex Trainers and headed toward the door. "Come on, Pumpkin." Her dog trotted out of the stockroom, where, apparently, by the little skip in her trot, she'd been pestering Bear again.

When Charli reached the door, she stopped and turned. "Deliveries should start tomorrow. If you could make a space where our crew can easily find it, it would be most appreciated." With a little zing in her step, she cruised outside onto the boardwalk. Behind her, she heard the distinct blast of an F-bomb being dropped.

The summer sun dipped below the hilltops as Reno leaned back in the saddle. Beneath him, the big quarter horse relaxed and rested his weight on one hip. Reno pushed down the brim of his hat to cut the glare while he looked out over the cattle grazing across the hillside.

Most days he was accompanied on the ride to check the stock by one or the other of his brothers. This evening, he'd slipped out before either of them had gotten off work from their day jobs. Jackson, a San Antonio fireman as well as a member of the local volunteer fire department, tended to have long and irregular hours. Jesse—the area's only veterinarian—showed up on time and without fail unless he was out on a call.

This evening, Reno just needed a little quiet time to reflect. Although, if you asked any member of his family, reflection was the one thing on which he spent entirely too much time.

He smiled as two calves trotted to their mother, then butted heads to be the first to start their evening meal.

The Wilder spread had been tough for their father to maintain when his sons had enlisted in the Marines. When Jared, the oldest, had been killed, it almost killed their father too. With the exception of Jake, the youngest, who was still deployed to Afghanistan, the rest had come home one by one to help out. But by then it had been clear their father had lost the heart to run the store or ranch. Or even breathe.

One morning, about two years before, he'd left for the store earlier than usual. When Reno arrived a few hours later, he found his father in the stockroom sitting at the small desk in the corner—head down on his crossed arms. For a moment, Reno thought the big man was taking a quick nap. But it had quickly become apparent that Reno had been alone in the room. His father, who'd been a giant-hearted man, had taken his larger-than-life spirit and left the earth.

Beneath him, Cisco let out a huge horse sigh as Reno himself let out a long exhale. That day, his father's death had devastated him far more than when he'd been five, and his birth mother had walked out of their ratty drug-infested apartment in Nevada and never returned.

She hadn't always been a shitty mother. He vaguely remembered times when she'd hold him, stroke his face with her bony fingers, and promise things would be okay. But more often than not, she'd walk around in a meth-induced haze and forget he even existed.

Joe Wilder had started out his uncle, but when Reno's mother abandoned him, the man didn't hesitate for a moment to take Reno in and make him one of his own. To add him to the brood of four boys he'd already sired. Joe had become a father, a friend, a mentor, a role model.

A hero.

Reno had spent a lifetime trying to show his appreciation.

In his will, his father had equally divided up the ranch and requested his sons join their mother and build their lives, homes, and families on the land that had meant everything to him. The land his family had owned for generations. In tribute to the man who laughed often and loved large, Reno and his brothers had created a special place up on the hill.

Reno's gaze swept the hillside and found the rustic fence that surrounded two graves. His father and big brother were buried there—side by side—beneath that large live oak. Nowhere on this land gave Reno a bigger sense of inner peace. He inhaled a deep breath of clean air, damp grass, and the pungent scent of cattle moving across rich soil. He took a moment to feel the spirits that moved across the land, and he smiled at the memory of his father's laughter as he first began to teach Reno to rope and ride.

The first few tries had been a disaster, as Reno's feet could barely stay in the stirrups, and the lasso seemed too long and heavy to keep in control. But he'd kept at it. The first time he'd popped a loop over a calf's head, his father had rewarded him with a smile and cheered like he'd hit a home run. From then on, Reno knew he was right where he belonged and, most importantly, how to please the man who, by Reno's good fortune, had become his dad.

Behind him, the sound of hooves beat at a fast clip across the meadow. He turned in the saddle to find Jackson and Jesse in a race. Laughter played on their faces. From the moment he'd been brought into the Wilder home, Reno had busted his ass to become a part of the family.

To be one of the boys.

He'd learned he hadn't needed to try so hard. From Jared to Jake, who'd been a newborn, they'd all accepted him from the moment he'd walked through the door, a scared little five-year-old. Before he'd known it, they were all tangled up in the things brothers do. Fort construction, squirrel hunting, fishing, not to mention more wrestling matches than their mother could referee.

With that unbreakable brotherly bond, Reno just couldn't believe that either of the two racing toward him could agree so enthusiastically with all the changes being made to the town they loved so much.

Both horses slid to a stop—too close to call a winner—and Reno's peaceful moment disintegrated.

"I beat your ass," Jackson boasted.

Jesse tugged the Stetson down over his longish blond hair. "You're blind. I got here a whole head in front of you."

Jackson turned to Reno for final confirmation.

"You're kidding, right?"

"Friendly competition, bro."

Jesse laughed. "Told you I won."

Reno shook his head, tapped Cisco's flanks with his heels, and moved forward. "You're both losers."

To his minor irritation, his brothers followed, bickering back and forth over who was the bigger badass. Reno was the oldest now, and a lot of responsibility came with the job. The position meant that once in a while he had to crack his brothers' hard heads together and make them apologize. Luckily, tonight was not one of those moments, and, finally, they both followed him across the field in a quiet compromise.

"Dickerson lost a heifer and calf last night," Jesse said, as the horses set their hooves into the earth and climbed the north face of a hill heading toward

Reno's property. "He called me too late. Stubborn old coot."

"That's too bad," Jack chimed in. "You could have at least saved the calf."

"Yeah." Jesse shook his head. "Sometimes, you've got to be smart enough to give up the old ways."

"Speaking of . . ." Jackson yanked off his ball cap and whacked away the dust on his pant leg.

"Watch yourself." Reno knew where this conversation was headed, and he had no intention of playing along.

"What?" Jackson grinned. "I was just going to say that . . . Sweet Pickens had added a new sauce to the menu."

"Uh-huh."

"Don't puss out, Jack," Jesse said. "We already had this conversation earlier, and it had nothing to do with barbecued brisket and ribs."

Reno looked skyward, hoping someone would take pity and rescue him from the torture he was about to endure. Unfortunately, no lightning bolts flew from the sky, and Jackson persisted.

"Just wasn't looking to get my ass kicked tonight," he said, then looked at Reno. "You see the new roof on the senior center?"

"Yep."

"Looks good."

"Yep."

"Did you check out Ms. Brooks climbing up and down that ladder all day?" Jackson asked with a grin that said he knew he'd just hit a nerve.

"Nope."

"She looked pretty damned good if you ask me."

"Don't recall asking."

"Figured you would have sent her packing by now," Jackson said.

"You know the old rule: Keep your friends close, your enemies closer."

"She's off to a good start," Jesse said.

"A good start at what?" Reno pulled Cisco to a stop. "Destroying our town? Butting her nose where it doesn't belong?"

"Pissing you off," Jackson said.

"Yep," Jesse added. "She's doing a fine job of that."

"I'm askin' her out," Jackson declared.

"Are you crazy?" Reno could not believe what he was hearing. "First you sabotage me by loaning her your apartment, and now you're going to ask her out?"

"Sorry, big brother, I didn't know you were interested in her."

"I'm not." Reno gritted his teeth.

Jackson pulled his horse around. "You sure about that?"

"She is pretty damned hot," Jesse chimed in.

"You've both lost your minds. She's temporary, and she's trouble." Reno kicked Cisco into a gallop toward home, leaving his brothers behind. The last thing he'd ever do would be to get involved with someone who had absolutely no respect for tradition. Or even just a sense for the vibe of a place that had no need for commercialization.

No matter how damned hot she might be.

The closer he got to his own barn, he thought of the woman who'd be sleeping in his upstairs apartment that night wearing a skimpy pair of shorts and a barely there tank top with a pile of wild curls tangled on top of her head.

As much as his brain denied, denied, denied, his body tightened in agreement with his brothers.

Charli Brooks was indeed a very hot woman.

Now all Reno had to do was find a way to put out the fire.

Chapter 5

"It's nice here, isn't it?"

Charli jumped. Caught in the act of poking around the garden behind the house, she looked up to find a beautiful woman with a warm smile, sharp blue eyes, and a big blond hairdo walking toward her. At her side was a brown goat with a pink ribbon around its neck.

"Hello," Charli said, while Pumpkin chased Bear around the lawn.

"Welcome." The woman extended her hand, and their palms met in a firm handshake. "Jana Wilder. I spoke with you on the phone about your staying here."

"Oh! It's so nice to finally meet you." Charli smiled and looked down at the goat, which stood like a well-behaved pet. "Who's your friend?"

"This is Miss Giddy," she said. "We've been pals since the day she was born. Her mama didn't make it. And well, I guess with me holding her feeding bottle, she kind of figured I was a good enough replacement."

Miss Giddy bleated out a welcome that made Charli laugh. "Can I pet her?"

"Oh sure. She's a friendly sort."

Charli reached out, then pulled back when the goat nudged her hand with its horns.

"Don't be afraid," Jana said. "That's just the way she says howdy. She's a cashmere."

"Like the sweater?" Charli petted the animal's long neck.

"Exactly. When my husband was alive, we had a small herd. But after he died, it became too much to work the cattle and keep up with combing the goats too. So we sold them. I just didn't have the heart to send Miss Giddy away."

"She's very sweet," Charli said, then laughed when the goat nodded in agreement.

"So . . . you like my son's garden?"

"It's lovely." Charli joined Jana Wilder on a stroll through the gravel paths between raised beds in the garden behind her landlord's home. "I've always dreamed of having one just like this."

Jana looked up. "What stopped you from making it happen?"

Charli leaned down and tested the ripeness of a Roma tomato. "My father is career military. We moved a lot."

"Really? What branch?"

"Marines. He's a lieutenant general."

"Impressive. All my five boys have served in the

Marines, with various ranks," Mrs. Wilder said with pride. "My youngest, Jake, has just been promoted to staff sergeant. He's still deployed to Afghanistan. We lost our oldest in the Helmand Province. Just outside Camp Leatherneck."

A chill ran down Charli's back. She knew Camp Leatherneck—the largest Marine base in Afghanistan—and she knew better than to ask what had happened. The area was known to be riddled with IEDs and Taliban fighters. If someone wanted to talk of their loved one, she always held the door open. But for some it was just too painful. She'd seen countless families lose a loved one to the war. She knew the pain of loss and the slow process to heal.

In Charli's mind, the eldest Wilder son was a brave young man who had enlisted, fought, and died in the name of freedom. People had loved him. People missed him. And in the hearts of America, he was and would always be a hero.

"I'm so sorry for your loss." Without knowing much at all about Jana Wilder, Charli hugged her. She was not at all surprised when the woman hugged her back. For several breaths, they remained in a quiet embrace before Charli leaned away and said, "You must be very proud of him."

"Jared." Jana Wilder smiled and nodded. "He is—was—a special boy. Always challenging the others to step it up. Do a better job. Take a bigger challenge. He and Reno were the closest in age. They shared a room and were inseparable." She sighed. "I know Reno still blames himself for not being assigned to the same operation. He believes he could have saved his brother had he been there. Most likely, I'd have lost them both."

A mother's nightmare times two.

"Reno can be a bit sullen." Her slow Southern drawl flowed smooth as butter. Though Charli could imagine that with five sons, the woman had learned to raise that drawl into a meaningful threat. "I'm sure you've seen that in him already. Jackson and Jesse think they can tease it out of him. But it will have to be something else. Something completely unexpected."

Reno. So *that* was his name. Charli couldn't help but picture that devastatingly handsome face and wonder where he'd gotten such a unique moniker when it appeared that the rest of his family all had names that began with J.

"All my boys have grown up to make me proud. Reno just needs to learn to laugh again. And I . . ." She gave a twist to a large zucchini until the stem snapped. "Try to shake up his somber little world every chance I get."

"Well, that would explain offering the use of the apartment to me."

"Oh yeah." Jana chuckled. "He wasn't happy about that."

"Tell me about it."

Jana's smile brightened. "I would have warned y'all, but his bark is worse than his bite."

Charli wasn't so sure.

"Now this is going to make a tasty meal." The older woman held up the huge vegetable. "Ever had stuffed zucchini?"

"I can't say that I have."

With a wink, Jana said, "Then you come by to-morrow night for dinner."

"Oh. Well thank you, but I'm not sure what time we'll be done working on the senior center so—"

"Tastes just as good heated up. If you can't make it, I'll send some home with Reno for you."

Charli smiled. "I'd appreciate that." But from the intimidating looks the grumpy Mr. Wilder pointed in her direction, she'd be smart to give it a poison test first.

Later that evening, Charli discovered a new love that had nothing to do with the male persuasion and everything to do with the Adirondack chair she'd settled into on Reno Wilder's back veranda. The glass of locally made zinfandel and Texas twilight added to her love affair. Entertainment came from the very vocal and territorial hummingbirds battling for dominance over the multiple feeders that hung from the patio roof.

With the man of the house out of the vicinity, she allowed herself to relax. She kicked her feet up onto the matching footstool, let out a long sigh, and chuckled as Pumpkin, exhausted from playing with Bear, collapsed on the lawn and passed out. Charli sipped her wine and listened to the orchestra of the crickets hidden in the surrounding trees and grass.

She'd enjoyed her conversation with Jana Wilder, and she'd learned a lot about the Wilder family without even asking. One thing she'd learned during the weeks she'd spent rejuvenating the small towns of America was how easy it was to become immersed in people's lives. She learned to like them, care about them, and she wanted to continue her newfound relationships. At the end of the projects, when she had to climb back up into the Hummer and drive out of town, she always left with an overdose of melancholy.

Always on the move.

She'd never wanted to live a vagabond life, but that's exactly what had happened. One of these days—just like she'd promised herself—she'd stop somewhere and stay put.

With a glance up at the stars emerging from the darkening sky, she realized Sweet was the exact type of place she'd like to stay. Open up shop. Start a new life. Plant some roots and never have to worry about being the new girl again.

She settled back into the chair a little more and sighed. Yep. Planting some deep roots sounded really nice.

In the distance, the soft thud of hooves came closer. She searched the now-barely-visible meadow. Probably one of the cows—whom she'd discovered are curious animals—coming up to take a look. Instead, the shadowy outline of a horse appeared out of the darkness with its rider sitting tall in the saddle. The sound of a gate on rusty hinges creaked open, then slammed shut. When the hooves clip-clopped across the gravel drive, Charli got up from her comfy chair to investigate.

By the time she reached the barn, the rider had settled the horse near the stalls. He took a deep breath, which expanded the broad shoulders of plaid shirtsleeves rolled to the elbows above muscular forearms. He tipped the straw hat back on his head, swung a long leg over the saddle, and stepped down to the ground. His spurs jangled.

No. Way.

Charli stood in the shadows of twilight, mouth agape, heart pounding.

Reno Wilder wasn't just a shop owner. He wasn't just a man's man whose gruff exterior sent out warning signals a mile wide. He wasn't just a former Marine.

Reno Wilder was a genuine freaking cowboy.

Good. God.

Her sharp intake of air gave her away, and he slowly turned—mouthwatering sexy dripping from every single masculine pore. Charli's heart took off in a race. She couldn't even think straight enough to grab hold before it completely went off the radar.

A groan rumbled from that wide, tight chest. "You need something, Fancy Pants?"

"You're a cowboy."

"I'm a rancher."

"You ride a horse," she said, stating the obvious. But for the life of her, sensible words were out of reach.

"Hard to be a rancher unless you can."

She folded her arms, leaned a shoulder against the barn door, and watched him move the stirrup aside to unhook the cinch. His movements were sure and steady. He lifted the saddle and pad from the animal and walked a few steps to place it on a stand. Even while trying to reengage her man-ban mission, Charli couldn't help but notice the way those well-worn jeans cupped his spectacular back-side.

"What about trucks or ATVs?" she asked.

The horse gave his arm a nudge when he reached to remove the headstall. With his large hand, he gave the animal an affectionate stroke on the neck that gave Charli a tug way down deep in her lemon yellow panties.

"Cows see trucks they think they're getting fed or going to the slaughterhouse," he said. "ATVs scare the crap out of them."

"Literally?"

"There you go asking questions again."

"If I don't ask, how am I ever going to learn?"

He turned to look at her like she'd lost a screw. "You want to learn about cow crap?"

She walked into the barn. "Not really."

He hung the leather piece on a hook, opened the stall door, and the horse wandered inside. He pulled a flake of hay from a cube outside the door and dropped it into a feeder attached to the inside of the stall. Then he grabbed a soft-bristled brush, and, while the horse happily munched away, he ran that brush methodically down the horse's sweaty back.

"Do you do that after every ride?" she asked.

"Yes." He exhaled. "It's his reward. Makes him feel good after a long ride."

Well, didn't *that* just put a different kind of thought into her head. "So you're all about feeling good?"

He braced his arms on the horse's back and dropped his head between them. Then he shook it ever so slowly, the motion catching shadows on the straw brim of his hat in the low overhead light.

Finally, he looked up at her. Exasperation darkened his face.

Could be just the play of shadows again.

She tilted her head to look closer.

Nope.

Clearly exasperated.

"If you'd like a lesson in horsemanship, I suggest you call Chester Banks," he said.

"Who's that?"

"He's an old cowboy who loves pretty ladies. I'm sure he'd be happy to show you a thing or two."

"Was that a compliment?"

With something that could be roughly considered a growl, he tossed the grooming brush back on the shelf, closed the stall door, and walked out of the barn.

She followed.

"Don't you think it's rude to ignore someone when they've asked you a direct question?"

He stopped halfway across the gravel drive and turned so fast she almost ran into the back of him. He smelled of hardworking man. And horse. And she was surprised at the jumping beans that began to leap around in her stomach and start a march toward her lower abdomen.

"Pardon my rude behavior." His tone dripped with sarcasm. "My mother did raise me to have better manners and to be honest. So yes. That was a compliment. And now I'll bid you a good night."

He disappeared into the house, and Charli

watched until a light came on in the back. She watched as his shadow passed by the window shade. She watched as he unbuttoned his shirt and pulled it off.

Her heart sprang up into her throat.

Watching that shadow play was like paying a quarter for a peep show. Only *she* got it for free.

He thinks I'm pretty.

Butterflies did a dance around her heart before she could swat them away.

Behind the shade, his shadow unbuttoned those soft, worn, butt-hugging jeans and slid them down his lean hips. Charli sucked in a big gulp of air, then headed back to the veranda and her glass of wine.

With all the estrogen doing a conga line through her blood, she needed a drink.

Well, she really needed something else.

But she'd settle for the drink.

Reno turned on the shower and stepped beneath the hot stream. He braced his palms on the tiled wall and let the water cascade over his head and down his back while he waited for the tension to leave his body. A long time passed before he finally got the message that it wasn't going to happen, and he grabbed the bar of soap. Minutes later, he toweled off and pulled on his most comfortable jeans and a clean white T-shirt.

Ignoring thoughts of the woman who'd invaded his property, his life, and his sanity, he went downstairs to feed Bear and enjoy a cold beer on his back veranda. Nothing soothed his soul like watching the stars and moon float in the velvet sky. Or the scent of the dew on the grass. Or a warm breeze on his face. Or the quiet calm of a summer night.

As he passed through the kitchen, he flipped on the radio and smiled at the George Strait song. "The Man in Love with You" had always been one of his favorites. He'd heard his father sing it to his mother countless times. Once, he'd even caught them dancing on the back patio while a summer storm beat down on the roof and his father hummed the tune. It didn't play on the radio all that often anymore, but the lyrics still warmed a place in his heart.

After grabbing Bear's bowl and filling it with dog crunchies, he swiped a cold longneck from the refrigerator, popped the cap, and went out the back door. The veranda was dark, and he was greeted by the sound of crickets from the nearby bushes.

"Bear," he called. "Dinner." After a few moments of the dog being a no-show, he called again. It wasn't unusual for his dog to be out running the meadow. Looking after the cattle was his canine job. But after another few moments, a streak of worry sped up Reno's spine. He whistled.

"I think he's asleep."

The soft, feminine voice startled him. Across the veranda, Charli Brooks lounged in one of his Adirondacks. With her feet tucked up beneath a yellow cotton sundress and a glass of white wine in her hand, she looked far too relaxed and, oddly, right at home.

"What are you doing here?" It seemed like he asked that question of her a lot.

"Your mother came by to pick some zucchini."

With, he was sure, a mess of Southern hospitality burning on her lips. "That hardly answers my question."

"She told me I could make myself at home."

"Of course she did."

"Earlier, I stopped by the store," she said. "Bought some groceries and a nice bottle of zinfandel. There appeared to be no place nicer to enjoy a glass of wine than on your veranda." She lifted her glass. "So here I am."

"Yep. Here you are." The snark in his tone didn't stop her luscious lips from tilting into a smile.

"Sit down and drink your beer, Mr. Wilder. It's been a long day." Her chin lifted slightly. "And I promise not to bite."

It wasn't her teeth he was worried about.

"Just for the record," she said in a soft, slightly humored voice. "I'm not easily intimidated. So save the scowls for someone else."

In total exhaustion and defeat, he dropped down to the vacant Adirondack.

"Who's this singing on the radio?" she asked.

The beer halted halfway to his mouth. "Seriously?"

"I work all the time and don't get to listen to the radio that much. In fact, I'm not even sure Los Angeles has a country station. But I really like this. So if you don't mind?"

"George Strait."

"Pretty music."

"Mmmhmmm."

She pursed those full lips, sipped her wine, then closed her eyes and listened to the end of the song.

He couldn't keep his eyes off her mouth. Or her face. She looked so damned . . . relaxed. *How the hell can she look so damned relaxed when I'm wound tighter than a coil of barbed wire?*

When Dierks Bentley came on the radio going "Sideways," everything in Reno's brain scrambled.

She opened her eyes and blinked. When she leaned forward, a whiff of sweet perfume tickled his nose.

"I should probably warn you that I was brought up by a military father," she said. "And I have a brother following in his footsteps. So unless you have a military assault rifle tucked in your pocket, how about we call a truce for the five and a half weeks I'm here."

"In our family we fight until someone cries uncle."

"I'm not much of a fighter."

Yeah. He got that. Soft eyes. Soft skin. Rhinestones on her sandals. Fancy Pants was a total girly girl. Probably more the kiss-and-make-up type.

He exhaled a long hard breath.

And the problem with that?

Nothing.

Kissing and making up had always been one of his favorite pastimes.

"Tell you what. I'll keep my weapon in my pocket"—he gave her low-cut sundress a long once-over—"if you put away your tools."

She laughed. "Mr. Wilder, you do have the funniest way of turning a phrase."

Funny?

Him?

Now there was something he'd never been called.

She stood, reached down, and lifted Bear's food bowl with a little shake. Reno wondered if she knew he could see straight down the top of her little sundress.

Not that he minded.

He'd already seen the woman in a tight skirt and blouse, and tight shorts and T-shirt. He knew how she was built. And as much as she irritated the hell out of him, she was damn fine to look at.

"Here, Bear," she sang out. "Dinnertime."

Reno watched in surprise as his dog came trotting up onto the veranda, with the poodle in tow. "So that's where he's been. Your dog is a bad influence."

She laughed and gave both dogs a pat on the head while they both ate from the bowl. "Isn't that nice that he's sharing with her?"

"She's pushy," Reno grumbled. "And he's too polite to push aside those silly pom-poms."

"Pumpkin's not pushy. She's a free spirit."

Reno took a pull of beer—licked a lingering drop from his lip. Her eyes tracked his every move. "Like you?"

That got him a laugh. "Hardly. The general would never have allowed something so . . . frivolous."

"The *general*?" He lifted the beer for another drink. "Literally? Or is that a nickname?"

"Literally."

"What branch?"

From the table between them, she picked up a matchbook and lit the candle in the center. The flame flickered behind the red glass, and shadows danced. "Marines."

"Jesus." His bottle banged on the arm of the chair. "Don't tell me your father is Lieutenant General Thomas Brooks."

"The one and only."

"No shit?" He leaned forward. "How'd you survive that growing up?"

She shrugged a slender shoulder. "He wasn't home much. The military is his life."

"And that left you out in the cold?"

"My brother and I. Maybe you know him too. Lt. Nicholas Brooks? Second Battalion, Alpha Company?"

"*Quick Nick?*" Reno chuckled. "I know him well. He's a good man."

Charli smiled. "He's a great brother."

"I take it he's still in?"

"Pretty sure he's a lifer." An expression of concern shrouded her pretty face. "I worry about him every day. I'm the big sister. It's always been my job to look after him, especially after our mother died."

A pang of familiarity jabbed his heart. "I'm sorry for your loss."

She gave him a direct look. "As I am yours."

Ah, so his mother was talking to strangers again. He wondered if Charli meant the loss of his father, his brother, or the love of his life. Then again, it didn't really matter. All three were devastating. And none were open for discussion. "Thank you."

He leaned back in the chair, drained the bottle of beer, and gave her comment and concern careful consideration. "Your brother will make it home," he said, confident the statement was true.

"Safe and in one piece, I hope."

"I'd count on that if I were you. I've seen him in action. He's smart. He's strong. And he's fast. Not to mention he can tell a hell of a good story."

"I know. I always thought he'd go into journalism or write fiction. He had such an imagination when he was a kid." Her face lit up, and she gave a little laugh. "Which kept him out of trouble more times than not. He could wrap our nannies around his little finger so fast, they wouldn't even know what hit them."

She'd been raised by nannies. That must have sucked.

As if she didn't have a care in the world, she curled her hand around the wood post, leaned out toward the lawn, and glanced up at the stars. A dreamy look came over her face, and he wondered what put it there. But as soon as his own imagination began to wander, he reined it back in.

What this woman thought, wanted, dreamed about, disliked . . . whatever . . . it wasn't any of his business. He needed to remain on guard. Because the one thing that *was* his business was how hell-bent she seemed on changing everything.

That she was so damned attractive made his resolve an even bigger challenge. Any other woman, any other night, and he'd take advantage of the warm evening, the candlelight, and the floral scent floating on the air.

Charlotte Brooks was off-limits.

With a sigh, she came back to the table, lifted her nearly empty glass, and finished off the wine. He noticed the soft curves to her arm, her long, feminine fingers—the complete womanly package that stood before him.

Everything inside him responded.

"Well, I guess I should let you get to whatever it is you were about to do," she said with a tilt of the empty glass and a smile. "Thank you for not kicking me out."

Reno didn't know how to respond to that, so he said nothing. But as she walked past him, he caught another whiff of her perfume. He closed his eyes against the images that leaped into his mind—of her naked on his cool white sheets. Of her arms reaching up to him. Of him following her down onto a big, soft bed.

He pushed out a breath and opened his eyes.

When she reached the end of the veranda, she stopped and turned.

"Oh. I almost forgot."

God, the woman was like Columbo—almost out of his space, then she's right back again, asking more questions and torturing the hell out of him.

"The mural in the little girl's room in the apartment is beautiful."

"That's Izzy's room."

She tilted her head, and a cascade of deep brown hair fell over her bare shoulder. "Izzy?"

"Isabella. Jackson's little girl. She's two."

"Well, she's a lucky little girl."

"Uh-huh."

"Who's the artist? I'd love to have them paint a mural in the senior center."

"I don't think he'd be interested."

She folded her arms. The movement pushed her breasts higher.

Yeah. He noticed.

"Why not?" she asked.

Reno hadn't felt like a fifteen-year-old boy since he'd been a fifteen-year-old boy. But all those adolescent hormones came rushing back to him now. Times a hundred. "You are the most inquisitive damned woman I've ever met."

"Thank you. So why wouldn't the artist be interested?"

"That wasn't a compliment." Because he didn't consider himself an artist. *"And he's busy."*

Realization dawned. Her arms dropped to her sides. "Oh my God. *You* painted that mural?"

"No."

"You did too. I can tell by the look in your eyes."

"You hardly know me well enough to *read* my expression."

"You're not that cagey, Mr. Wilder. You're probably the most forthright person I've ever met."

"I'll take *that* as a compliment."

"Honesty is a virtue. But too much isn't necessarily polite." She took a few steps closer. "You painted that mural, didn't you?"

"Maybe," he modestly admitted.

"Wow." She looked at him in such a direct way he wanted to squirm. "I am speechless."

"Thank God."

For some reason, she took that as an invitation and returned to sit beside him. "Who knew you had a fairy-tale castle and a knight in shining armor inside you. How long did it take to paint?"

He shrugged. "A few days."

"A few days?" One perfectly arched eyebrow lifted. "Hmmm."

"No."

"Why not?"

"I'm busy."

"You're stubborn." She leaned toward him and studied his face.

He leaned away. "What the hell are you looking at?"

"I'm trying to figure out what other hidden talents you might have beneath that persistent scowl."

Her intensity made him uncomfortable. He stood and moved away. "Don't look too deep, Fancy Pants. You'll only be disappointed."

"I doubt that." She followed him to the edge of the veranda. Came so close he could feel the heat radiating from her body. "I'll see you tomorrow, Mr. Wilder."

To his relief, she gave him a quick smile and walked toward the end of the veranda. But she stopped. Again.

Damn.

"Oh. And make sure you bring your paint and brushes."

"I'm not painting a mural."

"Uh-huh." She gave him a little finger wave. "Nighty-night."

Sass.

The woman had too much for her own good.

Reno watched her walk away, hips swaying gently beneath that little yellow sundress. Her silly poodle trotted happily behind her. Much to his surprise, he realized he liked sass in a woman.

He looked down at Bear, who lay stretched out on the grass watching the she-dog's twitching pompom tail. His dog gave a little whine, then looked up as if to say he'd been sucked in by poodle power.

"Yeah." Reno shoved his hands into his pockets and watched Charli's little yellow dress disappear within the darkness of the barn. "We are so screwed."

Chapter 6

Anyone would agree that a cast-iron skillet was primarily used for cooking. And even though Reno was currently stirring a pan full of scrambled eggs, he considered using the appliance for other purposes. Like whacking his brothers over their meddlesome heads.

"What crawled up your pant leg last night?" Jackson asked while grabbing a jug of milk and tub of butter from Reno's refrigerator. "You took off awful fast."

"Yeah." Jesse popped some bread into the toaster and turned with arms folded across his chest.

"Brilliant addition to the conversation, Jess." Reno flipped the eggs and added a handful of shredded cheese. "One would hardly know you're an educated man."

"I beat you at chess last week."

"Not everything's a competition."

"Come to think of it . . ." Jackson grabbed the glasses from the cupboard. "You took off about the time I brought up asking Ms. Brooks out on a date."

Reno shoveled equal portions of eggs onto three plates, then set them on the table. "I took off about the time you started asking stupid questions."

He sat down at the table as Jesse popped nicely browned toast on each of their plates while Jackson poured three glasses of milk. Within seconds, they were all seated and getting some nourishment before they each began the first of their many jobs.

"You boys ought to know better than to draw me into a conversation that involves *her*."

Jackson looked up with a smile and a mouthful of toast. "Can't even say her name?"

"Don't need to," Reno said. "She seems to be the hot topic of conversation these days."

"Hot. There's that fitting description again," Jesse said, receiving a glare for his lame efforts.

"Have we honestly resorted to middle-school infatuation?"

Jackson laughed. "Hell yes. Don't get women like that around here often."

"Women like what?" Jesse asked, but the smirk on his face said the question was anything but innocently asked.

"Hot," Jack answered.

"Oh dear God." Reno shoved a bite into his mouth and took a sip of strong black coffee to wash it down. "Are we done here? Because there are cattle waiting to be fed."

"Saw her jump into that big-ass Hummer this

morning." Jackson waved his fork in the air. "She had on a pair of Daisy Dukes and some little white tennis shoes."

Jesse's brows jacked up his forehead. "That's all?"

"Don't know." Jack shrugged. "That's all I could see."

Reno's gaze ping-ponged between his brothers, and it was all he could do not to laugh. They'd known exactly how to bait him since the day he'd appeared in their home, and they'd been told he was their new brother. He didn't know whether to smash their fool heads together or join in this ridiculous conversation. Maybe if he did, they'd see he couldn't care less, and they'd give up.

Head-smashing did have its benefits. But he was already exhausted, and the sun had barely come up over the hilltops.

"She likes Izzy's mural." He leaned back in his chair and sipped his coffee. "Asked me to paint one for the senior center."

"That's a great idea," Jackson agreed.

"You going to do it?" Jesse asked.

"Hell no."

"Why not?" was simultaneously asked.

"Because . . ." Reno paused. No matter what response he came up with, he'd come off sounding like a jerk. And he didn't need to give these two jackasses any more ammunition.

"Mom would say *because* is not an answer," Jesse said.

"Because I don't have time."

"Bullshit."

"We'll gladly take over the feeding, so you can go

lend a hand," Jesse said. "You could manage a few hours each day or in the evenings."

"Change is a comin', brutha." Jackson grinned. "Ready or not. Like it or not. It's a comin'."

"And how are you going to feel when the tourism peaks, and they tear down Bud's Diner to put up a McDonald's. Or an Applebee's? Or a Sonic Drive-In?" he asked.

"Why would they do that?" Jackson asked. "They've got plenty in San Antonio."

"Thirty-plus miles away, little brother." Reno sprinkled more pepper on his eggs and took another bite.

"I'd prefer Bud's Belgian waffles to a McMuffin any day," Jackson admitted.

"Well, there you go," Reno said, enjoying a sense of triumph for having brought a little logic to the discussion.

For several moments, they ate in peace. Then Jesse looked up from slathering orange marmalade on his toast. "So . . . you going to paint that mural for the hot chick?"

Reno took a long drink of coffee that gave him time to bite back his immediate response.

He loved those seniors as much as anybody. But there was no way in hell he would help Fancy Pants ruin his town. Sure, a mural might be nice, but once he lent a hand, she'd expect more. Just like how she always came up with a goddamned gazillion questions. The woman didn't know when to quit.

Maybe he'd paint a mural once the production crew left town. But as long as *she* was there, he would not go near that senior center. He wasn't about to help her send his town into a spiral from which it might never recover.

No way in hell.

Midmorning, Charli stood inside the senior center trying to politely refuse a salted caramel cupcake. Two things you could never put in front of her? Chocolate and caramel. Gertie West was tempting her with both.

"Little darlin'," Mrs. West implored, "this here cupcake will give you all the energy you need to finish out your day."

"Mrs. West—"

"Gertie."

Charli smiled. "You know, *Gertie* . . ." The smile slipped from the woman's face. Charli knew refusing her offer would not only hurt her feelings, it would crush them. Southern hospitality deserved respect. "I think I could actually eat *two* of those cupcakes. They look delicious."

Gertie's smile came back, and Charli bit into the cupcake with a long sigh. She was going to weigh a ton by the time she left town. The cupcake was so moist and delicious, she really didn't care. "You have got to teach me how to make these," she told Gertie, whose ample chest puffed up with pride.

"Secret's in the butter. Gotta have the real thing from cream fresh off the cow."

Somehow, Charli couldn't see herself churning butter or milking a cow, but she smiled and winked. "Your secret is safe with me."

As Gertie drifted away with her platter of cupcakes to distribute to the rest of the crew, Charli got back to stapling new fabric onto old seat cushions. One of the most important shortcuts to make sure a redesign came in under budget was to reuse anything possible. The chairs in the large meeting space were sturdy. With a fresh coat of paint, they looked good as new.

Charli smoothed her hand over a wrinkle and popped in the last two staples. She looked up at the bare wall that ran the length of the room and wished the stubborn and grumpy Mr. Wilder would change his mind. He was very talented. His creative eye and attention to detail could add a nice spin to this room that the seniors would enjoy for years and years to come.

The front door opened, and Charli popped her head up, hoping he'd changed his mind. Instead of a sexy rancher entering the room, it was an old bow-legged cowboy with his Wranglers starched so stiff, she wondered how he managed to move. His black felt hat was tipped up at the brim, and determination knitted the grayed brows above a pretty spectacular nose as he headed right toward her. She rose to greet him.

"Howdy there, purdy lady."

"Howdy yourself."

He stuck out a hand gnarled with arthritis. She extended her own hand, which he lifted to his wrinkled lips and kissed the backs of her fingers.

She chuckled. "You must be Chester Banks."

"How'd ya know?" His grin said he was pleased she'd heard of him.

"Let's just say your reputation precedes you."

She gave his hand a squeeze. "How can I help you today?"

"Heard you was wantin' some ridin' lessons."

She wanted to ask where he'd heard that bit of misinformation, but she knew. No doubt a certain dimpled cowboy had planted that speck of nonsense in the old guy's ear. Still, she wouldn't want to hurt the old gentleman's feelings. "Well, I would love that, but I doubt I'm going to have much extra time."

"Got yer evenin's off, doncha?"

Crap. "Sometimes. It depends on what projects we're working on."

"Well, next time you get a few, you give me a call. I got me a new bottle of Dickel, and I'm willin' to share."

"Dickel?"

"George Dickel. Good old Tennessee Whisky. It'll give ya a kick in the knickers."

"Well, I'll definitely remember that, Mr. Banks. Thank you for the offer."

He lifted her hand and gave it another kiss. "You can call me Chester, darlin'."

"I think I can call you Mr. Flirtatious."

"That you can." He gave her a wink. "Yep. That you can."

Talk about local color. Charli chuckled. At that moment, the front door opened again. She didn't know what to expect after Chester's amorous invitation. When a tall, dark, and devastating cowboy dressed in paint-splattered jeans and a baby blue T-shirt in the same condition entered the room, she couldn't have been more surprised.

In his hand, he held a red toolbox that Charli hoped was filled with paints and brushes.

"Aw shucks," Chester said. "Here comes Mr. Party Pooper."

Reno tipped his battered, straw, cowboy hat at Gertie and walked up to where Charli stood fending off Chester's romantic intentions.

"You trying to fix up a date for Friday night, Chester?" His deep voice brushed over Charli's skin like a feather, tickling her senses into full alert.

"As if you didn't know," Chester said. "What are *you* doin' here?"

Reno held up his toolbox. "Ms. Brooks asked me to lend a hand."

"She ain't got enough help?" The jealousy in Chester's gravelly voice was clear.

Charli couldn't help but be entertained by the men bantering among themselves as if she weren't standing there taking it all in. "Mr. Wilder has offered . . ." She looked up at him. "Right?"

He gave a quick nod as if he needed to respond before he rescinded the offer.

She sighed in relief. "To paint a mural for us." She tucked her arm through Chester's and led him toward the door. "Promise me you'll come back in a couple of days to see the finished piece."

"I sure will," Chester said, then turned around and sent a glare in Reno's direction. "I got my eye on you, Wilder."

When Charli closed the door behind her ardent admirer, she turned back to Reno. "What made you change your mind?"

"Call it a moment of temporary weakness," he said. "Which wall?"

She pointed to the largest.

"Figures." He carried his toolbox toward the back and flipped open the latches.

Charli walked through the room bustling with commotion and went to where he'd hunkered down. His big hands were busy removing a rainbow of paints and soft-bristled brushes.

Excitement moved through her as she watched the emotions play across his handsome face. She recognized that he didn't want to be here, but at the same time he seemed eager to create.

She bent down beside him. "What are you going to paint?"

He didn't look up. Just continued to remove the paints, brushes, and a roll of cheesecloth with big strong hands that seemed more capable of wielding a hammer than a small paintbrush.

"What do you *want* me to paint?"

"Oh, no. It would be a sin to take away an artist's creativity. That should come from passion and inspiration."

"Told you I'm not an artist."

She leaned her head back and got a good look at him. She had a feeling Reno Wilder was many things he'd never admit to. One of them being passionate.

She could imagine when a man like him decided to express himself, how powerful that might be. And to be on the receiving end . . . The thought alone gave her a delightful shiver.

"I beg to differ," she said. "What made you paint the castle for Izzy?"

"She's a princess. Always wearing tutus over her jeans and sneakers." His dimples flashed. "When she stays with Jackson, she even sleeps with a little tiara on her head."

"That's adorable."

"She is."

"And you love her like crazy, which is why you painted the castle."

"Yeah. She's only two and pretty much already has me figured out."

At least someone did.

"Where's Izzy's mother?"

"She lives here in town." He looked down, removed another brush from the toolbox. "They're divorced. Joint custody. Breaks Jackson's heart every time he has to take Izzy back home." His head snapped up, and those dark eyes narrowed as though he realized he'd just been trapped.

"What?" she asked.

"You're tricky."

"I don't know what you mean."

"You ask so many damned questions, a person doesn't know when you're getting personal."

"Sorry. That wasn't my intent. It just seemed like a natural flow to the conversation."

"We're not having a conversation."

"We're not?"

"No. You're telling me what you want painted on this wall, then we're done."

She rose.

His eyes followed her all the way up.

"Surprise me."

* * *

Two hours after closing time at the store, Reno put his old red truck into gear and found himself drawn back to the senior center. With little extra time during his normal busy days, his passion to paint was a curse as well as an amazing release.

He could thank his mother for discovering his gift about six months after he'd been in their home. When he'd arrived, he'd been a scared, angry, little boy. His new parents had resolved his anxieties by giving him an abundance of love and the security that he'd never again be alone or abandoned.

His brothers—as ornery as they could be when the sun was shining—would reach out in the dark of night to calm his fears. When nightmares shook his skinny foundation, those boys would grab the blankets off their beds, and, side by side, they'd all sleep on the floor. They never teased him. Never called him a sissy. They just drew him into the brotherhood and let him know he belonged.

Though the anger had subsided, it often came back in the nightmares that woke him in a sweat. As someone who immersed herself in a parade of crafts over the years, his mother recognized that any type of creativity was a way to soothe the soul. She'd tried different methods to engage him, but it wasn't until she'd put a paintbrush in his hand that he'd found his instrument. The first time he'd put that brush to a bare wall, he knew he'd found the perfect medium.

As he parked his truck at the curb of the senior center, he knew that the scene he'd chosen to create would enhance the space and lighten the moments spent within those walls.

That's why he'd gone against his initial foot-dragging on the project. Not for any other reason.

Certainly not because *she'd* asked him to.

When Reno opened the door to the senior center later that evening, he stepped back in surprise. Though the quitting-time bell had rung for most folks, the senior center remained abuzz. Amid the chaos, Charli sat in a corner, her head bent over a sewing machine as she pushed fabric through the pumping needle. Beside her on the floor sat the tiny little blonde who always seemed to have a clipboard plastered to her chest. At the moment, she'd moved the clipboard aside and was busy pinning pieces of fabric together.

Earlier in the day, while Reno had been in the midst of the activity, he'd had a chance to watch Charli in action. He hated to admit that her passion was infectious. She displayed the same quickness and efficiency her brother did on the battlefield. There seemed to be nothing she couldn't or wouldn't tackle. She'd been up ladders, down on the floor, sewing, painting, and hammering. And all the while, she kept up that constant, inquisitive banter.

Why do they call it the Lone Star State? How big is the biggest ranch? What's the difference between Texas- and Kansas-City-style barbecue? Are there really scorpions here?

At first it drove him nuts. He couldn't concentrate. Couldn't figure out what to put on that blank wall staring back at him—daring him to come up with something fresh and creative.

After a while, he became numb to her repartee.

Well, maybe not numb. It was hard to be anesthetized by a moving cyclone. He'd had to mentally remove himself from the chaos—much as he'd needed to in Afghanistan. Stand back and close his eyes until he regained focus. Instead of battlefield rocket fire, he'd heard the tap-tap of hammers. The whir of the sewing machine. And laughter.

Little by little, the image revealed itself in his mind like a dissipating fog. When the entire vision opened up, he'd smiled and dipped the brush into a jar of paint.

Now, he managed to slip into the room as unnoticed as possible. While he dabbed in layers of shadows and highlights, he lost track of time.

From the corner, the drone of the sewing machine came to a halt. Reno glanced over his shoulder to see Charli raise her arms above her head and stretch like a cat. She'd kicked off her tennis shoes, and one dainty bare foot rubbed over the top of the other. Brush poised in the air, he couldn't help but watch in fascination.

Any warm-blooded male—as his brothers had proven—would be mesmerized by the way she looked. The way she moved. She was confident. Comfortable in her skin. And that skin was mighty attractive.

There were others—men on her crew, men in the community—who paid close attention to what she did. She was the type of woman who would make other women jealous. But Charli Brooks had an uncanny way of warming up to people, making them feel comfortable around her.

Comfortable enough to spill details of their lives. He had to be careful of that.

She'd caught him off guard about Jackson's past. God only knew what she could wheedle out of someone if she put her heart into it.

"That's looking good," she said, coming up behind him. "You're really very talented."

Much as he tried to remain indifferent, the compliment washed over him.

"I'll be honest," she said. "I really didn't know what to expect from you."

"You said yourself that the seniors deserve a nice place to gather. I agree. So, however I might feel, I'm not about to take that out on the folks who come here to relax and enjoy themselves."

"I apologize." Her eyes did a quick scan over him. "I underestimated you."

Before he had a chance to respond, she meandered away, picking up this and tucking away that.

Thoughts scattered in a million directions—most of her and how he might have totally underestimated her as well—he went back to his work. It took a while for him to refocus his attention on the art and not the girl. What seemed like mere moments later, he heard her saying good night to her crew. And then they were alone.

"You can go ahead," he said, dabbing highlights on a section of sky. "I'll lock up when I'm done."

"I'll stay," she said.

"No need."

A sigh of exasperation pushed from her lungs as her hands went to her slender hips. "Most people like me, Mr. Wilder. I don't know why you don't. But I guarantee by the time we roll out of town, you'll have changed your mind."

She grabbed a pink hoodie from the counter, shoved her arms through the sleeves, picked up her poodle, and walked out the door.

For a moment, he stood in her wake, surprised at the abrupt quiet.

"You'll change your mind," she'd said.

Exactly what he feared.

Chapter 7

*E*xhaustion attacked every muscle in Charli's body. Every square inch told her it was time to go home, take a shower, and get some sleep. But she'd made a promise she intended to keep.

As the daughter of a general, she'd learned that a promise—no matter how big or how small—was made to be kept. She'd learned about broken promises the hard way. Like when her father would promise they'd spend time together when he returned home—and they didn't. Or when she'd hear a soldier promise his loved ones he'd return from the war—and didn't. Or when her mother had promised she was just going to the store and would be back in no time—and wasn't.

As Charli knocked on the door of the little stone bungalow on Maple Sugar Road, she knew her promise to visit was just as important. Even if it was only for a glass of sweet tea, cookies, and a little decorating advice.

The door swung open, and she was met with a wide, lipsticked smile from Gladys Lewis and her blue-haired sidekick, Arlene Potter, whom Charli had tagged the "Dynamic Duo." As the current senior center and Sweet Apple Butter Festival president and copresident, the ladies were rarely seen apart. They never ceased to amaze everyone with their *energy*—a term loosely translated by some in town as a proclivity for gossip.

Gladys had cornered Charli after the meeting at the community hall to set up a little tête-à-tête with some of the women in the community—a practice not uncommon in the small towns Charli had the opportunity to visit. She considered the meetings a bonus—a chance to get to know the community a little better and maybe uncover some wishes and dreams the residents had for the place where they lived.

It was a far cry from the isolation she felt in her Studio City apartment, where she was surrounded by young professionals who were rarely home and had little time for beverages and conversation. The get-togethers were a chance to learn, and also to help a few overcome some design issues in their own homes.

She entered a small living room bursting with women of all ages clustered together on anything they could find to sit on—a piano bench, folding chairs, even an upside-down bucket.

"Hello, ladies." She gave a quick little wave. While her hand was up, someone literally thrust a glass of tea into it and stuck a silver tray of cookies beneath her nose. She laughed. "Now there's the Southern hospitality I've been hearing about." She snatched a sugar cookie from the tray and sat down in the empty chair.

"We're so glad you could join us, Ms. Brooks," Arlene Potter said, then took a seat on a barstool near the kitchen. "And we promise not to keep you too late. We know you've had a long day."

"Please. Call me Charli." She looked at the eager faces and noted that Jana Wilder was among the crowd. "I'm happy to be here. Design is my favorite subject."

"Men are *my* favorite subject," said a tiny little woman with strawberry red dyed hair and a face creased with enough laugh lines to know she'd enjoyed every moment of her probably eighty-plus years.

Everyone laughed as they passed around the cookie tray.

"What's your name?" Charli asked.

"Gertie Finnegan."

"There are a lot of Gerties in this town."

"Popular name in our day."

"Well, it's nice to meet you, Gertie Finnegan. And I'm rather fond of that subject too."

"You got a husband?"

How did this turn into a discussion about her personal life in zero to thirty seconds? "No. I don't."

"Boyfriend?"

Charli laughed. "Nope. Not one of those either."

"You like girls?"

"As friends."

Gertie gave her a sharp nod. "Just checkin'. We got lots of lookers in this town in case you want to take one home with you. Jana's got a few boys. I'm sure she wouldn't mind if you snagged one of them."

If Gertie only knew what Jana's dark-haired son really thought of her, she'd never even make mention. "I'll keep that in mind." Charli took a sip of sweet tea to wash down her laughter. Leave it to the senior set to get right to the point.

"Well, I'm sure you're all not really interested in my love life so—"

"Honey, this is Texas," Mrs. Potter said. "We're interested in *everybody's* love lives."

That got a round of nods and laughter that oddly made Charli wish she was a part of a community where everyone knew your name and most likely knew how many times a week you engaged in whoopee. Okay, maybe not the last part.

"Well, I *love* design," she said, tiptoeing out of the sticky subject. "Especially when I can help nice ladies like you work out some issues in their homes. So let's get started. Who wants to go first?"

A woman with apple cheeks and a polka-dotted blouse raised her hand. "I've got two teenaged girls who share a room. One's a princess, the other is a jock. How can I decorate a room that will suit both?"

"That's a great question. And believe it or not, *not* the first time I've heard it." Charli put down her glass and cookie, crossed her legs, and leaned in. "The best approach is to find a color they both agree on. For instance, if they agree on blue, the princess will probably want baby blue and the jock will probably want navy. You settle somewhere in between. Maybe an aqua or Mediterranean. For fabrics, you want to stay basic. No flowers. No polka dots. Then you let each girl accent her side of the room with her favorite things. A vase of flowers for the princess. An athletic trophy for the jock. When you're done, it will all meld, and they'll be able to enjoy it without its being too girly or too tomboy."

From there the conversation moved on to how to give the hubby a place to recline without a recliner, how to choose a shade of orange that didn't look like a pumpkin, and how to inject a little femininity in a household of six little boys. The group shared laughter and tea, and they even playfully fought over the last cookie. Charli couldn't remember a time when she'd enjoyed herself so much. The women of Sweet made her feel right at home, and Charli completely forgot that she'd already put in an eleven-hour day on the job site.

As she stood talking to a middle-aged woman named Flora about the best stain-free fabrics, Jana Wilder joined the conversation.

"Thank you so much for spending some time with us tonight," she said, clasping her hands together. "I know how hard you work and that you must be just exhausted."

Charli covered her hands with her own. "Don't you worry about that. I'm used to it. Besides, I don't know when I've ever been able to sleep so well. It's so quiet out at your son's place."

"I think that's why I go over there so often. The boys somehow still end up in my kitchen arguing about who's smarter, bigger, or badder." She laughed. "They always ask if I miss them. But how can I when they won't go away?"

"You do miss them though."

Jana nodded. "I can't tell you how awful it was when they all enlisted. Not that I wasn't proud, but when you're used to five boys ransacking your refrigerator in the middle of the night, or having to separate them when they're wrestling on the floor . . ." A deep sigh lifted her shoulders. "Of course, my husband was still alive then, so I wasn't completely on my own. But after Jared was killed, he retreated into himself so much that . . . I might as well have been alone."

"That must have been a very difficult time."

"It was. I miss my husband more than I can ever express. And losing my firstborn almost took me down. But I'm learning that I can always carry them with me in my heart and my memories." She paused, and the look of utter loss that darkened her light features was enough to break Charli's heart.

"A few days ago," she continued, "I told Reno we all have to move on. He's fallen into an emotional rabbit hole, and, well . . . I guess I'm going to have to lead by example. That's why I came here tonight. I'm ready to take a step into the future."

"Good for you." Charli gave her hands a squeeze.

"You've inspired me. I've decided to make over my house. Give it some new life. Starting with my bedroom. My husband, bless his heart, took the Western lifestyle literally. While I do love the ranch style, I'm ready for something a little more romantic. And maybe a little . . . fun. So it's good-bye to John Wayne, hello to the new me. Whoever that is."

The design rebel in Charli exploded with ideas, and she hadn't even seen Jana's house yet. "I'd love to help."

"Oh, sugarplum, bless your heart. Y'all have got enough on your plate." She glanced away and came back with a grin. "But maybe if I could ask your advice now and then?"

"It would be my honor. Maybe I could come by and help you put together a plan. Then you could get those big strapping sons of yours to give you a hand."

Jana's perfectly arched brows lifted. "Are you sure you don't mind?"

"Are you kidding? This will be an absolute blast. Nothing would make me happier than to help you take the steps toward your new future."

Blue eyes so different from her oldest son's brightened. "Then it's a deal. But only if you let me repay you by inviting you to our big summer barbecue. You and your entire crew are welcome."

"We accept." Charli thought of all the things that could go wrong if she showed up and invaded Reno's space again. Though her self-imposed ban on the other sex loudly protested, something inside her tingled with the idea that maybe something could also go very right.

A Texas sunrise was really no different than a Memphis or Hawaiian sunrise. But something in those gleaming golden rays made Charli jump out of bed even when every muscle in her body screamed in protest.

She wasn't due at the senior center until nine o'clock, so she'd made arrangements to drop by Jana's to take a look. See what they could come up with if they put their heads together over coffee.

After a quick breakfast, she skipped the long, hot shower her body craved for a quick lather and rinse. On her way out the door, she scooped up Pumpkin and her design bag. As her tennis shoes hit the gravel driveway, and she opened the door to the Hummer, she noticed a light on in Reno's kitchen.

Good.

At least she didn't have to worry about his being at Jana's. She'd walked out on him last night, so she guessed that meant they weren't on speaking terms. Not that he'd notice.

A little kick hit her in the heart.

She wanted him to notice.

When she looked at those dark, soulful eyes or those deceptively hidden dimples, it was like being hit by ten thousand volts of raw electricity. Her heart raced. Her fingertips tingled. And the sensation that shot through her core down to all those womanly parts that rarely got a workout was pretty much indescribable.

She knew it was wrong, wrong, wrong, to spend even one nanosecond with those kinds of thoughts. Or feelings. Hadn't she learned her lesson a bajillion times? But Reno Wilder was a big strong man with an amazing physique. And all those *womanly* parts couldn't help but wonder what kind of magic he could work if only given a little encouragement.

Or if he'd at least get that stick out of his butt.

As she thrust the gears into DRIVE, the tires kicked up a little gravel on her way down Rebel Creek Road beneath the canopy of live oaks toward the heart of Wilder Ranch.

Several minutes later, she turned onto Jana's road

and braked to allow the golden brown chickens to waddle to the other side. Without an obvious place to park, she stopped the Hummer next to the huge wooden barn, which looked big enough to house an entire wagonload of Budweiser Clydesdales. As soon as she opened the car door, Miss Giddy greeted her with a bleating hello and a little butt of her horns. Her pink satin bow looked a bit bedraggled as Charli gave her a good rub on her head.

Jana opened the front door of an amazing ranch-style home faced with rock and rough-hewn posts. The front veranda spread across the length of the house, and, much like Reno's, was accented with comfortable chairs and colorful flowers.

"Welcome to Wilder Ranch."

With one arm tucked around Pumpkin and the other hand clutching her design bag, Charli stepped up onto the veranda. Jana immediately enveloped her in a warm hug.

Motherly.

That was the one thing Charli recognized in the woman. It made Charli yearn for her own. No matter how many years passed, she missed her mom as much as if she'd lost her yesterday.

"Good morning." As best she could with arms full, Charli returned the embrace.

"Don't be too shocked when y'all come inside. This isn't the SouthFork Ranch and we aren't the Ewings," Jana said. "We're just simple, hardworking folk."

"I never judge in any manner," Charli reassured her. "In fact, if anyone came into my apartment, they'd probably never guess a designer lived there."

"You don't practice what you preach?"

Charli shrugged. "Mostly I'm never there. When I was just working on my own, I didn't have the time. Plus, it's a small apartment. Hardly anything to get too excited about."

"You don't like living there?" Jana's voice tilted an octave, as if she was surprised.

"I spent my whole life moving around. An apartment just feels so . . . temporary."

"I've never lived in one, so I wouldn't know. But I can tell you it is nice to have a big house and a lot of land to get lost on. Sometimes I look at all this and think it's too much space. Too much work." She glanced out over the pasture, the rolling hills, and the tall, shady trees that dotted the property.

"But everywhere I look, I see my husband. He put up all that fencing before our boys were even born. As a new bride, I remember watching him from the tailgate of our old Chevy truck. As he worked in the sun, he'd take off his shirt, and those muscles would just flex in ways that made my heart race." She gave a small sigh and chuckle. "Sometimes he'd take a break and we'd cool off in the creek."

"That sounds wonderful. And romantic."

"Oh, it was."

Jana's smile confirmed everything Charli believed about love and marriage—that through the hard times came the good times. And that those good times would carry you through the rest of your life. Charli never saw that side of her parents' marriage, but from the way her mother had loved her father, she believed it must have existed.

"Well, that's enough woolgathering for the moment." Jana opened the front door. "How about we go inside and let you put down that big bag."

"It's my design stuff," Charli said, stepping inside a large foyer with adobe floor tiles that still had a lot of life left in them. "Samples. Photos. And . . . wow. This is beautiful."

Photographs in carved wood frames lined the walls and recorded the history of a blossoming land and growing family. Charli studied them all until her eyes landed on one that included all the Wilder boys wearing their full-dress military uniforms surrounded by their beaming parents.

"Is this your husband?"

"Yes. That's Joe." Jana sighed, and Charli sensed a moment of deep heartache.

"He's very handsome."

Then Jana chuckled. "He was definitely what girls now call a hottie."

"No wonder you watched him so closely." Charli moved closer and studied the photo a little more. It didn't take an Einstein to recognize that while four of the handsome young men were blond-haired and blue-eyed like Jana and her husband, Reno was the standout, with dark hair and eyes.

"On the right is Jake, the baby. And that's my Jared, the oldest, there on the left."

Joe, Jana, Jared, Jackson, Jesse, Jake and . . . Reno. Hmmm.

"Jared looks just like your husband."

"Almost a complete replica, temperament and all. He was such a good baby. But once he learned to walk, look out. He was into everything. He and Reno were very close. They both liked to work with their hands." She sighed. "They'd planned to build a side furniture business when they got out of the military."

For a moment, she stood silently looking at the photo, and Charli could almost hear her heart break all over again. The woman had said she was ready to move on, but that didn't mean it wouldn't be difficult.

"Now. In this room the furniture was tasteful— once upon a time." Jana waved Charli into a family room filled with dark, heavy furniture, and boy-resistant fabrics. Horseshoes had been welded into lamp bases. Antlers had been used to make a chandelier. And a movie-theater poster of the movie *Tombstone* was placed next to the flat-screen TV.

"But it's seen the rearing of five rambunctious boys. That coffee table has always been to blame for the scar at the corner of Jesse's eye. *Not*, mind you, the fact that he was nine at the time and trying to perfect an Olympic backflip."

"Is that where the saying "Boys will be boys" came from?"

"Obviously from a mother who knew them well. I always wondered what would last the longest, the boys, the furniture, or me. Come on. I'll give you the nickel tour of the rest of the disaster that is my home, and you'll see that the furniture has survived the longest."

"Your home is very comfortable," Charli said.

"And *you* are very polite." Jana chuckled, then led the way down the hall past several smaller bedrooms on one side of the home to the master suite on the opposite end.

Instead of seeing a bland room with bland walls and heavy, man furniture, Charli saw possibilities. "What's the budget for your makeover?"

Jana folded her arms and her index finger came up to tap her chin. When she finally gave a number, Charli knew she'd have to work her magic to give this nice woman what she wanted. Or maybe *needed* was a better term.

"I have some ideas," Charli said. "And since you mentioned coffee, do you mind if we sit down at your kitchen table? I have some samples to show you. Then we can pull our visions together and come up with a plan."

"I not only have coffee, I have some butter biscuits and homemade raspberry jam."

"Well, I'd be willing to see if I can help you get rid of a few of them." Charli followed her hostess into a kitchen scented with maple and baked goods. She abruptly stepped back when they found Reno, Jackson, and Jesse helping themselves to the warm biscuits. They all looked up—two of them with surprise, one with a scowl.

Yeah, like that was anything new.

All three stood, as their mother had most likely trained them to do when a lady entered the room.

"Oh you boys!" Jana said, scolding them even while she smiled. "I made those for our guest."

"Sorry." Jesse's apologetic expression was obviously one he'd used with his mother many times.

"There's still enough for the both of you." Jackson held up a platter piled high with golden biscuits.

"Have a seat," Jana told Charli. "I'll grab coffee."

"We already have coffee," Jackson said.

Jana's gaze sliced to the counter. "And you left me an empty pot. Sorry, Charli, it will only take me a minute to brew another."

"No problem." Charli accepted the chair Jesse had pulled out for her. She sat down, resting her design bag against her ankle and Pumpkin on her lap. "I've got about an hour before I need to be at the senior center."

Reno lifted a biscuit to his mouth, took a bite, and chewed thoughtfully. "You always bring your dog with you everywhere you go?"

She blinked. Glanced at the mop of brown, white, and black fur curled up on the rug near the back door. "Do *you*?"

Jackson stood, grabbed his empty plate from the table, and dumped it in the sink. "Think she's got your number, brother."

" 'Bout damn time somebody did," Jesse added as he also stood and scooted the chair back under the table.

Jana turned from the counter with a smile. "New pot's brewing. Jackson? Jesse? Can you come grab a box from the top of my closet?"

"It takes both of us?" Jackson asked. To which his mother gave him a disgruntled "Yes."

"We'll be right back." Jana tugged her two muscular sons from the kitchen.

Jana's quick departure was an obvious attempt to toss Charli and Reno together. Charli knew this by the little eyebrow wiggle she did on her way out the door. To hide a laugh, Charli grabbed a packet of sugar substitute from a bowl in the center of the table and shook the contents to the bottom of the packet.

"Must be a heavy box," Reno mumbled, setting his fork down on the plate.

"Or maybe she just needed to give them a time-out."

His head came up, and those dimples flashed. "Wouldn't be the first time." His eyes searched her face, then settled into a bold stare. "So what brings you here today? I thought you'd be knee deep in projects at the senior center by now."

"Some construction projects gave us a late start. So I came over to help your mother."

"What exactly does my mother need help with?"

Charli settled back in her chair and noted his rumpled hair. Windblown? Just out of bed? Finger combed? Didn't matter. It looked good on him. "She's decided to give her home a makeover, and she asked for my advice."

His eyes narrowed so fast, it took Charli back a notch.

"She's going to do what?"

"You know." Charli shrugged. "Change things up a bit."

His hand tightened around the biscuit, and jelly squished out between his fingers. "Why would she want to do that?" His voice never rose above a whisper, but the growl beneath his words made his feelings clear.

"Why wouldn't she?"

"Because there's nothing wrong with it the way it is."

"But you don't live here anymore. So why does it matter if she changes the color of the walls?" Charli had never been one to intentionally push people's buttons. But something told her that unless someone was brave enough to poke at the bear, the bear planned to hibernate through the rest of his life.

It was obvious that his family cared and worried about him. Maybe they cared too much to carry a stick with enough of a point to make a difference. She wasn't sure what chaos in the universe kept flinging her and this man together, but he'd thrown down the gauntlet, and she'd picked it up. Today, he left her no choice but to give him a spirited nudge.

"Just because *you* don't like change doesn't mean everyone else has to keep things the same."

A muscle in his jaw clenched. "You sure make a lot of assumptions for someone who really knows nothing about me."

"Maybe I don't yet. But I'm learning."

"Well . . . don't look too close." Something other than anger darkened his eyes as he leaned in. Something a little sad. Maybe even a little anxious. "You might be very disappointed."

He got up from the table and set his dishes in the sink. "If you'll excuse me, I have cattle to feed," he said, then grabbed a frayed straw hat from a rack on the wall and settled it over his rumpled hair.

Charli watched him walk out the door with dog in tow. She watched through the panes of glass until his boot steps faded away. Her chest lifted on a slow, thoughtful intake of air.

Reno Wilder might be many things.

Disappointing would not be one of them.

Chapter 8

On a hot Friday night, everyone headed into a cool building for a cold beer and some dancing. Seven Devils Saloon—aptly named for the types of alcohol served—was everybody's favorite place to cut loose. In this old-style dance hall, you could count on beautiful women, jealous cowboys, and even a brawl or two.

Reno rarely engaged in anything other than conversation and a couple of longnecks. Which did not mean he was any kind of saint. When loneliness and need took control, he wandered outside the city limits. The distance gave people less to gossip about. Unlike his flashier brothers, he did not like being the center of attention.

He'd watched the senior center closely for most of the day. When Charli left, he'd gone over to finish the mural. Tomorrow, they'd have their big reveal of the project, and he didn't want to disappoint the elders in his community. He also didn't want to run into Fancy Pants if he could help it. She rubbed him the wrong way.

She was far too curious.

Too meddlesome.

And far too sexy.

From the moment he discovered she'd be sleeping just a few steps away from him, he hadn't been able to sleep. He'd always had a creative mind, and it had been pushed to the limit conjuring up images of Charlotte Brooks. Mostly naked. Eyes closed while a smile of satisfaction tilted her full lips.

For a man trying to remain cognizant of the fact that she was trying to change everything that mattered, she was like an F4 tornado with a great pair of legs. For the duration of her stay, he intended to keep his distance and his sanity intact.

Looking forward to a night of mindless entertainment, he parked his old truck in the space at the end of the crowded lot on the outskirts of town and headed toward the old-time saloon. The guitars of a live band twanged through the window screens as he pushed open Devil's big heavy door and stepped inside to join the others for a few moments of respite from the long week.

As he glanced around the huge, wood-floored hall, the band's cover of Luke Bryan's "Country Girl Shake It for Me" charged his eardrums. At peak volume, the song had inspired a group of tight-Wranglered, tank-topped cowgirls to hit the floor for a line dance. The cowboys holding up the walls gawked in appreciation.

Reno stood just inside the door letting his eyes adjust. He lifted a hand at the round of "Hey's" he received. The décor in Devils was little more than bare walls, an oak bar, neon beer signs, and some banged-up tables and chairs that frequently flew across the room. It was a loud and rowdy bar that usually amped up around 10:00 P.M. Most who stood inside now would close the place down, then stumble home to sleep it off.

He scanned the area, looking for a place to land. Someone to talk to. A pretty girl to flirt with. Feminine laughter drew his attention. His gaze locked onto the shapely brunette perched at the bar in a little red sundress that barely covered the tops of her thighs. Obviously enjoying herself, she placed her hand on the arm of Ben Marshall, Aiden's older brother and local connoisseur of women—and she laughed with Chester Banks, Sweet's oldest living playboy.

Damn.

She'd not only invaded his turf, she'd brought out the riffraff.

"When you get up on them ponies, you gotta settle in with your butt, look straight ahead," Chester Banks told Charli as he gave her a verbal riding lesson. "Otherwise, they can't feel where you want 'em to go."

"So what you're saying is you lead them by your butt?" Charli didn't mean to sound dense, but she'd never been on a horse in her life, and what Chester was telling her didn't make sense.

"They're directional," the handsome man with the short brown hair said. "If you look left, they're going to go left. If you put pressure on them with your right knee, they're going to move away from the pressure. They can feel how the body shifts, and they take their signals that way."

"I thought the reins were like a steering wheel."

"Hell, no," Chester said. "You keep off a horse's face as much as possible. You let the reins touch his neck, and he'll know where to go. You sink down in the saddle, he'll know when to stop."

"They sound like very smart animals." Charli lifted her drink to her lips. A large hand snagged it away. Shocked, she watched as her glass with the pretty pink drink and colorful umbrella floated across the bar and got dumped into the sink.

"What the hell did he do that for?" Chester asked.

Charli sighed. "He hates me."

Moments later, Reno Wilder came back and shoved an icy longneck bottle with an orange slice garnish in her hand. "No girly drinks allowed in here. This is as pantywaist as you're allowed to get," he growled, then turned away and walked toward the back room, where a group of rowdies were engaged in a game of pool.

Fascinated, Charli watched his backside retreat—broad shoulders, narrow waist, lean hips, big boots going thunk-thunk-thunk on the hardwood floor.

He gave an amazing view, coming or going.

"I think you might be right. He hates you," Chester said. "Want me to go kick his ass?"

Charli laughed at the image that brought to mind. Seriously, Chester might be pushing ninety, but he could probably do some severe shin damage to that long, tall cowboy. "No thank you. I like to handle the ass-kicking myself. Would you excuse me?"

She slid off the barstool, gave an "I'm okay" nod to her crew, who were whooping it up and letting it go at a nearby table, and followed Mr. Grumpy to the back room.

She found him in a cozy spot between two big-breasted, big-haired women wearing skintight tank tops and painted-on Wranglers with belt buckles the size of serving platters. Charli felt out of place in her sundress and flip-flops. Lucky for her, she'd never been intimidated by big things, big people, or dark glares.

She walked up to him and smiled when he looked away. *Yeah buddy, like that was going to make her disappear.* "Can I talk to you?"

"No."

"Why not?"

"I'm busy."

"I can see that." She addressed his busty bookends. "You ladies don't mind if I have a chat with Mr. Wilder, do you? It seems we have a conflict about the redesign for his hardware store."

The women gave her a territorial glare, then shook their big blond heads.

Charli smiled. "Thank you so much." She grabbed the obstinate man by the front of his plaid shirt, curled her fingers into the fabric, and gave a tug. When she had him a safe distance away, she stopped and looked up into eyes unusually bright with amusement.

Or maybe that was irritation.

Hard to tell.

"Quite cowardly of you to hide behind the Barbie twins."

He leaned in and spoke over somebody singing about loving this bar. "In case you haven't noticed, I'm not really the type to hide."

"Right." She wagged her longneck bottle. "Why'd you steal and trash my drink?"

He looked at her as if she might be just a bit touched in the head. "It had an umbrella in it. That's just wrong in too many ways to count."

"I like umbrella drinks."

"I suppose you also like puppies, world peace, and long, moonlit walks on the beach."

"I do." She didn't let his derogatory remark land. "But luckily, my IQ equals more than a carrot stick, and I never plan to pose nude for *Playboy*."

"Now that's too bad." He flashed his dimples, lifted his beer, and tilted the bottle at her. "I'd actually buy that issue."

"To add to the collection under your bed?"

That got a laugh.

"You got something to say?" He took a pull from his beer, watching her over the bottle. Then he lowered that bottle and his tongue came out to lick away the drop of ale that clung to his lip. "I've got a game waiting."

Charli didn't know why the brush-off stung. She knew he didn't like her. Could barely tolerate her. He'd done nothing to make her think otherwise. And still, there was some twisted desire deep inside her for him to change his mind.

"You can have your beer back." She thrust her bottle into his rock-hard abs. "Other than an occasional glass of wine, I don't really drink."

"You were drinking when I walked in."

"A Shirley Temple."

"A what?"

"A nonalcoholic drink."

His dark brows shot up his forehead. "Do they even know how to make those here?"

"Apparently."

He watched her. Waited for any other gems of information to spout from her mouth. Then glanced over his shoulder when someone in the back called his name, and said, "You're up."

He gave them a nod and angled his bottle toward the pool room. "Gotta go."

"Take the beer." She held out the bottle, completely devoid of anything else to say.

"Keep it." His gaze took a slow ride down the front of her sundress. Then he leaned in so close she could smell the clean scent of shampoo lingering in his hair. "It's Friday night."

Bells, whistles, and emergency sirens clanged in her head as her man ban tried to put up a deflective shield. "What does *that* mean?"

He gave her a wink and flashed a dimple as he walked away.

Charli crossed her arms, rested the cold bottle on her heated skin, and leaned her weight on one hip as she watched him retreat into the pool room.

Seemed he was always walking away from her.

She briefly wondered what it would take to make a man like Reno Wilder want to stay.

* * *

Several hours and three beers later, Charli felt the buzz light up her electrical system. She had no question now what Reno had meant by, "It's Friday night."

Seven Devils had exploded with energy. The big dance floor was shoulder to shoulder. The bar was standing room only. The picnic-style tables were jam-packed with groups of men and women flirting, arm wrestling, laughing, and in general taking a walk on the wild side.

There were several couples toward the rear of the place making out, and the competition in the pool room had amplified into a hoot-and-holler fest. From what she'd been able to tell, Reno Wilder was a very popular pool shark.

The alcohol cha-cha'd through her veins as she watched him for the umpteenth time lean over the table and skillfully smack the little white ball into a whole bunch of other balls. She couldn't really care less about whether stripes or solids fell into the pockets; she was far more intrigued by the rear pockets on Reno's jeans. Not to mention the muscles that played in his shoulders and forearms as he drew back the stick.

She laughed and hiccuped. The bleached blonde to her left flashed her a *Seriously?* glare.

She wasn't drunk. Tipsy? Hell yeah. Enjoying herself? Absolutely. Even when most of her crew had picked up and gone back to their perspective loaner homes, she'd chosen to linger. After all, it was Friday night. All she had to do tomorrow was put some finishing touches on the senior center and host the reveal. Easy cheesy.

She'd never been in an environment like Devils before. She never thought she'd fit in with a roomful of hell-raisers looking for a good time, but she found she kinda did. They were different than the store owners who looked to her for help. The people surrounding the bar, dance floor, and pool table didn't expect anything from her other than to have a little fun. And she was doing her best to keep up her end of the deal.

When a couple of women in blue jeans and snap-front Western shirts dragged her out onto the dance floor, she learned to do the Electric Slide in flip-flops. For the Tush Push, she'd kicked off her shoes and dared to boogie barefoot. By the end of the song, she'd come out laughing with toes intact and a vow to buy a pair of boots before she visited Devils again.

And all the time, she couldn't help but keep looking over her shoulder at the tall, dark man leaning over the pool table.

Common sense and past experience told her to keep away. But he was like a fishing lure, and she was just an old largemouth bass. Admittedly, she was weak for a man who held tradition and memories so close to his heart, he'd give up everything, including his own happiness, to hold on. Those dark eyes of his held secrets and heartache. And within their depths, she often thought she saw unity.

But she'd been wrong before.

When he popped the last ball on the table into the pocket, the crowd cheered. Charli watched as, with a big grin, he leaned over, swiped up the money lying on the felt, and accepted a kiss on the cheek from Bambi with the big belt buckle. Charli decided she'd spent enough time ogling. It was probably time to call it a night. She carried her beer over to a rare open stool at the bar.

"You want another one of those?" the bartender asked.

"I'd probably better have coffee."

"If you're serious, I'll put on a pot."

"Thanks." In the meantime, she planned to finish the . . . she lifted the bottle and looked at the Blue Moon label. She'd always thought of herself as more of a teetotaler, wine connoisseur. But by the bottom of the first bottle, she'd decided she liked beer. She'd probably be bloated as hell tomorrow, but tonight, she'd been down with the nice orange-colored brew drifting through her bloodstream.

Reno folded his winnings into his pocket and headed toward the door and home. Alone. As usual. Even though he'd had several offers for companionship.

Absently, he scanned the room, wondering if Charli had left. He'd caught her in his peripheral vision now and again—dancing, or talking, or laughing. To his surprise, she'd managed to fit in with the hell-raising mob.

When his gaze hit the bar, there she sat—her hand wrapped around a bottle of Blue Moon, her chin propped up with her palm, looking like she could pass out any second. Before he could stop himself, he was zigzagging through the crowd.

"Weren't you supposed to turn into a pumpkin at midnight?"

She looked up and gave him a smile that melted a frozen chip off his heart. He'd never had a woman smile at him like that since Diana—like she was genuinely happy to see him.

Then again, maybe it was just the beer in his system.

"Is that an insult to my poodle?"

He chuckled, leaned a hip against the bar. "You got a comeback for everything?"

She grinned. "I try."

"You're pretty good at it."

"Wow. Is that a compliment from Mr. Grumpy?"

"I'm not grumpy."

A husky laugh, which made everything inside him tighten and swell, escaped those pretty lips.

"You so are grumpy. And you have the most amazing dimples." She reached up and trailed a finger down his cheek. "You really should show them more often."

He didn't flinch when she touched him. In fact, he liked it so much he wanted to grasp her hand before she could pull it away and make her touch him some more.

Then again, maybe that was just the beer in his system.

And maybe he seriously needed to quit blaming the two bottles of beer he'd had much earlier for his reaction—or attraction—to her.

"Are you flirting with me, Ms. Brooks?"

She looked up, batted those full, thick eyelashes, and tilted her head. "Maybe."

Blood raged through his veins when he looked at those cherry red lips that matched her skimpy little sundress. He wondered what it would be like to kiss them. To find out if they were as soft as they looked.

He inhaled a deep breath meant to calm him down.

It did not.

"I don't know what to say," he admitted.

"Say you're flattered."

"I'm flattered?"

"Thank you." She twirled her index finger around the rim of her bottle. "So where'd you get a name like Reno anyway?"

"From a mother who was so high she couldn't remember anything except the city she was in."

She leaned her head back. Her eyes assessed him. Her luscious mouth parted just enough for a small gasp to escape. "I've met your mother. She hardly seems the type."

"She's not. But she didn't give birth to me," he admitted openly though he didn't know why. "Joe and Jana were my aunt and uncle. They adopted me and became my parents out of the kindness of their hearts." And that was about all he planned to tell her. Ever.

"Then you're a very lucky man."

"I am." He gave a nod to her empty bottle. "You about ready to get out of here?"

"The bartender is making coffee, so I can drive home."

"Caffeine will only make you a wide-awake drunk."

Her smooth brows crinkled together. "I'm not drunk."

"Uh-huh." He glanced over his shoulder, looking

for her design crew, but they all seemed to have disappeared. "You got a purse or something?"

"In the Hummer. Why?"

"I'm taking you home."

"Oooh, I like the sound of that."

He couldn't stop the smile that pushed at the corners of his mouth. "Only so you don't put anyone's life in danger."

"Well, that's too bad."

What did she expect? That he'd take her home, and they'd do the wild thing?

He didn't like her.

He didn't like that she could look at him so direct and find a way to extract pieces of his life before he knew what the hell he was saying.

He didn't like that she had practically everyone in town mesmerized with her pretty words and false promises.

He just didn't like a damned thing about her.

When he took her arm to help her from the stool, the warmth of her soft skin beneath his hand brought everything together like the eye of a hurricane. And he had to admit the one thing he'd been denying since she slipped out of that big yellow Hummer and poked her high heels into Ernie McGreavy's grass.

He wanted her.

Bad.

Charli had never been one to lack for things to say. Her mother had once told her she even talked in her sleep. On the ride back to Reno's ranch, she was unusually quiet. Until she realized her silence probably made him happy. And she could think of a dozen better methods to make the man smile.

"At the bar, I heard a song something about a truck, and a beer, and a girl in a red sundress." She floated a Vanna White hand down the front of her dress. "Ironic, isn't it?"

When he glanced across the dark of the cab, she could swear a smile tilted his lips.

"Completely."

"Of course, there was also something in that song about a kiss and a creek at 2:00 A.M." The beer tingle in her veins squashed down her man ban and gave her an extra boost of bold. Not that she needed one. Just being around him took all her professionalism and her cool and turned it inside out. Common sense? Pffft. Gone. Hormones raging? Oh yeah. Which begged the question—why were women so intrigued by the unattainable man? "Didn't I see a creek on your property?"

The dashboard lights reflected off the buttons on his shirt and the side of his face as he turned his head with a *What the hell?* look on his face.

"You whip off your clothes there, and you're likely to become mosquito bait," he said.

"Well, that's not very romantic."

"You know the difference between fantasy and reality?"

"Of course. But it's my job to mingle the two."

"I know I'll regret like hell asking this but . . ." His fingers flexed on the steering wheel. "How so?"

"Well . . ." She kicked off her flip-flops and tucked her feet up. "Sometimes when I meet a client, they bring me a box or a binder full of pictures of things they like. Images that inspire them no matter how far out of their reach they might seem. It's my job to bring those fantasies to life."

"Sounds frivolous."

"Oh, it is." She leaned toward him and grinned. "Very often it's decadent. Like a rich chocolate parfait eaten in bed on a Sunday morning after a night of drinking champagne and making love."

He leaned his head back and looked at her like he didn't know what to make of her.

"Don't tell me you've never done that," she said. Not that she ever had.

"I'm not much of the parfait type."

She gave him her most innocent look and poked the bear some more. "Not even when you can lick it off someone's body?" She'd never done that either. But she was willing to try.

He coughed.

She laughed.

Damned if she wouldn't break him out of that shell somehow.

"Most of the time I mingle fantasy and reality in the form of creating environments where families can bond over meals, or quiet time, or even game time," she said. "Before I started this job, I created a game room for a family of eight that was like *The Jetsons* meet *Happy Days*. It was a bit extreme, but I created all kinds of nooks where they could all just gather and have fun. The mom and dad complained that as their children were getting older and had so many activities, they were rarely home. So they wanted someplace the kids would want to come. Maybe bring their friends over."

She laughed, remembering the way those kids' eyes lit up when they saw the room. "I called them after a few months, and the mom said their game room had become the neighborhood hangout, and now they needed to create a space for the parents to have some quiet time."

"What did you create for them?"

She sighed. "I wasn't able to work with them because of the schedule for the show. So I had to hand it over to a designer friend."

"Sounds like that bothers you."

"It does. When you work in someone's home for weeks or months, you feel like you become a part of them. You get to know them. Sometimes, they become friends. I liked being in that house with all those kids running around. It was fun." She glanced out the side window at the passing rows of trees to mask a pang of longing. Sometimes, the task of creating those warm family environments made her realize what she wanted but didn't have.

"Anyway." For a distraction from the ache in her heart, she reached forward and turned the volume up on the radio. A male country artist came on singing about wanting to know what he had to do to win someone over. "Is this a classic truck?"

"No." He kept his eyes trained on the road ahead. "It's just old. It belonged to my father. I have a newer one in the garage. I just like this one."

She could relate. Sometimes, the connections you had to objects were all you had left of a person. She had her mother's jewelry box. Though it had been given to her empty, she could still imagine the baubles her mother had once stored there. A few times she'd even let Charli play dress up in those dangly earrings and huge necklaces. "I like old things."

"Right."

She looked up and noted the frown tightening his brow. "You sound doubtful."

"Hard to buy from someone who's single-handedly trying to change everything old about this town."

"I didn't choose to come here and change things, you know. I was *asked* to come here. I'm just doing my job. *And* I'm doing my best to preserve the soul of Sweet while giving it something that will make it more attractive to those who want to come in and spend their hard-earned cash. People in Sweet have to make a living, you know."

"Sweet was never meant to be a tourist attraction."

"But it would bring in more revenue."

"Everything can't be about money."

"Why do you like to argue all the time?"

He turned his head, gave her a long look. "I don't."

"You argue with me every chance you get."

"Because you piss me off about 90 percent of the time."

"Good."

"*Good?*"

"Yes. That leaves at least 10 percent in my favor."

He laughed. And by the expression on his face, that surprised him.

"Do you always just say whatever the hell you feel like?"

She tilted her head and studied the sudden Grrrr look on his face. "Don't you?"

In response, he turned the truck onto the bumpy

gravel road that led to his house. They rolled to a stop and parked by the barn. After he shoved the gearshift into PARK, he said, "Look. I offered you a ride so you didn't injure yourself or anyone else. That's it. I don't want to talk about the age of my truck, or argue with you, or figure out why you're so outspoken."

He grabbed the keys from the ignition and got out before she could respond. A bit dazed, she sat there, expecting him to disappear inside his house without another word. Instead, he came around to her side of the truck and opened her door.

"Maybe it doesn't matter to you . . ." she said, dangling her legs over the edge of the seat. "But I had to learn to be outspoken, so I wouldn't be completely ignored. The general wasn't the most attentive father a girl could have. In his fleeting moments at home, I had to make him aware of me. Whether he wanted to or not."

His eyes searched her face for a long, breathless moment. Then his face softened. Silently, he held out his hands.

Her heart skipped as she placed her hands in his and slid down from the big red truck. Her bare feet hit gravel cooled by the night air, and her toes dug in.

They were breast to chest, and she swore she could feel his heart beat. When she thought he'd let go, he held on and drew her closer. She knew that even as he did so, the conflicts in his soul battled for dominance. She, on the other hand, had never been a woman to let a good thing go. At the moment, they might be like fire and gasoline, but something in his eyes said Reno Wilder was a man worth fighting for. And her heart was more than willing to take a chance.

His gaze swept her face, fell to her mouth, then came back up to her eyes and held. His thick dark lashes lowered on a slow blink. When she thought her heart would knock through her rib cage, he cupped her face between his strong hands, lowered his head, and brushed her mouth with his warm lips.

"I'm sorry you had to fight for your father's attention," he whispered against her mouth. "But you definitely have mine." Then he kissed her so slow and sweet, she thought her hammering heart would shatter. For a moment, surprise immobilized her, and she could do nothing more than stand there while he fed her a tender kiss.

His lips were soft yet possessive. Commanding yet gentle. When his long fingers slid into the hair at her temples and tilted her head for better access, she wrapped her arms around his waist. His lips tested, and teased, and made her want more, more, more.

Then he was gone, and her arms were empty.

He lowered his hands to his sides and turned to leave.

"Wait a minute." She reached out and grasped the firm muscle of his forearm. "That's it?"

"Yeah." He looked over his shoulder. "That's it."

While everything inside her buzzed and snapped, he was content with one kiss?

"Are you serious?"

"To be fair, I've been pretty up front about everything." He turned—halfway toward escape. "You can't say I didn't warn you."

"Then what was that kiss all about?"

His broad shoulders lifted. "Momentary insanity."

"Bullshit."

"Call it what you want." His dark slash of brows pulled together, and the silver at his temples glinted in the moonlight. "It won't happen again."

Bullshit. She wanted to argue or prove him wrong, but, for the moment, she'd let it go. "Will you be at the senior center reveal tomorrow?" she called to his retreating backside.

"Don't count on it."

Charli grabbed her purse off the seat of the truck and walked into the darkness of the barn. There she turned and, with a skip in her heart, watched those long legs and slow gait put space between them.

She considered herself a *reasonable* woman.

Reasonably smart.

Reasonably cautious.

Reasonably patient.

Reasonably tolerant.

Reasonable did not come to mind when she considered the flood of feelings she'd quickly developed. He was a physically beautiful man. But that wasn't all that attracted her to him. It was what went on behind those soulful eyes and deep within that broad chest. She was intrigued as hell by the curiosity of the man's mind and heart and the glimpses she caught of the passion he'd locked away.

When he reached his back veranda, he called for Bear. The Australian shepherd appeared and danced around until Reno leaned down and gave the dog some love. Charli sighed as they both disappeared in the darkness.

Walk away now, Cowboy. But this isn't over.
Not by a long shot.

Reno closed the door behind him. Without turning on the lights, he walked into his room and sat down on the bed. Bear jumped up and lay down beside him while he sat there in the darkness, wondering exactly when he'd completely lost his mind.

Tonight, when he'd walked into that bar and seen Charli sitting there with Ben Marshall, something in his blood began to boil.

Something that felt a whole lot like jealousy.

Which was completely insane.

And then to kiss her?

What the hell was I thinking?

He ran his hand through his hair and flopped back on the bed. Bear crawled closer and snuffled against his side.

He couldn't blame the alcohol in his blood because that had burned off hours ago. He couldn't blame loneliness because between Jackson and Jesse he barely got a moment alone. And he couldn't just blame the fact that he was attracted to her because he'd been attracted to women before and often hadn't acted.

For several minutes, he lay there, thinking so hard his head began to ache. When his reason became clear, he pushed a tight breath from his lungs.

It was the look in her eye when she'd made the comment, *"I had to learn to be outspoken so I wouldn't be completely ignored."*

Charlotte Brooks was *not* the type of woman who should be ignored.

He reached down and stroked the top of Bear's head, receiving a contented doggie groan for his efforts.

The look in Charli's eye was one Reno had seen over the years when he'd looked in the mirror.

He recognized the sense of abandonment.

The hurt.

The need.

He related.

And so he'd kissed her.

When he'd lifted his head and looked into her expressive eyes again, he'd wanted to pull her back into his arms and never let go.

And that just plain scared the hell out of him.

Chapter 9

"So why doesn't someone as pretty as you have a man?" Arlene Potter, copresident of the senior center asked, as Charli stood in the midst of the chaos the production crew called the *load in*.

"I could ask you the same thing, Ms. Potter." She set a vase of yellow roses in the center of the new round table she'd placed in the center of the gathering room. Surrounded by cameras and a dozen helpers all scurrying about to put the finishing touches on the place before they opened the doors to the members for the big reveal, Charli had little time to chitchat with the little blue-haired woman. But her mile-long list wouldn't stop her from doing so.

With the exception of the man of few words, Charli had learned that Texans liked to talk. They were inquisitive and friendly. And when they asked questions that might make a normal person blush, Charli took them in stride. She knew they meant no harm. In fact, the entire community, with the exception of one stubborn man, made her feel very welcome.

Ms. Potter chuckled. "Well, most folks think I've got one foot in the grave, but I ain't done lookin' yet. Just always turns out the ones that flip my petticoats are already taken. When you get to be my age, you just gotta wait till someone either passes or moves on."

Charli crossed the room to fluff the new front window curtains. Ms. Potter, in her button-down floral dress and squeaky orthopedic shoes, followed. "You have your eye on someone now?"

"Naw. I'm takin' a break," Ms. Potter said. "Had my eye on that cute Aiden Marshall when he came back from Afghanistan, but that darned Paige Walker snatched him up before any of the rest of us got a chance."

Charli smiled. She'd met Aiden and Paige, both were in their early thirties and crazy in love. "So I take it you prefer younger men?"

"I like 'em young. Or old. Long as they don't have hair growin' out of their ears or nose and don't snore like the dickens."

"Ah. Well, that leaves at least half the population in this town."

"Yeah." Ms. Potter pushed her wire-framed glasses up the bridge of her nose. "So why don't you have a man?"

"I had one," Charli admitted.

"What happened?"

How to explain he'd been just another of her impetuous choices that had gone nowhere but heartache? Charli shrugged, then squatted to lift the curtain hem to inspect the seam. "He works in the movie industry, and—"

"An actor?" Ms. Potter's gray brows lifted.

"Actually, he's a documentary director. His job took him away for weeks and months at a time, then an opportunity to film in Africa came along and—"

"You never got to sleep in the same bed?"

Charli chuckled. "Something like that."

"You lookin' for a man?"

A sigh lifted Charli's chest. Even though she hadn't been looking, she might have found one. "Not really."

"Can an old woman like me give you a bit of advice?"

"Sure."

"Always keep your peepers open." She tapped her temple. "Smart women are *always* lookin'. Otherwise, you end up like me, old and alone and lusting after men less than half your age."

"What do you do if you have your eye on one, and he won't look back?"

"Pffft. That's easy." Ms. Potter gave her a wink and a shoulder wiggle. "You just turn on everything you've got to full volume and blind him with your amazingness."

"What if I don't have any amazingness?"

"Oh you've got buckets full. Just take a look around this place and what you've done to it. You took a shabby run-down building and turned it into something . . . well, amazing."

"Thank you, Ms. Potter."

"No need to thank me. You just get those batteries charged up. Use your secret weapon. And don't take no for an answer." She teetered toward the door. "I'll be waitin' for the reveal outside with the rest of the folks."

Charli watched the woman slip out the door with a pat on the back to a few of the crew and smiles for everyone. Then she turned her attention to the wall mural that had mysteriously been completed. The scene was idyllic—a distinctive Hill Country panorama with rolling hills, live oaks, tall grass, and a farmhouse with a huge windmill. Just the type of place where you wish you could escape to relax.

"Ms. Broo—I mean, Charli?" Sarah, her assistant came up with her clipboard pressed to her chest. "Everything's in place. The cameras are staged. Are you about ready for the reveal?"

Charli dragged her gaze away from the mural. "Why didn't you join everyone at Seven Devils last night?"

Sarah pushed her glasses up her nose. "I offered to babysit Pumpkin, so you could go."

"Hmmm." Charli dusted off a sparkle of glitter from the shoulder of Sarah's plain white shirt. "From now on, you don't babysit anyone. Pumpkin will be fine on her own. From now on, you join the rest of us."

"I'm not really a bar person."

Charli tilted her head and studied the girl. A little attention to detail, and she could be a knockout. "Have you ever been in a bar?"

"No, ma'am."

"Well, you certainly can't judge until you've experienced it, can you?"

"No, ma'am."

Charli leaned in and whispered. "You know what I did last night?"

Sarah shook her head.

"I drank three beers, danced barefoot, and kissed a man." *Like a big fat fool.*

Sarah's eyes widened. "You did?"

"I did. And I lived to tell the tale." She gave the girl a one-armed hug. "Some of us were brought up strict. Some of us are just plain shy. But you never know a shoe fits until you try it on."

"Are you saying I should go to bars, drink, dance, and kiss men?"

Charli chuckled. "No. But I am saying it's okay to broaden your horizons. You never know what you might find out there. This is Texas. We're here for another five weeks. There's bound to be enough fun to go around."

"Okay."

"So next time you'll join the crowd?"

"Okay."

Charli laughed. "You sure?"

"If you think it's a good idea."

"Well, I always think it's a good idea to experience new things. But other than that, don't listen to a word I say. Because as sure as there's an armadillo squished on some Texas highway, I will lead you in the wrong direction."

Sarah laughed. "You're funny, Ms.—"

"Ah. Ah."

"Charli," she said, correcting herself. "So are you ready for the reveal?"

Charli slid another glance to the mural. "Give me about fifteen minutes, then it's a go. Okay?"

"Sure. I'll let everyone know."

As the last crew member slid a chair beneath the new game table and disappeared out the front door, Charli looked around at the final project and took a deep breath. Pride replaced the air in her lungs.

Everyone had done a bang-up job. The senior center was fresh and vibrant, with pops of red and yellow and blue. It was a happy place the members could come to share a meal, enjoy some good company, and take away their worries for a while.

Everything was perfect.

Except for the one person missing who'd contributed immensely to the project. If he thought he was going to sit over in his dusty hardware sanctuary and miss out on all the fun, well, she'd just have to make him think again.

"This is going to backfire on you, brother."

Deep within the stockroom, Reno pushed aside a recent delivery of pressed-tin ceiling tiles to be used for the candy-store redo. He looked up at Jackson, who'd pulled up a chair to watch. "What are you mumbling about over there?"

"You—the meticulous one—haphazardly pushing aside all those boxes for the production company instead of using your usual tag-and-stack method for easy locating. One might think you had ulterior motives."

"They're taking up my stockroom. I'm just trying to make room for other things."

"Uh-huh." Jackson leaned back and grinned. "All the more reason to tag and stack, don't you think?"

"I *think* that *you*—Mr. Messy—don't work here, so you can hardly proclaim to know what's best."

"Yep." Jackson nodded. "Going to backfire. Like a poorly packed grenade." He made an explosion sound, then grinned.

"Are you enjoying yourself at my expense?"

"Don't I always? I thought you'd be in a great mood today. Heard you made some serious bank at the pool table last night."

The change of subject was a relief. Reno nodded. "I did. Popped it into Mom's savings account this morning."

Jackson pushed the chair away and gave Bear a rub on top of his furry head. "You'd think the yahoos at Devils would catch on to the fact that you're one step short of a pro."

"I'm not going to complain. Just helps out Mom." Reno shoved aside another case of tiles. "You want some coffee?"

"Sure. I don't have to be at the station until later."

While Jackson followed him into the front of the store, Reno pulled down two mugs from the rack above the coffeepot, filled them, and handed one to his brother. "Been a pretty mild fire year so far."

"Yeah, but we're heading into August." Jackson took a quick sip. "Things will change."

Coffee in hand, Reno leaned his back against the counter and crossed one ankle over the other. "I always figured you'd seen enough action in Afghanistan. Who knew you'd come home and go looking for trouble by fighting fires."

"You know me. I've always been physical, like

Jared and Jake. You and Jesse got all the brains."
Jackson shrugged. "Until now, I always thought you
were the smartest."

"Until *now*?"

"Gonna backfire."

"Are we back to that?"

The bell jingled, and Reno looked up as Ray Calhoun came through the door. "Howdy, boys."

"Mr. Calhoun," Reno returned. "What can I do
for you today?"

"Oh. Thought I'd come in for that faucet I ordered.
Hazel's been after me to get the guest bathroom finished before the holidays."

"Faucet?"

Ray looked at him a little funny. "Yeah. That
brushed-nickel two-handle job. Must have ordered
it about a month ago. Shoulda come in sometime last
week."

Last week had been the peak of insanity with the
arrival of the production company and their endless barrage of deliveries. Reno glanced back at the
stockroom and the disarray of boxes and pallets and
crap he'd kicked out of the way in his frustration.
He couldn't remember Ray's order. More than likely,
he'd shoved it in some dark corner along with the
hordes of production company purchases.

"Let me check the purchase order." He clicked
the mouse and waited for the computer monitor
to warm up. For the first time, it was unlikely the
spreadsheet would be any help. His *misplacement*
of things had quickly become a catastrophe. And
while he might have had a bit of conscious effort in

the mayhem, it was likely he'd only set himself up for problems. "That should tell me where I stored it."

Jackson leaned over, made an explosion sound, then grinned.

The bell over the door ting-a-linged again. In a state of semi panic, Reno looked up as an orange poodle trotted into the room and, with a sissified growl, jumped right on his poor, unsuspecting dog.

"There you are." Charli appeared in the doorway, wearing a snug pair of jeans and a soft summer blouse that looked like two handkerchiefs tied together. She turned on a smile that sent his thoughts to last night and how soft and warm her lips had been. How sweet she'd tasted. And how much sleep he'd lost.

"Mr. Calhoun. Jackson." She clapped her hands together like someone had given her a double scoop of ice cream. "You're here too. It's time for the senior-center reveal. You boys don't want to miss out, do you?"

Jack lifted an eyebrow. "I believe Reno here had every intention of doing just that."

"Don't be ridiculous." She crossed the store and curled her fingers around Reno's arm as if to prevent him from escape. "Since your brother played such a big part in making the design a success, I'm sure he wouldn't miss it for the world." She looked up at him, batted those damn long eyelashes, and gave him a smile. "Would you?"

Evil.

The woman had pure evil running through her veins.

"You did what?" Jackson lowered his coffee cup and looked at him as if he'd lost his mind.

Indeed, he had.

"Didn't he tell you?" Charli said, jumping in to interfere. Again. "He painted a mural on the wall in the seniors' dining room. I saw the one he painted for your little girl, and I begged him."

Reno pictured her begging for another reason entirely—one that had nothing to do with a damn wall and everything to do with—

"Well, big brother, aren't you just a walking contradiction."

"I did it for the folks," Reno said as a poor defense.

Jack's gaze slid to Charli and did a quick up and down. "Uh-huh."

"I'm looking forward to seeing it," Ray said.

"He wasn't easy to convince," Charli added.

Jackson hooted a laugh. "Wait till the other boys hear about this."

"You *don't* have to share," Reno said between gritted teeth.

"Oh yeah. I totally do."

"They'll be so proud of you." Charli looked up at him with those damned insightful eyes. "I know that your mother is."

Shit. "My mom knows?"

"Everybody knows," she said. "You didn't expect me to keep something like that a secret, did you?"

Yes.

"Just an FYI," Jackson said. "My brother is a pretty private man. Doesn't like to share his cereal. Doesn't like to advertise his talents or his personal doings. Like the time when his heroics saved another soldier. He never told a soul until the day they honored him with a medal."

"Jack." Reno growled out a warning, to which his brother suddenly became hard of hearing.

"I'm not surprised," Charli said.

"Did you know," Jack continued with some kind of twisted death wish, "he won't even date a woman in this town for fear they'll be all up in his business? Although you might want to ask him sometime about the time he disappeared for two days and got too tied up to check in."

Ray laughed.

"Well, that was thoughtless," Charli told him.

Reno flinched at the memory of his encounter with a newly assigned Deputy Ginger Baker and her handcuffs. Who knew such a small-statured woman had so many fantasies to live out?

"Well, I'm just about as excited as a person can get to see this reveal." Jackson headed toward the door and held out his arm, waiting for Charli to take it. "Shall we?"

"Oh. We shall." She flashed Reno a "See, I knew I could get him on my side" grin and joined Jackson, while *her* dog continued to torture *his* dog with a game of nip and run.

Like dog, like owner.

"Come on, Mr. Calhoun," Jackson said. "Big brother."

Reno wondered if he was too old to short-sheet his brother's bed. "You go on ahead without me. I've got work to do."

Charli stopped halfway out the door and came back. "Nice try, bucko."

When she took his arm in a death grip, Reno realized he was surrounded by bossy women and back-stabbing brothers.

Minutes later, Reno was surrounded by cameras, a production crew, his family, and members of the community, who ooohed and aaahed over the senior-center redesign and the mural he'd painted. To say he felt out of place at the reveal was an understatement. He didn't want to be there, and he'd tried to stay in the background. The more he tried, the more Charli dragged him into the middle of things.

"She's amazing, isn't she?"

Reno turned and looked down to the little blond-haired assistant. "Who?"

"Ms. Brooks, of course." She gave him a timid smile. "I mean Charli. She insists I call her that, but I'm not quite used to it. Her being my boss and all."

"And what kind of a boss *is* Ms. Brooks?" he asked, looking for any tidbit of ammunition on the woman who seemed to sneak past his defenses every chance she got.

"She's the best." She looked up at him like he'd taken leave of his senses.

Most likely he had. What else would explain him painting for three days on a project that took up all his spare time? Or kissing a woman he had no business kissing?

"She doesn't act superior if you know what I mean. She makes you feel so comfortable, like you could tell her all your secrets, and she'd really listen."

Yes, she'd squeezed a few out of him too.

"And I love the ideas she comes up with," the

assistant continued. "I love the enthusiasm in her voice. I could listen to her talk all day."

After only a week of knowing the woman, Reno had to admit that her bubbliness was infectious. Even when he wanted to tell her to shut the hell up and go about her business, he felt inclined to sit her down on his lap, tuck her head beneath his chin, and listen to her yammer about nothing. And everything.

Interesting. That's what she was. She'd been raised by the meanest son of a bitch that wore a Marine uniform. Yet she'd come out a warm and witty woman who seemed to genuinely care about people she barely knew.

He glanced across the room to where she stood in front of a camera holding the hands of senior-center big shots Gladys Lewis and Arlene Potter. Excitedly, she showed them the new kitchen the crew had installed. Today she wore jeans and a blouse. Last night she'd worn a little-nothing dress. The rest of the week she'd worn shorts, a T-shirt, and sneakers. With the exception of the day she'd rolled into town looking like she'd stepped out of a Nordstrom's display, she'd blended in with her surroundings. Well, not exactly *blended*, but she'd taken an approach that put her on the same level as those who worked and shopped in his little town.

It wouldn't take much effort to imagine her as one of those superwomen who worked, took care of a family, and made sure the man in her life knew he was well loved with little to no effort.

His chest lifted on a harsh intake of air. He needed to stop thinking thoughts like that before he got in too deep. He'd had a love like that once. And he'd been damned lucky to find it. He wouldn't be foolish enough to believe it could ever happen again. It was much easier—less painful—to exist on the outskirts of life. To be more of an observer than an actual participant.

"Are you all right, Mr. Wilder?" the assistant's gentle touch on his arm snapped him from his thoughts.

"Absolutely," he responded, even knowing the word was an absolute lie.

Chapter 10

With the senior center wrapped up and time on the clock dwindling, Charli jumped right into the work on the candy store. Cavity central resided in a cinder-block building with an overhang out front that gave her the perfect opportunity to step back in time. To re-create a look that had been lost to modern design. Since the interior of the store was a throwback to the 1800s, Charli knew the exterior had to match.

Lucky for her, the inside was in pretty good shape. With the exception of rearranging a few things, tin ceiling tiles, a little paint, some old-fashioned soda-fountain photos, and new display glassware, there was little to do. Her whiz-bang crew could get the place painted and the ceiling tiles up in a day. Then they could focus on the exterior and maybe even complete the project ahead of schedule. That would give them the opportunity to use the extra time on a more difficult project, like town square.

On this warm Saturday evening, the community's focus seemed to be on Sweet Pickens Bar-B-Q or anywhere else in town that served a good meal. Charli's stomach growled as she sat cross-legged on the wood floor of the candy shop and gave in to temptation by popping a sourball into her mouth. Her lips puckered as the candy rolled around on her tongue. If she couldn't have something slathered in a tangy sauce, she could at least survive on sugar.

"Can't find them."

Charli glanced up from her task of wiping off the new apothecary-style jars. Max strolled into the store, wiping a streak of barbecue sauce off his cheek from the gigantic sandwich in his hand. Her stomach grumbled again. "Can't find what?"

"The tin tiles." He pointed up to the bare white ceiling.

"They're at the hardware store."

"You would think so, right?" He sat on a stool beside her. "But I just came from there, and the man in charge said he couldn't find them."

A frown pulled her forehead tight. "Didn't we get a delivery confirmation?"

"Again. You would think."

"So this means what? We have to reorder and wait several days for delivery? And if you say 'You would think' one more time, I'm going to snatch that sandwich out of your hand and eat it myself."

"Are you hungry?"

She couldn't stop the eye roll. "Duh."

"Oh. Sorry. Didn't know."

"Grumbling stomach . . ." She pointed to her belly. "Dead giveaway. So . . . the tiles?"

Max shrugged. "Guess we could go take another look. I don't want to place another order. We're already on a tight budget."

"No kidding. Next time I try to talk you into more bang for the buck, I give you permission to kick me. Do you want to go back to the hardware store, or do you want me to go?"

"Neither will do us any good. Wilder was closing up shop a few minutes ago. We'll have to wait until tomorrow."

"Tomorrow is Sunday. Which means the hardware store will be closed, and if we do need to re-order, we won't get a one-day jump on delivery." She crunched down on the sourball, and a headache began to pound between her eyes. "Which means we'll be off a day, and I lose the extra time I need for other projects."

"Shit happens, Charli." Max shoved the last bite of barbecue sandwich into his mouth and wiped his face with the crumpled napkin. "Sometimes you just have to roll with the punches and put in a little overtime when necessary."

"Says the man with a full stomach."

"Want me to go get you something to eat?"

She sighed, leaned forward, and banged her forehead on the floor. She knew the senior-center redesign had gone too easy and that she'd pay on another project down the line. Nothing ever went smoothly in this business. "No. You go ahead and enjoy your Saturday night. I'll see if I can get hold of Reno to open up the store, so I can take a look."

Max tilted his head, and his ball cap slid a little to the right. "You sure?"

"Yes."

"Okay." He jumped up awful fast, like somebody who already knew she'd let him off the hook.

God, she was such a sucker.

As the producer of the show, wasn't it *his* job to make sure things went smoothly?

"Have a good night," he said with a wave on his way out the door.

"You are so funny, Max Downs."

When the door closed behind him, Charli looked up at the ceiling, trying to come up with another plan in case things went completely upside down. After a few moments' consideration, she shook her head. She wanted those ceiling tiles. Nothing else would do.

She didn't have Reno's number, so she'd just go over to the hardware store and look behind the chain-link fence to see if she could spot the boxes she needed. If not, she'd call Jana to get his number and have him open up the store. He wouldn't like it, and he'd most likely be agitated with her for interrupting his Saturday night plans. But since she already pissed him off about 99 percent of the time anyway, what was another 1 percent?

On most Saturday nights, Reno chose to stay home and relax or hang out with friends and family. Tonight, when he called to see what everyone was up to, he discovered that his mom already had plans, Jackson was on duty at the fire station, and Jesse had a date with his new veterinary assistant. Which meant, of course, Jesse would be looking for a *new* veterinary assistant in a few weeks.

Staying home wasn't an option because, as sure as he was named after the biggest little city in the world, Charli would come out of the apartment to harass him into a conversation. Then he'd end up spilling even more information about himself. She would have made a great spy. A man would give over top secret information and not even know until she was bouncing merrily on her way.

To avoid her, he decided to head over to Ginger Creek to meet up with Cheyenne—one of the women he knew who liked a good time with no strings attached. As he headed toward the highway down Main Street, he gave the hardware store a quick glance. When he noticed a light on in the back, he tapped the brakes. Damn. He must have forgotten to turn it off when he left earlier. He made a quick Uey and pulled around back. He left the engine running as he slid the key into the lock on the chain-link fence and hurried toward the delivery door.

When he reached for the handle, the door was already ajar. He knew he hadn't left it unlocked. A snap of alarm shot up the back of his neck. He had two choices: call Deputy Brady Bennett and suffer the man's wry sense of humor or walk inside and take a chance on who'd broken into his store.

Robberies were nonexistent in Sweet. Other than the usual five-finger discounts, the only time they ever had any problems was a few years back when a couple of high-school kids hid inside the bathroom of the Touch and Go until Walter Riggins closed the place down for the night. The teens snuck out with some cigarettes and a keg of Keystone. A night in the pokey and thirty days of community service cured them and any other takers from being so reckless.

Reno didn't figure teenagers would break into a boring hardware store, so he eased the door open and stepped inside as quiet as he could. It only took a second before he heard a curse and the sound of sliding boxes. As he stepped farther into the stockroom, it was apparent his *burglar* nicely filled out a pair of jeans. With his arms crossed, he stood back and watched her shove things around. The more she shoved, the more agitated she got. The more agitated she got, the more the F-bombs flew. Before she could do any damage, he cleared his throat.

Caught in the act, her head snapped up. Her beautiful mouth dropped open, and her eyes went wide. Dirt smudged her cheeks, and he had to refrain from laughing at her look of utter surprise.

"Looking for something?"

"Yes. My damned tin ceiling tiles."

Oh goody. And she was pissed off too.

"I already looked back there."

She put down the box in her hands and brushed her palms together. "Well, if you had a better storage system, I'm sure you'd be able to find them. This place is a mess."

"I can find things quite easy."

"But not my ceiling tiles."

"Nope. Not your ceiling tiles." He tilted his head and, intrigued, watched her climb over several boxes of faucets and plumbing accessories until she came to stand before him.

"I never pictured you as the cat-burglar type," he said, letting his eyes roam down her body, past the handkerchief blouse that looked like all he'd need to do to remove it would be to give her a little twirl.

"I have many talents."

His gaze skimmed her body again. When everything inside him tightened, he knew he couldn't allow his imagination go *that* route.

Too dangerous.

And he hated cold showers.

"One of them," she said, "is organization. A skill which *you* obviously lack."

"You break into a man's place of business, then try to make *him* feel guilty for not having a system up to your standards?"

"I didn't break in."

"I locked the door on my way out tonight. You don't have a key. If you don't call that breaking in, what do you call it?"

"Your mother has a key."

Shit. There goes all my leverage.

He was going to have to have a heart-to-heart with that woman.

"So you waited until I closed down for the night, called my mother, and had her drive all the way over here so you could snoop around my store?"

"No." Her hands went to her shapely hips, and her chin came up. "My producer came over here earlier to get the boxes. *You* said you couldn't find them. He came to me and said you had left for the night. So *I* was faced with a time-and-financial dilemma, and I called your mother. Then *I* met her at the senior center and . . ." She whipped a key ring out of her front pocket and jingled the keys.

"My mother just let you come in here all by your-self?"

She dropped her head back and sighed. "Do I look like I'd break in and steal . . . faucets? Or, God forbid, a plaid shirt or some faded silk flowers?"

Personally, Fancy Pants"—he leaned in—"I don't know what you're capable of."

"Good. I like keeping a man on his toes."

A rumble gurgled through the space between them.

"Was that you?"

She looked down. "Was what me?"

"That noise. It sounded like a growl."

"Well, according to you, I *am* a ferocious cat bur-glar."

"Funny." He looked her up and down. She looked tired, hot, and hungry. "When was the last time you ate?"

"I don't know." Her bare shoulders lifted. "Maybe this morning?"

"Maybe?"

"Probably."

"It's eight o'clock at night."

"And yet I still don't have my ceiling tiles."

"If your boxes are in here, I'll find them tomor-row." He took her by the arm and led her to the door. "Right now, you need food."

She tugged back. "I *need* my boxes."

"Fine. First you eat. Then we'll come back and find your damn boxes."

Her stomach growled again.

"Okay." She looked up at him, and he realized she was allowing herself to be led. Her stomach had done the talking for her; otherwise, she'd never let him get the upper hand. "*If* you promise to come back."

Promises weren't something he made often anymore. But for some stupid reason, he felt compelled.

"Promise."

Last damn time he'd try to play good guy.

While Sweet Pickens bustled with hungry diners, Hank Williams Jr. rocked the sound system. Reno sat at one of the many well-used picnic tables across the bench from Charli, watching her lick barbecue sauce from her lips. When she wrapped that luscious mouth around a tender rib, Reno thought it might be the most erotic thing he'd seen in a long time.

And didn't that just identify him as certifiable.

She had sauce across her cheeks. Sauce on her fingers—which she managed to lick now and again. And sauce on her chin. Reno was used to taking women to dinner only to have them order a salad, then pick at it like it was full of thigh-busting calories. He couldn't remember the last time he'd seen a woman dive into her meal with such gusto and not be self-conscious.

He liked that.

He didn't know what that said about him, and as she lifted another rib to her lips, he didn't care.

Her straight white teeth dug in and tore off a bite. "This is the best barbecue I've ever had."

"When you end up wearing most of it, that's always a good sign."

She laughed. "Do I have sauce all over my face?"

"Oh yeah."

She grabbed her napkin and gave her face a good swipe, but left a smear near the corner of her mouth. "Better?"

"Not so much. Here." He reached across the table and used his thumb to wipe it away. When he looked up again, she was staring at him like he'd morphed into a circus clown. "What?"

"That was pretty intimate."

He looked down. Looked back up. "What'd I do?"

She pointed to his hand. "You sucked my sauce off your thumb."

"I did?"

"Yes." She set the rib down on her plate and reached for the stack of wet wipes in the center of the table. "You know, for a man who likes to keep himself an arm's length away—"

"I don't do that."

"Oh yeah." Her eyebrows lifted as she nodded. "You do."

Man, he'd never had anyone nail him so dead on before. Did she have some kind of superpowers or something? Or was she just that intuitive? He stuffed a French fry in the glob of ketchup on his plate and took a bite. "Like I've said before, you really don't know me, and—"

She snagged the rest of his fry from his hand, stuck it in her mouth, and chewed. "I'm getting to know you, Reno Wilder. Now, you might not like that idea . . ." She snitched another fry, jabbed it in his ketchup, and waggled it in the air at him before her teeth clamped down. "But I find it's much easier to work with a client if I know a little bit about them."

"I'm not your client."

"Yet."

"Ever," he insisted. "What's it going to take to get it through your pretty head that I'm not interested in partaking of the insanity you and your crew are forcing on this town?"

"Stop patronizing me." She smirked. "And what's it going to take to get it through your thick skull that you are the only one in this town who doesn't want this change?"

"Dynamite."

She laughed. "I'm sure I can pick up a bundle at the nearby hardware store. They have everything there from hacksaws to satin ribbon."

A smile he couldn't stop lifted his mouth. "Stop insulting my store."

She leaned forward, and her breasts came in danger of smushing into the barbecue sauce on her plate. He wondered if he'd be allowed to lick that off too.

"Then make it a real hardware and feed store," she argued in an amused tone. "Not Wilder's *five and dime*."

"For your information," he pointed his fork for emphasis, "yesterday I sold two plaid shirts *and* a bunch of those silk flowers you keep making fun of."

"Wow." Her eyes danced with laughter as she dug into another fry. Off *his* plate. "You'd better hurry up and put that in the bank. Can't have money like that lying around."

A charge of electricity snapped up his spine. Damn. He hadn't had this much fun in a long time.

Fancy Pants might be a huge pain in the ass, but she could definitely give as good as she got.

He liked that in a woman.

"Fancy seeing you two here. Together."

Reno looked up to find Aiden and Paige standing beside the table, arm in arm, like a solid force nothing could divide.

"Hi," Charli said in a way-too-perky voice for someone who moments ago was going head-to-head with him. "Did you guys try that lamp trick I told you about for your foyer?"

"Lamp trick?" Reno smirked. "I'm afraid to ask."

"We did," Paige replied, then turned to him to explain. "Charli showed us this really cool way to turn the old cranberry jug we had sitting by the door into a neat little lamp for the hall table. Aiden is a genius with tools." She looked up at the man by her side, and no one needed to guess how much she loved him. If Reno weren't so damned happy for the two of them, he might be jealous.

"What are you guys doing here?" Reno asked. "Thought you'd be over at the Ashfords' playing poker."

"Nope. We're celebrating." Aiden looked at Paige and smiled. "Our *official* engagement."

"He *officially* asked me last night," Paige gushed. "By the creek. On bended knee."

"Oh, how romantic." Charli's face lit up as Paige dangled her hand and flashed her solitaire ring. "And how beautiful."

The dinner in Reno's stomach turned over as he remembered the night he'd asked Diana to marry him.

It hadn't been a glitzy affair. She'd been a quiet

girl, and his proposal had followed suit. But he could still remember the exhilaration that had run through his veins when she'd said yes. He'd planned to spend the rest of his life with her. But fate and a twenty-thousand-pound truck had other plans. So here he was, sitting with a woman who couldn't be more different, and doing her best to turn his nice, quiet existence upside down.

Ironically, at the moment, he had to admit to enjoying it.

"Congratulations." Reno shook Aiden's hand, truly happy that Paige had never given up on him, even when Aiden had given up on himself.

"When's the big day?" Charli asked Paige.

"Well, we'd like to get married in Town Square because that's where everything fell into place after Aiden came home," Paige said. "So we thought maybe a couple of weeks from today. But we know you have the square scheduled as one of your redesigns, and we wouldn't want to interfere."

"Interfere?" Charli's head went back like that was the most preposterous thing she'd ever heard. "If you can put together a wedding in two weeks, I can finish the project by then."

Reno watched as Charli calculated everything in her head so fast, he could almost hear the bell ring when she came up with the solution. Without her saying a single word, he knew exactly where her mind had gone. Her smile slipped—just a hint. Then it came back so bright, he thought he'd need sunglasses.

"I'll make it happen," she finally said. "I just have one favor to ask."

"Anything," Paige replied.

"Can I be invited?"

Paige's face lit up even more if that were even possible. "Are you kidding? Of course you're invited."

Charli slid two fingers across her frilly little handkerchief blouse. "Then I cross my heart. Town Square
will be done in time for you two to get married."

Paige squealed and scooched onto the bench
beside Charli. Before Reno got caught up in all the
dresses and flowers and froufrou talk, he looked up
at his perplexed friend. "I think they're going to be
busy here for a while. Want to join me for a beer?"

"Yeah." Aiden ran a hand through his hair and
chuckled. "Guess I won't be needed again till the
wedding day."

Reno stood, slapped a hand on his friend's back,
and guided him toward the bar. "Nope. All you
gotta do is show up, tell her she's beautiful, and say
I do."

"That's easy," Aiden said. "Paige is the most incredible woman I've ever known. I can't wait to be
married to her."

The bartender slid two bottles of Shiner Bock in
front of them. Aiden lifted one and took a drink.
"I wasted too much time thinking all the wrong
things."

"Like?"

Aiden shrugged. "Like I didn't deserve to be
happy. Like I was supposed to live my life under a
rock because I hadn't stopped my best friends from
dying on that Afghani mountainside. Like I had to
stop living and let the world go on without me."

Reno swallowed down his beer hard. He understood those thoughts. He *lived* those thoughts. But could he ever step outside his comfort zone as Aiden had? He didn't know.

"Thought you didn't want anything to do with all this changing-the-town stuff," Aiden said, changing the subject. "So what are you doing here with Charlotte Brooks?"

"Good question, my friend."

Reno turned his back to the bar, propped the heel of his boot against the rail, and watched Charli laugh and express herself to Paige with smiles and hand gestures.

He didn't know exactly what had made him bring Charli here tonight other than he could tell she'd been hungry. He only knew that the more time he spent with her, the more he liked her.

The changes she'd made to the senior center had been good. Unlike what he'd expected, she hadn't torn the place apart. She'd made it a better, happier, livelier gathering place. She'd brought smiles to the faces of those who spent time within those walls. The group had been so pleased, they'd made her an honorary member.

She was actually quite an incredible woman.

Aside from all his grumbling, Reno realized he had to be honest with himself. He liked her. But in five weeks, she would be gone. She'd pick up her measuring tape and her staple gun and head back to her real life. He didn't know what she had waiting for her there; he only knew he couldn't picture her anywhere but here in Sweet.

If he let himself get too close, he knew he'd get involved.

If he got involved, he'd get attached.

If he got attached, he could very well lose his heart—and lose her too.

And with all he'd already gone through, that might be a pain he'd never survive.

By the time they left Sweet Pickens, it was late. But Reno had promised Charli they'd go back to the store and look for her ceiling tiles. So here he was rummaging through boxes and scanning labels while she sat perched up on his desktop, legs swinging, and keeping up a conversation that distracted him at every turn.

"I think I'm going to put a lucky horseshoe up at the top of the entry to the new gazebo," she said.

Reno pushed aside a carton of paint rollers and looked up. "What constitutes its being a *lucky* horseshoe?"

"You know, I'm really not sure." She grinned. Bit her lip in deep thought. "I guess I'll have to Google it."

"Or you could just ask a horse."

"Ooooh. Did you just make a funny?" She laughed. "I like it." She lifted her hand to brush her hair back from her face. "Maybe I could just ask a certain aging bowlegged cowboy. He's been dying to get me alone."

Reno hated to admit it, but he'd like to get her alone too. But then, that's exactly what he had right now, wasn't it? And what was *he* doing while they were alone, and she sat there looking so kissable? Searching for boxes.

Total waste of time.

"Chester has a reputation, you know." He moved a case of smoke detectors, thinking it was a good thing they weren't active. Because every time he looked at Charli, he felt like he might spontaneously combust.

It wasn't anything in particular she did or said. And it didn't help that he'd had several talks with himself about keeping his distance. Something about the woman just turned his head. Flipped his switch. And tempted him to ignore all the warning bells clanging like a three-alarm fire. "I hear when Chester was younger, he had the ladies lined up," he said.

Her brows drew together. "His wife must not have appreciated that."

"Probably not." He chuckled. "Though it would be hard to figure out which wife that would have been."

"So Chester was a repeat offender?"

"Most folks lost track at six marriages. The last one anyone could remember was Loretta La Fleur. Rumor was he met her in a Cajun bar in New Orleans. Of course, rumor also hinted that old Chester had paid for her favors and liked them so much he married her."

"Whatever happened to her?"

Reno shrugged. "After she left, Chester kept pretty tight-lipped. But rumor has it she'd never divorced her previous husband and went back to Louisiana."

A smile tilted Charli's mouth. Everything male in him responded.

"I know the story seems funny," she said, "but

I can't help think how sad it must be to marry so many times. I know some people go into marriage these days thinking if they don't like it, they can just get a divorce. But that's like claiming defeat before you even get the *I Do's* over with."

"Some would say that's old-fashioned thinking," he said though her thoughts echoed his own.

"I know. But that's okay with me. I'm not the type to change my opinions because of peer pressure."

She glanced down, then back up. Something in those amazing eyes reached into his chest and wrapped his heart in warmth. He put down the box in his hands and stepped out from the mire of cardboard containers.

"You'd probably be surprised to know I'm a lot more like you than you might think," she said.

"How's that?" He took a step closer.

"I believe strongly in tradition. I believe in family and friends and doing what's necessary to keep it all together. And I believe that marriage is something sacred and that people should work hard and fight to keep the love they shared in that exact moment when they exchanged their vows."

Her candid admission made him swallow.

"I was really young when my mother died," she continued. "When I look at my father today, I can't imagine what she saw in him. But somewhere . . . in the back of my memories . . . I remember hearing them together when Nick and I were supposed to be asleep. I remember them talking to each other in loving voices. I remember their laughter. And I know, regardless of my father's frequent absences and his sometimes unpleasant behavior, they truly loved each other. Neither of them would have given up on a marriage I didn't really understand."

She gave a sad laugh and shook her head in a way that made her long, loose curls dance.

"I know my father's a son of a bitch. But he loved my mother. He was never cruel—just difficult. And it broke his heart the day she died."

"What happened to her? If you don't mind my asking?"

"I don't mind. I like talking about her. It keeps her alive if you know what I mean."

He nodded.

"She was wonderful. Whimsical. Completely the opposite of my father."

She gave a little laugh. As she talked, Reno noted how her face lit up with the happy memories. The kind that for him were the most difficult to remember amid the tragic results.

"My father always said I reminded him too much of her. I never thought that was a bad thing. But apparently *he* did. I was eight when she died. It was so . . . unexpected that it took a long time to sink in and realize she was never coming home."

Reno knew that feeling only too well.

She glanced away, then looked back at him again and sighed. "My father was coming home after several long months in which Nick and I had both gotten the chicken pox, then Nick broke his arm in a bicycle race. My mom had been doing double duty, taking care of us and basically being shut in the house for a couple weeks. The cupboards were bare. She'd gotten the lady next door to watch us for a few minutes while she rushed off to the store to get the stuff to make my father's favorite meat loaf. On the way home, she was killed by a drunk driver."

Her voice broke, and she paused. "Hard to imagine someone could be that inebriated at four in the afternoon and rip away the life of someone who was so loved. The man who killed her wasn't even injured."

"I'm so . . . sorry," Reno said, knowing that the words were inadequate.

"Thank you." She gave him a tentative smile. "It was horrible. But the tragedy can't erase all the wonderful things she did in her life. It can't erase what a wonderful mother she was. Or how lucky Nick and I were to have her. Even if it was only for a short time."

Emotion knotted in his chest, and he recognized that he too was lucky. His feet moved before he could tell them to stop. In a blink, he was standing before her.

Tilting her head back, she looked up and lifted her hand to touch his cheek. "What is it, Reno? What's got you so tangled up inside?"

He placed his hand over hers, closed his eyes, and savored the softness of her palm against the rough stubble of his beard. He wanted to say it was *her* who had him tangled up, but right now he could think of better things to do with his mouth than talk. He lowered his head and pressed his lips to hers.

Because he was a man who never took what wasn't offered, he ended the kiss and leaned away. Her hand on the back of his neck stopped his retreat. She looked up at him with understanding, desire, and need.

"Kiss me again, Cowboy."

Permission granted.

Again he bent his head and covered her mouth with his own. On a slow intake of air, he blotted out everything in his mind but her—the sweet scent of barbecue that lingered in her hair, the softness of her skin, the slick slide and tangle of their tongues. She tasted like honey, and passion, and promise.

She swayed against him and slid both her hands up and around his neck. He stepped into that warm space between her thighs. Pulled her up and against him. Beneath the thin handkerchief blouse, her nipples tightened and pushed against his chest.

A simple tilt of her head gave him better access and turned up the heat. The kiss turned urgent, wet, and visceral. Fire spread through his body and made him light-headed. He welcomed the loss of control, grabbed hold of her with both hands, and drew her firm against the bulge straining against his jeans. As his body reacted to hers he completely forgot why he'd tried to convince himself to keep his distance.

Her fingers weaved into his hair.

His hands slipped beneath that flimsy little top and connected with soft, warm, bare skin. He slid his palms up. His thumbs brushed the underside of her breasts. She moaned in his mouth, and sensation tingled in his fingertips.

A hard knock on the back door broke them apart.

"Wilder?" the deep voice on the opposite side said. "That you in there?"

"Shit."

Reno ran a hand through his hair while he looked

at Charli, her lips moist and red from his kiss. He wanted to ignore the man at the door, take her in his arms, and kiss her again.

"Who is *that*?" she asked with a little giggle.

"Brady Bennett."

Her eyes widened. "*Deputy* Bennett?"

"The one and only."

"What do you think he wants?" she whispered.

When he looked at her rumpled hair, her well-kissed lips, and flimsy little blouse askew, he couldn't have cared less about what the good deputy wanted. "Guess we'd better find out."

He opened the door. "What's up?" he asked when he found Brady standing back, hand hovering above his sidearm.

"Took you damn long enough." Brady dropped his arm to his side. "Thought maybe you were being robbed."

Reno stepped out the door, hoping the darkness would be a screen for any *evidence* going on below his belt. "Nope." He popped the P and figured if he got Brady the hell out of there, maybe he and Charli could get back to business. "I was just—"

"Deputy Bennett." Charli slipped beneath Reno's arm and turned on the charm. "How nice of you to check on things at this late hour. It's really nice to know all our materials are safe with you on patrol."

Brady touched two fingers to the brim of his Stetson. "Ms. Brooks."

Reno didn't like the way his childhood friend and a favorite of the single ladies in town was looking at her. Then again, it wasn't all that different than the way most of the men in town looked at her. Men who included his own brothers.

"Mr. Wilder and I were trying to find some items he misplaced." She flashed a smile and clasped a hand to the front of the blouse he'd just had his hand up. "I hate to admit that our production company seems to have overrun his stockroom."

"Uh-huh." Brady looked at Reno. Looked at Charli. Then looked back at Reno and smiled. "Guess I'd best let you two get back to your *search*."

"Thanks for stopping by." Reno began to shut the door as Brady stepped away.

"Oh. And Wilder?" Brady turned back again. "You might want to tuck in your shirt."

Reno looked down, and sure enough, his shirt looked like he'd had it about halfway off. He smirked. "Yeah. I'll get right on that."

Charli looked up at Reno and grinned. "Busted."

"Big-time."

Once he closed the door, she curled her fingers into his shirt and leaned in. "Now. Where were we?"

Fortunately—or unfortunately, however he chose to look at it—the cool air and the sight of a deputy badge flashing at him in the dark of the night brought all his senses back.

Charli wasn't the type of woman a man *did* on top of a desk the first time. She deserved to be treated like a lady. And as much as it killed him, he knew the fun and games were over.

At least for now.

"I was about to take you to your car so you can go home and get some sleep."

Her bottom lip came out in a sexy little pout. "What if I told you I wasn't tired?"

He sucked in a deep breath and let it out slowly. He could think of at least a thousand ways to wear her out.

"You won't think that come morning." He reached down and took her hand in his. "Didn't you say you were working tomorrow, so you can get Town Square done for Paige and Aiden's wedding?"

Her slim shoulders lifted, then dropped with an exaggerated sigh. Her nose wrinkled. "Yes."

He reached behind her and grabbed his hat off the hook near the door. "Then it might be best to call it a night."

"But what about my ceiling tiles," she asked, as he began to close the door behind them.

He glanced back at the jumbled mess of a stockroom and flipped off the light. "I'm afraid they may be lost forever."

Chapter 11

$\mathcal{S}$unday morning, Charli woke up and slid out of bed. She'd never wanted to sleep in more.

Well, that was a lie.

She wanted to sleep in every day, but most days weren't her "day off," when she *should* be able to sleep in. But last night's encounter with Paige and Aiden changed that. In order to give them their dream wedding, Charli knew she had to move fast. Push hard. And do some general scrambling to get things done.

To Charli's delight, Paige had agreed to let her decorate the newly renovated Town Square for the wedding. Which meant Charli would also need to rework her dollar allotments for each project. Which meant she would have to do some returns of smaller items and come up with something equally awesome for less.

She rubbed her eyes and stretched. God, she was tired already.

Yet how could she not jump at the chance to give the adorable couple the wedding of their dreams? Former Army Ranger Aiden Marshall had survived multiple deployments to Iraq and Afghanistan and had lost his best friends in the process. When he'd come home, *he'd* been lost, and Paige's love had saved him.

Charli sighed.

She'd move glaciers if need be to give them a wedding of pure heaven. They deserved nothing less.

From the top of the comforter, Pumpkin stretched her little poodle paws and yawned. Her pink tongue clacked against her tiny teeth as her mouth closed.

"Come on, sleepyhead. We've got work to do."

Pumpkin gave a slow "you've got to be kidding me" blink, then laid her head back down.

"I'm making scrambled eggs," she taunted in a singsong voice.

The dog's fuzzy topknot came up, and when Charli shuffled from the room, Pumpkin leaped from the bed and followed.

When Charli got to the kitchen, she grabbed the glass carafe from the coffeemaker and went to the sink. She flipped on the faucet, and, as the carafe filled with water, she glanced out the window to the bright sunshine peeking over the hilltops. Being on the second story did have an advantage for the amazing views. Her gaze shifted from the wide-open meadow, where cows grazed, to the movement she'd caught in Reno's garden.

She snapped off the faucet and watched as the man moved about the raised beds with a large wire basket. He looked at ease in that garden. At peace.

And she really hated to go annoy him. But that wouldn't stop her.

Last night, they'd shared something more than just amazing kisses. They'd had a moment where she thought they'd truly connected. It had been brief, but she hadn't imagined it.

After Deputy Bennett's interruption, Reno had crept back into that dark place where he seemed the most comfortable. No matter how she teased or taunted, he'd not taken the bait. Much to her total disappointment, he'd been a complete gentleman. And when the opportunity for a good night kiss arose, he'd given her a smile instead.

A while later, when she'd arrived at the ranch, his truck was nowhere to be found. She'd marched up the stairs to the apartment, then spent half the night wondering where he'd gone.

Around four in the morning, she'd woken to the sound of tires pulling into the gravel drive. She'd been too tired to get up and go look, but she figured he'd finally come home from wherever he'd been.

Where *had* he been?

A girlfriend's?

Maybe.

Her eyebrows scrunched together.

She hoped not.

She hadn't seen him with anyone, nor had his mother mentioned that he was seeing someone. And though he had kissed her socks off last night, she couldn't imagine that the women of Sweet would let a man like him slip through their fingers.

Just one more solid reason she should be sticking to her man-ban resolution.

Charli poured a scoop of coffee grounds into the filter compartment, punched the ON button, and went in search of her flip-flops. After she washed her face and made some semblance of her unruly morning curls, she poured two steaming mugs, spooned in sugar, and headed down the stairs. Pumpkin, sensing Bear wasn't far, ran ahead.

As Charli made her way across the neatly clipped yard, her flip-flops made a snick-snick-snick sound and gave away her surprise appearance. Well, that and the fact that her dog had pounced on Bear and proceeded to engage him in a game of yap and tag.

The garden gate creaked as Charli nudged it open with her hip and stepped inside. Reno's head came up, and she couldn't tell if his intense glare was caused by the bright sunshine or if he was unhappy about the intrusion.

"Morning," she said, and received a dark-headed nod. "I brought you coffee." As she joined him in the tomato, onion, and jalapeno aisle, she handed him the mug.

His hair was damp, and the silver at his temples gleamed in the sunlight. The fresh scent of soap clung to him. Though he'd apparently showered, his dark eyes looked sleepy, and a beard shadowed his jaw. His jeans were faded and worn and hugged his lean hips with just the right amount of snugness. A clean, slightly wrinkled, white T-shirt lay over his broad shoulders, and the sleeves cupped a pair of sizeable biceps.

As he accepted the mug from her hand, his gaze slid from her eyes down the length of her body. He took that trip slowly, like he wasn't in any hurry. When his gaze came back up, a smile tilted that sensual mouth, and those rarely seen dimples made an appearance.

Charli sipped her coffee if only to calm her racing heart.

"Thank you." His voice was low and rough. From lack of sleep no doubt. His lips pursed over the rim of the mug, and he sipped. "Perfect."

Okay, it was only a cup of coffee and two spoonfuls of sugar, but the compliment made her smile.

"Careful you don't get bit by mosquitoes," he said. "There's some spray over there by the gate."

"I've always been pretty fortunate." She glanced down to her sleep shorts and tank top. "They don't seem to like me. Even when we were in the Bayou last fall."

"Lucky you."

She looked him over again, from his boots to the eyes that watched her with interest. Desire. Hunger.

Yes.

Lucky her.

"I guess I just don't taste very sweet."

"That would be a matter of opinion."

"Is that a compliment?" She laughed. "Because I'll take it."

Those amazing dimples flashed again.

"Are you flirting, Mr. Wilder?"

"Nope." He sipped his joe. "Just being polite."

A grin swept her mouth. "Uh-huh." Why the possibility sent a sizzle of exhilaration through her electrical system was anybody's guess. Then again, when a man like Reno showed any kind of interest at all, a woman would be out of her mind not to care. And isn't that what always got her into trouble?

He started to move down the aisle. She followed.

"So what's with the mile-high wire fence?" she asked.

"Keeps the whitetail out. They'll eat most anything, and within a couple of nights, they'll ravish your entire garden."

"*Ravish.* Now there's a fascinating but seldom-used word."

He chuckled as he reached for a Roma tomato and tested its ripeness. She couldn't help but remember what those large hands and strong fingers felt like on her skin.

"Gardening in Texas is a challenge," he said. "If the deer and other critters don't get to it, the drought and heat will."

"Yours seems very prosperous."

"The fence . . . and my mom help."

"Yes. I talked to her out here the other day. She seems to really like getting her hands in the dirt."

He moved farther down the aisle, pulled off a ripe cherry tomato, brushed it against his shirt, and handed it to her. She popped it into her mouth, closed her eyes, and moaned when the sun-warmed sweetness burst in her mouth.

"From the watering system to the layout, my mom helped plan out the garden. It's hers as much as it is mine."

"Tomatoes, green beans, okra, sweet potatoes . . . you have quite the crop."

"We share," he said. "Anyone who's down on their luck, we share vegetables and beef."

"Because that's what neighbors do?"

"Absolutely."

"I can't imagine that happening where I live. Once I actually saw two women in the seafood aisle of Trader Joe's arguing over who deserved the last package of salmon."

His dark brows pulled together. "You're kidding."

"I wish I was."

"I could never live somewhere like that."

"I often wonder why I do."

He brushed off another cherry tomato and popped it into his mouth. "You come up with an answer?"

She shrugged. "Originally, I moved to California to get as far away from my father as possible. I went to college at Pepperdine—for which I might be re-paying student loans the rest of my life." She chuckled. "I made friends there, and I just stayed."

"Friends are a good reason to stay."

"I don't see them that much anymore. Most are married. A few have kids. Everybody's busy. And then there's all the travel involved with my job."

He shook his head. "Sounds lonely."

At the sound of understanding in his tone, she looked up. In his eyes, she recognized that kindred spirit again. "Yeah. I guess it is."

Then he looked at her with a directness most people never mastered. "So why do you stay?"

A sigh lifted her chest as the deeper meaning behind the simple question sank in. "I don't know."

A myriad of emotions grabbed hold of her heart,

and the reality of her feelings pumped new energy. She might not have all the answers, but one thing she did know? She was always open to new adventures.

Maybe it was time to rethink this merry-go-round she called life. Maybe it was time to push the button and get off the ride. She glanced at her surroundings—the beautiful rolling hills, the green meadow, and the amazing man looking at her like he was genuinely interested in what she had to say.

Maybe it was time to make a different plan.

"I was planning to make some scrambled eggs."

He reached down, pulled a sweet onion out of the ground, and handed it to her. "Maybe you could add some of this."

"Maybe you'd like to share?"

He gave her a hesitant look, then finally said, "Sorry. I've got plans I can't cancel."

With an über polite "Have a good day," he picked up his overflowing basket of vegetables, and, once again, she was left with nothing but a view of his retreating backside.

An hour later, Charli finally pulled herself together enough to get in the Hummer and head into downtown to start her work on the candy store. This morning, she'd treated herself to an omelet of vegetables fresh from Reno's garden. Seated in his brother's kitchen looking out the window at the picture-perfect scenery outside had been wonderful. Eating alone took away some of the flavor. She'd wanted conversation. Instead, she got a begging dog whose cute little paw-waving dance made her hard to refuse.

It wasn't until Charli was headed down Main Street that she realized most of her conversations with Reno were focused on her. He shared little of himself. A situation she'd make sure to remedy the next time she had the chance. There were too many mysteries about the man. Other than the fact that Jana and Joe Wilder weren't his birth parents, that he'd been named after a city, and that he'd lost both his brother and father in a short period of time, she knew squat. But it didn't take Einstein to know there were stories galore locked up behind those warm brown eyes. Secrets that had dug their claws into his soul and wouldn't let go.

In her mind, he was like the treasure in an Indiana Jones movie. If she wanted to capture the prize, she would have to don her fedora and go on a little expedition. The risks might be high, but even Indiana got a happily ever after.

Didn't he?

She eased the Hummer to a stop in front of Goody Gum Drops, gathered up her dog, and walked up to the door. She slid the key she'd been given into the lock, stepped inside, and set Pumpkin and her purse down. She turned. And gasped.

The entire ceiling had been covered in the missing ceiling tin tiles.

Charli raised her hand to her mouth and walked farther into the store, looking up at the impeccable workmanship. There could be only one person who could have installed those tiles. Her heart gave a quick thump against her ribs.

So he hadn't been out all night with a woman or carousing around town. He'd been working. For her. So she could meet her deadlines and move on to provide the perfect place for a wonderful couple's wedding.

This morning, he hadn't said a word.

Tears filled her eyes.

She didn't need to go on an expedition to find out what kind of man Reno might be; he'd just confirmed what she already knew in her heart.

For the candy-store reveal, Reno made sure he wasn't within coercion range. He'd suffered through one, and that had been enough. Plus, he didn't want anyone to know he'd been involved in any way. Especially his brothers. He'd never hear the end of it. They were bad enough now as it was.

Guilt and nothing more had made him go back to the hardware store the night he'd taken Charli to Sweet Pickens. Guilt had made him drive the boxes of ceiling tiles over to the candy store. Guilt had made him put the damn things up.

Nothing more.

In the past few days, he'd done a good job avoiding her—even if there had been a couple of times he'd taken the longer route just to catch a glimpse. He'd managed not to be within arm's distance, where he could catch the scent of whatever flavor-of-the-day body lotion she wore. Or where he could view those naturally ripe lips of hers inviting him in for a taste. Or lose his mind again and pull her into his arms.

It had seemed necessary, so he'd developed a mantra: *Do not get close. Do not get involved. Do not get attached.* And when his brothers were around, he added: *Do not give them any kind of ammunition to fling at him like monkey shit in the zoo.*

He needed to use his military skills and stay in neutral territory to save his skin. And his sanity. Not to mention his heart.

No time seemed better than now as he sat on horseback and rode out to check fence lines with Jesse at his side.

"Heard Goody's was having a candy sale today after the big reveal," Jesse said in his discreetly meddlesome manner. "Thought maybe you'd want to go over there and pick up something for Izzy."

Reno tipped his hat farther down on his forehead to avoid the sun's glare. "Maybe *you* could go get her something."

A grin tilted Jesse's mouth. "You know I'm a chips and salsa guy. I'd have no idea what to pick out."

"Just buy something pink, and I guarantee it will be a hit."

"What if I buy the wrong shade of pink?"

"She's a two-year-old, for crying out loud." Reno shook his head. "You think she has a preference over light or dark?"

"I think you're the one with the sweet tooth, and you'd do a better job."

Reno pulled Cisco to a stop and glared at his brother. "Are we really arguing over what kind of candy to buy our niece? Or are you just butting your nose in where it doesn't belong?"

"Nose is exactly where it's supposed to be. In *your* business." Jesse tugged the reins on Ranger, the big bay he preferred to ride even though the horse had a stubborn streak. "Shelly Dworshak brought her schnauzer in yesterday for a rabies vaccine. She said she saw you and Ms. Brooks sharing barbecue, and you looked mighty cozy."

Reno felt his eyes roll and hit the back of his head. "Shelly Dworshak is a nosy woman who wears Coke-bottle glasses and wouldn't know a possum from a raccoon."

"No need to be so insulting. Or get so defensive." Jesse leaned back in the saddle. "Unless you got something to hide."

"Nothing to hide, little brother." He kicked Cisco into gear, and the buckskin took off at a gallop. Damn. Reno needed to watch his responses. His brothers were pros at yanking out information, then making of it what they wanted. Any kind of defensive tone with them was like confirmation.

Jesse caught up, turned his horse, who did a side-step while his rider pried deeper. "Thought you'd want to know that Mom invited the delightful Ms. Brooks and her crew to the barbecue."

"Well, that was nice of Mom."

"Those parties can get out of hand once in a while, you know."

"Stop going around the block, brother. Say what you mean."

"Not often you go home alone afterward."

"And what makes you think I'd go home with Ms. Brooks?"

"She's hot?"

"Then why wouldn't you or Jackson try to go home with her?" Aside from the fact that he'd have to kill them.

"Because we weren't seen eating barbecue with

her. Because we didn't spend three days painting a mural for her even after we swore we were pissed off that she and her TV show were here to rape and pillage our town. Because—"

"Jesus, Jess. You've got an imagination on you."

"Jesus, Reno. You've been throwing out "Back the fuck off" signals since the minute she moved into Jack's apartment."

He had?

Oops. Time to detour. "How old are you?"

Jesse's blue-eyed glare made him want to laugh. "Thirty-two."

"No shit? I could have sworn you were still in high school."

"Funny."

Before he urged the horse into high speed, Reno did a quick spin on the conversation. "So how's it working out with your new vet assistant?"

Jesse threw out an arm to stop him, grasping Reno by the shirtsleeve and almost yanking him from his mount.

"What the hell are you doing?" he asked, but he knew. Damn it. He knew.

"We love you, bro." A rare look of concern pushed down on Jesse's brows. "And there isn't a single one of us that doesn't want to see you happy. Diana was a wonderful girl, but she's gone. It's time for you to open yourself up to the great big world out there. Dad and Jared may be gone, but do you think for one minute they'd want you to mourn them forever?"

"I—"

"Hell no they wouldn't. Dad would kick your ass if he knew you'd practically quit breathing the

day he died. Jared would call in the noogie patrol
until your head burned." Jesse let go of his shirt
and clamped his hand over Reno's shoulder. "You
busted your ass your entire life to prove you were
one of us. But, Reno, you're the *best* of us."

His throat went dry.

"Do you remember when you first came to live
with us, and you'd have those nightmares and wake
up screaming?"

"Hard to forget."

"Do you remember how we'd all lie down on the
floor together to protect you from whatever haunted
you in the night?"

"Yeah."

Jesse's grasp on his shoulder tightened. "We're
still there, man. And we all want to see you move
past what's holding you back. Your life started out
rough. We want to see you live the rest with a smile
on your face."

Reno took in his brother's words—let them sink
deep down into his soul. Without warning, emotion sprang up into his eyes and misted his view of
the brother who'd seemed to grow wiser when he
hadn't been looking.

"Give yourself permission to exist, big brother,"
Jesse said. "You deserve to live. Even if others can't."

Like Charli had said about her mother, he felt
lucky to have had Diana in his life. He glanced
across the field and could picture her riding her
horse at breakneck speed, lasso overhead, smiling
as she chased down a wayward calf at branding
time. She'd been the quiet one at family dinners. The

thoughtful one on special occasions. His confidant. His friend. His lover.

And when she'd died just a few months after his father, he'd wanted to die too.

Living was one thing. But Reno knew a woman like Charli deserved better than him.

Nobody wanted—or needed—damaged goods.

Chapter 12

The grass in Town Square tickled the bare bottoms of Charli's feet as she walked over to the gazebo area and approached the man who stood with one booted foot propped up on a picnic bench. Overhead, the grackles gathered in the trees, fluttered their wings, and bombarded her with squeaks and whistles.

"I know we're on a mouse-sized budget, Sam, but I want elephant-sized results."

Sam, the landscape manager, bent his head over the plans and rubbed his brow with a free hand. "I can't—"

"No. No. No. I don't want to hear 'I can't.' I want to hear"—she lowered her tone to sound like a man—"wow, Charli, this is a really astronomically impossible feat, but I'll make damned sure you get what you need."

He chuckled. "Does anyone ever tell you no?"

"Well, they try." She grinned. "But the results can be really ugly, and I'd rather not discuss the messy details."

"Fine." Sam gave a huge man sigh. "Then you'll have exactly what you want—providing that elaborate gazebo you ordered gets done on time."

"This morning I brought the workers donuts. Later, I'm hitting up the bakery for cupcakes," she admitted. "If I see a weak link, I have a stash of energy drinks in the cooler."

"You are one determined young lady."

"I know you've only been here for a couple of days, Sam, and you haven't gotten to know the community yet, but there's more than just a park here. It's more than just a place where people picnic or sit beneath the stars to listen to a band. This is the conduit for keeping the community connected. It's the place where couples are united. Where lives are celebrated."

"Sounds like an old-fashioned movie."

"Maybe it is. But I'm quickly learning that sometimes keeping tradition alive is what keeps people going—even when they want to give up."

He shrugged. "Makes sense I guess."

She could tell he wasn't fully convinced, so she told him Paige and Aiden's story and how they would have their wedding there in just a few weeks. Sam, being a vet who'd done time in Desert Storm, quietly nodded. "I get it now. You'll have your vision. I promise."

When Sam went back to his projects, Charli took a slow look around the square. With all the activity going on and progress being made in each project area, she nearly cried with relief. When it all came together, it would be a spectacular place for the residents of Sweet to enjoy for years to come.

One day, she hoped to come back and see it all for herself. Maybe she could even make it back during the Sweet Apple Butter Festival. She heard that was quite the party.

"There you are."

Charli turned toward the friendly voice. Jana Wilder—hair and makeup perfectly groomed—walked toward her, lugging a large plastic beverage cooler and a bag of red Solo cups. Beside her on a sparkly leash, Miss Giddy displayed a perky blue satin ribbon around her neck.

"Hi. What are you doing here?"

Reno's mother smiled. "I was on my way over to the assisted living center. I take Miss Giddy there to visit once a week—animals being a good source of therapy and all. I just couldn't think of y'all being out here in this hot sunshine without some sweet tea to cool you down. So here I am."

"That's so nice of you." Charli's thirst went into overdrive. "And hello to you, Miss Giddy."

The goat said *"Meh-eh-eh"* in return, and Charli laughed.

"How about we go over there to that table under the tree and call everyone over." Charli relieved Jana of the cumbersome, heavy cooler.

"That'll do," Jana said. "It'll give me the chance to invite them all for the barbecue this weekend."

"Are you sure you want *everyone* there? That adds a lot of people to your list."

"Oh, sugarplum, don't you worry. The whole town's invited."

"The *entire* town?" As they walked across the lawn, Charli's eyes widened at the prospect.

"You bet. Joe started the tradition to celebrate Jared's first birthday."

"But—"

"I know what you're thinking," Jana said with a wistful smile, as Charli set down the cooler. "But after that first gathering, the party took on a meaning other than just a birthday party. When each boy was born after that it became a celebration of life. When Joe and Jared died, nobody wanted to have the party anymore. I insisted. I wasn't about to quit celebrating how much they meant to me, or how much they'd given me in the years I had with them. There will always be loss. And there will always be new life—like my granddaughter Isabella. So the party goes on—in their memory and for the memories yet to be made."

Charli felt the warmth of the woman's smile and sincerity all the way into her heart. "You have an amazing outlook on life."

"Not always. I won't lie and say I don't get lonely. Or mad as hell that those I love have been taken away from me." She shook her head. "But each day I wake up, and I make myself find something new to be thankful for. And that gets me through. Now, if I could just get my son to feel that way."

"Which one?"

"Reno."

"Ah. He's a tough one." Charli hesitated, knowing most things about people's lives were private and meant to stay that way, but more than just a little something about that man drew her in and made her care. "I hate to pry, but—"

"What happened to him?" Jana finished.

Charli nodded. "He briefly mentioned that another woman gave birth to him."

"Well now." Jana's head went back, and her eyebrows lifted. "Isn't that interesting."

"What is?"

"My boy doesn't share that information with many people outside of those who already know him. He must feel comfortable around you."

"Oh no. Far from it, I'm afraid."

"He doesn't trust easy." Jana's bright eyes darkened. "If he knew I was telling you any of this, he'd skin me alive."

"I promise I won't say a word."

"I know you won't. I told my boys what a good girl you were from the moment I laid eyes on you."

Jana softly patted her cheek, and Charli felt honored that someone who didn't even know her could see that she always tried to do the right thing. Even if sometimes she took the long way around.

"Reno's birth mother was Joe's youngest sister," Jana said. "She'd always been a wild child and let anyone who'd listen know how, as soon as she got old enough, she planned to escape anything to do with cattle or small towns or the family who'd raised her." Sunlight danced through the leaves overhead and across Jana's turquoise blouse as she opened the bag of cups and pulled out a stack. "No one heard from her for a few years. When her parents finally got a call, it was from the Las Vegas police. They'd arrested her on drug charges and prostitution."

Charli's heart sank right into the pit of her stomach.

"She did two years behind bars. Everyone hoped that would give her time to think. But the minute she was released, she disappeared again. Six years later, Joe and I received a call. Seems Angela had gone on a binge and taken off with some guy. Until that moment, we didn't even know Reno existed."

Jana paused, bit her lip as though remembering the emotion she'd felt that day.

"She left Reno all alone in her apartment. When neighbors didn't see her around for a few days, they called the police."

"Oh my God. How old was he?"

"Just five." Her eyes watered. "Makes me want to cry just remembering what he went through." She waved her hand in front of her face a few times to dry the tears.

"He'd been alone in that filthy apartment for four days with only a half-empty jar of peanut butter and tap water to drink. He was such a smart, brave little boy. He kept himself clean. Made sure he ate small amounts in case she didn't come back for a while. And he stayed inside where he considered it safe. When the police came, it took them hours to convince him it was okay to open the door and let them in."

Jana paused again and gathered up the emotions obviously tearing through her at the memory. "Two hours after Joe and I got the call, we headed to the airport to go get him. He was such a sweet little thing. So grateful to finally have someone to look after him. But also so scared he would lose us and end up right back where he'd been. He feared Angela would come get him and drag him back to that mess."

"What about his father?"

"No one knows who he was. Angela never told. I'm not sure she even knew. Or cared."

"Poor baby." Charli felt sick inside. All this time, she'd been complaining that her father hadn't given her any attention when Reno had literally been abandoned.

Jana nodded and began pouring sweet tea into the cups. "Six months after he came to live with us, we started the adoption process. We weren't about to give Angela any leeway to come back and snatch him away. We loved him like our own. And from the moment he walked through our door, our boys accepted him as one of them."

Charli laid her hand over Jana's arm. "He was so lucky to have you."

"*We* were the lucky ones."

"What happened to Angela?" She refused to call the woman his mother. Dogs treated their babies better.

"About a year after the adoption was final, she called, looking for him."

"She didn't know he was missing for over a year?"

"She didn't care. Why all of a sudden she had a change of heart we don't know. And it didn't matter. He belonged to us. There was no way in hell we'd give him back."

Charli had heard the term *Mama Grizzly* before, and when she looked at Jana Wilder, that's exactly what she saw. Someone who would defend her family to the death.

"Angela died when Reno was fifteen. When we told him, he just nodded. He never shed a tear. But inside, I knew he cried. For years, he blamed himself for what had happened. Thought he wasn't lovable. Didn't deserve to be loved."

"How could he do that?" Charli asked, stunned. "He was just an innocent little boy."

"Sometimes, the brain has trouble catching up with the heart. No matter how many times you tell someone it wasn't their fault or how much you love them, it just takes a little longer to get the message."

Jana called out to the team of workers and production crew, who put down their tools and headed in the direction of a refreshing drink.

Miss Giddy gave a vocal "*Meh-eh-eh*" and began to dance around the closer they came. Obviously, Miss Giddy was a goat with good knowledge that she'd soon be the center of attention.

Before the crew arrived, Jana took Charli's hand and held it tight. "I know my boy's got eyes for you," she said.

The statement surprised her. "Oh, I don't think—"

"He's my son. I know him better than he knows himself." She gave Charli's hand a squeeze. "Don't you let him push you away. He'll try. And he's damned good at it. But that wonderful soul of his could use a little breather. And, sugarplum, *you* just might be it."

Stunned to the toes of her worn sneakers, Charli watched as Jana turned toward the workers and began to hand out cups of sweet tea. Then she glanced across the expanse of grass and landscape construction to the hardware store across the street.

At that moment, the man in question came out the door with a huge bag of feed tossed over his shoulder. He slung it down to the ground and leaned it against the wall by the front window. As if he could sense her watching him, he looked up. While her heart played Skip to My Lou, and for what felt like an eternity, they both stood there watching each other not move. Finally, he broke the spell with a two-finger salute to the brim of his cowboy hat and went back inside the store.

In that moment, Charli dove headfirst off the man-ban wagon.

She waited until her heartbeat slowed back to normal before she joined her crew for a quick break. But she could not keep her gaze from straying to that dilapidated-looking building and thoughts of the man inside.

She wished she knew a little practical magic. Had a little mystical power. But the only thing that seemed to have any chance of working on a man who seemed to have put his heart in solitary confinement was pure, undiluted, feminine power. She'd always been inventive when it came to design; now she needed to put that creativity to good use.

Reno might need a little breather, but Charli planned to make him breathless.

A person could call himself ten kinds of stupid and still not listen to reason. As Reno headed over to Town Square, he figured he might have lost a few more brain cells between leaving the door of the hardware store and the curb on the other side of the street.

He had no business leaving the store for even a moment. There were accounts to review. Orders to place. Customers who wanted to make purchases.

Packages to deliver. Which was what he was about to do, and that was his total lame-ass excuse for walking across the grass toward the woman he wanted nothing to do with and whom he also couldn't get off his mind.

To further prove his stupidity, he fully realized he could have and should have waited for someone from her crew to come pick up the boxes of landscape lighting. But noooo. He had to take it upon himself to deliver.

He'd always had a level head. Always been the one to pull his wild brothers out of scrapes and catastrophes. Always been the brother everyone relied on. Because he had good common sense.

What a load of bullshit.

At the moment, his common sense was the size of a sunflower seed and stuck so deep in the ground, it had no chance of growing.

The grass beneath his boots was dry and crunched with every step. Ernie McGreavy must be having nightmares about his carefully tended carpet of green. There were holes everywhere, not to mention the craters created by a backhoe currently riding across the lawn and doing further damage.

Nothing looked like the old Town Square.

The gazebo had been torn down. In its place was a new foundation and piles of two-by-fours. The picnic benches had disappeared. And a border of bright yellow plastic CAUTION tape surrounded the entire block.

Somehow, he avoided getting in the way of workers and machinery as he walked toward a pair of Daisy Dukes and the shapely owner, who was currently on her knees digging in a flower bed, planting drought-resistant shrubs.

He tilted his head for a better look, feeling not in the least like a total stalker, just a man who appreciated a nice view.

Or at least that's what he told himself.

As he came up behind her, he noted the haphazard way she'd pulled all that silky brown hair into a messy knot on top of her head. He took in the way the muscles in her legs flexed as she leaned forward and dug in the rich, dark layer of soil. Appreciated the sheen of perspiration that dampened the back of her slender neck. The tops of her shoulders were turning a painful shade of red. And as she jammed her trowel into the ground, she mumbled beneath her breath.

"You forget your sunscreen?" He set the boxes down behind her.

She sat up and turned, looked up at him, and squinted against the bright sunlight. "What?"

"You're getting burned." He pointed to her shoulders, trying to ignore the drip of sweat trickling between her breasts.

She glanced down. "Oh. Thanks. Sorry. I don't mean to be cranky, but it's pretty hot out here." She swiped the moisture from her brow with the back of her arm and left a streak of dirt across her forehead.

He wasn't sure why that was so sexy, but well, it just was.

Tearing his gaze away from the front of her tank top, he looked at the work going on around the park. "Doesn't look like there's a chance you're going to be done in time for Aiden and Paige's wedding."

"I know you hope I'll fall flat on my face and fail." She looked at the activity around her—the backhoe scraping off a layer of grass to create an area for the new playground, the hammering of nails going into the elaborate Victorian gazebo, the studs being cut for the braces on the new picnic tables. "But I guarantee it *will* be done on time. I've never let anyone down before. I'm not going to start now with your friends."

She stood, brushed the dirt from her hands, then planted them on her hips and looked up at him. The sunlight hit her eyes, and, for the first time, he realized they weren't just dark, they were rich maple honey with flecks of gold and copper that flashed at him like the sparks of an electrical storm.

"I know you hate what's going on here," she said, "but—"

"I didn't say I *hated* it."

"Really?" She tilted her head. A lock of hair slipped from its knot and fell across her smooth shoulder. She reached up and swept it behind her ear. "You could have fooled me with all that frowning and growling going on."

"I don't growl."

A smile tilted those pretty lips. "You totally growl." She reached down and picked up her planting trowel. "So I'm sure something important dragged you from your cave, or you wouldn't have come over here."

"You're awful prickly today, Fancy Pants."

"No, I'm not."

He shrugged. "Okay."

"Wow. You're going to give in that easy?"

"I never give in."

"Never?"

"Ever."

"Seriously?"

He couldn't help smile. "Dead serious."

She grinned like someone had given her a fresh scoop of ice cream with colored sprinkles. "Then you're on."

"And you're not making sense."

"Sure I am. I'm taking that challenge."

"I don't remember issuing one."

She took a step closer. "We've pretty much established that other than a moment or two of wonderful insanity or a break in hostility, you don't like me much."

He wasn't sure how he felt about her anymore. Parts of him wanted to strangle her pretty neck or kick her cute backside all the way out of town. Other parts wanted to pull her into him and kiss her all damn day long. And then there were other parts that just wanted to grab her, back her up against a tree, and go primitive.

"So I'm taking the challenge of making you give in," she said.

"Give in to what?"

She stepped even closer and got all chesty, like a bulldog looking for a fight. "Me."

He laughed. "Not going to happen."

"Really?"

"Nope."

Her head tilted again, exposing that sweet, soft skin. He really wished she'd quit doing that. "Want to make a bet?"

"I don't take money from women."

"Good, because I don't want your money."

"Then what *do* you want?" he asked, knowing that what *he* wanted right at that moment was to tear off that little tank top and put his hands all over her.

"If *I* win, I get to make over the hardware store with no whining or interference from you. If *you* win, I leave your precious dusty conglomeration of paraphernalia alone." She stuck out her hand. "Deal?"

"How will I know who wins?"

"Oh, you'll know." She grinned. "Believe me. You'll know."

Well, didn't that just sound intriguing as hell? If only to find out exactly what she had in mind, he engulfed her hand in his and shook on a bet that was too stupid for him to believe that he'd taken a part in.

"So what's in the boxes," she asked, still latched onto his hand.

He looked down. "Landscape lighting."

"You mean the landscape lighting that supposedly you couldn't find?"

"Yep."

"Just like the ceiling tiles you couldn't find, then somehow they mysteriously appeared on the ceiling of Goody Gum Drops?"

"Yep."

She tugged on his hand and drew him closer. And all he could do was get lost in those electrical flashes in her eyes.

"I'm onto you, Reno Wilder."

"You're delusional, Fancy Pants."

"Uh-uh. You're not half as tough as you think. And don't worry. I won't tell a soul." She reached up, patted him on the chest. "But believe me, you only get a temporary reprieve. Because I plan to be on top very soon. So you'd better watch your stuff."

While he wondered exactly what part of his *stuff* he was supposed to watch, she gave him a sassy little grin and strutted away.

An unexpected chuckle rose from his chest.

As much as he'd liked to be pissed off about everything, he couldn't. Because at the moment, all he could think about was Charli.

On top.

In his favorite position.

Wearing nothing but a smile.

"If you dare to stray from the expected, you get a big old mouthful of sweet, delicious heaven."

Immersed in the patriotic "Don't Mess with Texas" décor, Charli sat around a big table in the heart of Bud's Nothing Finer Diner surrounded by blue hairs, big hairs, and no hairs. Age—and obviously hairstyles—had no boundaries when the topic turned to the potluck dishes everyone had chosen to bring to the Wilders' celebration on Friday night.

"I got a crate of honeycrisp from Paige's orchard last fall," Hazel Calhoun continued to tell Gertie West, "and I swear on the *good book* they're a better choice than Granny Smiths."

"What did you call that recipe again?" Charli asked, intrigued, and suddenly inspired to order a slice of Bud's fresh apple pie.

"Apple, cinnamon, and walnut rolls with cream cheese," Hazel said, as proud as a mama bear.

"Mmmmm." Charli's mouth watered. "I'm looking forward to tasting those."

"They won't beat my sweet-potato fries and apple-butter dipping sauce," Gertie West proclaimed. "That butter's been a blue ribbon winner for two years' running."

While the argument over whose recipe reigned supreme, Charli couldn't help wonder a little bit more about Jana Wilder's get-together for the entire population of Sweet.

"So what goes on at this party?" she asked.

"What *doesn't* go on?" Ray Calhoun jumped into the female-dominated discussion. "Obviously, if you listen to the womenfolk, it's just a bunch of eatin'. But there's dancin' too. And entertainment." He hooted a laugh. "Old Chester's been known to tip back a bottle of Dickel, get a little crazy, and haul his scraggly old bones out for a skinny dip in the creek."

A mental image of the ancient cowboy in nothing but his boots brought forth a giggle. "Does the entire town actually show up?" Charli asked.

"Nah," Ray said, " 'bout a third do, though. Those Wilder boys built their mama the biggest smoker grill I ever seen. Looks like a damned military tank. But it sure does make a sweet barbecue." Ray licked his lips.

"And you said there was dancing?" Charli asked.

"Always a local band," Gertie said. "Think this year Jana rounded up Moonshine Mayhem."

Again, Charli laughed. "Well, that sounds lively."

"Yeah, they play down at Devils once in a while when they're in town. Singer sounds a little like Brad Paisley."

"Who?"

They all looked at her as if she'd popped a brain cell.

"We don't have many country stations in L.A.," she explained.

"Well, who in blazes would want to live somewhere like that?" Hazel Calhoun said. "Country's the only music anymore that has something to say."

From what Charli had heard since she'd been in town, she'd have to agree. She thought about the truck song she'd heard when Reno drove her home from Devils. She liked that and the one she'd heard on his back veranda. Country music talked about loving, and losing, and telling your boss to shove it. It spoke of heartache, and happiness, and how to walk the line. "I heard a song I really liked by George—"

"*King* George," they all said.

"Bless his heart," Hazel added.

Charli couldn't help but be impressed that someone who made music for a living could create such devotion from those he sang for. But this was Texas. And if Charli had learned one thing about the great state, it was that things grew big there—including hearts.

One heart in particular interested her more than the rest.

She lifted her coffee cup, took a sip, and flagged down the waitress to order a slice of that pie.

In just a couple of weeks, her and Reno's relationship had gone from growls and demands to a bit of laughter, and even kisses. He'd helped her with her projects even when he didn't want to. And as much as his hands stayed in the pockets of his jeans, his eyes danced all over her body like he wanted those hands to follow.

She didn't know him well, and yet she felt like she'd known him all her life. And while she understood the pain of losing his father and brother, she couldn't understand why he'd chosen to put a "hands off" sign on his heart. Something else—something beyond devastating—burned inside him and kept him from finding happiness.

"You bringing anything to the party, dear?" Gertie asked.

"Absolutely." Charli dug her fork into the flaky crust of the apple pie and slid the sugary treat into her mouth. Friday night, she had an opportunity to change things up. To make him notice. *She* was going to follow Arlene Potter's advice and turn up everything she had to full volume. She planned to bring her secret weapon. Even if she didn't know exactly what it was yet.

As much as she'd often wished her upbringing could have been different, she appreciated that she'd been brought up with a military mentality.

Fight for what you believe in.

Fight for honor.

Fight for love.

And when it came to Reno Wilder, she was prepared to fight dirty.

Chapter 13

After a long week of putting in hours at the store, moving cattle, and helping put everything together for the party, Reno was surprised he had any energy left. But as he buttoned up his shirt and set his favorite Stetson on his head, energy zapped through him like he'd stuck his finger in a light socket.

In past years, he'd offered to help his brothers man the party grill, which often took up most of the evening hours. This year, he'd assigned himself to other projects that might not be so time-consuming. Tonight, he'd decided to take a break and try to enjoy himself for once.

What had changed?

Everything.

Each morning when he awoke, he had thoughts running through his head that were often accompanied by a throbbing erection. Those thoughts always included Charlotte Brooks. Naked. Half-naked. Fully dressed. But mostly naked.

It had become a habit. She'd become a fever in his blood he couldn't ease. An itch he couldn't scratch.

A dream he couldn't make real.

But that didn't stop the dream from coming night after night after night.

Stretched out by his boots, Bear gave a colossal groan.

"Sorry I can't take you this time, boy." He bent down and gave the dog a good rub. "You'd either get stomped on the dance floor or lost in the shuffle."

Bear's head snapped up. He whined, jumped to his feet, and trotted out of the bedroom. Moments later, a knock on the door rose above Jake Owens on the radio complaining about some girl only kissing him when she was drunk. In Reno's mind, that didn't necessarily have to be a bad thing. As long as she knew what she was doing and remembered it the next day.

And when a man started trying to make explanations for a song, he needed to wake the hell up and get out a little more often.

He nudged an anxiously wiggling Bear aside and opened the front door. In a flash of orange, Pumpkin dashed inside, took a running nip at Bear's ear, then disappeared into the back of the house. Bear followed.

"Would you mind if Pumpkin stayed here tonight?"

Reno swung his gaze back toward the door and did his best to keep his tongue inside his mouth.

Standing in the doorway with the waning sunlight highlighting her from behind, stood Charli, in a floaty, short, and sexy sundress. Her dark hair floated down over her slender shoulders and wide, halter-style straps in loose, sexy curls. The creamy color made him think of the famous Marilyn Monroe dress, and he wished for a sudden breeze to lift the fabric and give him a glance at Charli's long legs. His gaze traveled down the deep-cut cleavage-revealing front of her dress to a pair of red Western boots.

He swallowed.

"Would that be okay?" she asked, her lips sparkling with a sheen of gloss. "I mean, I don't want to intrude. But our dogs seem to have a good time together."

His gaze snapped up, and he noticed that in her hands she held a large bowl of something that smelled sweet and delicious. Or maybe that was just her. "What?"

"Our dogs? Pumpkin gets bored waiting for me up in the apartment. And since I don't know how late your mother's party will go—"

"Late," he said. "Sometimes the last stragglers don't leave till sunrise."

"Really?"

"That's why Mom always holds it on a Friday night." *Damn she looks good.* "Gives everyone the weekend to recuperate."

"Well, then, do you mind if Pumpkin hangs out with Bear until I come home? I expect to be back long before sunrise."

"No problem." His eyes took another slow ride down her body. "You need a lift?"

"No thanks." She flashed him a smile. "I'm picking up Sarah, my assistant, on the way so we can have a little girl talk."

"About?"

"Boys." She gave a throaty chuckle that turned him inside out. "What else?" With a casual wave, she stepped off the veranda. "See you later, Cowboy."

Reno leaned a shoulder against the doorjamb and watched her sashay toward the Hummer parked near the barn. She sure had all the right moves. No doubt she'd be the hit of the party.

Something in his chest gave a hard thump.

He didn't like that notion at all.

When she finally drove off, he closed the door, grabbed his keys, and with a "Behave" threat to the dogs, who were too busy playing tag to care, headed toward his truck.

The closer he came to his childhood home, the more the cars began to clog the parking lane, and the more he realized he would need to figure out how to keep the male population of Sweet away from Charli.

He had no right.

And he didn't care.

But if anyone was going to dance with her tonight, it would damn well be him.

Charli had been to military soirees, Beverly Hills bashes, and Mardi Gras masquerades, but she'd never been to anything like the Wilder BBQ Blowout.

Jana had said the party was a celebration. An understatement to be sure. Beneath the live oaks, people gathered in groups under multiple strings of decorative lights. In the barn, there were fabric banners in playful colors. Tables were covered with blue cloths and adorned with watering cans full of bluebonnets and sunflowers. Dishes of potluck delights dotted the tabletops with a tasty array of homemade favorites. Charli added her bowl of Chinese chicken salad to the mix, then guided Sarah over to the beverage table, where galvanized buckets were filled with ice, bottles of soda, and sweet tea. Hay bales were strategically placed for folks to gather or kids to use as launch boards.

When Reno strolled into the barn beside his brothers, Charli caught his eye, smiled, then casually went on about her business like her heart wasn't about to leap from her chest. Everything about the man made her stand up and smile. Made her feel like there was the possibility of light at the end of the tunnel.

For so long, she'd focused on survival, then her career. When she thought she'd found love, she'd learned that there were men out there who were less than honest with her and themselves. She had no doubt that Reno was the most honest man she'd ever met. Honest to a fault to be sure. What woman wouldn't want to be with a man so honorable, so traditional, so loyal? A man so tied to family and friends that he would sacrifice his own happiness.

From the corner of her eye, she saw him stop, lean down, and hug an elderly woman sitting beside a gentleman in a wheelchair. When he rose and saluted the man, Charli's eyes misted.

"I've never seen anything like this before," Sarah commented.

"Me either. It's fabulous." Charli glanced over the heads of the people in line in front of them. "Someone needs to do a magazine spread on this event."

"I can't believe Mrs. Wilder puts this together all by herself."

"I'm sure she has plenty of help. After all, she has three muscular sons here to give her a hand and a fourth who, I'm sure, wishes he were here."

"Where's the fourth one?"

"Still in the Marines. Deployed, I'm sure, risking his neck so we can party. Kind of makes you feel guilty, doesn't it?"

Sarah nodded. "*Really* guilty."

Charli wrapped her arm around Sarah's shoulder. "I'm pretty sure he wouldn't want us to feel that way. Not if he's his mother's son. I know my father has never regretted a moment he's spent wearing a uniform."

"Still."

"Uh-uh, young lady. This is Mrs. Wilder's way to celebrate. You're wearing a pretty dress with your hair all fixed up, and you're even wearing your contacts."

"I feel naked."

"You look amazing. And I want you to have a good time tonight. Is that clear?"

"Yes, ma'am."

Charli corrected her on the name usage. Tonight was no time for formalities. Charli had something a lot less conventional in mind. With that at the forefront of her plans, she accepted a red Solo cup filled with raspberry lemonade and led Sarah out of the barn and into the festivities.

Outside, the decorations were just as appealing. Galvanized buckets filled with wildflowers brightened up the wooden fence posts. Colorful piñatas hung from the shady oak trees. And colorful paper lanterns were crisscrossed on rope over a makeshift dance floor. A four-piece band played an energetic tune, with the singer proclaiming *all you have to do is put a drink in my hand* from atop the bed of a flatbed truck. And the scent of sweet barbecue wafted and curled through the air from an enormous, smoking, kettle grill.

People stood in groups chatting and laughing, or gathered around long picnic tables snacking on pulled pork, tender brisket, and corn on the cob.

Charli noticed Jana on the veranda taking it all in. Judging by the smile on her face, she was enjoying every moment.

That smile made Charli happy. Anyone who'd suffered the losses she had, who worked hard at being a good mother, and who outdid herself for the community deserved to smile. She was quite the woman, Charli thought, watching her go inside the house on the arm of a handsome silver-haired man. Charli thought her own mother would be very much like Jana Wilder.

When a pang of loss hit her heart, she took a deep breath and turned to Sarah. "There's so much going on, I don't know where to start," she said. "Are you hungry?"

Sarah bit her lip, as if trying to decide.

From out of nowhere a spectacular-looking young man popped up in front of them. He looked to be in his midtwenties, wore a plaid shirt that fit snug over bulging biceps and Wranglers stacked perfectly just above his boots. His straw hat was a bit worn but sat perfect over his short brown hair and shaded his bright green eyes.

"Hi," he said in a deep voice. "I'm Zack."

Charli nearly laughed when she realized that he hadn't even noticed she was standing there. Those green eyes were set only on Sarah. And wasn't that just about as perfect as things could get.

Her assistant returned his smile in a more timid version. He told her how pretty she looked, and the conversation was off to a running start. Neither noticed when Charli slipped away and crossed the yard toward the house.

"Hey. I've been looking for you."

Charli turned at the sound of Paige's voice. "Uh-oh. What'd I do this time?"

Paige laughed, tucked her arm through Charli's, and, together, they walked toward the big, ranch-style home.

"Jana sent me to find you. She wanted you to see the progress she's made on redecorating her bedroom."

"Wow. She works fast."

"I think she's just finally ready to move on. In Texas, when we move, we do it in a big way."

"Sometimes it's easier to move fast. Doesn't give you the time to overthink what you're doing."

"Tell me about it." Paige chuckled. "When Aiden came home from the war, I knew I had to hook him with lightning speed before he let the dumb idea that he was no good for me stick in his head forever."

"No good for you? You two are perfect together."

"We are. But he lost so much in Afghanistan, and he blamed himself. The big dummy had convinced himself that he didn't deserve to be happy."

Sounded familiar.

Paige could have easily been talking about Reno.

"So how'd you get him to change his mind?"

"Well, I helped him find a missing piece of his puzzle; and then I didn't give him much time to think. Aaaaaand I also kind of told him that I wasn't going anywhere, so unless he wanted a full-time stalker, he'd better hook up with me."

Charli liked Paige. And she was sure that if she were to stay in Sweet, they'd become good friends. "Sounds like Aiden made a very smart decision."

They stepped up onto the wide veranda, and Paige opened the front door. "Ah, you know, we've loved each other since we were kids. He just got a little lost along the way. It was my duty as the person who loved him most to show him the way home."

Charli's chest lifted on a sigh. "That kind of love doesn't come around often."

"Happens more often than you think. Come on, let's go find Jana."

Charli followed Paige through the entry and took a quick glance at the gallery of photos lining the walls. When she came to a framed eight-by-ten of Reno and a beautiful blonde holding each other close and grinning like there was no tomorrow, she stopped. "I don't remember seeing this one the last time I was here."

"You were probably just looking at the other side and missed these," Paige said. "That's Reno and Diana at their engagement party."

Diana?

"When was this taken?" Charli asked.

"About two and a half years ago." Paige rubbed away a smudge on the glass.

"Did they get married?"

Paige sighed. "They didn't have time."

Charli's heart stuttered. "What happened?"

"I wouldn't feel comfortable telling you, but it's common knowledge, so it's not like I'm gossiping."

"I would never think that about you."

"Reno and Diana had been a couple for a long time. Everyone knew they'd get married. It was just a matter of when. Still, when he proposed, Diana said it was like something from a storybook. He loved her so much he planned it out to perfection."

Charli was curious what *perfection* meant to a man like Reno, but she didn't ask.

"By then, Jared had died and that drew Reno and Diana even closer. An engagement seemed like the next step, and it gave everyone a moment of happiness. But then Joe died, and Reno was just . . . lost. Diana became his whole world. They decided to move up the wedding because it seemed as though everyone needed something to celebrate when all they'd done for so long was mourn.

"A few days before the wedding, Diana and her sister drove to Austin to pick up her wedding dress. On the way home, she texted Reno to tell him how excited she was to start their new life together and how much she loved him, then . . ."

Paige's voice broke off. Charli reached out and clasped her hand.

"And then," Paige continued, "she hit a semitruck

head-on at sixty-five miles an hour. Diana and her sister were both killed instantly."

For a moment, Charli just stood there, not knowing what to say or do. The sorrow that reached down deep into her soul and gave a hard yank brought tears to her eyes. Her throat dried up. "My God," she finally managed to say. "So in just a few years' time, he not only tragically lost his brother and father but also the woman he loved?"

Paige nodded. "Diana died just a few months after Joe."

"That explains so much." Charli could still remember the anguish that tore at her heart the day her mother had died, and that had been over half a lifetime ago. She couldn't imagine how these tragic losses must still haunt him.

Paige gripped her hand. "Don't let his grief swallow him alive. I know you two have only just met, but—"

"I'm not sure he's really interested in me."

"He is. Anyone who's known him for any length of time knows he's definitely interested. When you came into this town, all ready to shake things up and make some changes, he was just as determined to keep them the same. He only wants what's best for the entire town. In his mind, that's keeping things the way they were. For him—in happier times."

"I see that now," Charli said.

"Besides Aiden, Reno is one of the most loyal people I've ever known. When we all started seeing him help you make those changes—even against his own wants and desires—we all knew there was a spark."

For Charli, there was more than a spark. The attraction between her and Reno crackled like a three-alarm fire.

Voices came from down the hall, and Paige paused to look over her shoulder. When her blue eyes came back, they were bright with optimism.

"If you feel anything for him at all, don't let him push you away," Paige said, being the second person in as many days to give Charli the same advice. "Take it from someone who knows. He'll continue living the rest of his life inside that shell that tells him he doesn't deserve to be happy. But then the rest of the world will miss out on an amazing man. And you—if you're looking for it—will miss out on an incredible love."

Love?

Charli's heart stuttered.

She hadn't known the man long enough to be in love with him. Had she? Was there any truth to love at first sight? Sure, she'd read stories of married couples who fell in love the moment they'd met and had been happily married for eons. But she'd always just thought those were fairy tales. Like "Cinderella" or "Snow White."

"Come on." Paige smiled and tugged her down the hall. "Jana went romantic cowgirl on her bedroom makeover, with a pair of Texas Long Horns painted white and bedazzled with pink rhinestones. She even made curtains from the ruffles of wedding gowns. You're going to love it."

Bull horns and rhinestones?

An unlikely match.

Just like her and Reno.

* * *

While the band covered the new Jason Aldean tune, Reno took his turn at bartending. He'd traded off an hour ago with Jesse, who'd promptly disappeared with Angel Martinez—not the current veterinary assistant, who was currently chatting up Jackson while he tried to dance with Izzy.

No one needed to watch reality TV when you lived in a small town. There was enough going on to keep everyone entertained. And with all the whispers and eyeballing going on, apparently *he'd* become the current topic of gossip. Not that he hadn't been in that spot once or twice before. Wasn't his favorite place to be, but without even trying, he'd become a repeat offender.

The other element in the newest buzz about town was currently dancing on the arm of Chester Banks, who had to look way up into her pretty face. Which meant Chester was at about breast level and enjoying himself immensely. Reno would have intervened, but Charli seemed like she could handle herself well enough with the near ninety-year-old. But Chester had better watch himself if those arthritic hands started to roam.

Annoyed that he hadn't found time to snag a dance or two with Charli himself, Reno popped the cap off a bottle of Southern Star and poured a shot of Jack Daniel's for Lila Ridenbaugh. The lifelong Sweet resident had worn her skimpiest tank top and, breasts thrust out to kingdom come, posed herself against the bar in a suggestive manner.

"So when do you get off work?" Lila asked, slamming the Jack and taking a pull from the longneck.

She made a big show of licking a drop from her red-painted lips.

Once or twice in his younger, dumber days, he might have thought about taking Lila up on her invitations. Luckily, he'd refrained. Lila had a track record a mile long—married three times and had four kids. All with different fathers. Seemed Lila had a little trouble staying in one place for any length of time.

"I'm not really working. Just giving my mom a hand."

"Can't Jesse or Jackson work the bar? I'd like to show you a new dance step I learned."

By the suggestive tone in her voice, Reno knew that any dancing she had on her mind would be of the horizontal type. Lila was a nice person, but he had no intention of being baby daddy number five. Or six. Or whatever.

"Jack's busy with Izzy and Jesse"—he glanced around the barn—"seems to have disappeared. So it looks like I'm it for now."

"Then maybe you can get me a bottle of whatever *that* is."

Reno's head turned toward the sultry voice on the opposite side of the bar, and his heart kicked up a notch. Charli stood right beside Lila, leaning into the bar—giving him an eyeful of cleavage and Lila a run for her money.

"Mike's Hard Lemonade?" He held up the bottle. She nodded. "Thought you said you weren't much of a drinker, Fancy Pants. This has a little kick to it."

Lila's nose wrinkled like she smelled something bad. "That's pansy-ass stuff. Maybe she'd like something with a bigger boot to keep up with the rest of us Texas girls."

"Oh, I'm not looking to get drunk," Charli said with the sweetest smile. "That's just so . . . distasteful."

Lila took the remark for exactly what it was. Then, as if she wanted to make a point, she leaned across the bar, wrapped her fingers in Reno's shirt, and planted a hard kiss on his mouth. Lucky for him it was a quick look-what-I-can-do show of possession and not a let-me-ram-my-tongue-down-your-throat display of affection.

"You let me know when you're done here, handsome. I'll be waiting." She lifted her nose in the air, gave Charli *the look*, and sauntered off. Hopefully in search of someone who might actually take her up on her offer.

"Hmmm. I don't think she likes me very much," Charli said with a smirk on her lips.

Reno wiped away the remnants of Lila's lipstick and tossed the napkin in the trash. "Some local girls don't like outside competition. Lila's looking for husband number four." He popped the cap on the lemonade and handed her the bottle. "Or maybe it's number five. I've lost track."

"Are you applying for the job?" She lifted the bottle and took a drink.

Reno watched the way her delicate fingers wrapped around the glass and the way the bottle pressed against her lips. After that, it was impossible to ignore the immediate reaction inside his jeans. "Oh, I'm damned sure there's a better man than me out there for her."

"Not that I think you and baby mama would be a good pair, but why do you always sell yourself short?"

"When it comes to Lila's affections, I'll sell myself short all day long." He chuckled and handed a wine cooler to Maude Perkins, who then headed in Chester's direction. "Other than that, didn't know I did."

"Maybe that's not such a bad thing." Her dark eyes assessed him, and her lips tipped up in a smile. "I guess it's better when a man doesn't feel the need to puff his chest out all the time. Machismo does have its limitations."

"Exactly what constitutes too much?"

"Oh, you know . . ." She turned around and eyed the crowd. "See that guy right there?" She pointed her bottle toward Alec Lightfoot, one of the area's most notorious players.

"Yeah."

"He has a look in his eye that says he *might* be able to get the job done. But the smirk on his lips discounts anything he has to offer because he'll tell everyone in town whom he nailed the night before. When you ask the woman on the other side of the story, she'd probably be reluctant to admit she jumped between the sheets with him because it was an embarrassing waste of her time. In other words, men like *that* are usually flashy big talkers and—"

"Lousy in bed."

"Yes!" She laughed. "Not that I would know anything about that."

He smiled, then stopped himself from wondering who had been the big talker in *her* life. He didn't want to travel down that road. Even thinking about her in another man's arms drove him bat-shit crazy.

"Personally, I think all guys like that need to wear a thick chain around their neck like a big gold warning sign," she said.

Reno laughed. Sometimes, talking with Charli made him spill his guts. Sometimes, it made him think about and wish for things he didn't deserve. And sometimes, talking with her was just plain fun. "So you're against hairy chests? You prefer the smooth gym-rat type?"

"Well." She took another pull from her lemonade, licked her lips, and smiled. "If I get to play Goldilocks and have my pick, I do have a confession." She leaned in and whispered. "I've seen *your* chest. And it's just right."

She gave him a wink, then took her lemonade and strutted away in her floaty, attention-grabbing sundress and red boots. With each sexy sway of her hips, her shiny hair swung across her bare back, and all he could think of was threading his fingers through those silky locks and drawing her in for a kiss. As she reached the barn doors, she glanced at him over her naked shoulder and smiled.

Everything inside him jumped to full alert. The muscles in his neck tightened. His heart pounded. And an erection that literally stole his breath swelled inside his pants.

He wanted Charlotte Brooks. And he wanted her bad.

Enough of the wordplay. Enough of letting his imagination contrive what it would be like to make love to her.

She'd opened the door, and he had every intention of stepping through.

What seemed like hours later but was probably only a few minutes, Reno finally found someone to replace him at bartending and went in search of the hot woman in the cool dress and red boots.

As always, the party picked up once the sun went down. Most of the families had taken the little kids and gone home. Those who remained were looking to have a little fun—big-kid style. He finally spotted his target out on the dance floor on Jackson's arm doing a two-step to "American Saturday Night." She'd caught on to the dance fast and appeared to be enjoying herself. Unfortunately, by the grin on his face, it looked like his little brother was enjoying himself as well.

A bit too much for Reno's taste.

Reno eyed Jackson's ex on the veranda, saying good-bye to his mother. He rushed over to snag Izzy in her pretty sunflower dress.

"Unca Weeno!" Izzy held out her plump little-baby arms.

"There's my girl." He snatched her up, bussing her chubby little cheek with a noisy kiss. "Looks like you're about to take off," he said to Fiona, Izzy's mother. A tall, beautiful blonde who'd tolerated his brother's nonsense for far too long.

"I think it's about time I got Izzy to bed," Fiona said. "She didn't have a nap today."

"Noooo!" Izzy wrapped her arms around his neck and pressed her cheek against his. "I wan Unca Weeno!"

He hugged her tight, thinking of all the dreams he'd once had for a family of his own—happy that at least Izzy had entered his life. Being an uncle wasn't anything like being a dad, but his love for this little girl made it easier.

"How about a dance, sugar? Would you like that?"

She gave a quick succession of nods, and her golden curls bounced like springs.

"One last dance?" he said to Fiona. "Then I can grab Jackson for you."

Fiona smiled, knowing she'd been had. "One more dance. And thank you."

Reno held his giggling niece in his arms and joined the others on the dance floor. He made grand dance gestures, which only made Izzy giggle more. As the Brad Paisley song hit the midway point, Reno spotted Jackson and Charli in the center of the floor. The two laughed and leaned in to speak into each other's ears. And that made Reno's feet move just a little quicker.

"Daddy!" Izzy held her arms out when she spotted Jackson, who turned with a big smile.

Reno knew he could fault his brother for many things but not for the love he had for his daughter, or for trying to do right by her mother. Jackson had given the marriage his best shot, but his problem stemmed from the one woman who'd gotten away and taken his heart with her.

"There's my princess!" Jackson swept her into his arms.

"Fiona's looking for you," Reno said, handing Izzy over. "Past someone's bedtime apparently."

"Ah. Duty calls." Jackson gave a bow to Charli. "Thank you for the dance, my lady."

Charli smiled, obviously charmed by Jack's gallantry. But more than likely by the cherub who held out her arms to Charli—a perfect stranger—for a good-bye hug. His niece was an affectionate little thing, and Reno was glad to see Charli respond without hesitation.

Reno stood side by side with Charli, watching Jackson waltz Izzy off the dance floor.

"He's so good with her," Charli commented above the music.

"He adores her. It's just too bad things didn't work out with her mother."

"What happened?"

"Long story." He opened his arms. "How about a dance?"

"Hmmm. I didn't even get a chance to check out your brother's chest."

"No need. I've got one you'll fit just perfect against."

When she smiled, he needed no further invitation and pulled her into his arms. To his pleasure, the band swung into Chuck Wicks's "All I Ever Wanted," which had a slower pace that gave him the opportunity to enjoy the sensation of finally having Charli in his arms.

Beneath the smooth fabric of the sexy dress, her curves called out to him to come play and explore. To find out where she liked to be touched and where she *loved* to be touched. She fit perfectly in his arms, like they'd been made just for her. Which was the last thing he'd thought the day she rolled into town in her big yellow Hummer, and he'd wanted her gone.

A moment of sorrow grabbed him by the heart, and, for the first time, he pushed it away. He was going to live in the moment. Even if it killed him.

"I like this music." She smiled up at him, and it was hard not to get lost in her eyes.

"Beats rap or hip-hop."

"I like that all the songs have a story," she said.

Their bodies found the perfect rhythm, and, for Reno, the friction of rubbing against her only increased his desire. "I like the way you smell."

"You do?"

He nodded. "Must be some expensive perfume."

"I don't wear perfume. Only scented body lotion. Tonight, I'm wearing peaches and cream."

"Mmmm. I love peaches." He lowered his head, ran his nose up the length of her neck. Beneath his hand, a shiver danced up her spine. He spoke close to her ear, "Ripe . . . juicy . . . peaches."

A little moan vibrated in her chest. "And cream?"

"Cream definitely enhances the flavor. Makes me want to lick up every last drop."

Her head tilted back. "Are we talking about food?"

"Nope."

"Hmmm." Her eyes brightened. "Then there's probably something I need to tell you."

A hundred erection-busting thoughts raced through his head.

She slid her hand up the front of his shirt. Wrapped her arm around his neck and pressed her breasts against him. "Tonight, I was in such a hurry to get to the party I forgot . . ." She leaned in closer, stood on tiptoe, and whispered in his ear. "To put on panties."

As she slid back down to the heels of her boots, everything inside him swelled, expanded, and damn near exploded. He fought the urge to lower his hands, clasp a handful of her backside, and see for himself. His grip tightened around her waist.

"No panties?"

She smiled. "Nope."

He took a quick glance around them. Definitely not the place to back her up against a fence post and ride her hard.

Not his style anyway.

"You continue to surprise me," he said, failing to keep a grin in check.

"Is that a good thing?"

"Very good."

The heat of her body warmed his hands, and the desire to slip them beneath that thin fabric and touch her skin was almost too much to deny.

"Perfect." Her fingers stroked his shoulder. "But I'm willing to bet I can put an even bigger smile on your face and make those dimples pop."

"Hard to beat imagining you naked under that dress."

A second later, as he was trying not to haul her up over his shoulder and cart her off somewhere private, she took complete control of the situation. He was a man who liked to be in charge, but he didn't mind admitting her confidence was a big turn-on.

"Since everyone is already staring at us, wondering what we're whispering about, and I know you're not the type who likes to advertise his goings on . . ." She gave a casual glance over her shoulder, smiled, and waved to Hazel and Ray Calhoun. When her eyes came back to his, they were full of sexual promise. "I'm going to back away real slow like we're just done dancing."

"Okay."

"Then I'm going to get in my car and go home. Give me a five-minute lead. If you're interested . . . I'll be waiting."

If he was interested?

There wasn't a muscle or bone in his body that wasn't vibrating with fascination.

Before he could tell her he really didn't give a shit what people thought right now, she slipped from his arms, gave him a nod, then tossed him a sexy smile.

"Thank you for the dance," she said mildly as though she hadn't just told him beneath that floaty little dress she was absolutely naked or that she'd be waiting at home ready to put a smile on his face.

And because he was a man who hadn't had fun in a very long time, he decided to play her game. He gave her a two-finger salute from the brim of his Stetson as she walked away. She cut right off the dance floor, he went left.

For the moment, their directions might be vastly different, but once he got her back in his arms, he'd make damned sure they were on the same course.

Chapter 14

No panties?

That had been the best she could come up with?

Some secret weapon.

Charli didn't need confirmation that she'd completely lost her mind. Flirting was one thing, but to tell a man she barely knew she wasn't wearing any panties *and* to let him know she'd be at home waiting for him to show up?

Yeah, that hardly reeked of desperation.

She might as well have walked around with a blinking red sign that read "I'm hot for you" or "Take me, I'm yours" or any number of similar phrases that screamed Loserville.

Pathetic.

She'd made some bad romantic decisions in her life, but she'd never been the aggressor in a relationship before. And if this turned out disastrously, it would be the last time she tried it. And then she'd have to get a big old ladder and climb back up on that no-man wagon.

While she maneuvered the road home, she slowed to a crawl, grabbed the tube of peaches and cream lotion from her purse, and slathered on a fresh layer. Might as well smell tasty too. Just in case. When the road straightened out, she dumped the lotion back into her purse.

Maybe the possibility of humiliation was frightening, but how could she say she didn't know Reno? Outside of her father and brother, she might know him better than any man she'd ever known. She knew his life, his passion, his heartaches, his losses. She knew he believed he didn't deserve to enjoy his life. And she knew he deserved to be happy more than most. Her attraction to the man had grown into something more. And she cared.

God, how I care.

Just the sight of him flipped her stomach like she was on the world's largest roller coaster. When he flashed those rarely seen dimples, she melted like a Hershey bar in the summer sun. For her, it had become far more than just his amazing face, tall, powerful body, or, heaven forbid, those dimples.

She was crazy about his heart.

As she turned the Hummer onto Rebel Creek Road, she reached down, shimmied out of her underwear, and tucked them inside her purse. Not an easy task while tires spun and gravel flew. She parked the Hummer near the barn and turned off the ignition. In her rearview mirror, headlights sped up from behind. Her heart did a double somersault.

The red truck came to a sliding stop. Beneath her hand, her door flung open.

"You drive slow." His voice was rough.

"You came."

Those dimples flashed. "Not yet."

Lust darkened his eyes as he pulled her into his arms and crushed her against him. His mouth came down and opened against hers, and he fed her hot, gut-clenching kisses. His fingers tangled in her hair. And then his hands were everywhere. Touching. Exploring. Testing.

He rocked his hips and slowly thrust against her. The woman in her responded to the hot man pressed against her from breast to thigh. A warm flush tingled up her chest. She didn't think she'd ever experienced anything like the crazy need that swirled through her stomach and into her heart.

As she wrapped her arms around his neck and devoured his kiss, he pressed her up against the side of the Hummer and slipped his hands up beneath her dress. His moan filled her mouth when his long fingers cupped her naked bottom.

He lifted his head, and a whoosh of air pushed from his lungs. "My God, you weren't kidding."

"Why would I kid?" She traced her tongue across his bottom lip. "When I want you so bad."

Dark brows pulled together. Then his mouth came down on hers again. His kisses became feverish—hungry—as though any moment she might disappear, and he'd starve. He tasted wild and hot, like a man who could deliver on all those seductive looks he'd been giving her when he thought she wasn't looking.

The rapid throb of desire pulsed through her blood and gathered low in her belly as she speared her fingers into his hair and knocked the hat from his head. When the black felt Stetson hit the gravel, she figured she'd probably committed some kind of Texas sin.

Lucky for her, he didn't seem to mind.

The moonlight shone down and glinted in the strands of silver at his temples. His slick tongue delved deep in her mouth, stroking, caressing, teasing, promising.

And then he was gone.

A rush of air swept across the moisture on her lips and cooled her heated flesh.

"Are you sure about this?" he asked, even as his heart pounded against her own. "Tell me no. Right now. Tell me no, and I will stop and walk away."

She looked up at him, at the doubt creeping into his eyes. She couldn't let him stop. Not for her. Not for him.

"Don't do that," she whispered. "Don't deny whatever this is between us. Please. I want you." She lowered her hand from his chest. Slid it down the front of his shirt, past the big silver buckle, to the zipper on his jeans and cupped his long, hard erection. "And you want me."

"I do."

"Besides, if you stop now, I'll sue for false advertising."

"I'll be damned if you aren't the sassiest woman I've ever met." He chuckled in a deep, husky tone. Then he lowered his mouth and gave her a slow, sexy lick up the side of her throat. "Wrap your legs around me." His breath rasped hot and moist against her ear.

"Yes, sir." She did as he asked, locked the ankles of her boots together and felt his erection pulse against her flesh. His fingers dug into her backside as he lifted her and carried her toward the front door of his house.

"Where are we going?"

"A gentleman doesn't take a lady standing in the driveway up against a truck."

"I wouldn't mind."

His boots stopped moving, and he looked deep into her eyes. "Next time. But for what I have planned for you, you're definitely going to want to get horizontal."

Well, if that didn't stir everything up inside her like a warm bucket of butter, nothing would. "I like the way you think, Cowboy."

Between feeding her wet, hot kisses, he somehow managed to unlock the front door and push it open. Bear and Pumpkin were sprawled out on a leather sofa, and their fuzzy heads popped up as the door crashed against the wall. Reno practically fell through the opening, but he managed to stay on his feet. His firm grip on her naked bottom never wavered.

Charli had been curious as to what the inside of his house looked like, but at the moment, she wasn't the least interested. As they moved through the living room into the hall, she caught a vague sense of a huge stone fireplace, adobe floor tiles, lots of warm wood, and traditional leather furniture with nail-head trim.

Reno paused in the hallway and pressed her backward against the wall. She slid her legs down his muscular thighs until the toes of her boots touched the floor.

"You win," he said, his voice a rough whisper. "I give."

"I like winning." She gave him a playful grin, knowing what it took for him to let go of his past. She lifted her face and kissed the shadow on his jaw. "I'm always up for a celebration. And I think . . ." Her hands wandered south. "I deserve my prize."

He made a low sound in his throat—half growl, half surrender—before his mouth slashed across hers in a fiery kiss that hit her ignition switch like a fully charged torpedo. She threaded her fingers through the sides of his soft hair and held him tight to her lips while his tongue caressed and plundered. When he pulled back, his broad chest expanded on uneven breaths.

On a slow rotation, he turned her to face the wall and settled her hands flat against the surface. He pressed his full length into her back. "You're so soft. So beautiful." In a smooth motion, he lifted her hair to fall over one shoulder. "And you smell so damned good."

The quiet words were spoken low and close to her ear, and she felt the vibration between her legs. She swallowed hard as he slid his work-roughened hands to the buttons at the top of the halter dress at the nape of her neck and methodically released each one. As the dress fell to her waist, he trailed his fingers down her back. When she thought she couldn't take his unhurried movements much longer, those warm strong hands slid up the bare flesh of her stomach and cupped her breasts.

He trailed kisses down her neck to the sensitive spot near her shoulder and sucked her skin into his mouth. A hot flush of tingles spread up from her core into her belly.

Beneath his skillful touch, her nipples peaked and ached for the warmth of his mouth. When she moaned deep in her chest, he slipped those magical hands down her waist, taking the dress with him. The fabric fell into a silky pool around her boots, and Charli realized that while she stood there naked, he remained fully clothed.

"Not fair," she said, as his mouth and tongue did a slow glide down the length of her spine, and his hands cupped her rear end.

He came back up—his chest pressed into her back. His hand skated down her belly. His fingers slid lower and parted her flesh, touching her in that warm dampness where she craved him most.

"What's not fair?" he murmured against her ear.

She could barely think, let alone breathe. "You're still dressed." She panted, glancing over her shoulder. "I haven't even touched you."

"You want to touch me?" His dimples flashed with a teasing smile.

"Yes."

His hand moved away, and she ached at the loss of his touch. Then he turned her to face him.

"I'm all yours," he said, arms held out.

That was all the invitation she needed. She had no finesse as she tore at the buttons on his shirt, yanked the fabric from his pants, and pushed it from his shoulders. She pressed her breasts into his hard chest. The short dark hairs tickled her nipples.

Her hands touched him everywhere. His skin felt hot and tight, and she wanted more.

She kissed him hard, like he was a last meal. Then she lifted her head and looked up. His heavy-lidded gaze looked back.

"Boots. Off."

He complied, then waited for her next instructions. She didn't know what was more fun—being in command or giving up control. Both, in her mind, were going to be more satisfying than she could ever have dreamed.

Hot liquid lust burned through her veins and set her need for him on fire. She flipped open the big belt buckle, unbuttoned his pants, and pushed them down his muscular thighs. His boxer briefs went next. And then she just looked at him.

He didn't waver beneath her heated gaze. He just stood there with that tight, muscular skin, jutting erection, and let her look.

And she did.

But looking alone wouldn't ease the ache between her thighs. She reached out and took him in her hand, squeezed gently, and smiled when he dropped his head back and groaned. She leaned forward and pressed her mouth to his chest, licked his flat brown nipple, and said, "I'm ready to collect that prize you owe me now, Cowboy."

A deep chuckle rumbled in his chest. "Yes, ma'am." He lifted her into his arms, carried her into his room, and tossed her on the king-sized bed. He followed her down.

If she thought this would be quick, she'd be wrong. Reno took back control. He fed her slow, wet kisses while his erection pressed into her lower half and tempted her with heat and promise. He kissed her neck on his way down to her breasts, where he paid very careful attention to each one with long laps of his tongue and gentle pulls of his hot, moist mouth. Those languid strokes sent a flurry of need between her legs.

"I want you, Reno." She reached for him, tried to pull him up and over her. "I need you."

"Mmmmm." He gave her nipple a slow lick, then gave her a gentle nip. "Happy to comply."

Instead of moving up, he went down and put that amazing mouth and tongue to work between her legs. If she'd thought he'd taken his time at her breasts, he proved he was in no hurry now.

He licked. Stroked. Sucked. Until she couldn't take the heat anymore. Her midsection tightened, and the slow burn headed north from her toes up her legs.

It would be so easy to let that fire singe her until she couldn't breathe, but she didn't want to take that trip alone. She squeezed her inner muscles to stop the wildfire, reached beneath his arms, and tugged. "You promised."

He stopped. Looked up. "But—"

"I need *you*, Reno. Inside me. Right now."

With a smile, he moved up, leaned over her, and opened the nightstand drawer. He tore open the foil packet, and she took the condom from his hands.

"Let me do that." She pushed him to the mattress, straddled his thighs, and rolled the condom down to the base of his penis. Then she leaned down, brushed the tips of her breasts across his chest, and watched a smile spread across his face. She kissed him. And squeezed him. And teased him. Right up to the moment he grabbed hold and flipped her on her back.

"I want *you*," he said. "Right now." He parted her legs and slid into her with a long, hard thrust that stole her breath.

She gasped. Or moaned. Or something, then grabbed his firm butt with both hands and locked her legs around his waist. "You feel amazing. Don't stop. Don't even slow down."

With a long groan, he plunged into her again. Deeper this time. Touching all those amazing places that lit her up like a carnival ride. His thrusts alternated between slow and fast. He rotated his hips, kissed her neck and breasts until her breathing quickened, and everything inside her tightened. Her entire world centered on him and where their bodies were joined in intense pleasure.

His thrusts came faster, his breathing shallower. He reached beneath her, grabbed her bottom, and lifted her hips. He drove harder. Her heart pounded in her ears. Scorching flames licked at her core and lit the fuse.

"Oh . . . God." Her words came out a strangled moan. As he pounded into her body, he unleashed a sexual storm of beautiful and intense sensations that rolled over her in a long, sweet climax. She rode out the throbbing pulsations, holding him tight between her legs and arms as he thrust one last time with a long groan that sounded of pleasure and pain.

Together, their hearts pounded until their ragged breathing began to ease. He kissed her. Told her she was amazing. Then he rolled to his side and tucked her into his arms.

Charli knew she could stay right there forever. As she allowed herself to settle into a nice little fantasy, the dogs came barking down the hall and jumped up onto the bed like a pack of wild hyenas.

After great sex came a great appetite. Especially when that amazing tumble between the sheets had taken hours and happened three times. The fourth time in a long, hot shower. And the sun hadn't even come up yet.

Reno scrounged through the refrigerator in search of something quick to eat, while Charli perched herself up on the granite countertop and watched. Somewhere during round two she'd kicked off her red boots. Now she wore only the shirt he'd worn earlier—sans buttons. For a brief, foolish moment he couldn't decide what looked tastier, the ingredients for the omelet he was about to make, or her.

He turned, looked at her, and smiled.

He was no fool.

"Need some help?"

"No," he said, breaking the eggs into the skillet. "You just sit there and inspire me."

She picked up an apple from the basket on the counter. "You want me to talk dirty to you?"

He laughed. "Yes."

"Okay. I'm thinking about grabbing that jar of honey from your cupboard and dripping it slowly on your—"

He crossed the kitchen, wrapped his arm around her, and pulled her to the edge of the counter between his legs. Then he crushed his mouth down on hers and kissed her. Her hands came up to his bare chest, and she moaned into his mouth. He leaned away with a smile. "I've decided actions speak louder than words."

"Awesome." She grinned. "But can we eat first? I'm starving."

"Whatever the lady wants." Reluctantly, he turned back to the eggs bubbling on the stove.

"The lady wants *you*." She bit into the apple with a crunch. "After the eggs. So when did you get that tattoo? I didn't notice it until . . . well, you know."

Until he had his mouth between her legs. Yes. He knew. And he planned a return trip. Soon.

He rarely thought of the wings of freedom inked onto his upper back anymore even though the meaning was as powerful to him today as it was the day he leaned over that chair and let an artist put meaning to his work.

"I had it done while I was on leave after my first deployment. The brothers and I all made a trip into Austin. There's a guy there who does amazing color work." He chuckled, remembering the night they'd all invaded the tattoo shop. The laughter. The winces of pain. Calling each other good-natured names. "Yet somehow we all came out with traditional black ink. And we all had the same general idea. Same motto. Just in different locations. Jared had it on his leg. Jackson put it on the back of his shoulder. Jesse has it on his biceps."

"And yet you covered both your shoulder blades."

He shrugged. "That was me. Always trying to prove I belonged."

"Your brothers have always known you belonged."

"Yeah. Getting the tattoos was the very last thing we all did together as brothers." He didn't want to bring up old memories when he'd just begun to create new ones.

She slid down off the counter and came up behind him, tracing her fingers across the wings and the word FREEDOM. Shivers tingled up his spine at her touch.

"Beautiful."

"Thanks. The guy is really talented."

"Yes. He is. But I wasn't talking about the artwork."

She flattened her palm against his back and rested her cheek there. Her breasts pressed into him. Then she wrapped her arms around his waist. A sense of calm—of unity—settled into his soul. He hadn't felt that kind of peace in . . . forever.

He set the wooden spoon down on the counter and took her in his arms. The kiss went from sweet and tender to hot and hungry. He turned off the stove, lifted her up onto the granite counter, and stepped between her thighs.

There were a million places on earth he *could* be, but nowhere else he *wanted* to be.

And right there in the middle of his kitchen with a half-cooked omelet on the stove and two dogs stretched out on the floor watching, he showed her his appreciation.

Chapter 15

Nothing felt better than having a warm woman in your bed.

Unless that woman happened to be trying to sneak out.

"Where do you think you're going?" Reno grabbed Charli's wrist as she carefully tried to slip out from beneath the tangled sheets.

"I have to go to work."

He glanced at the clock radio. Seven o'clock. "So early?"

"We only have a week left before Paige and Aiden's wedding, and there's still so much to do." She grabbed her dress up off the floor. "I need to take a shower and wash my hair first."

"Yeah. I guess you can't really go to work with honey in it."

"Well, I could." She grinned. "But there would be that whole explaining thing."

He pulled her back down to the bed and moved her on top of him. "You need some help?"

"At the job site?"

"Uh-uh." He kissed the corner of her mouth. "Taking a shower."

She giggled. "Then I'd never get to work."

"That's the whole idea." He kissed her neck. Cupped her warm, firm breasts in his hands.

She kissed him back, and when he reached down and pressed her groin against his growing erection, she moaned. He thought he'd had her. But just as things started to get interesting, she slipped from his arms and danced away from the bed.

"I really do have to go."

That's when the truth hit him hard.

He'd sworn he wouldn't get close. Wouldn't get involved. Wouldn't get attached. Because one day soon, she was going to drive out of his life. And everything he'd allowed himself to dream would be lost.

All the darkness in his life would descend once again.

He watched as she slipped the dress over her head and tugged on her red boots.

Charlotte Brooks was a different kind of woman than he'd ever been with before. She was nothing like Diana, who was sweet and quiet and took things in life as they were handed to her. Charli just reached out and grabbed it. She was nothing like the other women he'd been with, who were either looking for a husband or just a good time. She had a fire in her—a spark—that was hard not to admire. But he should have known that when you played with fire, you either got singed or burned.

She buttoned the top of her halter dress, then leaned down and kissed him. "What are your plans for tonight?"

He shrugged. "Haven't really thought about it."

"Doesn't matter." She kissed him again. "As long as they include me. See you later, Cowboy."

With a quick little wave she called to Pumpkin, then she and her dog left.

He folded his arms behind his head and lay there listening to the silence. He'd never noticed it before. Now that he had, he realized he didn't like it so much.

Charli had blown into his life like a hurricane. In just a few weeks, she'd blow out just as fast.

Which meant there were choices to be made.

Did he grab hold of all that swirling velocity and enjoy it for a short time? Or did he let it go now and save himself from the eventual devastation?

Charli managed to take her shower and wash all the sticky honey from her hair in no time. She yanked on a pair of shorts, tank top, and tennis shoes. Grabbed a granola bar and Pumpkin and headed toward the Hummer. As she tossed her purse and dog onto the front seat, she glanced over at Reno's truck—door still wide open. She smiled. He'd been everything she could have imagined and more. The idea that he'd been hiding all that passion for so long made her sad. But the knowledge that she'd been on the receiving end when he'd finally let it go—well, that made her extremely happy. And satisfied.

Man, was she satisfied.

She'd give it a few hours before she started to go through withdrawals from his touch, his kiss, his every damn thing that made him Reno. She loved hearing him laugh. The deep, throaty sound made her heart sing. She wanted more.

Before she climbed inside the big yellow monster of a vehicle, she grabbed her purse, smeared the tube of coral lipstick across her mouth then went to his truck. She closed the door, leaned in, and kissed the driver's side window. When she pulled away, she grinned at the mark she'd made.

Silly?

Juvenile?

She didn't care.

With Reno, she felt like a giggly, flirty sixteen-year-old.

Until he put his hands on her.

Then she felt all woman.

When her tires hit Main Street, she stopped at Bud's Diner for a coffee to go. Someone seriously needed to open up a "real" coffee place. Then again, most of the residents of Sweet would probably argue that a double-shot caramel latte with whipped cream wasn't "real" coffee. They'd argue that coffee needed to be strong enough to put hair on your chest. Maybe she wasn't all gung ho to have to wax between her breasts, but she did love that the people in this town were of the hearty, good-natured sort.

Well, except for Lila Ridenbaugh, who was going to be a very *un*happy camper when she discovered that a woman who couldn't shoot whiskey had gone home with the man she'd had her eye on to be her next baby daddy.

Charli pushed open the door to Bud's Diner, and the little bell above the door gave a merry jingle.

"Hey, Charli!"

She smiled at the round of greetings from those seated at the counter or around tables sipping a hot cup of joe and forking up fluffy pancakes slathered in butter and syrup. Her stomach growled so loud she would swear everyone could hear.

"Good morning," she called back on her way to the counter, where Paige stood pouring a fresh cup for Max.

"Hey there." Paige greeted her with her usual chipper attitude. "How are things going?"

"Excellent. We're right on schedule, so you don't need to worry about your wedding venue. It will be ready and gorgeous."

"I'm not worried. I trust you one hundred percent." Paige reached beneath the counter and brought up a clean mug. "And you're coming to my bridal shower, right?"

"Wouldn't miss it for the world." Charli smiled. She hadn't been to a bridal shower in years. In the past, they'd varied from cozy settings with crazy little games like dressing the bride in toilet paper to snobbish affairs where all that mattered were the dollar signs on the gifts. Still, it remained a tradition in which Charli would one day like to partake—as the bride.

Paige slid the clean mug in front of her and filled it with steaming dark brew. "Please don't feel obligated to bring a gift. That's not why you were invited."

"I know." Charli poured in some sugar and took a careful sip. "And I really do appreciate being included. It will be fun."

"As long as my sister doesn't spike the punch, like she did at Helen Grace's seventieth birthday party," Paige said. "That quickly became an out-of-control old-lady drunk fest."

The mental image of a bunch of tipsy old ladies made Charli chuckle. "Well, I'm looking forward to it however it turns out." She turned to Max, eyeing his sausage links and eggs over easy. "Did you order me a plate?"

"No, but you'd better grab something." He stuffed a bite of crispy English muffin into his mouth. "It's going to be a long day."

"I wasn't going to eat. Thought I'd just get over to the job site."

"Of course you're going to eat," Paige said, handing her the laminated menu. "What'll you have? I'll make sure Bud gets it up quick."

"Surprise me." Charli knew anything that would be served up would be delicious and hot.

"Great. I'll get you some protein and a little sugar. That will keep you going for a few hours," Paige said, then called out to Bud through the order window, "Flop two. Side of dicks and a stack of Vermont. On a rail," she added.

Max choked on a bite of sausage. "What did she say?"

Charli laughed. "I don't know. But I'm betting

it will taste great." She sipped her coffee. "Did the rubber playground mulch arrive?"

Max nodded. "Got a text that they delivered it straight to the site this morning."

"Good. That will get us moving a little faster today." Charli sipped and let the strong chicory roll across her tongue. "We need to make our Friday deadline."

"I got a call last night," Max said in a voice she hated to hear.

"From?"

"The top."

"Oh. Bad news?"

Max shrugged, set down his mug and took a bite of egg. "They want us to head right to the next location from here. No stop back home in between. Apparently, with the price of gas and freight charges, they're trying to shave off some expenses."

The thought of leaving clenched her stomach. She didn't want to go—not when she'd just found the best place on earth.

If pressed, she couldn't divide that meaning between Sweet and the arms of the man she'd just left in tangled sheets. Both gave her what she'd been searching for her whole life.

A place to call home.

"It is a pretty expensive show to produce," she said.

"But look at *Extreme Home Makeover*. Look how long that's been at the top of its game. What does that say about us?"

"Two different concepts, Max. You can't compare a show that helps people in need with a show that just wants to pretty up a town." Paige delivered her hot plate with a smile, then moved on to help another customer. "I mean, yes, I believe in what we're doing and that it helps the residents and business owners with their bottom line. But it's not like we're helping to save the life of a sick child. God. I'd love it if we could do that."

Max looked at her, thick brows drawn together. "You're not invested in this show."

"Bullshit. I'm totally invested. I'm just a realist. I think change is good." An image of Reno flashed through her mind. "And sometimes it can be freaking awesome. And I give a hundred percent to this job. But, Max, at the end of the day, if this show goes away, who's going to miss it? Other shows will come along to take its place. Other hosts will waltz into people's living rooms and convince them that mirrored ceilings are the newest thing. No one will miss me, or you, or the next big design star. A year from now, they won't even remember our names."

"Wow." Max leaned back and looked at her like she'd lost her mind. "That's cynical. Especially coming from you, Pollyanna."

Charli took a bite of her heavily syruped pancakes. The flavor burst across her tongue, and she couldn't help but think of all the luxurious breakfasts or breakfast conversations she'd missed in place of a quick cardboardy granola bar while driving at top speed to their most recent job site. She thought of being able to sit across from Reno every morning and share a fresh pot of coffee while talking about the day to come.

She was thirty-one years old, and until now she'd

only thought of *home* as being somewhere you had to frequently leave. Like her cold, empty apartment in Studio City. Or the various military houses where she'd spent her childhood. As a temporary fix, she'd focused on her career and not the many lonely nights she spent thinking of all the homes she'd decorated for other families to play in and be happy.

But she was thinking now.

And after last night in Reno's arms, she looked at life in a whole different light. She *wanted* it all. Love. Family. Home.

"I'm not cynical, Max. But show me a cemetery headstone where it says BELOVED MAKEOVER SHOW HOST or BELOVED TELEVISION PRODUCER."

His bloodshot eyes assessed her. "What, in your all-the-way-around-the-block manner, are you trying to say?"

"Those headstones read BELOVED WIFE, BELOVED HUSBAND, BELOVED MOTHER or FATHER, BELOVED FRIEND."

"And that means?"

"TV shows, no matter how entertaining, don't matter. What does matter is love. Family. Friends."

Charli glanced around Bud's filled-to-capacity diner at the faces she'd come to know over the past few weeks. The people she'd come to care about. They made her feel welcome. Included. Needed. She thought about Reno again and that amazing peace he brought to her wandering soul. And she realized, just maybe, she *could* have it all.

Hours later, Charli stood in the hot sun, with her hands on her hips. The sweat rolling between her breasts made her itchy and uncomfortable. The situation at hand made her tense and cranky.

"I need black-eyed Susans," she said to Sarah, who looked up, cheeks flushed from the red alert heat of the day.

"The landscaper ordered daisies."

"Which are nice," Charli admitted, "but they don't have the pop of color I'm looking for. Plus, Susans are a more hearty plant that will thrive in cold or heat. And God knows it gets hot in Texas." She pulled her damp shirt away from her skin, hoping a little air would flow beneath and cool her off.

No such luck.

"There are a gazillion ways to accent this amazing gazebo," she added. "But the bottom line is it has to be beautiful no matter what time of year it happens to be. A lot of activities take place here—weddings, birthday parties, town gatherings. It needs to be photo-op pretty from January to December."

"That makes sense."

Charli smiled. She loved it when someone validated her ideas. "Did you have fun at the party last night?"

Sarah nodded with a big smile. "I met someone."

"Zack?"

Sarah sighed. "Zack."

"Wonderful. Want to share?"

"Not yet. I know we're only here for a short time, and I don't have any . . ."

"Expectations?"

"Yeah."

"But you like him, and you had a good time."

A smile lit up Sarah's pretty face. "I really like him, and I had a really good time."

Charli wrapped her in a one-armed hug. "Beats dog-sitting any day, right?"

"Well, I do adore Pumpkin." Sarah glanced down at their feet, where the poodle lay in their shadows panting like a wild rabbit. "But yeah. Pretty much a lot better."

After a few minor adjustments to the landscape order, Charli grabbed a rake and headed over to the playground area to help spread out the rubber mulch. She loved the product, which not only kept its color longer but protected the kids as well.

"You're working too hard."

Charli looked up to find Jana Wilder heading toward her with—thank God—a huge cooler she hoped was filled with icy sweet tea. "Deadline's creeping up fast," Charli said, taking the cooler before the teetering cups in Jana's arms spilled onto the grass. "Let me help you with that."

"Thanks." Jana eagerly handed over the heavy container. "I drove by earlier, and I just couldn't help notice how hot everyone looked. So I promised myself that as soon as I got done returning the Calhouns' folding chairs, I'd bring y'all something cool to drink."

"You're a saint."

"Now don't go spreading rumors."

"No Miss Giddy today?"

"Oh, she'd wandered out into the meadow and got herself all muddied up. I didn't have time to clean her up with everything else."

Ice knocked against the interior walls of the cooler

as they walked toward one of the new picnic tables. With a grunt, Charli set it on top. "I figured you'd be home trying to clean up after the party."

"The boys took care of that this morning. Then I got them busy painting the living room. Had them haul all the furniture out first. Not much going back in."

Charli smiled and accepted a cold glass of tea. "You're really getting into this redecorating thing."

Jana began filling more cups and waved the hot and thirsty crew over. "You were right, just a change of paint color can really revive an old room into something brand-new. I've been living with those white walls and dark wood for so long I had no idea. I don't know exactly what I'm going to do with the living room, but I'm starting with a nice shade of sand with a splash of poppy."

"Well I love the whimsy you brought to your bedroom. Even I would never have thought about using wedding-dress ruffles on curtains. And the pink, rhinestoned bull horns? Classic. You could create an entire business just by making them."

"I could?" Jana's bright blue eyes widened.

"I think you may have some real hidden talent."

"Coming from you, that's quite a compliment."

"I never say something I don't mean." Charli took a long drink and wiped her mouth with the back of her hand. "Where did you find those architectural columns?"

"I actually have a stash in the barn loft. I've been collecting old stuff that strikes my happy for years. It started taking up too much room in the garage, so Joe made me move it up to the loft."

Charli lowered her cup. "How big is your *stash*?"

Jana shrugged. "Pretty much takes up most of the loft."

"Judging by the size of the barn, that's a huge loft."

"Yeah, it's all packed in there pretty tight. Last time I had Jackson carry something up, he stood at the top of the steps and yelled down "There's no damn place to put it.""

A tingle of eagerness shimmied down Charli's spine. "Jana. I absolutely have to see your stash."

"Oh, sure. Come by anytime."

Charli thought about Reno. She hadn't seen him all day, but when she'd left him in bed that morning, she'd kind of invited herself into his plans for the evening. "Tomorrow is my day off. Can I come look then?"

"Sure. I'll be home all day." Jana handed the last cup to Sarah. "But you've probably seen this kind of stuff a million times in your work."

"Actually, I've never had the privilege of seeing someone's collection of what *strikes their happy.* Mostly I order stuff from catalogs or stores."

Jana laughed. "Then you need to hang around me more often. I know all the good places to go."

"Which are?"

"Yard sales. Flea markets. Blow-me-down barns that no one dares walk into except crazy old me. I like stuff. I like it old. I like it with character. And I like it at a good price. Best four days out of the year is when the Route 127 Corridor Sale starts."

"I've never heard of it."

"What? Sugarplum, we are talking over six hundred glorious miles of yard sales. From Michigan to

Georgia and everywhere in between." Jana's smile was huge. "It's like dying and going to bargain heaven."

"I think that's definitely something I need to put on my to-do list." Charli admired Jana's enthusiasm as well as her hidden design talent. She remembered the FOR SALE sign she'd seen on the two-story Victorian on the way into town. A definite fixer-upper, but with more potential on its front porch alone than most new houses had under their entire roof.

A plan sparked.

Maybe her thoughts moved faster than they should. Maybe she—as always—saw the end results. The big reveal of her life, so to speak. And maybe anyone with half a brain in their noggin would tell her she'd booked first class on the crazy train. Still, she held on to that ticket and climbed on board.

"Does two o'clock tomorrow work for you?" she asked.

"Yep. I'll even make us some cobbler."

Charli placed her hands on Jana's shoulders. "You might want to hold off on any rewards until you find out exactly what I have in mind."

The summer sun hung low in the sky as Reno watched Charli pull the Hummer up to the barn and head upstairs to the apartment—the place where she would remain for only another few weeks. He couldn't help notice that she looked hot and tired. And while his nerves jumped, he hoped his plans would not go awry.

Postparty, he'd spent most of the day putting the

Wilder Ranch back together and hauling furniture from his mother's living room so she could "spread her wings." He didn't know why she'd become so hell-bent on redecorating the house. He didn't see anything wrong with it.

The sofas, chairs, and tables he'd hauled outside brought back memories of sitting around with his family, playing board games, munching on popcorn while watching movies, and huddling together on the sofa as a thunderstorm rolled through. It was a childhood most kids took for granted—even his brothers. But he knew every moment they'd spent doing such simple things together was special.

Something to be cherished.

Air pushed from his lungs as he stuffed the remaining contents of his surprise into the saddlebags and snapped the flap closed. Life should never be marginalized—exactly the reason he'd pulled his sorry ass out of bed this morning and decided to take a chance.

Before that, he'd lain there, strangled with thoughts and fears that threatened to suck him under. He'd never been the kind to just give in. He'd battled the worst life had thrown at him. Though at times the worst claimed temporary victory. Still, he'd always managed to come back—ready to put one foot in front of the other to make it through another day.

Until Diana died.

He stared out the window, not really seeing the green rolling hills or the stands of oaks shadowing the ground. In his mind, he pictured the semitruck bearing down on the woman he'd loved. Colliding with her compact car. Mangling everything until it became unrecognizable.

Pain seared through his chest as breath-stealing as the day he'd received the call that she and her sister had been killed.

From that moment, he'd cursed life—dared it to take him down. Instead of complying, life had laughed in his face. Dared him to live another day. Pushed him to open his eyes and see the joy that stood before him if only he'd grasp it.

He'd lived in darkness for too long. He could see that now.

Charli had changed everything.

She brought something to the party that made him feel things he'd never felt before. Or at least not in a long time. He didn't know how to sort through the tangle of emotions that churned in his chest. He only knew he wanted more.

He flung the saddlebags over his shoulder and looked down to Bear, who sat with pointed ears perked up. "Sorry, buddy. You need to stay home this time. I'll see if your girlfriend wants to come visit."

Bear rubbed his nose with a paw and sneezed.

"Yeah, I know she's a pain in the ass. But don't tell me you don't like her just a little."

The dog stood, stretched, and wagged his tailless butt.

Reno chuckled. "That's what I thought."

He reached down and gave his dog a good rub between the ears, then headed out the door.

Inside the barn, he tended business, taking his time until he heard the water shut off in the apartment above. He gave her a few minutes, then he climbed the stairs and knocked.

The door creaked open. A happy glint brightened her eyes. "To what do I owe this pleasure?"

Much like the first time he'd knocked on her door, her warm brown hair was pulled up into a messy tumble of damp curls on top of her head, and her coconut scent danced through the air between them. This time, however, instead of being bundled up in her robe and looking like a marshmallow peep, her sweet curves were loosely wrapped in a big fluffy towel. One little twirl was all it would take to unravel her naked into his arms.

While he had big plans for the night, he wasn't above taking advantage of a gift when it was handed to him.

"I needed to see you." He grabbed hold of the towel and drew her against him.

"I wanted to hold you." He lowered his mouth to hers. "And kiss you."

With a sweet sigh, her arms slid over his shoulders and wrapped around his neck.

Much to his delight, the towel sailed to the floor.

The softness of her breasts pressed against his cotton shirt, and he wished he were without clothes as well.

"And I wanted to touch you." His hands smoothed down her warm, damp body. "All over."

"Then please . . ." she whispered in a husky voice. "Be my guest."

He moved her inside the apartment. Kicked the door closed behind him. And gave himself permission to touch her wherever his hands could land. He swept her into a wild, unrelenting kiss. Her mouth softened, and his tongue swept between her lips, claiming her, giving her more of himself than he'd ever intended.

She moaned her pleasure and smiled against his mouth. "So why are we just standing here in the middle of the living room when we could both be naked in the bedroom?"

His hands covered her bare bottom, and he gave it a gentle squeeze. "Because there's no way in hell I'm doing it in my brother's bed."

She laughed, and the sound played across his skin. "I didn't think about that."

"And," he said, sliding the backs of his fingers down the gentle slope of her breast. "Because we have plans."

"We do?"

He nodded. "Get dressed. Long pants. Those fancy red boots. And a sweater."

"That's all?" She leaned in and brushed the side of his neck with quick little kisses. "No shirt? No bra? No . . . underwear?"

He smiled, remembering how hot he'd gotten when she'd told him she hadn't been wearing panties. When he'd raced home and found her naked beneath that soft dress, he'd about come all over himself.

"Surprise me." He gave her a soft swat on the bottom, then watched her sashay away. He loved to watch her—walk, laugh, smile, frown—didn't matter. She might very well be the most animated woman he'd ever known. And for that he considered himself a lucky man.

Chapter 16

Charli took no time at all to throw on a pair of jeans, tank top, boots, and grab a lightweight hoodie. She left her hair up in the messy bun and didn't bother with makeup. She didn't think Reno would care—or want to wait for her to get all glammed out. If she judged the size of his erection correctly, he had hot and messy written all over his thoughts.

Not that she minded.

Hopefully, the slathering of frosted-cupcake body lotion she'd put on would make him not only hot but hungry.

She called to Pumpkin, then realized her dog wasn't in the bedroom. Grabbing her hoodie, she went out to embrace the man waiting to show her a good time and found him pinned on the sofa.

"No wonder Bear is always exhausted if she's this amorous," he said, while her tiny apricot poodle licked his chin as if she'd found her very own dessert.

Charli couldn't stop the giggle that bubbled up

from her chest. His tone might have held a shadow of Mr. Grumpy, but the smile on his face said he didn't mind at all. In Charli's world, that said a lot about the man.

"Well, you can hardly blame her. Bear does have the same certain *something* as his owner."

His head cocked, and his smile turned into a grin. "Did you just compare me to a dog?"

"No, silly boy." She reached out her hand to pull him up. "Just the animal magnetism."

He came up off the sofa, wrapped her in his arms, and buried his nose in her neck. "God, you smell good. I could just eat you up."

She kissed him. "That's the plan, Cowboy. Now let's get going before you ruin your appetite."

With a chuckle, he reached down and took her hand in his. Locked their fingers together. "Just in case you think of running."

She looked up and noted a sudden seriousness on his face. "I'm not going anywhere."

"For now."

She didn't want anything to ruin tonight. Not when she'd been thinking of him all day and imagining scenarios where she'd never have to leave Sweet. Or him.

"I thought you were taking me on a date," she said. "Our *first* date."

"I didn't show you a good time last night?" The smile was back, and so were those amazing dimples.

"You did. Several times." She tugged him toward the door. "Now let's drop Pumpkin off with Bear, and you can show me some more of those amazing acrobatic feats."

"Always give a lady what she wants."

"Smart way to stay out of trouble."

They hit the stairs side by side, and Pumpkin took off on a run toward the house. When they got down to the barn level, Charli noticed two horses just outside the doors, tied to the big, pine hitching post.

"Uh-oh. Is *that* our transportation?"

"Yep."

"You do know I've never ridden a horse before, right?"

His dimples flashed. "Thought you were giving it a pretty good go last night."

She gave him a playful punch in the arm. "That doesn't count."

"*I* was counting." He took her in his arms as they reached the horses, which looked much bigger and scarier up close. "You know I wouldn't ever put you in danger. Right?"

"Depends on how much of a smart-ass I've been."

He pressed his brow to hers. "You're always safe with me. Even if you do drive me crazy."

A slow leak of air pushed from her lungs. She knew that. But those animals looked . . . She turned to glance at the blond horse nuzzling her arm. Dark eyelashes swept down in a flirty wink. Charli laughed. The animal suddenly looked kind of cute and harmless.

"This is Bonnie," Reno said, giving the horse a smooth stroke down her long neck. "She's been around as long as I can remember. She's gentle and so trained you don't even need to pick up the reins to tell her where to go. She's the horse Izzy rides."

"Well, if a two-year-old can master riding, then I guess I can too."

"That's my girl," he said to her, not the horse. "Wait here, I'll go let Pumpkin in the house."

"Okay."

He gave her a short, sweet kiss, then walked toward the back veranda. She tilted her head just slightly and watched him go. The man did look amazing from the rear. He looked over his shoulder and smiled at her as if he'd read her thoughts.

And he looked damn good coming too.

In more ways than one.

Bonnie gave her elbow another nudge, and Charli lifted her hand to pet the animal's strong neck. The hair beneath her fingers wasn't nearly as soft as it looked. In fact, her nearly white mane felt wiry to the touch. In those few quiet moments of shuffling hooves and horsey snuffles, Charli felt like they bonded. Or at least she hoped they did.

"All right, let's hit the trail." Reno clapped his hands together.

"Where are we going?"

"A pleasure ride."

"Well, doesn't that just sound like my slice of pie."

Reno laughed, then showed her how to mount the horse—which was fairly easy because, Lord knew, she was a tall girl. Moments later, as she got used to sitting in the saddle, Reno went to his own horse, put his foot in the stirrup, and swung his long, muscular leg over.

He settled a straw cowboy hat over his dark hair. His boots looked like they'd seen many ranch miles.

And the tight T-shirt and jeans combo, well, wasn't that just about every woman's fantasy?

"What's your horse's name?" she asked.

"Cisco."

"Like *the Kid*?"

"Yep." He made a clicking sound. Both horses turned their heads and started toward the gate that led to the big meadow and beyond. "He's a champion cutting horse."

"What's that?"

"A performance horse. It's a competition where the horse and rider cut one cow from the herd without letting it return. My dad and Cisco brought home a lot of trophies. He's made some pretty good earnings over the years."

"I'd like to see that kind of competition."

He turned to look at her. "You would?"

"Of course. I'm always willing to try something new."

"Well, Fancy Pants, you are about to do just that."

She didn't seem to mind him calling her Fancy Pants anymore.

Reno smiled to himself.

Guess she realized at some point it had gone from a slur to a term of endearment.

The horses prodded along at an easy clip, in no hurry to get anywhere, and neither was he. With Charli at his side and a warm breeze at his back, he figured he could be riding anywhere, and it wouldn't matter. On the plus side, her curiosity kept him entertained.

They'd just passed a small herd of Whitetail that made her gasp. Moments later, she pointed, and asked "What kind of trees are those?"

"Take your pick. You've got some live oaks, lacy oaks, cedar elm, and on the banks of the creek, you have some cypress and pecan. And those"—he pointed to the clusters of cacti—"are the Texas state plant. Prickly pear cactus. Which are edible. My mom makes an excellent jelly with them."

"Mmmm. Sounds delicious." She took a long look around. "I never knew Texas looked like this. I always imagined it flat and dry, like in the John Wayne movies."

"You watched the Duke?"

"Didn't everybody? Of course, in a young girl's heart, he really couldn't hold a candle to Brad Pitt in *Legends of the Fall.* And then there's Daniel Craig in *Cowboys & Aliens.* And let us not forget Johnny Depp in *Rango.*"

"Wait a minute," he said. "Rango is a lizard."

"I beg your pardon. He's a *chameleon.* And the fact that you even know who Rango is gives you extra points."

He laughed, tipped his hat back, and gave her a hopeful look. "So you're saying you like cowboys?"

"Yes." Her dark eyes licked him up and down. "So you're saying you watch cartoons?"

"Busted." He gave Cisco a little kick. "I've already got a date with Izzy to see the new Disney princess movie."

"Be still my heart." She fanned herself, then stopped suddenly. "Wait. Should I be jealous?"

"Only if you refuse my offer to come along. I do look pretty tempting with melted butter and Raisinets stains on my shirt."

She whoaed Bonnie, then crooked her finger. "Come here."

He sidestepped Cisco closer and was rewarded when Charli curled her arm around his neck, leaned in, and gave him a kiss. "I wouldn't dream of taking your attention away from your adorable niece. But I *would* offer to lick off your butter and chocolate."

He leaned closer and framed her face with his hands. "You have a deal."

Her gentle laughter floated across the meadow as they got the horses going again. Something settled into Reno's soul that he wasn't sure he'd ever feel again.

Peace.

How that was possible when only a few weeks ago he was ready to run her ass out of town on a rail, he didn't know.

But, she'd been right. He'd damn sure changed his mind.

"So Cisco belonged to your father?"

"My dad owned Cisco's mom. He was there from the moment Cisco was born, and he trained him from that day forward." He reached down and gave the horse a pat on the neck. "They made a great team."

"They say you can tell a lot about a man from the way he treats his mother," she said. "I'd have to add you can tell a lot about the way a man speaks of his father too."

He shrugged. "Wasn't anything I wouldn't have

done for him. For either of them. They saved my life. They were amazing parents."

"And you're still trying to pay them back."

He looked up—saw the admiration in her eyes. "I'll be trying to pay them back until the day I die."

He could never do enough to prove how much he appreciated being rescued that day when he was a scared, hungry, little boy. He'd never forget the comforting arms that surrounded him and made him feel safe or the house they'd brought him to, where he felt an immediate sense of homecoming. The day Angela had died, people asked him how he felt. He'd felt nothing. Just because a woman could give birth to a child didn't make her a mother. Just because a man could get a woman pregnant didn't make him a father. Reno knew he'd been lucky because in every sense of the terms *mother* and *father*, he'd found Jana and Joe.

They'd raised him to be caring, smart, and self-sufficient.

His father had taught him to be a man.

His mother had taught him to love.

And he'd never stop trying to prove his appreciation.

He and Charli rode in silence for a hundred yards, then he asked, "You hungry?"

"Starving."

"Then kick that pony into gear and follow me."

Together, they worked as a team. Reno grabbed the saddlebags and set them down on the blanket he'd spread out on the ground next to the creek while Charli held the reins of both horses until he had everything in place. When he removed the tack, the mare and gelding wandered off to munch grass.

"Won't they run away?" Charli looked up at him, concern tightening her voice.

"Nope. All I have to do is whistle, and they'll come back from wherever they roamed."

"Well, they're better behaved than Pumpkin then. She just ignores me when I call."

"Yeah, she does have the tendency to be a bit of a wild child."

"She probably gets that from me." Laughter rumbled deep in her chest. "I'm probably a bad influence."

"Is that so?" He snaked one arm around her and pulled her close, aware of the desire that rode up his thighs and settled in his groin.

"Yes." She kissed him, then nipped his bottom lip. "And if you'll show me what you've got in those bags, I'd be happy to give you a demonstration."

"Guess if I want a real show, I'd best feed you first."

"I hoped you'd say that. Because I'm starving."

"How's this sound?" He opened the flaps and pulled out the contents, holding each bag up as he called them out. "Barbecue brisket sandwiches and coleslaw from Sweet Pickens. Fresh Dutch apple pie from Bud's Diner. And cabernet from the Sweet Oak Wine Cellar."

She looked at the banquet he'd set out on the blanket and licked her lips. "Heavenly. Only one thing would make it taste even better."

"What's that?"

She closed the space between them. Her cupcake

scent drifted like a sweet bouquet beneath his nose. While his heart thumped against his ribs, she slid her hand up the front of his shirt and curled her fingers around his nape. The heat of her hand sent a warm shot of desire down through his chest.

His hands clutched the paper bags—fingertips tingling. Every cell craved that perfect union of bodies that made him feel more complete than he'd ever dreamed. It was all he could do not to grab her, tear her clothes off, and go all he-man.

Her hand slid down past his buckle to his zipper. She stood on tiptoe and kissed the underside of his jaw as her palm pressed against his erection. "If I can use you as a plate."

The bags fell from his hands. "The hell with dinner."

He crushed her to him, claimed her mouth, and forgot about anything but the raw, aching need to be one with her. To be deep in her slick, moist heat. To feel her long arms and legs wrapped around him, holding him close.

With a sigh of sensual surrender, she softened in his arms. God, he loved that about her. One moment she could be sassy, fully in charge of the situation—and him. The next moment, she was like a warm pat of butter, eager to be molded by his hands and lips. He kissed her with not so much brute force as desperate need.

Far sweeter than any dessert he'd ever tasted, her tongue met his—playing a game of hide-and-seek he was only too happy to let her win. His erection swelled beneath the heat and pressure of her hand. "Put your hands behind your back."

Her head came up, eyes heavy-lidded. "Why?"

"Do you trust me?"

"Of course."

"Then put your hands behind your back." He trailed his fingertips down the front of her little white tank top, brushing her hardened nipples.

Slowly, she put her hands behind her back. Her breasts thrust forward. Her nipples rigid against the thin fabric.

His mouth watered.

As much as he wanted to tear away that cotton barrier and have his way, he didn't want to hurry. A woman like Charli was meant to be savored like a perfectly aged whiskey. He wanted to feel the rush. Taste the burn. Enjoy the journey.

He reached up and released her hair from the elastic band. The dark locks fell around her shoulders in a cloud of loose, silky curls. In the waning sunlight, she looked like a forest nymph. "So beautiful." He took a strand between his fingers, lifted it to his nose, and breathed in her confectionary scent. His arousal intensified, and he closed his eyes to regain control.

When he opened them again, he found her biting her bottom lip. Leaving a red spot he had no choice but to kiss away.

That meeting of lips and tongues nearly stripped away his intent to go slow. He took his time— touching her with gentle, possessive hands—the full curve of her breasts, the long line of her throat and waist. With his mouth, he coaxed and teased. When she began to moan and lean closer, a bullet of white-hot lust shot into his groin.

He slid his hands down her sides, then slipped them beneath the edge of her shirt. When he caressed the warm flesh at the small of her bare back, the tips of his fingers tingled. He lifted the top over her head and smiled when she stood there for him to see without trying to cover herself.

He bent his head, lowered it to the side of her throat, and inhaled her luscious scent. His mouth opened over that sensitive spot just below her ear, and he softly sucked. Eyes closed, her head dropped back while his parted lips trailed to her cleavage. His palms tested the weight of her breasts while he licked and suckled her nipples until they were wet and erect.

"Appetizers are over." She unlocked her clasped hands from behind her back and yanked his shirt from his jeans. "I *have* to touch you."

Only because he wanted to feel those amazing breasts against his bare chest did he allow her to pull the shirt over his head. Her soft hands caressed the muscles of his shoulders, bunched in anticipation of her touch.

"More," she said in a husky whisper, and reached for his buckle.

"Me first." His fingers made busy work of stripping away her denims and tiny blue panties beneath. And then he stepped back, looked at her for a long, breath-stealing moment before he sank to his knees and drew her to his mouth.

With one hand braced on her backside, he parted her slick flesh with the other and found her with his tongue. She dug her fingers into his hair and let out a long "Ahhhhhh" while he worked her swollen erect nub. Beneath his hands, the muscles of her derriere clenched and released. Her breathing came quick and breathy, and he could feel her climax build.

"No, no, no." She moaned. "With you. I want to come with you."

He gave her a long slow lick, then looked up. "You sure?"

"Yes." She clutched at him, pulling him to his feet. "I waited too long to have you. I don't want to do anything alone anymore." She grabbed the waistband of his pants, undid the buckle and zipper, and pushed the denim and boxer briefs down his legs.

He toed off his boots, then they both stood there naked. She wasted no time in taking matters—and him—into her own hands. One touch of those fingers curled around his solid erection was enough to make him buckle at the knees. She leaned in, flattened her tongue against his erect nipple, and moaned. Then her soft hand stroked him slowly from head to base. He pushed into her palm, and, when he couldn't take the heat anymore, he knew he had to get *into* the kitchen.

He swept her off her feet, laid her on the blanket, and followed her down. Braced on his elbows, he moved over her. Her greedy hands were all over him. Her mouth tantalized. Her legs opened wide to welcome him in. The plump head of his erection nudged her slick opening, and she moaned her pleasure. Her impatience.

"Please, Reno." Her teeth nipped his earlobe. Her hot breath brushed his cheek. Her words escaped on a breathless plea. "I want you so much."

Need and desire tangled in his throat, and he couldn't speak. His only response was to give her what they both wanted. Needed.

He sucked air into his lungs as he pushed into her. Strong. Steady. Complete. Her uneven breath whispered across his temple as he moved inside her, increasing the rhythm. Friction built. Heat engulfed. His heart pounded in his ears as intense pleasure grabbed him and turned him inside out. He whispered her name. She locked her legs around his back. Lifted her hips. And met his thrusts.

And then she tightened her legs and came over him and around him with a long moan. Her muscles contracted, gripping him tight inside her as wave after wave of release washed over her. A deep groan rumbled in his chest, and he joined her in that sensual state of bliss. With his head thrown back, he gave her all of him—body and soul—as he thrust into her one last time.

Later, they swam in a deep pool he and his brothers had long ago created within the creek. They played. They laughed. They made love again. When a breeze kicked up, and their bodies grew chilled from the cool water, they finally ate their dinner and drank their wine.

While Charli's sexy side was there to see in every move she made and every smile she gave, Reno also drew out her playful side. After several glasses of smooth cabernet, it didn't take him long to discover yet another facet of the woman who took his breath away on so many levels.

Together, they lay on the blanket, looking up at

the stars, when she asked, "Will the dogs be okay in the house tonight?"

"There's a dog door in the laundry room, so they can always go outside if they need to. They have food and water. And as we discovered last night, they enjoy lounging on the sofa. So I'd say they're covered." He leaned his head back, and through the darkness looked at her. "Why?"

"Can we stay here tonight?" She turned on her side and smoothed her hand along his chest.

"Here?" The touch of her fingers sent a shiver of pleasure through his body. "Beside the creek?"

"Yeah."

"I didn't bring sleeping bags. This blanket is all we have."

"But if we snuggle, it will cover both of us, right?"

"Sure." He liked the idea of that. "You're not afraid of spiders or snakes. Or *scorpions*?"

She looked up at him with big, trusting eyes. "You'll protect me, won't you?"

"With my life."

"Then can we stay till morning?"

"If that's what you want."

"I do. I love it here. It's so quiet. So peaceful. It makes me feel like . . . I belong." She rolled to her back and sighed. "I never have, you know. We moved so much. I was always the new girl. A mystery for the boys. Competition for the girls. Our neighbors were always nice, but they might as well have had the same faces and names. I never really got to know any of them. I've come to know the people in this town better than anyone I ever lived next door to." She leaned forward and pressed her lips to his in a tender kiss. "I always longed for somewhere like Sweet. But I never believed a place like this actually existed. I can understand why you would never want to leave."

Maybe all the time she spent in the small towns she traveled to fulfilled some deep need in her soul. Maybe they were just a substitute for what she *really* wanted, he thought.

Charli had a need to belong.

Maybe they weren't all that different after all.

"Maybe you don't have to leave this time," he said.

"That would be nice. Then again, life is never really that easy, is it?"

"Depends on how bad you want it."

"I want *you*." She smiled against his mouth.

And without a doubt, he wanted her.

He stretched his arm out, and she moved in close, with her head on his shoulder. They snuggled. Which was a word he'd never used before. But damned if he didn't like it.

She felt so good in his hands—against his heart. As they lay there together beneath the moon and the stars under the canopy of ancient oaks, he was glad he'd taken the risk.

The rewards went far beyond sexual.

She made him feel again.

Desire again.

Dream again.

But even as satisfaction floated in his veins, he didn't fool himself into believing that the day she packed up and moved on would be easy.

Letting her go would be anything but sweet.

Chapter 17

When one awoke in the morning beside a creek with a canopy of fluttering green leaves overhead, nestled in the arms of a deliciously sexy, good-hearted man, one had no choice but to be in the best mood of her life.

Charli—in the best mood of her life—excitedly turned the Hummer onto the long, tree-shaded drive that would take her to her new friend Jana and the treasure-filled barn loft.

On horseback, she and Reno had taken the leisurely route home from the creek, and she had fallen even more in love with the place. Who knew one could have places to picnic, swim, and just relax and enjoy the beautiful surroundings right in your own backyard? From the balcony of her Studio City apartment, she saw rooftops and heard the sound of car tires and screechy brakes from the street below. Or heaven forbid, her neighbors fighting. Again.

She loved the peace and quiet Wilder Ranch offered. But most of all, she loved the man who'd shown it to her.

Yeah.

Love.

Wow. The sensations that created in her heart were inexplicable.

She thought she'd been in love before. In high school, when her father had actually managed to keep them in one place for nearly a year, she'd met Del Matthews. A sweet Southern boy who'd played varsity football, ran track, was a straight A student, and seemed like everything he appeared to be on the surface. But then her father had given her the bad news that they were moving. Overseas this time. No chance to nurture a budding relationship with a boy she'd never see again.

Then there had been John, who'd never been a very steady kind of guy. He actually *liked* to pick up and move around. Which was why, she guessed, he'd chosen to be a documentary filmmaker. They were polar opposites. Because of that, she'd never understood her attraction to him. In the end, she'd written it off to the fact that she'd been tired of being alone. Tired of talking to herself when she came home from work. At least he'd been someone with whom to have a conversation. Even if it always managed to be about some tragic incident that spurred an idea for a new documentary.

When his opportunity to film in Africa had come along, she'd been happy for him. And happy to move on. Even if that had meant more lonely nights.

After John—and the realization that without conscious effort she continued to select men who were incapable of returning her love—she'd imposed the ban on men in her life.

Then Pumpkin had come into her life, and she hadn't been lonely anymore. Well, at least not for company. Though it was hard to keep a conversation going with a poodle whose only real concern was what kind of Scooby snacks were in the cupboard and the dangers of getting shaved a little too close beneath her tail.

Reno changed everything.

He'd shown her something she hadn't known— the comfort of stability. Tradition. Loyalty. With both a father and a brother in the military, she recognized honor and knew that particular virtue lived strong in Reno's heart. Though passion dwelled in every cell in his body and he might have very strong feelings about things, he never lost his temper and exploded. Not like she'd seen her father do a million times.

Reno handled things in a quiet manner—even if he expressed it between gritted teeth. And he listened—intently—to anything she had to say. He might not agree with her, but he always gave her the opportunity to speak her mind. A trait, she was sure, he'd learned from his past and from the parents who'd obviously adored him.

A man with patience and virtue these days wasn't just hard to find—it seemed impossible.

Reno had all that and more.

And she'd fallen quickly and helplessly in love with him.

When she neared the house, chickens squawked and scattered to the sides of the gravel drive. She eased the Hummer into a space near the barn, parked, and was greeted by Miss Giddy, who trotted up for a pet on the head.

Jana came out onto the veranda. "Howdy," she said with a wave. "Push that old goat aside and come on in. I've got something to show you."

Charli gave Miss Giddy a nuzzle and tried not to feel bad at the goat's sorrowful bleat when she walked away. When she stepped up onto the veranda she noticed her friend's jeans and T-shirt were splattered with paint. Poppy red paint. Looked like Jana had been busy.

After a brief hug, Charli followed her into the foyer and immediately noticed that all the photos had been taken down off the walls.

"What happened here?"

"I'm going to repaint," Jana said with a sweep of her hand. "Then I'm going to reframe the photos and hang them from some wire fencing I found out at an old ranch near Luckenbach last year."

"What kind of wire fencing?"

Jana grinned. "Vintage double loop. Practically had to arm-wrestle a woman from Nebraska for it."

Picturing the scene in her head, Charli laughed. "Seriously?"

"Yep. No way was I going to let that fencing out of Texas. It belongs here. Has just the right amount of rust to prove it."

"Well, it definitely sounds like a wonderful design application."

"Hopefully, you'll say that when you see the living room." She opened up the French doors to a newly painted room. Charli walked inside, mouth gaping in amazement. "Wow. Are you kidding? You did all this in one day?"

"And night. I actually never made it to bed. Just too darned excited to see the results."

"You are my kind of lady."

The walls had been painted a sand color and accented with a splash of poppy. The comfortable leather furnishings were placed in well-thought-out locations. And the style hinted of Old West without being cheesy.

"What do you think?" Jana asked eagerly.

"I think you're amazingly talented."

Jana beamed with pride.

"*And* I think . . ." She picked up an old pewter pitcher filled with silk bluebonnets. "I'd kill to find these kinds of accents."

"Well, let's sit down to that cobbler I promised, then we can go out to the barn. I'm sure you're going to be surprised."

"Goody. I love surprises." She followed Jana into the kitchen.

Everything about Sweet had been a surprise. From the historical buildings to the friendly folks to the amazing man with whom she'd fallen in love. Everything seemed to have been just waiting for her to arrive and fill her heart.

The apple cobbler was still warm, and the home-made cinnamon ice cream on top had melted to just the right texture as Charli slid a spoonful into her mouth. "Oh my God, this is good."

"I'm so glad you like it. It's the boys' favorite." Jana placed her bowl on the chicken-deco placemat and sat down on the opposite side of the table.

"Then I'm lucky I got here first. And please don't judge if I ask for a second helping."

"I'd be pleased if you did. Paige is always so wonderful about sharing her honeycrisp apples. Most people don't know they're good for baking."

"They're delicious."

Jana took a bite. "How are things coming along with Town Square. Think y'all will have it ready for the wedding on Saturday?"

Charli nodded, letting the ice cream melt in her mouth. "Even if I have to work through the night every night until then. I'll make it happen. She and Aiden deserve a beautiful wedding."

"They're a remarkable couple." Jana chuckled. "That girl has been in love with him since she rode around on her little pink Stingray bike with sparkly handle streamers."

"Their love story is really something."

"Almost didn't happen."

"I heard."

"For some reason, we raise our Texas boys to be a bit stubborn."

Tell me about it.

"Take my Reno. I know you've seen his ornery side."

She'd seen his naked backside too but she certainly didn't plan to share that info with his mama.

"He can be . . . determined. But I've never met a man with a bigger heart."

Jana smiled, spooned a dollop of cobbler into her mouth. "Looks like you got him to come around."

"What makes you say that?"

Jana reached out and patted her hand. "A mother just knows these things."

Hopefully, his mother didn't have a clue how many times they'd *come around* or the deep feelings Charli had developed in her heart.

"I think we're communicating better now," Charli said.

"Well, that smile on your face tells me there's something more than a *little* communicating going on."

Charli turned the question on Jana. "What about you?"

"Me?"

"Yes, *you.* And the handsome silver-haired man I saw you with at the party?"

"Martin Lane?"

Funny how with all the gray-haired men in town, Jana knew exactly whom she meant.

"He moved into town a few months ago. Bought the old Pritchard place. Ten acres. Easy ranching." She chuckled. "Course he's a big-city boy who can't tell the back end of a steer yet. But he'll learn."

"What's his story? Where's he from?"

"He's divorced. Lived in Seattle until about a year and a half ago. He was married thirty-five years. When the youngest moved out, he and his wife realized they hadn't nurtured their marriage all those years, and they had nothing left in common."

"That's too bad. It's so sad to see a relationship fall apart like that."

Jana set down her spoon and looked up—her eyes a deeper shade of blue. "Happens more often than folks know."

"Well, it's nice that he's made friends here already."

"He's a very nice man."

Charli recognized that look of denial. She'd seen it in her own face a time or two over the past weeks. "Is he someone . . . special?"

"I'm not sure. We like each other. We've shared supper a few times but . . ." Her slender shoulders lifted. "I'm not sure either of us is ready to take such a big step."

"So you're just taking it slow and easy?"

"My mama always taught me that if you wanted a perfectly cooked stew, you set the pot on low and let it come to a full boil real slow."

Charli laughed. "I'm not sure I've ever heard that saying before."

"My mama was an odd bird. Guess I take after her."

"Well, I think you're just wonderful."

"And I think you're too free with your compliments."

"As a woman, I reserve the right to use my frequent complimenter miles. Especially when it comes to a fabulous design, pair of shoes, or really nice people."

They shared a laugh, then the smile slipped from Jana's face. "I'd appreciate it if this particular discussion didn't go any farther than these walls."

"You have my promise. But can I ask why?"

"It's just . . . not information I'm sharing with the boys."

"Why not?"

"Because as unsure as I am about moving forward and maybe going out on a few dates, the boys are *not* ready for me to take that plunge."

Disbelief vibrated through Charli's bones. "You don't think they want you to be happy?"

"Depends on whose version of happy you're talking about. They all loved Joe so much, I don't think they can imagine anyone taking his place."

"But another man wouldn't take the place of their father. Surely, as grown men, they would know that."

"Well, sugarplum, the head may know what's right, but sometimes the old ticker takes a different route. Reno's the perfect example of that notion. Boy's been trying for years to take one step forward. But he always seems to take two steps back. His head knows he has to move on, but that heart of his tells him it's comfortable right where it sits—all wrapped up and alone."

A rush of air pushed from Charli's lungs.

Jana ducked her head and caught Charli's eye. "Something tells me he might be taking those two steps forward now."

"Yeah, but he's a slow walker."

"Maybe you just need to get him to trade in those boots for a pair of running shoes," Jana said.

"If you weren't his mother, I'd say maybe I just need to hide his clothes until he came to his senses."

"Well I *am* his mother, and I say that's a damned fine idea."

"Things just aren't ever as easy as they should be, you know?"

"I do." Jana nodded her head. "You two would certainly face some mighty big challenges."

"I know. It's hard to maintain a long-distance relationship. I actually tried it once."

"Obviously, it didn't work out."

Charli wiped a drip of ice cream from the placemat with her napkin. "That's an understatement. We were two totally different people going after two totally different things in life. It just became painful after a while." And she would never want that to happen with Reno.

"Sometimes it's a blessing when those things come to an end," Jana said.

"My job doesn't make it easy." She laid the napkin back on her lap. "Sometimes what I want for my heart and what I want for my career are completely different. I get ideas in my head of how to mesh them together, but—"

"You said you don't really like living in your apartment. Maybe you need a change."

Charli looked up. "Can I be totally honest with you?"

"Of course."

"I'd love to stay in Sweet. I'd love to make it my home."

"Why don't you?" Jana asked.

Charli shrugged. "Guess I'm just waiting for a sign from the universe."

Jana chuckled as she stood and took the empty bowls to the kitchen sink. She turned with arms folded. "Now you're sounding a little bit like Reno.

Like I always tell him, you can't reach the goal line with one step forward and two steps back. You have to keep moving."

"What does he say to that?"

"Well, I'm his mother, so he tempers it with a lot of 'Uh-huhs' and 'Sure, Moms.' Which translated usually means for me to mind my own tootin' business."

Charli smiled. "He's very lucky to have you."

Jana came back and sat down. She laid her hand over Charli's on the tabletop. "Patience is a virtue, sugarplum. But sometimes you've just got to grab the universe by the tail and give it a good swing in your own direction."

A cup of coffee later, Charli followed Jana and climbed the steps that led to the barn loft. When her feet hit the landing, she stopped and put her hand to her mouth.

"Oh. My. God."

A thrill shot up the back of her neck at the discovery of treasures jammed together beneath the rafters. The collection was everything she'd dreamed and nothing she'd imagined. In her mind, the universe kicked into a joyful chorus of Hallelujah.

Jana stopped with her hand on the rail. "What is it?"

Charli looked at all the wonderful things gathering dust. "Confirmation that the universe is not a farce."

In front of her were old country gates, antique chairs, headboards, dressers, architectural columns, porcelain signs, railroad lanterns, and God only knew what was hidden beneath the dusty sheets.

"Do you even know what you have up here?" Charli asked.

"A picker's paradise?" Jana laughed, but Charli had to agree; anyone who scoured the country looking for antiques to pick from old barns and properties would have a field day in here.

"Mind if I go in and take a look?" Charli asked.

"Help yourself. If you see anything you like, just holler. I'll give you a good deal," Jana added with a wink.

Charli waded between oceans of aged items with values she couldn't even fathom. "What were you going to do with all this?"

"Oh, I started out wanting to do what I'm doing now—putting it up for display in my home. But raising five active boys put a damper on that real quick. My collecting turned into a passion and well . . . here we are—years later—with a whole bunch of stuff and no idea what to do with it all."

In the midst of examining a set of oak and brass post-office boxes, Charli looked up. "I have an idea that might interest you."

"Shoot."

"Have you ever thought about opening a business?"

The surprised look on Jana's face said the idea had never even entered her mind.

Charli couldn't help but chuckle.

"I've been too busy raising my boys and being a wife to even dream of something like that. Got too much time on my hands now. So I'm definitely interested." Jana leaned against a tall Chippendale chest of drawers. "What did you have in mind?"

"I've always dreamed about opening a place that was part design center and part home-accessories store. Something that meshed the old with the new." She glanced around the treasure trove. "A place where someone could walk in and solve their design issues and pick up a cool tchotchke on the way out the door."

"This area could sure use something like that. There are several towns in the Hill Country that are full of antique stores. Sweet is sorely lacking."

"And everyone knows antique stores are a huge draw to an area. It could help increase tourism." Charli inspected an old leather bag with "Dr. Louis O. Anderson—1922" inscribed on the brass fitting. "From what I've seen, Jana, you have a real knack for decorating. I'm a believer that natural-born talent is often stronger than a framed degree."

"That's nice of you to say."

"It's the truth." She looked up. "I saw an old Victorian house on the way into town that would make a perfect storefront. If you'd be interested, I'd love to sit down and talk with you a little more about my idea."

Jana's chest lifted on a big intake of air. "Then how about we go back to the kitchen and have us a little chat."

A rush of exhilaration tickled Charli's heart.

She knew her feelings toward Reno were spinning into something deeper than she'd ever intended. He gave her a sense of belonging. A sense of hope for the life she'd always dreamed of. They had much in common, and she felt that he could possibly be the perfect mate to her soul. But though she knew he enjoyed being with her, she could feel him holding back. Pushing her away even as he held her close.

More than anything, she wanted to know that he could reach out beyond his loss—beyond his grief—and grab hold of what she had to offer. Though her heart wanted that chance at a future with him, she really had no control of what he'd decide to do. She could only be in control of her own destiny.

With or without him, she needed a plan.

At half past nine on Sunday night, Reno's house phone rang off the hook. Five minutes later, he climbed into his truck and found himself tooling down the road toward his mother's place. When he rolled the Chevy to a stop in front of the barn, he tipped his hat back and shook his head.

On the veranda, his mother and Charli—obviously soused on something stronger than sweet tea—were dancing barefoot to Dwight Yokum's "Guitars, Cadillacs" and giggling like schoolgirls. Their third dance partner was his mother's pet goat, all dolled up in ribbons and lace and a hat sitting crooked across her horns.

He stood back watching, reluctant to end their fun. Come tomorrow, they'd probably both have hangovers the size of the Rio Grande. For now, he didn't think either of them cared.

For selfish reasons, he was happy to see that they

got along so well. His mother could always use someone to put a bright spot in her day, and Charli was damned good at that.

She'd definitely put a smile on his face.

He hadn't seen her leave the apartment earlier, but he could definitely appreciate her now in her peasant blouse, cutoff jeans, and red boots. Her shiny hair hung down her back in a wild mass of curls, and his hands clenched with the desire to feel the silky strands run through his fingers.

Charli had many facets and more he was sure he'd yet to uncover. One moment she could be sweet, funny, and sexy, the next she could be giving him hell without backing down. She could dance on the porch with his mother and a goat or relate to his sorrow and loss.

If he could design a woman who'd be perfect for him, she'd surpass his own expectations.

He could imagine waking next to her every day. Sharing a sink as they brushed their teeth. Sitting across from her every night at the dinner table. He could imagine holding her when she cried and joining in when she laughed.

Without much coaxing, he could fall heart over heels in love with her. It would be so easy, he thought, as he watched her do a little heel-toe action, then swing her hips to the beat of the song.

Hell, if he was honest, he could imagine walking down the aisle, having babies, and growing old with her.

But those were all just dreams. And he knew that every dream ended in a nightmare.

In three short weeks, she'd climb up into that Hummer and drive out of his life—back to California or her next makeover location. Maybe even go back to some guy she'd left behind.

While the thought of her in someone else's arms made him go a little crazy, he tried to remain logical. Or at least as logical as his jaded mind would allow.

Besides, there would be plenty of time to agonize over what could have been when she was gone. And he would. Right now, he just needed to get her home and into bed.

The guitars of the song crescendoed, and the women on the porch fell into each other's arms while the goat continued to prance. Their sounds of amusement reached through the air and made Reno smile.

Hands in pockets, he made his way across the drive. When his boots hit the aged planks of the veranda where he'd once spent hours daydreaming and doing homework, Charli turned with a big grin.

"Hey, Cowboy. Did you come to pick me up?"

"Yes, ma'am."

She walked up to him—her steps a little wobbly in those bright red boots—grabbed him by the front of his shirt, and pulled him in for a kiss. Normally, he didn't show any kind of public display of affection. Especially in front of his mother. But since she'd been the one making the—margaritas, judging by the empty glasses on the table—and she'd been the one to call him to give Charli a ride home, he expected she knew Charli was a little trashed. *And* that there might be a little something going on between them.

"You're going to have a helluva headache come morning," he said.

"Pffft. Nonsense." She waved her hand like she was batting flies. "We only had a couple of teeny-weeny little strawberry smoothies. Right, Jana?"

"Right," his mother agreed. "Hardly any alcohol at all."

"Uh-huh." He skimmed his hands down Charli's bare arms. Felt goose bumps rise beneath his fingers. "You about ready to go?"

"I guess." She let out a big old sigh. "But I had sooooo much fun."

His mother came over, and the two of them embraced. "Come back next Sunday," his mother said. "We'll make *peach* margaritas."

"I think y'all have had enough tequila for a month," he said.

Charli giggled.

"What's so funny?"

"You said, *y'all*."

He tilted his head, looked down into her sleepy brown eyes. "Something wrong with that?"

"No." She leaned in and lowered her voice. "I think it's really hot."

"Hokay. Time to go nighty-night, Fancy Pants. You got a purse or something?"

"I'll get it." His mother disappeared into the house. The screen door banged closed behind her. Then she was back outside again with a pink leather bag. "Here you go."

"Thanks." He tucked her purse beneath his arm. After she gave the goat a hug, he steered Charli toward his truck. "Night, Mom."

"Night, sugarplum." She gave them a wave. "Thanks for a fun day, Charli."

"Thank *you*," Charli returned. "You'll think about what I said, right?"

"I sure will."

After Reno helped Charli up into his truck, he waited until his mother disappeared safely into the house. Then he slid into the driver's seat and started up the engine. Once they hit the main road, he asked, "What was going on with you and my mom?"

"We . . . bonded."

"I can see that." He chuckled. "I think you're the first person she's danced with since my dad died."

"Really?"

"Yeah. So . . . thanks."

"I really didn't do anything. A fun song came on the radio—something about ticks, I think—and we just jumped up and started dancing. Next thing I knew, we were out on the veranda." She flashed him a smile. "She just couldn't say no. I'm too irresistible."

He did a double take on those cutoff jeans, long legs, and her red boots.

No kidding.

Her stomach growled.

"Oops." She let out a giggle.

"Did you eat dinner?" he asked.

"We had cobbler."

"That's not much of a meal."

"It was delicious. Your mother's a wonderful cook." She slid closer, dipped her hand down the buttons on his shirt to his zipper, and leaned in to kiss his neck. "Mmmmm. I could snack on you all the way home."

He cleared his throat, which did nothing to alleviate his sudden erection. No doubt the woman rang all his bells and whistles, but he was pretty damned sure she wouldn't make it to his front door before she passed out. And he'd never been a man to take advantage of a woman unless she was an awake and willing participant.

"How about I take a rain check on that?"

She leaned away and looked at him through the darkness with a frown pulling her beautiful smooth brows together. "You don't want me?"

"I didn't say that."

"Oh. Sure." She slid to her own side of the bench seat and folded her arms. "I get it."

A moment of silence filtered through the cab as he waited for her to enlighten him on exactly what it was that she *got*. Instead, her gaze remained focused out the passenger window, and her lips remained sealed.

A million thoughts raced through his head—all of them starting with how much he wanted her—and ending with her leaving him and Sweet with nothing but a heartache.

"No, honey." He touched her arm, knowing he'd be a whole lot happier with her sitting a little closer. "I'm afraid you don't."

Thunk.

"Charli?" He eased the truck to the side of the road. By the time he put the gearshift in PARK, he didn't need to look closer to find the problem. She let out a snuffle and a snore. A chuckle vibrated in his chest, and he got them back on the road.

Minutes later, he carried her into his house and laid her on his bed. He slid off her boots, then debated whether to remove the rest of her clothes so she'd be comfortable. Deciding she'd never know the difference, he pulled the covers up to her chin.

For a moment, he gave himself permission to just look at her. He watched her gentle breathing lift her chest, her closed eyelids flutter. A small smile curled her lips. Even in her sleep and drunk off her ass, she was beautiful.

Inside and out.

Before he moved into stalker mode, he called her dog, who had remained comfortably stretched out on his leather sofa when they'd come through the door. Little dog toenails clicked on the hardwood floor as she trotted down the hallway, then came into the bedroom and looked at him as if he'd committed a felony.

"Don't give me that look," he said. "Get up there with your mama. Keep an eye on her."

Pumpkin sneezed, and her foofy ears flew up like flags made of cotton balls. Then, with a graceful leap, she jumped up onto the bed and snuggled against Charli's side. He leaned down and kissed Charli's forehead, then forced himself to turn off the light and walk out the door.

Not climbing into bed beside her might be the hardest *and* the dumbest thing he'd ever done. But with all the emotions churning inside him, he needed to give himself some distance. Get used to being without her around. He knew he was getting too attached. Even though he'd already found himself knee deep in wanting her, he had to keep a clear mind. A guarded heart. One foot on the road to reason.

At 2:00 A.M., she shuffled into the living room, naked, took him by the hand, and pulled him up from the sofa. Then she led him back to the bedroom.

He went.

Willingly.

Charli woke with elephants parading through her brain. She abruptly sat up, then lay back down just as quick. Slid one bloodshot eye open and peered around the room.

Empty.

She turned her head and glanced at the clock radio.

Nine o'clock.

Judging by the sunshine peeking through the slats in the window blinds, she knew that meant nine in the morning, and she was late for work. She threw back the covers, got out of bed, and went in search of the man who'd held her close all night. And some painkillers.

Her bare feet slapped against the hardwood floor as she went room to room. Each space was as empty as the next.

No Reno. No Pumpkin. No Bear.

In the kitchen, she spotted her purse on the granite counter and reached in for the bottle of Ibuprofen. When she turned to grab a glass of water, she saw the full coffeepot and the note propped in front.

Thought once you got up you could use a strong cup of coffee. Pumpkin is in the backyard with Bear. She's been fed. I'm at the store. Will try to catch up with you later.

Hope you have a good day,
R.

Charli knew she was late for work, and she'd pay hell trying to catch up. Instead of rushing off to the shower, she poured herself a cup of coffee, splashed in some sugar, and sat down at the kitchen table. She picked up the note and reread it.

Twice.

In all her thirty-one years, she'd never had a man leave her a morning note. Not even her father or brother. Not even her filmmaker ex-boyfriend, who'd snuck out in the middle of the night so he didn't have to say good-bye.

She turned the piece of plain white paper in her hand. The note was simple. It wasn't a love letter. And yet it tugged at her heart.

He cared.

Sure. He probably didn't want to. But he couldn't help himself. Reno was a man who wanted—needed—to look after someone. To be a part of their lives. To hold them. Love them. Even if he never asked for anything in return. She'd never met a more complex man. And she was sure she'd never meet anyone again who'd come close to making her feel like he held her future in his hands and heart.

She sipped the strong coffee, sat back in the sturdy chair, and glanced around the kitchen. Warm earth tones with a punch of red and solid furniture with a touch of masculinity. All could easily be softened up with paint, pillows, and rugs. There were few embellishments, yet the room felt comfortable, like she could sit there all day and never leave. It did not surprise her that she wanted to do just that. But the completion of a new Town Square awaited.

She took her coffee and strolled into the living room—surprised he hadn't created a mural in his own home. He had amazing talent. Then again, she had the feeling he didn't spend much time indoors. Maybe he hadn't made the time. Or maybe he hadn't been inspired yet. He had the perfect wall space, but it was currently hidden by a pair of bookcases. She walked up to check out his reading choices.

Fitzgerald. Hemingway. Steinbeck. L'Amour. Brontë.

The man certainly had eclectic taste.

She glanced across the bookshelf to a trio of picture frames attached by silver loops and was not surprised to see those he loved and lost.

Joe Wilder had been a dashing man, with a thick head of blond hair and deep blue eyes that sparkled with mischief.

Jared Wilder, in his Marine dress blues, had been equally as handsome as any of his brothers and had a smile that radiated sincerity.

Diana—the great love of Reno's life—had the unpretentious looks of the girl next door. She would be anybody's friend, Charli thought. A good daughter. A good wife. A good mother.

Charli's heart broke for the young woman who'd

been about to marry the man of her dreams, then lost it all in one crushing moment that ended her young life.

A slow breath leaked from Charli's lungs as she picked up the picture frames and looked into the faces of those who'd been there to help Reno grow into such an amazing man.

A man who deserved happiness.

"If he'll have me," she told them all silently, *"I'll take good care of him. I promise."*

How could she not?

Against everything she'd sworn herself *not* to do, she'd quickly fallen hopelessly, helplessly in love.

She only hoped that, eventually, he'd feel the same way.

Lunchtime rolled around, and Reno helped the rush of folks who'd come into the store for various odds and ends to get their week started. Mondays were notoriously slow. Well, most anyway.

Seemed the usual weekend shoppers had waited for the beginning of the week to come into town to see how far the renovations on Town Square had come. As far as Reno could see from across the street, they'd gone well.

The new playground had been installed with a variety of colorful playsets and the rubber mulch Charli insisted on to keep the kids safe. New wood and decorative iron park benches and picnic tables were in place. Final touches were being added to the gazebo. And work continued on the new waterfall and creek Charli and the landscapers had thought would be a nice addition.

It appeared the only thing missing today was Charli.

Not that he'd been standing at the window watching for her. But the few times a customer had made comments about the square, he'd glanced across the street, expecting to see her working away. Each time he'd come up empty.

Seemed Charli had been a no-show.

That had started him to worry.

He'd called the house, but there had been no answer. He'd call her cell phone but, hell, he didn't have her number. How was it that he'd made love to her numerous times and didn't have her damned phone number?

Around two o'clock, the activity in the store slowed, and he figured he could finally get to the long list of special orders he'd neglected these past few days. Either that, or he could jump in his truck and rush home to make sure nothing was wrong. While he contemplated the dilemma, the bell over the door jingled.

To his surprise, Charli strolled in, looking bright-eyed. As she came forward, her gaze flitted around the store.

"Stop that," he said.

She looked up. "Stop what?"

"Undressing my store with your eyes."

"Okay. I'd rather undress *you* anyway." A deep-throated chuckle bubbled up from beneath her really nicely fitted cotton top. "But not just with my eyes."

Great. There went all kinds of wicked thoughts flying through his head. "How's the hangover?"

Her slim shoulders lifted in a shrug. "Not an issue. I had a hair of the dog earlier this morning."

"You've been hitting the strawberry margaritas already? No wonder you look so relaxed."

"No, silly. After I had two cups of the wonderful coffee you made—and thank you very much for that—I took a shower and headed to Bud's. Paige made me a short stack smothered with strawberries. So since ten this morning, I've been on a caffeine-and-sugar high. I'm pretty sure the crash is going to be ugly."

Doubting anything she did could be considered *ugly*, he chuckled.

"Whatcha doin?" She leaned over the counter and propped her chin with both hands. "Ordering more plaid shirts?"

Once he managed to drag his gaze away from the abundance of cleavage she'd offered him, he caught the amusement in her brown eyes. "You're feisty today."

"I'm feeling good," she said. "Productive."

"Then to what do I owe this visit, Ms. Productive?" He moved the computer mouse, clicked on his purchasing spreadsheet, then gave her his full attention—an action far more satisfying.

"I came for my clock." She reached a hand across the counter and walked her warm fingers up his arm with a come-and-get-me grin. "Unless you can think of something better to do."

The idea of locking the front door and hauling her into the back room sounded like a great idea, but he'd promised himself he'd try to put some distance between them. To do his best to protect his heart even when he knew he'd pretty much already lost it.

"Being that you already slacked off enough for one day by sleeping in, and you have a project that needs to be done in just four days," he said, "I suggest we stick to the clock thing."

She sighed. "Okay, but it's not going to be nearly as much fun."

Understatement.

There wasn't anything more fun than getting tangled between the sheets with her.

He slid off the stool and headed toward the storeroom. She followed.

"So what's this clock look like?"

"It should be in a box about this big." She demonstrated the size with her hands. "It's for the gazebo."

"You're putting a clock in the gazebo?"

"Not *in. On.* It will sit near the top on the street side. It's solar-powered, but it looks like an antique, so it will fit into the turn-of-the-century design I'm going for."

"I hate to admit it, but you and your team have done an outstanding job so far."

"Thank you." Her smile burst into a full grin. "Now that wasn't so hard, was it?"

It was *hard* all right. Then again, he wasn't talking about a damned admission. "When I'm wrong, I'm willing to own up."

"I like that in a man."

He smiled and continued to look for her clock box amid all the other deliveries he'd received for her projects and had yet to put in order. Best to keep his hands busy searching so he didn't have time to think about where else he'd like them to be. She followed him from the stack of boxes to bundles of boxes all arranged in a haphazard formation. The sweet peachy scent of her lotion tagged along as an added form of torture.

"Can't find it?" she asked.

"It's here somewhere."

"Are you sure you didn't *unconsciously* misplace it?"

"Is that what I'm doing?"

"I'd prefer to think that I've just dazzled you, and you can't think straight."

He laughed. "Well, there is that."

"I get how you feel about this town, Reno. I truly do." Her fingers curled into the front of his shirt and she drew him close. Her luscious mouth hovered mere inches away. "But sometimes a little freshening up doesn't hurt. You like what we've done with the senior center, the candy store, and now Town Square. I hope you'll extend that same optimism when we get to your place. It's only a few weeks away, you know."

A few weeks away.

A few weeks closer to changing everything he loved about this store.

A few weeks of getting to know her better, falling for her a little more every day, only to have her toss everything out the window as she drove out of his life.

A few weeks until he found himself alone again. Wishing for something he couldn't have and wanting it badly just the same.

Maybe he was getting way ahead of himself. But the idea of another devastating loss tightened around his throat. Sent a cold chill up his back. And pushed him back behind the wall he'd erected to protect himself.

"Yeah, well, until then, you don't get to touch a damned thing. Here's your clock." He bent down, pulled out a rectangular box, and shoved it into her hands. "You might want to hurry so you can get that put up in time."

He warned himself not to look into her eyes, but he did it anyway.

A deep furrow pulled those delicate brows together over eyes clouded with confusion. "What's wrong?" she asked.

"Nothing. Just . . . burning daylight."

"And that's enough to make your *mood* do a one-eighty?" She settled the box on her hip and turned that confused look into a glare. "I don't think so. What's wrong?"

"Oh. You know. Just a good hard slap of reality."

"Sometimes it's hard to keep up with you, Reno. One minute we're good. The next I don't know where the hell you're coming from."

"Nobody's asking you to keep up."

"Wow." Her jaw tightened. "Really?"

At his stupid silence, she said, "Fine. Don't worry about me. I've got better things to do than deal with you and your P.M.S."

As she headed toward the exit, Jackson walked in and held the door open for her—behaving like the gentleman their mother had raised. *He*, on the other hand, needed a good whack upside the head.

"Nice to see you, Ms. Brooks," Jackson said.

She flashed him a hesitant smile. "Charli."

"You need help with that?" Jack held out his arms to take the cardboard box.

"No, thanks. I've got it." She turned her head and said to Reno, "Guess I'll see *you* later."

With an appreciative eye, Jackson watched her go. Then he turned back to Reno. "What's up here, big brother?"

"Working on purchases until she showed up to collect her clock."

"You could have offered to carry the box for her."

"Apparently, she didn't want help."

"Hmmm."

Reno glanced up from the computer monitor. "Hmmm, what?"

His brother lifted the straw Stetson from his head and shoved a hand through his hair. "Thought I saw something going on between you two at the party the other night."

"Guess you saw wrong." As cool as possible, Reno went back to perusing the company names and figures on the spreadsheet so as not to give his overly intuitive brother any ammunition.

"Bullshit." Jack grabbed a stool and sat down. "Don't make something up that isn't there, little bro. You'll only be disappointed."

"Yeah? Then how come you look like you're stuck in an emotional blender?"

"You know, I've known you your whole life, and I still can't make sense of some of the shit you say."

"Hell you don't." Jack laughed. "When I walked in, there was enough sexual tension in here to kill a whorehouse cat."

"Delusional. That's you." Reno pointed. "Look it up in the dictionary."

"So . . . nothing going on?"

"Nope."

"Cool." Jack's broad shoulders lifted. "Then I guess that gives me the green light to ask her out."

Tension knotted the back of Reno's neck. "What is it with you and Jesse wanting to take that girl out? She's here for three more weeks. Pretty damned sure she's not going to be interested in hooking up with either one of you."

"Why? Because she's already hooked up with *you*?"

"Yeah." A rush of air pushed from his lungs. "Satisfied?"

"Are you?"

Several heartbeats passed before he could answer, then he did so with the truth. "No."

"She's no good?"

He shook his head. "Not going to go there with you."

"I didn't mean in bed." The look on Jackson's face was one of utter disappointment. "Give me a little credit would you?"

"Sorry."

"I meant she's no good for *you*?"

"She's perfect for me. That's the problem."

"How so?" Jackson unscrewed the cap on the soda bottle in his hand and took a drink.

"For starters, like I said a minute ago, in three weeks she'll say *adios*."

"And you can't take another loss," Jack said bluntly.

The truth more than hurt. It knocked the wind from his lungs. "Nope."

"Maybe she'll decide she likes you enough to stay."

"Not a chance in hell. We're too different."

"How so?"

"Do you know who her father is?"

"How would I know that?"

"General Thomas Brooks."

Jack's brows shot up his forehead. "United States Marine Lieutenant General Thomas Brooks?"

Reno nodded.

"Get the fuck out."

"I'm serious. Do you know what that means?"

"That her father's a mean-ass son of a bitch?"

"Besides that."

Jackson took another slug of Pepsi. "Clue me in."

"Means she's used to moving around. Frequently. She took a job on a makeover show. A traveling job. One where she's never home. And she loves her job. Which means she's *never* going to be home."

"And that kind of moving-around-from-place-to-place lifestyle is *not* okay with you."

"We both want something completely different. She'd never be happy staying in a Podunk town like Sweet."

"Have you asked her that?"

"No need."

"You sure?"

Am I?

If the ache in the center of his chest was any indication, then . . . "Yes."

"Well, at least you put yourself out there." Jackson studied him for a moment.

"What?" Reno asked, curious as to the reason behind his brother's serious contemplation.

"I'm just trying to figure out where we screwed up in life so bad that it just seems like we're always going to be on the outside looking in. Why you and I are never going to have the kind of relationship Mom and Dad had."

Reno knew his brother referred not only to his loss of Diana but also Jackson's divorce from a perfectly wonderful woman. Fiona's only problem had been that she wasn't Abby Morgan—the woman Jackson had been in love with since he'd learned to tie his shoelaces.

"You're young," Reno said, even knowing it was a ridiculous statement because *he* was only a few years older. "It'll happen for you."

"Yeah? Well, I'm not going to lay money down on either of us."

Chapter 18

Forrest Gump had nothing on a box of chocolates when it came to weddings. Each was as different as the people who stood in front of friends and family and pledged their love. Charli had been to blow-out weddings in Beverly Hills, where the bride and groom simply selected a wedding planner, wrote out a check, and showed up on the big day. She'd also been to intimate weddings held on a beach where waves crashed on the shoreline as the couple recited vows they'd written themselves, then celebrated the night away under the glow of tiki torches.

The wedding of Aiden Marshall and Paige Walker had been traditional right down to the very simple wedding bands they'd exchanged.

As the couple stood in the new Victorian gazebo beneath thousands of twinkling fairy lights, they spoke the same time-honored vows as millions

before them. The bride wore a classic white gown.
The groom wore a timeless black tux.

There hadn't been a dry eye in the entire place.

Including the groom's.

Charli wasn't sure she'd ever seen tears spill from
a tough soldier's eyes before. Especially her father.
Even on the day he'd buried his wife.

Aiden had cried.

He'd been secure enough in his masculinity that
he could let the entire world know just how much
he loved the woman at his side. In Charli's eyes, that
made him an exceptional man.

Paige was a lucky, lucky woman.

As the celebration continued, and the dancing
began, Charli swiped a piece of cake and took her
plate over to a quiet picnic table. She kicked off
her shoes, then sat back to appreciate all the work
her crew had accomplished to make this wedding
transpire.

She studied the beautiful craftsmanship on the
gazebo, the perfectly laid pavers that led to multiple areas of the park and created a nice walking
path. She breathed deep the fragrance of the new
rose garden and scented blooms. And her ears de-
lighted at the splashing sounds from the new waterfall. Somehow, they had pulled it all together. And
it was magic.

That she was enjoying it alone? Well, that sucked.

She speared her fork into the fluffy marble cake,
pleased that the bride had forgone fondant for
buttercream icing. She adored buttercream. As a
habit, she seemed to indulge in the taste of things

that were overly pleasurable. Things—and maybe people too—that might not always be good for her.

Or her heart.

Her gaze traveled across the lawn toward the gazebo, where the community chatted, couples danced a waltz, and Reno stood with his brothers.

Stubborn ass.

She hadn't spoken to him in four days.

During daylight hours, he'd managed to stay inside the hardware store while she'd remained outside in the park. When she'd gotten home late, his lights had been off. In the mornings, she'd heard the roar of his truck fly down the gravel road well before the sun peeked over the hilltops.

They'd missed each other at every turn.

Accidental?

Nope.

She'd decided whatever had crawled up his pant leg and set him off needed to cool down. So she'd decided two could play at his game—though it was a lonely one. In just the few short days they'd been together, she'd gotten used to the sound of his voice. Anticipated his laughter. And basked in the warmth of his arms.

She missed him.

But she also knew that with a man like Reno, you couldn't push. He had to come at things on his own, in his own time. She was willing to wait for a little while. But if he thought he could just pretend like she didn't exist for very long, well, she wouldn't let that happen.

She was the daughter of a Marine general.

She didn't just let things go.

She went after them with combat skills and stealth reconnaissance.

If all else failed, she wasn't above resorting to tears.

A sigh slipped from her chest as she dug into the thick buttercream with renewed vigor. All she needed now was a pint of caramel-chunk ice cream, and she could just drown her frustration in saturated fat.

She took a bite, and the hairs on the back of her neck tingled. She looked up and forced the cake down her throat. "You've been avoiding me."

His dark eyes searched her face.

She watched him.

Waited for him to say something.

Anything.

All the while wishing he'd just reach down, pull her up into his arms, and kiss the living daylights out of her.

"You're right."

Yeah. Not really what she wanted to hear. "Well. You may have excellent Cheshire-cat vanishing skills, but at least you're honest."

Dark eyes guarded, lips flattened together in an impassive slash, his expression was unreadable. His hands disappeared into the pockets of his dress pants. His shoulders stiffened beneath his crisp blue shirt. His highly shined boots shifted in the grass. "You're upset."

"Whatever gave you that idea?"

"Your face is all scrunched up."

"Maybe I'm just tired."

"I don't doubt that. You and your team did an incredible job here. And I'm thankful you gave my friends the wedding they deserved."

"Thank you."

He glanced away. When his eyes came back to hers, they were shadowed with unspoken words. "Can we talk?" His voice was low. Apologetic.

Her heart dropped into the glob of buttercream in her stomach.

She knew that tone. Had heard it before. Maybe not from him, but she'd been the recipient of what was about to come often enough that she could almost recite it line for line.

The last thing she wanted to hear was him telling her that being with her had been a monumental error in judgment. So she had no choice but to beat him to it. Even though getting the words out might be impossible.

"Look . . ." She prayed the tempo of her heart would slow enough for her to speak in a rational tone. "You don't have to explain. I pretty much threw myself at you. Obviously, I forced you into something you either weren't interested in or comfortable with. It doesn't take a sledgehammer for me to get it that you . . ." She couldn't speak the words. "And that's okay." *Liar.* "Really. I understand. I'm—"

"Do I look like the kind of man who could be *forced* into anything?" His words came out in a growl.

"Not really."

"Do I look like the kind of man who'd be with a woman he wasn't interested in?"

His dark brows pulled together. Eyes churned

with turmoil. Hard to say what was going on in that handsome head. "Ummmm."

"No," he answered. "I'm not. I don't know what you *think* I'm going to say, but why don't you just give me a chance to say it anyway?"

She pushed away her half-eaten cake and tried to ignore the Mexican Hat Dance going on in her gut. "Okay."

"You scare the hell out of me, Charli." After a moment of silence that drew out like the evening tide, he folded his strong arms across that magnificent chest. His gaze pinpointed her until she squirmed and resettled on the picnic bench.

"I look at you, and all I do is want you," he said. "And not in just a sexual way. And that makes me start thinking about things I shouldn't be thinking. Wanting things I shouldn't want. You confuse me. And you tempt me until I can't think straight anymore. So I had to back off."

He took a deep breath like he was gearing up for round two.

Charli bit her lip to keep from bursting out with "*I love you*" or something equally as crazy.

"I had to give myself time to think."

"And what did you conclude?" Wow. She amazed herself at how composed she sounded.

He sat down on the bench beside her, and she scooted over to give him room. He smelled clean. Like soap, and aftershave, and warm, sexy male. His heat seeped into her, and they weren't even touching.

"I don't know." He looked away.

When his eyes came back to hers she could not

only see the confusion ripping him apart, she could feel it.

"I've been fighting myself for so long, I don't know how to do anything else. That's why the Marines were so good for me. I finally got a chance to fight something else. I got to fight *for* something for a change."

Fight for *me*, she wished silently.

"Then the endless shit cycle began. My brother was killed. My father died . . ."

His pause was so heartbreaking Charli wanted to wrap her arms around him and never let go.

"And when the woman I loved was killed, I thought maybe it was all my fault. Like somehow they all died because they knew me." His hands curled into fists. "Like I was the connecting factor, and they all disappeared from my life because they'd touched some evil part of me left over from when I'd lived with Angela in that crack house," he said, unaware that she even knew the whole story.

"Reno—"

"You're leaving in a couple of weeks," he said starkly. "When people leave my life . . . they don't come back. Logic tells me it's better to let you go now. To not get any closer."

She laid her hand over the bunched muscles in his forearm. "Sometimes you just have to take a chance. To live your life and let the shadows disappear."

"It's not that easy," he said, looking directly into her eyes.

She felt the edge of his fear deep in her soul. "I know." She touched his cheek. "But you have to believe you deserve to be happy. That's what everyone wants for you. You just have to want it yourself."

He gave her an almost imperceptible nod. Then his hand reached up and covered hers. "I missed you," he said.

"I missed you too."

In the distance, the band kicked into "Somethin' 'Bout a Truck," and Charli knew there was no time better than the present for him to take a step forward. They'd settled nothing, and fear still ruled his heart. But for the moment, maybe they could just put a bandage on all that was wrong between them until they figured it out.

"Hey," she said. "They're playing our song."

"We have a song?"

"We do now." She held out her hand. "Come dance with me, Cowboy."

His dimples flashed. And then he took her hand and tugged her close. "I think you might be good for me."

"That news is so twenty-four seconds ago." She grinned. "I've just been waiting for you to get a clue."

"I'm a little slow to come around sometimes," he said. "I don't have all the answers. I won't make promises. I don't know what will happen when—"

She pressed her finger to his warm lips. "How about we just take it one day at a time?"

A slow leak of air escaped his lungs. "Now you're talking." He leaned in and pressed his lips to hers.

The kiss was sweet. And Charli refused to concede that she had only a few weeks to convince the man that they belonged together.

* * *

The following Wednesday, Charli patted down the potting soil over the bluebonnets embellishing the new whiskey barrels in front of Sweet Pickens Bar-B-Q. Brushing the dirt from her palms, she stood back and looked up at the newly power-washed rock exterior, new corrugated metal awning, revamped sign, and fresh red trim paint.

On the outside, the place gave a big welcome. On the inside, comfortable new booths and a warm interior invited people to stay. The first improvement they'd made to the place was to move the huge BBQ pit out in front, where everyone could see the meat sizzling and the juices dripping. Nothing smelled better than mesquite chips and hot flames. Charli figured it was a main attraction, so why hide it?

As she had when she'd suggested an old-time soda fountain might be a good addition for Goody Gum Drops, Charli had come up with a few ideas for Mr. Carlson's restaurant.

She ducked into the building and found him helping her electrician hang the new chandelier she'd fashioned from Mason jars. Word had it that in the month of December, Mr. Carlson took on a distinctive persona. With his thick, snowy beard and round, rosy cheeks, Charli had no doubt the man would make a fine Santa Claus.

"Do you have a minute, Mr. Carlson?"

From the tall aluminum ladder, he looked down and smiled. "You betcha. Just give me a second here so Jimmy doesn't fry his fingertips."

Charli waited patiently while they hooked up the wires, then instructed her to flip the switch.

Warm amber light reflected off the stainless accent bars she'd used on the upper walls to make the ceiling look a little like a barbecue grill. She grinned proudly. "I like it."

Mr. Carlson climbed down the ladder and came over to stand by her. He looked up and grinned. "You outdid yourself with this one, young lady."

"It's kitschy without being too over-the-top."

"Customers are going to love it. We decided to start serving drinks in Mason jars too. Keep the theme going."

"That sounds great." She smiled. "I have a few other ideas if you're interested."

"How about I make us a cup of coffee, and we sit down over at the bar."

"I would love that." While he got busy at the coffeemaker, she slid onto one of the saddleback stools, feeling only slightly guilty that most of her crew was still putting in the sweat labor. When Mr. Carlson returned with two steaming mugs, she splashed in some sugar and took a sip. "Mmmmm. Good."

"Now, what ideas have you come up with?" he asked, sipping from his own mug.

"Well, to start off with, I've eaten your delicious food several times, and—"

"Yes, I thought I saw you in here a few weeks back with Reno Wilder. Looked like you two were having quite the conversation."

She laughed. "Mr. Wilder doesn't take easily to new ideas."

"Ah. But he's a man with a good heart. Last year, my Annie took ill and couldn't put in the hours at the grill. Reno was the first to step up and help out.

Then he talked those wild brothers of his into taking up the load too."

Another reason to love him, Charli thought. Not that she needed more.

"How is Annie now?"

"She's a peach. Healthy as a horse. Course, don't tell her I mentioned her and a farm animal in the same breath, or she'll have my hide."

Charli laughed. "I promise I won't. I'm looking forward to meeting her. She sounds wonderful."

"Salt of the earth," he said.

"I'm finding that most of the people in Sweet are the same. Which is why I'm tossing out ideas that might—no promises—help everyone increase their revenue by bringing in more tourists."

"I like yer thinkin' so far."

"Good. Then how does a chuck-wagon cooking competition sound? You could hold it right outside in your parking lot. In the big empty lot next door, you could add picnic tables and a stage for bands to entertain the guests while they wait for a seat in the restaurant. You could even hold a craft fair or antique show."

"Never thought about that before."

"Or maybe a chili cook-off."

He grinned. "Like that one too."

"And that Bar-B-Q sauce you make would be a wonderful item to have on hand to sell to those who'd like to take a bottle back home or give as a gift. You could call it . . . what's your first name?"

"Jack."

"You could call it . . . Snappy Jack's Sweet Picken's Sauce."

Mr. Carlson hooted a laugh, and his rosy cheeks turned a brighter shade of red. He grabbed her up in a hug that made her squeak.

"Darlin', you and those ideas need to stick around for a while."

As he set her back down on the barstool, Charli hoped she could do exactly that.

Reno moved around the kitchen, throwing fresh-picked vegetables into the hot skillet on the stove, grabbing plates from the cupboard, and watching the clock.

Two weeks had passed since Paige and Aiden's wedding. Two weeks in which Charli had spent the nights in his bed and the mornings in his arms. They'd danced that night at the reception, and he had never felt more complete than when she looked up at him and smiled.

She'd come home with him, and, from that night on, she and her little orange dog had never gone back to Jackson's barn apartment. Each night, they'd share dinner, stories from the day, and plans for the following. They did the dishes together, walked their dogs together, and settled in on the sofa to watch a movie together. They'd made a pact that for each action shoot-'em-up he chose, they'd watch one of her chick flicks. He found he could easily tolerate *27 Dresses* as long as she was snuggled in his arms wearing her skimpy little boy shorts and tank top.

They'd been like any other couple easing into a new relationship, getting to know each other. And what Reno had discovered he liked. A lot.

Charli made him laugh. Try to forget his past. And dare to look toward the future.

He glanced up at the clock again.

And that was the problem.

They were running out of time.

Stirring the vegetables in the pan with a wooden spoon, he glanced up as both dogs jumped down from the sofa and began to dance at the back door. Moments later, Charli came into the house looking gorgeously bedraggled. But she still had enough energy to give both dogs a little baby talk and affection.

"Tough day?"

She dropped her bag near the door and walked into his arms. "The Harvest Moon Mercantile reveal almost didn't take place."

"What happened? Bodine wasn't happy with the results?"

She looked up, tired but tempting. He kissed her soft lips.

"Oh, he was happy. But you know how it is with century-old buildings and Murphy's Law. Something's bound to happen. And did." She stuck her fingers into the pan and snatched up a green bean. She blew on it, then popped it into her mouth. "The carpenters measured all the new awning spindle posts the same. And, of course, the building had shifted so . . ."

"They didn't fit?" He watched her mouth move in a delicious way as she stole another bean and chewed.

"Not at first, but we got it figured out. However, it delayed the reveal for over an hour."

"From what I saw when I left the store, the place looked really good. You did a nice job. Especially with the new sign. It looks original."

"See." She grinned and slid her arms around his waist. "Makeovers don't necessarily mean pop art and loud colors. You have to choose appropriately for the era. A step back in time is just as important as a step into the future."

He seriously hoped he'd never have to step back in time. It had been too damned painful.

The vegetables were fork tender, so he removed them from the stove and pushed them onto the plates. Then he added some chicken hot from the oven.

"Ooh, that looks as good as it smells," she said. "I'm starving."

He put her plate on the table and held out her chair. When she sat down, he scooted it in for her.

"You know," she said, "I could get used to having someone cook for me. Especially when he's such a gentleman."

When he sat down in the chair beside her, she curled her fingers into his shirt and pulled him in for a kiss. She probably wouldn't be surprised to know that the thoughts running through his head while she kissed him were anything but gentlemanly.

Somehow, he managed to put those thoughts aside—temporarily—and sliced into the baked chicken. He hadn't eaten a thing since breakfast. The store had been busier than usual, and since the production crew supplies were dwindling, he'd made a good effort to put his storeroom back into some kind of order.

But he'd still be willing to put aside his hunger if she decided to let him have *her* as an appetizer.

"I've been in this business a while, but I learned a lesson today that I'm sure will be beneficial for future reveals." She set down her fork and sipped at her glass of chardonnay.

"What's that? Measure twice, cut once?"

"No." Her giggle that bubbled up made him smile. "Make sure your morning coffee is spiked with something ninety proof."

"I'd like to see that." He could get used to this— sitting beside her, listening to how her day went, watching the animation on her face as she spoke of research and textures and piecing things together that otherwise might never work.

In just a week's time, he'd no longer be able to look at her. Or touch her. Or kiss her any damn time he wanted. The best he could hope for would be an occasional phone call. Or text. Or e-mail. Or watching her come alive on that damned show instead of in his arms.

He hated to slip back into a doomsday frame of mind, but there was no getting around the fact that when she drove away, he would miss her like hell. Somehow, she'd slipped beneath his skin and into his heart. And he liked her there.

"But you don't need to worry," she said.

Lost in his thoughts, his head snapped up. "Worry about what?"

"That next week, when we start on the hardware store, we'll measure wrong. *Or* that I'll show up drunk."

He didn't want to think about next week. Or what

she planned to do to his store. Or about her leaving.

Charli got up from the table and took their empty plates to the sink. "Since we start on your store renovations in two days, I wanted to talk to you about some ideas I have."

Apparently, what he wanted didn't matter, and it seemed she was determined to carry this discussion through dessert.

She stuck the dishes under the running water, grabbed the sponge, and rinsed off the scraps she hadn't already tossed to the dogs. "I'm not sure I mentioned it, but we're running a little low on funds, and I'm close to being over budget."

Hope sprang up. "Does that mean you're going to forget about the store?"

"Of course not." She glanced over her shoulder as she stuck the dishes in the dishwasher. "It just means we might need to do things a little differently."

"Different how?"

"Well, since we're doing an inside and outside renovation, it would be a good idea to eliminate some of the overstocked or *unusual* items."

"Like what?"

"Like . . ." Drying her hands on the dish towel she turned. "Maybe the things that don't actually belong in a hardware store? Like . . . the barrel of yarn."

"That yarn is a special order for Mrs. Duncan."

"Then why didn't Mrs. Duncan take it home?"

"I think she said something about the color not being right."

"So . . . out of the kindness of your heart, *you*—the owner of a *hardware* store—special ordered something that wasn't even *hardware* related for someone. She didn't like it. And now you're stuck with it?"

Put that way, he had to admit it sounded pretty lame. "Pretty much."

"Perfect." A smile broke across her face. "Then the yarn can be the first item to go into the fire-sale box."

"*Fire sale?*"

"Or you could just call it a yard sale or even a clearance sale. But *fire* makes it sound more urgent, don't you think?"

"Why would I want to do any of the above?"

"To get rid of all those items that will probably sit in that store for the next decade. Which means you make no money, and all they do is take up space and collect dust."

"I never agreed to something like that. Hell, I never even agreed to the renovation."

"Oh, but you did. You made a bet." She grinned. "You lost."

Since he got *her* in the bet, he could hardly complain.

"I can see by the crinkles in your forehead and the dark shadows in your eyes that you aren't quite comfortable with this idea," she said.

"No shit."

"Then we won't do it."

And there was a one-eighty he didn't expect. "What?"

"We won't do a fire sale. We won't do the store renovations."

The pressure in his chest released like a dam break. "Seriously?"

"Seriously."

"Why the change of heart?"

"Oh, don't get me wrong, I haven't changed my mind. From the minute we drove into town, I wanted to fix that place up." She hung the dish towel on the hook near the sink. "But I can tell this is really bothering you, sooo . . ."

"What happens if you don't?"

Her shoulders lifted. "We've already done more than the usual. I'm pretty sure Max and the bookkeepers will be happy to cut expenses. We'll just change some of the intros and B-roll, and that will be that. The whole six-project thing was my idea anyway."

That didn't answer the question he'd really been asking. "No. I mean what happens if you don't? As in how does that affect your stay here?"

"We'll leave tomorrow," she said in a much too casual voice. "Go back to L.A. and work on the plans for the next location."

Leave tomorrow?

Fuck. That.

As much as he wanted to say, "Don't do the makeover," there was no way in hell he was ready for her to leave. Even if she didn't sound like it was any big deal to her.

Shit. A huge breath of air pushed from his lungs. "Go ahead and do the reno."

"Are you sure?"

"No."

"You're still not going to make this easy, are you?"

"Nope."

"Then how about I sweeten the deal?"

He dropped his gaze to her smile, and thoughts of kissing those full lips started to fly through his head.

"How about," she continued, "we have a fire sale, and half the proceeds go to charity."

He pushed aside the sexual images and thought about that for a moment. "I like that idea."

"And the other half will go toward the renovation costs."

He laughed. "You're asking *me* to put up the cash for something I never wanted done in the first place?"

She leaned her butt against the kitchen counter and crossed her arms beneath her breasts. Her chin came up in that stubborn way that drove him just a little crazy. "Yes."

"That makes absolutely no sense."

"It makes total sense."

"Are we fighting?" he asked.

"No. We're discussing."

"Sounds a whole lot like an argument to me."

"Fine." Her chin came up just a little higher. Her dark eyes narrowed ever so slightly. "If you want to battle this out, then that's what we'll do because—"

Emotion churned in his gut. He was done hearing what needed to be done to the store. He needed to stop her from talking.

Now.

Before he had to listen to any more, he got up from the chair and grabbed hold of her with both hands. Next thing he knew, she was over his shoulder and swearing like a sailor while his long strides moved down the hallway.

"What are you doing?" she squeaked.

"Getting you to shut up the only way I know how." He tossed her on the bed. She looked up at him with big eyes full of disbelief. He followed her down to the mattress and kissed her. For a moment, she resisted. Then he raised his head, gave them both time to catch their breath.

"Is this how you fight, Cowboy? You do your talking in the bedroom?"

"I don't want to fight with you." He caressed her cheek with the backs of his fingers. "I just want to love you."

She took several deep breaths, then curled her arms around his neck. "Then what are you waiting for?"

He probably needed to find a method of communicating, so she could have her say, and he didn't freak out. But for this moment in time, as he slid his hands up beneath her soft blouse and touched her warm bare skin, he couldn't think of a better way to have a heart-to-heart conversation.

Chapter 19

Call it what you wanted, but come Monday morning, the Wilder and Sons Hardware & Feed Fire Sale was kicking some major booty.

Charli stood back, watching the community line up with money in hand to cash in on some amazing deals and add to the coffers of the Wilder family's favorite charity.

Mrs. Duncan had even shown up and bought the yarn she'd ordered once upon a time. Seemed at half-off the original price, it was just the right color.

While Reno manned the cash register with a smile and small talk for everyone, Charli thought back on the past two amazing days they'd spent together. Not that they hadn't had amazing days and nights before that, but something special had happened. She knew how difficult it was for him to go through with the renovations. The more she'd pushed, the more he'd backed off. As soon as she'd agreed *not* to talk about the hardware store makeover until Monday, he'd relaxed. They'd ridden the horses out to the creek to have a picnic-style breakfast. They'd gone to a movie, where, in the dark, they'd held hands, and she'd laid her head on his shoulder.

They felt like a real couple.

If Charli had any reservations about being in love, they'd all been erased. The only question that remained was how deeply he felt about her.

His emotions bounced higher and further than she could keep up with. It was clear he cared about her, and he seemed happy to be settling into a relationship with her. They had fun. They could be joking one minute and discussing a serious subject the next. And their lovemaking was off the charts.

But love?

She didn't know if he was moving in that direction. Neither of them had spoken the words. While she knew it might be a little early to expect that from him, she did hope to feel a little more secure. Then again, hadn't that always been her problem in the past? Expect too much too soon? Or expect and not receive at all?

She glanced across the store to where he stood at the cash register handing back change to Chester Banks for the rope halter he'd just purchased.

Reno was the whole package.

And there was the essence of the problem.

Was he too good to be true?

Was she just setting herself up for another fall?

As easily as she could look at him and see herself spending the rest of her life with him, she didn't want to end up like her mother. She didn't want to have to continuously cajole the man she loved into loving her. She wanted him to give his love freely. Openly. And often.

Maybe that was just asking too much of him.

Maybe he'd never be able to move past his fears.

Maybe he'd never be able to break the habit of keeping others at bay for his own self-preservation.

Maybe he'd never let her get close enough to fall in love.

A long sigh slipped past her lips.

All were exactly the reasons she'd hesitated to tell him of her dream to move to Sweet and open up shop with his mother. He didn't look like he was in any hurry to promise her forever. And though she wanted nothing more than to be a part of this community, it was a very small town. She could be as boastful about picking up her life and moving to Texas as she wanted to be, but she wasn't sure she'd be so brave if Reno didn't want her in his life.

And so she'd wait.

Until the store renovations were finished.

Until they had nothing standing between them but the possibility of a future.

"Can't believe you got him to agree to this."

Charli's head came up to find Jackson Wilder standing beside her in dark blue pants and a shirt that bore the SAFD insignia. Even without the fire department uniform, Reno's younger brother was a stunner. A man more than one of her girlfriends back home would jump—literally—if they had the chance. His short hand-combed hair and suggestive smile would turn any woman's head. Any woman except her. Hers had already been turned.

"Believe me," she said, "he didn't agree easily. I had to use everything in my powers to get him to come to the dark side. And I wasn't beyond using bribery."

His head tilted. "Is that what they call it these days?"

"What do you mean?"

He shrugged. "You tell me."

Her spine stiffened. "Are you accusing me of using my body to get him to agree to the makeover?"

"I don't make accusations. I'm just keeping an eye out for my brother."

"You don't need to protect him from me."

Big, strong arms folded across the front of his shirt. "You sure about that?"

"Damned sure."

His chiseled lips lifted into a cautious smile. "Just checking."

"How did you even know there was something going on between us?"

"The smile he's been wearing. And . . . because he told me."

"He did?" Happiness leaped in her heart.

" 'Bout killed him to admit it."

And happiness was down on the mat.

"Look. I know you don't know me well, but I promise there is no way I would ever do anything to hurt your brother. I think he's been through enough."

"He has." Jackson nodded. "I guess that's why I keep my eye on him—not that he needs it. He can kick my ass sideways if he wanted to. He's a good man. I just want him to be happy."

"I want that for him too," she said.

"And yet . . ." His brows pulled tight over dark blue eyes. "You're leaving in seven days."

And didn't that just drop a bomb on everything.

Bare walls. Dusty floors. Empty shelves.

Reno stood inside his store and swallowed down the streak of panic clawing up his throat. In all the years he'd been in Sweet as a member of the Wilder family, he'd never seen the place barren. Echoes of his father's jolly laughter and heartfelt salutations had disappeared with each item removed.

Logic told Reno he was a grown man who shouldn't allow himself to be overrun with emotion, but there was still enough young boy left in him to be hit with a tidal wave that threatened to bring tears to his eyes.

"Are you okay?"

He turned at the soft touch on his arm and managed a nod.

"No, you're not." Charli wrapped her arms around him, enveloped him in her warmth. She looked up at him, gave him a tenuous smile. "I know this is extremely difficult for you. All I ask is that you trust me."

"I'll give it my best shot." Even to his own ears, his voice sounded raspy and unsure.

"Maybe it's best if you don't come around until it's finished."

"Are you locking me out?"

She reached up and cupped his cheek with her palm. Her dark eyes took on a seriousness he'd yet to see. "Yeah. I am."

"Wait a minute." He dropped his arms. Backed up a step. The sound created an echo in the cavernous room. "First you tell me you're going to change everything. Then you tell me I have to sell everything to pay for it. Now you're telling me I can't even be here?"

"Pretty much."

The smile curving her pretty mouth made Reno reach deep to keep the incredulity burning. "That hardly seems fair."

"I know. But you leave me no choice. A little birdie tells me that you will thwart all my efforts, and nothing will ever get done. So as much as I hate to, I'm giving you the boot."

He ran a hand through his hair and grabbed hold, trying to keep the top of his head from exploding. "Shit."

"You can do this, Reno." Her hand rubbed his back. "I know you can. And I promise, if you don't like the results, we'll put it back exactly the way it was minus the items we sold at the fire sale. And the dust."

"You will?" The tension in his face eased.

"Yes." She pointed a finger at him. "*After* the reveal is taped."

He let that ramble through his head a minute, surprised to realize that her offer calmed his nerves. Somewhat.

"Okay. Then we have a deal."

"We do?" Her head tilted slightly as if she didn't believe him. "And I didn't even have to promise sexual favors?"

He gave her a smile. "Those come without saying."

Her laughter danced over him and lightened the weight in his heart.

"Lucky for you I'm only too happy to comply."

He wrapped her in his arms. "Lucky for *us*."

A kiss seemed appropriate to seal the deal, but no sooner had their lips met than Jesse barged through the door.

"Whoa." He came to a halt and backed up a few steps. "Bad timing."

"Actually . . ." Charli grabbed him by the arm and pulled him into their circle. "You have *perfect* timing. I was just about to kick your brother out of here and lock the door."

Jesse ran a hand through hair that needed a cut months ago. "You okay with that, big brother?"

"She's not giving me a choice."

"I promised him sexual favors."

"Sweet." Jesse chuckled.

"Way to break the news that we're seeing each other," Reno said.

Charli clamped her hands on her hips. "Oh, like he and everyone else doesn't already know."

"*Everyone?*"

"Before you go," she said to Reno, "I need you to do something."

Reno turned to Jesse. "See how she orders me around?"

"Yeah." Jesse's brows lifted. "And I can tell you really hate it too."

Reno had no choice but to smile.

"Follow me, please," Charli said, leading them through the storeroom and out the back door. "See that stack of lumber right there? That's for you."

"What am I supposed to do with that?" Reno asked, wondering what the woman had up her sleeve now.

"Those wooden barrels next to the lumber are going to be used as a display. I need you to build a stand for them."

Reno laughed. "And now you have me *working* for you?"

"No." She flashed those straight, white teeth. "I'm giving you a project to do so you'll feel included and so you won't go crazy over the next couple of days."

"I can build that in an hour," Reno protested.

"Jesse? I'm charging you with making sure he takes his time and stays out of my way."

Jesse shrugged. "Might have to feed him a beer or two. Or take him out and tie him to a tree."

"If you tie him to a tree, do it toward dark, and give me the GPS location."

Jesse turned to Reno. "Lucky bastard."

Reno just smiled.

"And on that note, big brother, we are out of here."

Reno didn't fight the large hand that landed on his shoulder and led him out the front door. He was too busy imagining all the hot things Charli could do to him if he *was* tied up to a tree.

No sooner had he and Jesse crossed the street than an eighteen-wheeler pulled up in front of the store and parked, obscuring his view of the entire store.

"What the hell?" Reno stopped in his tracks.

Charli appeared around the front of the big truck's steel grille. "*This* is so you can't peek. It will be parked here all week." Her hands waved. "So consider this area *off-limits.*"

Jesse laughed. "She knows you pretty well."

"Yeah. I'm getting that." As his brother led him away, Reno went right back to the tree fantasy she'd planted in his imagination.

Day two of the store renovations arrived, and Reno watched Charli grumble as she rolled out of bed at o'dark thirty. He'd kept her up late. Not to be mean but because he knew their time together was drawing to a close, and he wanted as much of her as he could get. What he planned to do after she left? He had no idea. Didn't even want to think about it.

He'd learned the hard way that when people quickly disappeared from your life, their images in your mind began to fade. He didn't want Charli's smile to disappear. Or the look of passion in her eyes when he made love to her. Or the quiet peacefulness that settled on her face as she slept.

While she took a shower, he let the dogs out, then made a pot of coffee. When she came into the kitchen, wearing nothing but a towel, it was everything he could do not to unravel it and take her back to bed. He thought back to that first night, when he'd knocked on the apartment door and she'd answered all wrapped up in a fluffy robe and looking like a marshmallow peep. That night seemed so long ago, when in reality it had only been a little over five weeks.

How things had changed since then.

He'd started out wanting her gone. And now . . .

he just wanted her to stay. Even if there was still that ever-present fear in the back of his mind.

"How's the barrel display coming?" she asked.

"Piece of cake." He poured her a steaming cup of coffee. "How's my store?"

"*Icing* on the cake." She rose to her tiptoes, clutched her towel together, and gave him a kiss.

"You know," he said, "if you drop that towel, it will make breakfast a whole lot more interesting."

"Last *night* was interesting. Who'd have thought you could get so much mileage from a bandana?"

He curved his arm around her waist and pulled her close. "Stick with me, and I'll show you a million different ways to use a lariat too."

"Do tell, Cowboy."

At least she hadn't come back with a warning that she wouldn't be here long enough to find out.

He handed her the cup of coffee, which she set down on the table before securing the bath towel by tucking the tail between her breasts. Too bad. There went any hopes of its coming undone somewhere between coffee and biscuits.

"Is this a waffle morning? Or eggs?" he asked.

"Coffee and granola bar, I'm afraid. I need to get to the store early. It's a big day."

"Why?" Panic struck. "What's going on?"

"Well . . ." She sipped her coffee, filling the air with an uncomfortable pause. "For starters, we're tearing out the back wall to expand the square footage, then we're ripping the roof off to make a second story, and—"

"*No* tearing and *no* ripping. I never agreed to that."

"Really?" She batted her eyelashes. "Did you read the small print in the contract?"

"Holy shit, Charli." His heart raced. "Please tell me you're kidding."

"I'm kidding."

He checked her expression, which told him nothing. "You swear?"

"Cowboy, if I told you what we were doing to the store, you'd have an opinion a mile wide. I told you if you didn't like what we'd done, we'd put it back the way it was. How could we do that if we tore out walls?"

When he leaned over her to refill her coffee, she curled her fingers into his T-shirt and pulled him down to eye level.

"Trust me," she said.

He made an effort to do just that.

And then he took her back to bed.

In the course of a morning and afternoon, Reno learned that with the exception of the garden—which had taken a midsummer turn from dry to scorched—and riding out to check the herd, there was little to do around his place. After he rode back to his mom's house, he found her flitting around like a butterfly, singing to herself. Giggling at some private joke.

Weird.

It didn't take long before she sucked him into helping her move this or that. She'd asked him his opinion on whether a wreath would look better on the wall or a picture. If a red or gold candle looked better in an old lantern she'd rescued years ago from Shorty Blackstock's farm.

He'd finally escaped out to the barn, so he didn't have to help her hang curtains. Or break up little sticks and pieces of bark to decorate a wall mirror. Or, for crying out loud, make a silk flower arrangement. His penance was he had to suffer the ever-curious and amorous attentions of Miss Giddy, who today sported a bright yellow ribbon around her neck.

As the day crawled on, it seemed like he looked at his watch about every ten minutes. After several hours passed, he figured the term *stir-crazy* was probably a description that fit him well. Then again, so would the word *fearful*.

What would he do if he walked into the store and found everything that reminded him of his dad, gone?

How could he go in there every day and not feel his father's spirit? Hear his laughter? The memories faded more and more with each passing day. He didn't want to lose it all. Just the thought made him sick to his stomach.

He needed to keep busy. Keep his mind occupied, so it didn't have the chance to freeze with fear. But that didn't mean he wanted to help his mother inside the house.

Around three o'clock, he couldn't escape when she came into the barn, where he'd kept busy by restacking hay bales. The job was dusty and itchy, but at least it kept his mind off what was going on at the store. Or Charli's leaving once it was done.

"Sugarplum, you've been out here for too long

without something to drink." She held up a bottle of Shiner.

He pushed the bale of hay into place, ran the long sleeve of his shirt across his forehead, and accepted her offering. The ale went down cold, crisp, and refreshing.

"Thanks, Mom."

She joined him by plopping down on a bale and sipping on a bottle of root beer. "I know you've been avoiding the house because of all the changes I'm making. I just thought maybe it was time."

Admittedly, he didn't like seeing all the comforts of the home he'd grown up in taken down piece by piece, but that was only part of the reason he'd stayed outside.

"Or maybe I figured you'd have me sewing aprons and arranging flowers."

She chuckled. "I'd never dream of asking you to do anything froufrouish."

"Figured if you had something heavy you wanted moved or something put up you couldn't do by yourself, you'd ask." He pulled down a bale and sat beside her. For a moment, the only sound that rustled through the barn was the cooing of a pigeon who'd taken up residence in the rafters.

"So why are you out here in the heat doing a job that's already been done?"

He shrugged. Lifted the bottle to his mouth and took a long pull. "Hiding out, I guess. Realized without access to the store, there's not a whole lot going on."

His mother leaned back. "Are you bored, son?"

"Maybe."

"Maybe you've just gotten used to having a little company these days?"

He smiled. "You spying on me?"

"Don't need to spy. Anyone with eyeballs in their head can see you and Charli are smitten with each other."

"*Smitten?*" Reno laughed. He'd hardly call what he and Charli had *smitten*. Then again, other than hot for each other or short-term, he wasn't sure how their relationship could be labeled.

"You've been alone so long, it must be nice to have someone to talk to," his mother said.

"I guess."

"Someone to share ideas with."

"Sure."

"Someone to make plans with," she said.

"I don't know if I'd go that far."

His mother sighed. Took a drink from her bottle of soda. Then stood. "Guess I'd best get back to my work."

"Other than flower arranging, you need any help in there?"

She leaned down and kissed the top of his head. "No, sugarplum, you just stay out here and keep hiding. I'm sure that will solve everything."

As she walked away, he cocked his head.

What the hell was that all about?

Lately, his mother made less and less sense. Though Jackson still inhabited his old bedroom, and Izzy made an appearance a couple times a week, his mom probably just needed a little more company. After having had a houseful of rowdy boys, it must get pretty quiet in that big, rambling place.

He slugged down the rest of the beer and stood. Brushed the hay off the back of his pants and headed toward the house.

For his mother, he guessed he could put aside his testosterone for a few hours to hang curtains and play with flowers.

Maybe then he could figure out what was going on inside her head.

Chapter 20

Late Saturday afternoon rolled around with a clear blue sky and heavy anticipation. Only the final touches remained on the hardware-store makeover. Charli bustled around the interior, placing items on the shelves and making sure everything looked perfect. The nerves in her stomach had increased from butterfly flutters to California-sized earthquakes.

For most reveals, she naturally felt a little anxious—a little concerned that her designs wouldn't quite meet expectations. This reveal, however, was unlike any other.

This one was personal.

She couldn't bear to see the disappointment on Reno's face if she let him down. And as promised, if he didn't like it, they'd have to put it back the way it was. In twenty-four hours.

Impossible.

She prayed he'd like the results.

Once the reveal was over, she planned to tell him

that after her contract was up, she'd like to come back to Sweet and make it her home. She'd tell him about the discussion she and his mother had had about opening a business together.

She hoped he'd be encouraged by her plans. She hoped he'd want to take their relationship further. She prayed he'd be patient and understand that she might have to leave for a short time, but that she'd be back to make a life with him if that's what was in his heart.

But even for a girl who hit her knees on a regular basis, Charli knew that was a heck of a lot of hoping and praying.

Prereveal, Reno stood across the street from his hardware store, waiting impatiently for the moment to be over. Feeling like he had a ticking time bomb attached to his chest. While everyone around him buzzed with excitement, the muscles in his neck twisted, and his stomach knotted. Apparently, the town had planned a big wrap party for afterward, but he wasn't even sure he could make it through the next hour of waiting without tossing his cookies.

He knew the hard work Charli had put into his store, as she'd come home every night exhausted. She hadn't given him a single clue as to what might be going on within those old walls, and, admittedly, that had been killing him all week. He didn't like handing control over to someone else. Most often he'd come out the other side disappointed or devastated. But Charli had convinced him she'd do right by the traditions he held close to his heart. And he had to trust that she'd be true to her word.

If the wait for the reveal weren't nerve-wracking enough, sometime tomorrow she and her crew would pack up their tools and roll out of town.

So what the hell was he supposed to do then?

Ask her to stay? Chances she'd say no were pretty high. He wanted to believe she'd been telling the truth when she'd said she felt like she belonged in Sweet. But she had a career that moved her around. A lot. And she hadn't mentioned plans to make any one place permanent.

He could think he knew her, but did he really? How well could you get to know a person in just six weeks? Maybe her hooking up with someone on location wasn't that unusual for her. He gave his head a hard shake, knowing the thought was complete and utter bullshit before it had even spilled from his brain.

Over the past few years, he'd become a pro at dodging life. He made a great observer but not such a good participant. As his mother said, it was time to move on. But could he? And what was waiting for him if he did? He'd be a fool to think there were guarantees in life. He'd just like a little gut instinct to tell him what to do. Unfortunately for him, his gut was currently too nauseous to even speak the English language.

The only thing clear to him at that moment was that his life was about to change in a big way. And he just wasn't sure he was ready for it.

"Guess things can go back to normal now," Jackson said, hitching Izzy up on his hip while holding her little pink, pearl-handled purse in his free hand. The action did nothing to take away from

Jackson's masculinity and everything to make the single ladies in the crowd melt and wonder where they could fit into his life and how they could get into his bed.

"Depends on what you want to call normal," Reno said. In his *pre*-Charli world, normal equaled a silent house. No one to make him laugh. No one to hold at night.

Yeah. Normal sucked.

He glanced across the barricaded street to the gray-haired group from the senior center. It seemed so long ago Charli and company had invaded the town and taken over the ramshackle rock-faced building. And so long ago when he'd sworn to find a way to boot her and her ever-present cameras from his town. Who knew he'd end up helping her make the center a better place for the over-sixty crowd? He must have had sucker stamped on his forehead from the moment Charli pulled into town.

"You okay?" Jackson juggled Izzy's purse and her half-eaten cupcake so she could lay her sleepy head on his shoulder.

"Not sure. But if you asked my stomach, it would give you a definitive *no*."

Like a hurricane-force wind, Jesse joined them. "Did you see Mom?"

"Yeah. About ten minutes ago," Jackson answered.

"No," Jesse corrected. "Did you *see* Mom."

"Jess, she's right th—"

All their heads turned at the same time when they heard their mother's laughter. No. Scratch that. When they heard their mother giggle.

Holy shit.

Reno searched over the tops of heads and found her standing a few feet away from the senior-center crowd. With a man.

"Who *is* that?" Reno asked.

"Don't know," Jesse answered.

"He was at the party," Jackson said. "I saw him talking to . . . damn it."

"What?" Reno and Jesse said at the same time.

"I saw him talking to her near the dance floor. Then they both disappeared."

"Disappeared to where?" Jesse asked.

"How the hell should I know?" Jackson's growl brought Izzy's head up. She rubbed her eyes and started to whimper.

"I want Mommy."

"Okay, baby girl. Hang on just a second." Jackson kissed the top of her curly hair.

Fiona showed up at the sound of her daughter's whine. "She's had a long day," she said, taking Izzy into her arms.

"Thanks, Fi," Jackson said. "You're the best."

"Uh-huh." She leaned in and gave him a kiss on the cheek.

The whole scene twisted Reno's gut. Jackson and Fiona had made a good couple. But just like so many other things, it hadn't been meant to be.

"Let's go talk to Mom," Jesse said, after Fiona and Izzy were out of earshot.

"And say what?" Reno asked.

"And ask her about *Mr. Mysterious*," Jackson said, as if Reno had taken a shot of stupid.

"You know Mom," Reno said in defense. "He's

probably new in town, and she's always been a member of the welcoming committee."

"I don't think so."

Both Reno and Jackson followed the direction of Jesse's gaze to find their mother still talking to the man and . . . twirling a lock of her big blond hair.

"Uh-oh." Jackson took the first step. As they had when they were younger, Reno and Jesse banded together with their little brother, who was once again leading them down the path of trouble.

When they reached the other side of the street, Reno felt a jolt rip through his heart. The last time he'd seen that smile on his mother's face, she'd been looking at his father as he'd led her into a waltz around the kitchen. That had been before Jared had been killed, and their world had fallen apart.

"Let *me* talk to her." Reno curled his fingers into his palms to prevent his hands from shaking. "You guys are too wired up."

Beneath their breaths, his brothers mumbled and muttered, which only proved that he was the right one to do the talking.

When they walked up to where their mother stood with the stranger, Reno realized that the man had his hand on her back in a gesture of familiarity.

"Is this guy bothering you, Mom?" Jackson asked.

So much for letting Reno do the talking.

"Don't be silly," she said, looking none too happy that her boys had obviously crashed her party. "I've known Martin since he moved here a while back. We have a lot in common."

"Like what?" Jesse asked.

"I'm sorry we've not met before," the silver-haired man said. "Martin Lane. I bought the old Pritchard place about three months ago." He offered his hand, which Reno shook and Jackson and Jesse stared at before they finally reciprocated.

"I hope you'll excuse my boys, Martin. I raised them to have better manners."

"It's all right, Jana."

Jana?

Reno cringed. The stranger and his mother were on a first-name basis? And she was already looking at him like *that*?

Their mother patted the man on the arm. "You don't mind if I have a little chat with them alone, do you?"

"Of course not." Martin Lane bowed away. "I'll catch up with you later."

"Like hell he will," Jackson said, as soon as the man walked away.

"Jackson Jeremiah Wilder! What has gotten into you?" Their mother's glare cut to all of them. "What's gotten into *all* of you?"

Reno could see the flush of anger on his mother's cheeks. "You caught us off guard with Mr. Lane," he explained. "We just wanted to make sure you were safe."

"Of course I'm safe. How can I not be with three grown sons who don't think I'm mature enough to make friends with a new member of our community?"

"Pardon me for being up front, Mom," Jesse said, "but the way you were looking at him seemed like a little more than friendship."

Her hands slammed onto her hips. "So what if it is?"

"Are you sure you're ready for that?" Reno asked, trying to be as careful with what he said as well as the way he said it.

"Am I ready for what? To move on with my life? Funny *you* should bring that up, Reno." She looked up at him, then shared that frown with his brothers too. "The answer is yes. I'm ready to move on with my life. Because what's the alternative? The grave? I give that a big hell *no*."

Jackson blinked. "Mom, I don't think—"

"Exactly!" Her tone was knife sharp. "How dare you think I'm not smart enough to know what I want or what's best for *me*. *Me*. Not *you*. I've dedicated my life to you boys. Well, now it's my turn to have a little fun. And as grown men, y'all should understand that I'm not looking for someone to replace your father."

Reno's heart hit his stomach when her lip quivered, and mist floated in her eyes.

"I'm lonely," she said matter-of-fact. "All y'all have your own lives to do with as you please. Why can't I have mine?" A breath of air pushed from her lungs. "If you can't accept that now, then stay the hell away till you can."

With a go-to-hell glare Reno had *never* seen, she walked away.

"Fuck," Jackson said.

There were no better words to relay the emotion of that moment.

Reno shoved his hands into his pockets. The time bomb exploded. His mother was putting his father behind her. Charli was leaving. And now he had to walk into that store, where all his wonderful memories of the man who'd saved his life had been stripped away.

Fuck.

As the last rays of sunlight lit up the western sky in shades of pink and gold, the earthquakes in Charli's stomach rolled into hurricane-force waves of nausea and stress.

This was it.

The moment when the Sweet, Texas, episodes for *My New Town* came to an end. The moment when she'd find out whether Reno would be pleased with her renovations. The moment when she'd have to face whether they had any hope of a future together.

As the residents of the town gathered behind the cameras, and the Wilder family gathered in front, Charli immediately recognized that something was very wrong.

To maintain spontaneity, she'd purposely not spoken to the family beforehand. Now, as she led them to the mark where the cameras could record their expressions and reactions once the eighteen-wheeler was moved, she sensed a tension so tight, the air around them virtually snapped.

Charli squeezed Reno's arm and looked up into his dark wary eyes. Tonight, the splash of silver hair at his temples was seemingly pronounced, as if he'd grown new ones over the past few days. Hours. His dimples were completely buried.

"Everything okay?" she asked, knowing all was not.

He stared at the eighteen-wheeler still parked in front of the store and gave a curt nod that gave away nothing.

She looked at Jana, Jackson, and Jesse, who stood beside him—though they definitely were not presented as a unit.

Confused, Charli was hesitant to continue. Usually, the participants were nervous, eager, and maybe a little on edge. They were not often wearing explosive expressions with hostility stiffening their stance.

"Does anyone need a moment before we do the reveal?" she asked.

Reno's brows slammed together. "For what?"

"I don't know." She glanced at the family. "Maybe for everyone to find their happy place?"

"Let's just get it over with."

Reno's tone was sharp, and Charli wasn't sure why it was directed at her. But they were burning daylight, and even if the Wilder family wasn't quite ready, everyone else involved with the show was primed to get on down the road.

"All righty then." Apprehension tingled at the back of her neck.

There would be time after the reveal to figure out the problem. For now, even as insensitive as it seemed, she had a show to do. She glanced behind the cameras to where Sarah stood holding Pumpkin, who'd come along to join the party. Her assistant gave her a thumbs-up. Charli gave the "Let's roll" cue to Max, pushed aside her uncertainty, and reached deep for the enjoyment she usually achieved in a reveal.

The camera lights blinked on, and Charli pasted on her cheerleader smile. "Hi. I'm Charlotte Brooks. Welcome to *My New Town*. Today we're deep in the heart of Texas Hill Country, where, six weeks ago, our production crew rolled into downtown Sweet. With the help of the entire community, we took on the challenge of refreshing some of the historic buildings on Main Street. Wilder and Sons Hardware and Feed wraps up our project list. And we're glad you're here with us today for the big reveal."

She glanced at the silent and apprehensive family gathered around her and made some brief introductions to the viewing audience. Then, with a little professional wheedling, she coaxed Jana into making some comments about the entire experience. Reno remained silent, as did Jackson and Jesse.

For the first time since she'd joined the show, Charli was unsure of how to cover dead air. With Max behind the camera making a move-it-along twirl with his finger, she trudged on.

"I know you're all very excited to see what we've done with your store, so without further ado . . ." She gave the truck driver a whistle, and the diesel engine rumbled to life. The wheels rolled away from the curb. Slowly, foot by foot, the hardware store came into view. The crowd appropriately gasped. The Wilders remained silent.

Panic lit a fire beneath Charli's heart as she looked up into Reno's unreadable reaction. She turned to look at the other members of the family, who stood at her sides with identical blank stares.

They hated it.

For a breathless moment, dread hammered inside

Charli's head. Then Jana finally broke through the ice in the air.

"It's lovely," she said. "The daisy-filled red buckets hanging out front really add a sense of welcome."

"It looks the same, but better," Jackson added.

Jesse nodded.

Nothing from Reno.

"Oh." Charli released a heavy sigh. "I'm so relieved. Come on, and I'll point out what we did. Then we can all go inside to see how you feel about what we did in there."

"I'm looking forward to it," Jana said with little enthusiasm.

The hurricane in Charli's stomach leveled out to a tropical storm. While the cameras rolled, she led them all toward the store, pointing out the new cedar siding, posts, boardwalk, and metal awning. The paint trim had been sanded and reapplied with a fresh coat of white. And the front window now sported turn-of-the-century lettering including the established date from when Joe Wilder had first opened the doors.

Reno wrapped his large hand around a post as they moved up onto the boardwalk. He paused as she opened the front door.

"It's going to be okay." She took his hand. "I promise."

At his almost imperceptible nod, Charli stepped back and allowed the family to be the first to walk into the store.

The first thing Reno did was to look up at the back wall, where she'd put up barn-wood-framed sepia-toned photos. Jana had helped her go through the old photos taken at the hardware store throughout the years. In some, Joe Wilder was surrounded by his boys at various ages. Others were candid and taken while he assisted customers. A few were of Joe and Reno working side by side. Charli hoped the gallery would help keep alive a sense of the man who'd been such a positive influence on Reno's life.

"Oh." Jana gasped, while the boys remained silent. "The photos are just wonderful."

Wanting to hear something—anything—from Reno, Charli's heart took a plunge. Her eyes misted. While she recovered, she urged the family to discover the rest of the newly organized yet still relatively intact store. Including Reno's barrel display, which now contained bulk pet treats.

In a surreal state, she managed to follow them about, pointing out specific treatments, and almost absently making appropriate comments for the camera. But all she could wonder was why Reno had failed to react—even negatively. He seemed to be running on autopilot. And that really worried her.

"What do you think?" she finally asked him.

He avoided her eyes. "It'll do."

It'll do?

Yeah. Not really what she wanted or expected to hear.

And still, it told her nothing.

Heart racing, Reno stood in the middle of his store, trying to take in all the changes and trying to disregard the cameras shoved in his face. Beside him, Charli asked a question he could barely hear over the loud buzz in his ears. He managed to mutter some half-ass response past the knot in his throat.

Everything in the place appeared cleaner and more organized. Charli had obviously tried very hard to add warmth to what was otherwise a place to buy screwdrivers and alfalfa cubes. The tractor-seat stools and checkerboard tabletop presented a bit of whimsy. The photos of his father were a nice touch. The inclusion of the broken-down desk where the man had worked for years and taken his last breath proved Charli had paid attention to Reno's concerns.

But the spirit of his father was gone.

Reno could no longer picture his father behind the renovated counter or putting up stock on the new and improved shelves.

The buzz in his ears became unbearable, and Reno knew he had to get the hell out of there.

Without a word, he turned and walked out.

Panic shot through Charli's heart as Reno walked out. The despair that darkened his face as she'd tried to draw him into the conversation spoke volumes of what must have been going through his mind. Because the show was not live, she had the privilege to halt the taping. She sent a silent plea to Max, who called for the cameras to be turned off.

"I'll go talk to him," Jana said, her motherly instincts obviously stronger than whatever had transpired before they'd begun to tape the reveal.

"Let me," Charli said. "Please?"

Jana nodded.

Charli caught up with him just as he reached his truck. "Hey. Wait a second."

He disregarded her and opened the door. She put herself between him and the big vehicle. As if he'd been burned, he put distance between them. Crossed his arms. And seemed to completely shut down.

"Talk to me," she said. "What's going on?"

For a long moment, he just stood there staring at the pavement. Breathing in. Breathing out.

And breaking her heart.

"I can't help you if you won't tell me what's wrong," she said.

His head jerked up. "Maybe I don't want your help. Maybe you've done enough."

"Whoa." She lifted her hands. "There's no need to—"

"You shouldn't have pushed for this, Charli," he said.

"So . . . whatever is going on here is all *my* fault?"

"It must be easy to just drop into people's lives, change everything whether they want it or not, then take off," he growled. "You don't have to face the consequences that way, do you?"

"How can you say that? That's the worst part of my job." A cold chill ran up her back. "Because when I do *"drop in,"* I find people who have everything that *I* want. Yet it always seems to be out of my reach. All I've ever wanted was someplace to put down roots. Where people love you no matter how stupidly you behave. Somewhere—some*one*—to call home. It amazes me how easy something like that can be taken for granted."

He looked away.

"It's obvious you aren't happy with the changes I've made to your store. I apologize." She took a step back and leaned against the truck for support. "But I promised if you didn't like it, I'd put it back the way it was. And I will. So what's got you wound up so tight?"

"It's not just the store."

"Then what is it?" She wanted to reach out and touch him. Comfort him. But his body language screamed "hands off."

"I wouldn't even know where to start."

"Just start someplace," she said.

"Everything's wrong. Moving too fast." He shook his head. "Changing."

In her mind, Charli flashed back to the expressions and body language she'd witnessed just before the cameras started to roll. Then her mind zipped back even further to something Jana had said the day she'd shown Charli her treasure-filled barn.

"The boys are not ready for me to take that plunge."

Realization dawned. "Does this have something to do with your mother wanting to date?"

His head came up. Eyes narrowed. "You knew?"

She shrugged. "It may have come up."

A muscle in his jaw contracted once. Twice. "And you didn't say anything to me?"

"She asked me not to."

"Why?"

Charli pressed her lips together. "Oh. I don't know. Maybe because you'd react just as you're doing right now?"

"My brothers and I had a right to know."

"But it wasn't my place to tell you. It was hers."

Brows tight over tired, haunted eyes, he said, "You just don't get it, do you?"

"I get it. Clearly." She took a breath to keep from losing her cool because that certainly wouldn't help. And only honesty was going to get it settled. "I know your anger is misplaced. And I know this has nothing to do with anyone else. This is all *you*, Reno."

"What the hell are you talking about?"

"I know you loved your father, your brother, and Diana very much. And I know your grief has consumed you. But this isn't about them. This is about your not wanting to let go. You think if you move forward and live your life, you'll be disloyal to them. But you're wrong. If you live your life, their memories will thrive. Through you. Don't you think they'd want that?"

He looked away.

"You haven't grieved alone, Reno. Your mother has suffered too. Your father was the boy she fell in love with. The man she built a home and family with. And she misses him terribly. But if he's the man I think he was, he wouldn't want her to be miserable. And she isn't ready to lie down and die. She's ready to live the rest of her life with as much joy as she can find."

Charli took a breath. "You should be too." She planted her feet in preparation for the force of his bitter defense.

Though his body remained tense, when he finally spoke, it was clear the fight in him had deflated. "Nothing is ever as cut-and-dried as it seems."

"No. It's not. I'm sorry you've lost so many people you love," she said softly. "I wish I could bring them all back. I wish I could tell you that you'll never lose anyone you love ever again. But I can't. All I can tell you is that your mother deserves the opportunity to find happiness. And so do you."

Heeding her own advice, she took a chance. Took a step closer. Placed her hand on his arm and let the warmth seep through her fingers. "I'm in love with you, Reno."

His unreadable dark eyes searched her face.

"I know I'm a risk. I know there will be challenges . . . things to work out. I know I'm not perfect. I'll annoy you, piss you off, say stupid stuff, then take it all back. But I guarantee you will *never* find another woman who loves you more than me. If you're ready to take a chance and step outside that box you've built around yourself, I'm here."

He hesitated for several long, painful breaths that told her everything she didn't want to know but needed to just the same.

He wasn't ready to move forward.

At least not with her.

She'd taken a chance. Again. And she'd failed. Again. She'd jumped too soon. Let her heart rule her head. And now here she was, having the same conversation with a man who couldn't or wouldn't love her back. Her ridiculous man ban hadn't worked because the moment she'd met Reno, she'd jumped ship and dove headfirst into love. Again.

When would she ever learn?

"Charli, I—"

"No need to make excuses. I get it." She withdrew

her trembling hand. Sucked in a lungful of courage. "But as much as I love you, I'm not going to beg you to love me back. I'm not going to cajole you the way my mother did my father just so *you'll* be happy."

If she wanted to go that path, she could tell him right now that she'd love nothing more than to stay in Sweet. Make a life here. But really, what was the point?

"*I* deserve to be happy too." Tears stung her eyes, and she didn't even try to stop them. "And if you can't—or won't—make this relationship a two-way street, then we really have nothing more to say."

She took a step back. Waited several heartbeats for him to respond.

Say something, she pleaded silently. *Take me in your arms and make this be okay.*

He only stood there—motionless—and looked at her like he hadn't really heard a word she'd said. Or didn't care.

As she turned away, her body shook with tethered emotion. Her heart cried out for him to stop her. To tell her he was ready to take that step.

To tell her he loved her.

But he didn't.

He let her walk away.

The following morning, Reno stood inside his store looking around at all the changes. Exhaustion ate into his soul.

Until the early hours of dawn, he'd waited for the sound of Charli's Hummer to roll into the driveway and park near the barn.

That sound never came.

She'd never come back to gather her things. To tell him good-bye. To tell him what a stupid ass he'd been.

From the back veranda, he'd looked out over the yard, the garden, and the wide-open meadow beyond. He'd had an urge to run. To ride. To dunk his head in a cold bucket of water. When his pity party ended, he knew he needed to talk to her. Explain himself. Apologize. Figuring her and the crew would still be putting the place back together, he headed to the store.

It wasn't every day a beautiful woman told him she was in love with him—even with all his faults and fears.

She was right.

He'd been afraid to let go.

She was right.

He wasn't the only one who'd suffered from the losses. His mother had lost a husband, a best friend, a lover, and her firstborn son. Jesse, Jackson, and Jake had lost their big brother. And Diana's parents had lost not one, but both their daughters. And yet they'd all somehow managed to put one foot in front of the other and move forward. He had not.

She was right.

His mother deserved to find happiness. And no one had the right to stand in her way. His father had died. She hadn't. She deserved to live and be happy.

Realization didn't always come easy. Didn't always come when it should. Since the deaths, Reno believed his grief was a way to pay respect. To show his loyalty. But all this time, he'd been nothing but a coward. Hiding behind the grief. Making excuses for reasons not to live.

She was right.

He deserved to find happiness.

He glanced around the store. At all the thoughtful ways Charli had managed to preserve the spirit of what had once been the heart and soul of his universe. Of what she knew meant more to him than breath.

The realization came too late.

Charli was gone.

He'd lost again.

This time he had no one to blame but himself.

"I told her to leave it the way it was."

Reno turned to find his mother in the doorway. Bright sunshine poured in behind her, and church bells rang in the distance.

"I wondered," he said, glancing up at a photo in the center of the new gallery. The picture was of him and Jared sitting in a wheelbarrow laughing while their father held the handles. "I remember that day." He pointed to the photo and smiled. "Jared and I thought we'd come down and give Dad a hand in the store. Guess we were more trouble than help because Dad set us both in the wheelbarrow and wheeled us right out the door."

"I remember too. I took that photo," his mother said. "I'd come down looking for you two rascals. Right after I took that shot, your daddy wheeled you out to my truck and tossed you both in the back with a smack on the behinds for scaring the living daylights out of me with your disappearing act."

Smiling, Reno nodded. "I remember."

She closed the door and walked up to him. Cupped his cheek in her hand. "See that, son? That's what memories are supposed to do. They're supposed to make you smile. Warm your heart. They're not supposed to tear you apart. Those memories— those smiles—keep them alive."

"That's what Charli said."

His mother nodded. Patted his cheek. "She wanted to put everything back the way it was. Said she promised that's what she'd do if you didn't like the changes."

"She did make that promise."

"I told her to leave it. I think it looks wonderful."

"So do I."

"But that's not what you told her."

He shook his head.

"Why?"

"Because I didn't realize until I stood in here this morning that these are all just . . . things. They can't bring someone back. And they can't help you make new memories. They're just . . . objects."

She smiled. "It's so nice to see you finally get a clue."

"Took long enough."

"Better late than never."

At the moment, he couldn't agree. Because taking so long had now cost him more than he'd been willing to lose.

"I'm sorry about last night," he said, taking his

mother's hand. "I'm sorry to be so selfish that I couldn't see how lonely you've been."

"I know, sugarplum." She squeezed his hand. "I know."

A sigh of relief expanded his chest.

"I'm probably going to date," she said.

"Okay."

She gave him a wistful smile. "I might even fall in love again."

Surprised to discover how much that made him happy, he leaned down and kissed her cheek. "I hope you do."

Chapter 21

Something inside her had died.

Charli studied the little building in Lakeside, Oregon, that had been everything from a grocery store to a video store. Currently, it was being operated as a restaurant. A diner, to be exact. The exterior architecture was midcentury and the menu reflected the era's love of burgers, fries, and milk shakes. But due to the poor condition of the building, it looked unappealing, and the customers had dwindled. Like the other places she'd brought back to life, it needed her TLC.

Any other day, she could have come up with a quick design to make the best use of what already existed. Today, she could not.

The production crew had rolled into town a few days before. She'd done some preliminary sketches from photos the location scouts had given her. But as easy as black-and-white-tiled floors with red 1950s soda-fountain accents might seem, Charli couldn't get her mind off a certain hardware store she'd left behind.

As she sat out front of the diner on the curb, the sun broke through a layer of clouds and offered a ray of warmth on the late-summer day. Much to her surprise, the coast in Oregon was much cooler than the beaches in Southern California. And the gloominess did nothing to perk up her current funk.

She'd made a promise to Reno that she'd put the store back the way it was if he didn't like it. Well, he'd hated it. And then she'd skipped out of town, leaving it just as it was. Jana—whom she'd not talked to since she'd left Sweet—had convinced her that it would be fine. But Charli felt that she'd let Reno down.

And wasn't that the crux of her funk.

In the end, they hadn't aired the hardware store portion of the makeover. Any references to Wilder and Sons or the Wilder family had been expertly cut as though they never existed. Charli realized that was best. Later, down the road, she didn't want to have to see reruns that would remind her of what she'd thought she'd had with Reno, only to be fooled once again.

She hadn't gone back to the apartment to gather her things. T-shirts and tennis shoes were easily replaceable. But the love she'd developed for Reno? Not so much. Somehow, she'd move on without him. But it wouldn't happen anytime soon.

In the meantime, she needed to find her happy place. After that, figuring out the rest of her life should be easy cheesy. Then again, delusional was a very interesting place to dwell.

She'd much rather be in Sweet.

While the crew inside the diner pulled down everything to the bare walls, Charli put her head down, put pencil to paper, and began to sketch.

A ray of sunshine danced over the top of Charli's bent head as Reno parked his truck down the street from where the production crew of *My New Town* had set up shop. There were trucks and trailers everywhere. Commotion swirled around the oblivious brunette sitting on the curb, working away with her pencil and paper.

His heartbeat tripped all over itself at the sight of her. Though it had been only a week, it felt like an eternity since he'd held her in his arms.

If she'd take him back, he'd never let her go again.

She was worth any risk, and without her, he'd be miserable. He'd never told her how he felt. But that was a mistake he'd never make again.

He got out of the truck, closed the door behind him, and walked down the street. She didn't notice him until he sat down on the curb beside her.

"I'm not sure I'm ever going to get this right," she said, sliding the sketch pad over onto his knee. "What do you th—"

She looked up. Obviously expecting someone else, her mouth dropped open. "Reno."

He smiled. "Hi."

Confusion and surprise swirled in her eyes. "What are you doing *here*?"

"Looking for you."

"Why?"

"Because I love you, Charli." As he slid his hands to the sides of her face, the declaration set him free. "And I want to be here or wherever you are. I want to hold you so tight that I can still feel you after you leave. Feel your heartbeat against mine. Feel your breath against my cheek in the morning when I wake up."

Her beautiful face crumpled, and tears filled her eyes. He took her hands in his.

"You were right. About everything," he said. "I've been hiding for too long, thinking it was safer. Easier. Thinking I would be disloyal to Jared, my dad, and Diana if I continued to live when they couldn't. But then you came into my life, and you yanked the lid off that box I've been hiding in."

"Well, I am pretty good for ripping things apart." Her beautiful mouth lifted in a tentative smile.

"You're good for *me*." His lungs expanded, and his heart soared with liberation. "And I want to be good for you."

"I . . . don't know what to say."

"Say you still love me." His hands tightened around hers. "Say you'll give me a chance to prove myself to you."

"Oh . . ." Her hand lifted, and her warm fingers caressed his cheek. "Reno, you don't have to prove yourself to me. I do love you."

Relief and exhilaration filled that dark, empty space in his soul as he bent his head and lightly touched his mouth to hers. "At Paige and Aiden's wedding, I told you I didn't have all the answers. I told you I wouldn't make promises. Well, I still may not have all the answers, but I'll definitely make a promise to love you for the rest of my life. I'm so sorry I didn't tell you before. I wanted to. But—"

Her fingers trembled as she pressed them to his lips. "There are no deadlines on telling someone you love them." And then she smiled. "But if you don't mind, I'd like to hear it again."

"I'll say it as often as you want." He smiled all the way from his heart. "I love you, Charlotte Brooks."

In the back of the Hummer, Bear and Pumpkin were cuddled up as Charli instructed Reno where to turn. The quaint little bed-and-breakfast where she'd been staying had a beautiful ocean view and a romantic terrace. She didn't think the nice couple who owned the place would mind a few extra guests. Even if one of them had fur.

"Are you sure you've got someone to watch the hardware store while you're gone?" she asked.

"Got it covered."

"And you swear you like the changes I made?"

He clasped his hand over hers and squeezed. "Love them."

"And your brothers won't mind doing your share of the ranching?"

"I've covered them a mess of times. It's their turn."

"I'll admit. I am going to miss seeing you up on that horse with that hat and those spurs on." She smiled and leaned across the seat to steal a kiss. "You are one hot cowboy."

"If you like them that much, I'm sure I can arrange something."

She laughed. "At least I'll only have to wait a few weeks."

"Where to after that?" he asked.

"Home."

"Home?" He glanced at her, then turned into the driveway of the B&B. "You don't have another location after this?"

Her heart was so full she could hardly keep the smile to herself. "Didn't I tell you?"

"Uh-uh." His brows came together as he parked the Hummer and turned in his seat. In the back, Pumpkin and Bear popped up and wagged their tails. "How about you tell me now."

"The show goes on hiatus."

"For how long?"

"For me? Forever."

One dark brow shot skyward. "Some clarification would be helpful."

"I'm at the end of my contract. And I'm not going to return to the show."

His head went back. "Why?"

"Because I have other plans."

"Like?"

"I've always wanted to open my own antique-and-design shop. So I thought I might put an offer on that ramshackle Victorian on Main Street."

"In Sweet?"

"Yeah. I talked to your mom about my idea during our Margarita Fest. She might be interested in becoming my partner."

"Sounds like a great idea."

"I'm thinking of naming the shop Miss Giddy's Country Junk."

"You're naming it after a *goat*?"

"Of course," she said, making the idea sound so logical.

He smiled. "So that means you plan to stay a while?"

"I told you I love it there."

His dimples flashed. "And I love *you* there."

"Me too." She leaned toward him and ran her fingers up the buttons on his shirt. "Although I hear Jackson moved back into his apartment, so it looks like I might need a place to stay. Think you can be there for me?"

Her heart danced as he dragged her into his arms. "For the rest of my life."

"Candis Terry is an absolute delight!
I laughed, sighed, and fell in love.
You'll want to visit Sweet, Texas,
again and again—I know I do."

Jill Shalvis, *New York Times* bestselling author

Return to Sweet, Texas, in January 2014

Sweetest Mistake

Candis Terry

From the moment he became her toddler-sized-sandbox-knight-in-shining-armor to the day he went off to war, Jackson Wilder has secretly been in love with Abigail Morgan. She's his best friend and the first girl he ever made love to. With the sands of war at the bottom of his hourglass, he heads home to surprise Abby and finally professes his love. But as everyone knows, surprises can backfire, and upon his return Jackson discovers that his news comes way too late.

Abby has made some mistakes in her life but none as monumental as marrying a man she barely knew and sinking into a loveless marriage. When she hits the age of thirty, her job as a trophy wife comes to an abrupt end and there's no place for her to go but home. Abby thinks she's learned her lesson the hard way until she returns to Sweet. And a homecoming just wouldn't be complete without coming face-to-face with her biggest and sexiest mistake.

From Avon Books